Lisa Wingate's contemporary romances
Texas Cooking and *Lone Star Café*

"A delightful journey into the most secret places of every woman's heart. Everything a romance should be, yet so much more, *Texas Cooking* is a book that all women, young and old, will remember always."
—Catherine Anderson

"A delightful love story . . . heartwarming and vivid as its setting in the beautiful Texas hill country."
—Janice Woods Windle

"A practically perfect romance: soft, sweet, often uproariously funny, alive with people you'd want to know and places you'd like to be." —*Detroit Free Press*

"Lisa Wingate leaves you feeling like you've danced the two-step across Texas." —Jodi Thomas

"A beautifully written, heartwarming tale about finding love where you least expect it." —Barbara Freethy

"With a voice that is fresh and provocative, she's sure to touch the heart and reach down deep into the well of hope within each one of us." —Debbie Macomber

"Lisa Wingate dishes up fun and charm."
—Rachel Gibson

"A treasure. . . . Give yourself a treat and read this tender, unusual story." —Dorothy Garlock

"A remarkably talented and innovative writer, with a real feel for human emotion." —Linda Lael Miller

LISA WINGATE

Good Hope Road

FICTION FOR THE WAY WE LIVE

NAL Accent
Published by New American Library, a division of
Penguin Group (USA) Inc., 375 Hudson Street,
New York, New York 10014, USA
Penguin Group (Canada), 10 Alcorn Avenue, Toronto,
Ontario M4V 3B2, Canada (a division of Pearson Penguin Canada Inc.)
Penguin Books Ltd., 80 Strand, London WC2R 0RL, England
Penguin Ireland, 25 St. Stephen's Green, Dublin 2,
Ireland (a division of Penguin Books Ltd.)
Penguin Group (Australia), 250 Camberwell Road, Camberwell, Victoria 3124,
Australia (a division of Pearson Australia Group Pty. Ltd.)
Penguin Books India Pvt. Ltd., 11 Community Centre, Panchsheel Park,
New Delhi - 110 017, India
Penguin Group (NZ), cnr Airborne and Rosedale Roads, Albany,
Auckland 1310, New Zealand (a division of Pearson New Zealand Ltd.)
Penguin Books (South Africa) (Pty.) Ltd., 24 Sturdee Avenue,
Rosebank, Johannesburg 2196, South Africa

Penguin Books Ltd., Registered Offices:
80 Strand, London WC2R 0RL, England

Published by NAL Accent, an imprint of New American Library,
a division of Penguin Group (USA) Inc. Previously published in
an NAL Accent trade paperback edition.

First NAL Accent Mass Market Printing, April 2005
10 9 8 7 6 5 4 3 2 1

To my grandparents
Elvera and Norm,
Who made us believe
In love at first sight,
Who showed us young folks
How to dance a soft shoe,
Who taught us that
True love lasts a lifetime,
And beyond. . . .

ACKNOWLEDGMENTS

On any journey, it is the unplanned happenings that make the trip unique. The past year since the publication of *Tending Roses* has been a jump completely off the map. I have so many times been helped along by the grace of friends, the kindness of strangers, and the guidance of those who knew the world of book publishing much better than I did. I could write a volume about the good deeds and happenstances that have led to the publication of this second book, *Good Hope Road*. But that is another story, so I will settle for this quick list of wonderful people to whom I am indebted for many reasons.

My thoughts, prayers, thanks, and gratitude go out to the many readers of *Tending Roses* who took the time to write letters and e-mails, to share emotions, struggles, prayers, and encouragement, and to share the book with others. There are no words to express what your letters meant and what your recommendations meant to the success of the book. I am honored beyond measure, and truly blessed.

My heartfelt thanks go out to friends who helped with the research and editing of *Good Hope Road*—in particular Amanda Carter, for incredible proofreading; to Dr. Phil Webb and Pam Slagle, for invaluable medical consultation, and for not slapping me when I confessed that what I know about emergency medical treatment, I learned from watching soap operas. Thank you also to my treasured friend and favorite computer girl, Mandy Koger, for using your talent and expertise to create the Web site, www.LisaWingate.com.

My gratitude once again goes out to my wonderful agents, past and present, Lisa Hagan of Paraview, and Claudia Cross of Sterling Lord (Literistic). Thank you for holding my hand, yanking it when needed, and guiding me through the strange and awesome publishing process. Thank you also to the fantastic staff at New American Library, and especially to my editor, Ellen Edwards.

Thank you to all the booksellers, librarians, and book clubs who have so graciously invited me for book signings and speeches for *Tending Roses*. My gratitude also to all of the newspaper and television personnel who gave coverage to the book and to the story behind it. You have made this year everything I hoped for, and more than I ever dreamed. Special thanks to those booksellers who devotedly recommended and shelved *Tending Roses*, including Michelle, Lavone, Verna, Sharon, and many more, but especially Christopher Cleveland, for being the first bookseller to read a pre-market copy of *Tending Roses* and telling me there was a big audience out there for the book. What an incredible kindness that was.

Last, thank you to my family, to my aunts, uncles, brothers, parents, and grandparents on both sides, for helping to drum up publicity, for housing me when I came for book signings and speeches, and for each buying at least one copy of the book. Sometimes it helps to come from a big family!

My love and thanks also, and as always, to my husband and my two sons. You are my heartbeat, the three of you, the answer to my prayers, the thing I treasure most. How blessed we are to have one another.

CHAPTER 1

JENILEE LANE

There is a moth in a cocoon outside the window. It has been there for months, twisted by the wind, dampened by the rain, a reminder that the windowframes should have been cleaned and painted last fall. It is spring, and there is a tiny hole in the end of the cocoon, a small probe pushing through, sawing back and forth, struggling to free the creature inside.

The moth has labored for hours, and only now has it pushed two legs through the hole. Inside in the darkness, does it know why it must struggle? Somewhere in the mass of cells and neurons that make up its tiny body, is it aware that the struggle is God's way of pumping fluid into its wings? If not for the struggle, it would come into the world with a swollen body and flightless wings. It would be a creature without strength, unable to fulfill its purpose.

I wonder if it can sense the warmth of my hand on the other side of the glass as night falls and another spring storm blows in.

On nights like this, I do not sleep. I sit awake and listen as the storms howl through the valley. Like the moth, I have emerged in a place that was once beyond my imagining.

Outside, I hear a gust of wind, and I remember. I remember where I have come from, and it is as if every blessing in my life has been showered anew around me.

I fall to my knees, and I thank God for everything. Even for the wind. For the fragments of my life that survived it, and the fragments that didn't, and the things that were changed forever. . . .

On the afternoon of July 29, the entire town of Poetry, Missouri, was cast to the wind. The town rained down around me for what seemed like an eternity as the tornado receded into the sky and disappeared, spitting out what was left of Poetry.

I stood watching, thinking it was the most horrible, awesome sight I had ever seen, unlike anything I had experienced in my twenty-one years of living. If Daddy had been home he would have yelled at me for not having sense enough to go to the cellar. But once you start watching something so enormous and so vile, it pulls you in just as surely as if you were caught in the vortex itself. I don't know what it is that makes people want to look into the face of evil. . . .

"Oh, my God. Oh, my God," I remember saying. My mind couldn't comprehend what was happening. Only a few minutes before, I had been fixing dinner for Daddy and my younger brother, Nate, listening to an old Bob Wills record, and wondering if the coming storm would bring rain. I was thinking about leaving again—having that fantasy where I packed Mama's old suitcase and went . . . somewhere. The dream always came wrapped in a tissue-paper layer of guilt, so that I couldn't see the contents clearly. Perhaps that was a merciful thing, because I knew Daddy and Nate couldn't get by without me.

I heard branches slapping against the house as if the

oak tree knew about the dream and was angry. Outside
the window, a car sped by, a black Mercedes going too
fast on the gravel, like it was running from something. It
fishtailed back and forth on the curve, throwing rocks
against the yard fence before it straightened and rushed
onward.

*Probably one of those doctors or lawyers leaving the
resort on the lake,* I thought. *Probably doesn't want his
high-dollar car to get wet. They should stick to the paved
roads where they belong.*

The car disappeared down Good Hope Road, and the
wind came up, roaring like a freight train. Hail pounded
the roof, and debris whipped through the air, crashing
into the house and barn.

When I ran to the screen door, the sky was swirling
like a giant black cauldron. I watched as the cone of the
tornado slowly separated from the ground and disappeared into the sky. Not a half mile away, a wall of rain
was falling, but at our house the hail stopped suddenly.
The roar faded, and destruction lay everywhere—pieces
of wood and metal, tree branches, shredded furniture,
torn clothing, shards of glass glittering like diamonds in
the afternoon sunlight.

Bits of paper floated from the churning clouds, drifting, swirling, dancing, as if they had all the time in the
world. They filled the sky like snow.

The air was so quiet I could hear the papers falling,
rustling slightly against an eerie silence, like a battle-
field after the battle, when only the corpses remain. I
wondered where so much paper could have come from,
and if it had been blown all the way from Poetry, three
miles across the low hills.

The big oak tree in the yard moaned, its limbs heavy
with a crusty coating of fresh hail. I stared at the ice,
then turned around in disbelief, looking at our single-
story brick house and seeing everything as it had always
been—the peeling paint, the overgrown bushes, the torn

window screen where Nate sneaked out of his bedroom at night.

A piece of paper fell lightly on the screen and hung there, fluttering against the window like a bird trying to break free.

I remember thinking, *Why not us? Why not our house? Why is everything the same as it was yesterday, last week, last month, last year, ten minutes ago? Why wasn't anything destroyed, or changed, or carried away . . . ?*

I had the strangest sense of wishing that it had been. Then I realized how crazy that was. I should have been thanking God I was alive.

Turning around, I gazed at the wall of rain, now moving away toward the east, revealing the footprint of the beast—an enormous path of stripped earth and strewn debris, ending in a narrow swath of twisted trees just past Daddy's wheat field. From there, it carved a jagged scar toward the horizon, toward Poetry. Where farms had been, there was nothing.

I wondered how God could let something so terrible happen at all.

A mile down the valley, the pecan orchard that had hidden old lady Gibson's farmhouse stood splintered, the limbs hanging like broken bones. Near the road, a geyser of water sprayed into the air, mixing with the falling rain.

I realized the tornado had passed across the Gibson farm. Gasping the gritty air, I ran down the porch steps and across the yard. At the sound of the yard gate opening, Daddy's bird dog rushed from under the house and slammed against my legs, sending me sprawling into the litter on the grass.

"Get away, Bo!" I hollered, grabbing his collar as he tried to bulldoze his way through the gate. "Get back in the yard, you big, stupid dog!" Daddy's dogs were always big and stupid, and always trying to escape.

I held on as Bo plowed a furrow into the long,

scrappy grass outside the gate and pounced on a bit of paper blowing by. Scrambling to my feet, I dragged him into the yard and struggled to hook him to his chain while he cavorted with the paper, grabbing it, then dropping it and pouncing on it again. I caught a quick glimpse of a face. A photograph. A baby. A birth announcement.

Securing the chain, I snatched the photograph away, dried it on my jeans, then looked at it with the same horrible fascination that had forced me to stare at the tornado.

Somebody's baby. Just newborn. A girl. Seven pounds, six ounces. The space where the name would have been was torn away.

A coldness came over me, as if all of the blood in my body were draining to my feet and disappearing into the grass. For a moment I stood frozen. I didn't want to move, or think, or be. I didn't want to know what reality waited outside the yard fence, or who the baby was, or what might have happened to her. It was too awful to comprehend.

Come on, Jenilee. Come on. Get your head on straight. . . .

The voice in my mind sounded like Mama's. At least the way I remembered her sounding. I slipped the photograph into my pocket and ran across the yard, leaving Bo yapping at the end of his chain.

Come on, Jenilee, hurry up, the voice reverberated as I rushed to the shed to get the pickup, then realized that Daddy and Nate had taken the pickup to Kansas City that morning. There was nothing left but the tractor. I climbed on and started the engine.

No time to be afraid, just back it out of the shed and drive down to Mrs. Gibson's house. It's not the first time you've driven a tractor. Mama's voice sounded insistently in my head. But I wondered: If she were really there, would she worry about what Daddy would say?

Daddy didn't let the tractor off the property, and he hadn't liked Mrs. Gibson since her goats got in his pasture, and he shot them thinking they were deer, and she called the sheriff and had Daddy thrown in jail. After that, we didn't have much to do with the Gibsons. We didn't have much to do with anybody. Daddy had pretty well driven off all of the neighbors.

"Come on, Jenilee," I muttered, wondering how my mind could still be thinking all the normal things when nothing around me was normal. Everything had been changed in an instant. I could see the destruction, yet I wanted to deny that it had happened.

The tractor squealed an ear-piercing complaint as I stopped on the road and tried to put it into forward gear. It jerked into motion, the rumble of the diesel engine seeming to shake the hushed earth as I steered through the debris on the road. The wind blew damp strands of blond hair across my face, pasting them against the film of perspiration on my cheeks. Tiny drops of rain cooled my skin as I brushed the hair away and stared at the furrow cut by the tornado, watching it grow larger and more surreal as I sped closer. Overhead the clouds parted, and muted afternoon sunshine streamed through the hole, seeming out of place against the dark clouds and ravaged earth.

Ruined trees and stripped earth surrounded me as I reached the Gibson place. The air smelled of dust and plaster, electrical burn, wet dirt, freshly cut wood, and rain. It was an unnatural scent, like nothing I could remember.

The rain slowed, the sky seeming to hold its breath as I passed what remained of the Gibsons' orchard. Mangled sheets of rusty galvanized metal lay wrapped around shattered tree trunks and cracked fence posts. The farm was unrecognizable—the earth bare, the trees sheared off, nothing remaining but twisted trunks and broken branches dangling without leaves.

Breath caught in my throat. The foundation of Mrs. Gibson's farmhouse had been stripped clean. Beside the ruined barn lay a pile of splintered boards, a battered refrigerator, what was left of the farmhouse roof.

I ground the tractor to a halt in front of the overturned well house and killed the engine. I called out Mrs. Gibson's name, then listened for an answer, afraid to breathe.

Nothing but the drumming of the last drops of rain on the hood of the tractor and the *hiss-hiss* of water hitting the warm engine. Near the well, the spray from the pipes died to a weary, noiseless gurgle.

"Mrs. Gibson?" I hollered, jumping down, my tennis shoes sinking into the mud. "Mrs. Gibson . . . Is anybody here? Hello . . ." I climbed clumsily over a pile of broken boards that may have once been part of the yard fence.

I stopped again to listen. Nothing but the *click-click* of the tractor engine settling and the throb of blood in my ears. I swallowed hard, my mind racing.

"Mrs. Gibson?"

I could see the taillights of her car beneath the collapsed garage.

"Mrs. Gibson?" The tractor engine coughed, as if it might come to life again, and I jerked sideways, stumbling over a section of picket fence rammed into the dirt like spears. "Is anybody here? It's Jenilee Lane. . . ."

Something sharp clawed my knee as I pushed to my feet. I touched the trickle of blood that ran down my leg and disappeared into my sneaker, tracing a warm trail against the cold dampness on my skin. I pulled my hand away, looked absently at the watery red liquid on my fingers, listened again.

Silence. Nothing.

Closing my eyes, I let out a long breath. *Maybe she isn't home.*

A noise whispered through the darkness in my mind.

A sound almost too faint to hear. A baby crying. Maybe Mrs. Gibson was home, and maybe one of her grandbabies was with her. . . .

I stumbled toward the sound. "I'm coming! I'm coming!" I screamed. "Who's there? Is anybody there?" I scrambled over a section of the house wall, rushing to the backyard. "Hello . . . anybody . . ."

The sound came again, close by. Not a baby. "A cat," I whispered, slapping my hand over my heart, catching my breath. "Just a cat." The sound was muffled, as if the cat might be trapped underneath something. "Here, kitty, kitty. Where are you, kitty?"

The cat mewed again, leading me toward a pile of rubble.

"Here, kitty." I stepped closer. "Here, kitty."

"Hello?" The sound of a voice came so suddenly, I jumped backward. "Hello! Help us!" It was the desperate call of a child's voice.

I stumbled closer, seeing the opening of a storm cellar beneath the tangle of twisted barn siding and the remains of a pecan tree. Overhead, a huge tree limb dangled perilously from a power line that I hoped wasn't still live.

"Are you down there?" I pulled at the debris covering the door. The old boards slumped inward, buckling under the weight of the fallen tree. Dirt fell through the cracks around the edges as I struggled to move the larger limbs. I knelt beside the ventilation grille, my hands clearing away the damp, silty mixture of mud and last year's leaves. "Is someone down there?"

"Yes! Help us!" A tiny hand pressed against the ventilation grille. "Hurry! Granny fell down and ain't wakin' up. The flashlight's burned out. It's dark!"

"Hang on," I cried. Tears filled my eyes as in vain I pulled on the trunk of the fallen tree. *Oh, please. Please* . . . Letting go in despair, I sank against the pile as the child's hands beat against the grille.

"Get us out, please!"

"I will. I will," I promised, reaching through the branches and touching the hand on the screen. In the dim recesses below, I could see a little girl's face, black with dust, her gray eyes wide, terrified. "Wait here. I've got to use the tractor to move this tree. Don't be afraid. I'll be right back."

I heard her call after me and start to cry as I made my way back to the tractor, grabbed the winch line, then slowly returned to the cellar, dragging the hook. The door groaned and sank farther inward as I looped the line around the tree trunk and struggled to secure the hook with cold, trembling hands.

"Move away from the door!" I shouted. "I'm going to pull this branch off now. Hang on! You're almost out. You're almost out." *Almost out. Almost out. Almost out* . . . I stumbled to the tractor and turned on the winch. The winch pulled tight, then strained, dragging the tractor down in the front, making a low grinding sound. I closed my eyes, hoping. . . .

Then the tractor lifted, and the tree trunk tumbled free of the root cellar. The little girl inside pounded on the door again, trying to force it open.

"Hold on, I'm coming! Get away from the door!" I rushed clumsily through the maze of debris, imagining the heavy door crashing through the opening, or the branch overhead falling from the power line. Wrapping both hands around the cool metal of the cellar door handle, I threw my weight against it and opened the door halfway, as far as the mangled hinges would allow.

A cat hissed and dashed through the opening into the sunlight, then disappeared. Propping the door with my knee, I reached into the cellar. Tiny hands clasped mine, and the girl scrambled through the narrow passage. She threw her arms around my waist and clung to me.

"Where's your grandma?" I held her away and

looked into her silt-covered face as the door shifted against my knee. Tears fell from her white-rimmed eyes, turning the silt to mud, drawing lines toward her mouth as she struggled to form words.

"In-inside." She motioned to the cellar. "She fell down when . . . when the door blowed shut. She won't talk. Sh-sh-she don't wake up." The cellar door shifted noisily on its hinges, and she jumped, screaming and grabbing handfuls of my T-shirt.

"Get that board over there," I said, pushing her away from me. "Come on now, we have to get your grandma out. Get me that board so I can brace the door. It's all right." But I wondered if it would be.

She moved finally, tripping, then scrambling through the mud on her hands and knees, whimpering as she brought the board back. Overhead, the power line groaned, and she screamed, jerking her hands up to cover her ears.

"It's all right. It's not going to fall," I said, sounding stern. The cellar door creaked and shifted in the wind as I braced it and started down the steps. "You hold this door," I ordered, taking her hands from her head and placing them against the door. "You hold right here, but if that tree limb moves overhead, you get out of here. You understand?"

She stood motionless, staring into the darkness below me, not hearing.

I smoothed her dark, mud-streaked hair away from her face, making her look at me. "What's your name?"

"L-Lacy," she answered, her eyes vacant, as if her mind had gone somewhere to hide.

"O.K., Lacy," I said, trying to sound calm. "You hold this door. If it blows shut, or anything happens, you run down the road and get some help. Go about a mile and a half that way to the Millers' place, you understand?"

She nodded, but I wondered if she heard. I wondered if she was capable of finding help if the worst happened. She didn't look more than six or seven years old.

She braced her hands against the door, sobbing as I descended through the thin sliver of light into the darkness below.

The air, thick with dust and mildew, caught in my throat as I stared into the void. "Mrs. Gibson?" I whispered like a miner entering an unstable shaft. "Mrs. Gibson?"

A groan came from somewhere below.

I followed the sound, feeling my way down the uneven rock stairway as pieces of mortar fell from above and clattered downward, then landed in water. I barely heard them against the pounding of my own heart, so loud it seemed it would bring down the ceiling and bury us alive.

"Mrs. Gibson?"

Another groan. I reached the bottom of the stairs and my tennis shoes sank into water that smelled of dirt and old grease. Bending down, I crawled through the cool inky liquid, feeling my way along the slimy ooze on the floor, knowing she was close now. "Mrs. Gibson. It's Jenilee Lane. I'm here to help. Can you hear me?"

"Mmmm . . ."

I heard her moving nearby. Reaching out, I felt her arm. I held on, inching closer, hearing the water ripple as she shifted her body. I felt her try to rise, then sink against the floor again. Overhead, the door creaked dangerously, and I glanced at the shuddering sliver of light on the stairway.

"Watch the tree limb, Lacy," I called, trying to sound calm. My mind whirled at the idea of being trapped in the watery darkness. "Mrs. Gibson?" Gripping her shoulders with both hands, I shook her with a new sense of urgency. "We have to get out of here. The door is hanging by a thread up there."

She answered with a weary moan and muttered something I couldn't understand, and then said, ". . . angels," as she tried to shrug my hands away from her shoulders.

"No, now, come on," I said, amazed by the force of my voice. "Lacy is waiting up there, and she needs her grandma. You wake up and come on with me. We're going up these stairs."

Her words were only partially audible. ". . . wait for Ivy . . . to come back . . ."

"We have to go now! There's no help coming! We have to go now!" My voice boomed against the confines of the cellar. I wrapped my arms around her chest as far as they would go, trying to raise her by sheer force of will, but she only slumped against me, knocking me against the wall. I shook her hard, trying to think of anything that would convince her to get up. "There's a tree limb hanging over Lacy's head, and it's going to fall on her! We have to go!"

"Lacy?" she muttered, coming to life again. "W- where's Lacy?"

"She's upstairs," I said, encircling her with my arms again. "Come on, we've got to go now. Can you stand up if I help you?"

"I th-think . . ." Her voice sounded clearer and she slid her arm around my shoulders, swallowing a whimper of pain. Slowly, carefully, we climbed to our feet and moved toward the stairway, toward the light.

Overhead, I could see Lacy's face in the doorway. The door broke free from one hinge and bits of mortar clattered downward. Lacy drew back, then leaned inward.

"Move back, Lacy," I called. "Stand back out of the way and hold the door handle, all right? Your grandma's fine. We're coming."

Beside me, Mrs. Gibson groaned and slumped forward, her weight shoving me into the wall beside the steps. My head crashed against the uneven rocks, and a sound like thunder rattled through my brain. "Come . . . come on, Mrs. Gibson." I shook my head as my vision dimmed around a swirl of sparks. "We're almost there. We're almost out."

She straightened again, and we struggled upward, one step at a time, her feet dragging behind mine, my legs buckling under her weight until we reached the doorway. Bracing my back against it, I pushed it upward as far as I could, then helped Mrs. Gibson squeeze through.

"Move out of the way now, Lacy." I coughed, choking on the last breath of musty air as I climbed into the sunlight, and we crawled away from the cellar, then fell into the wet grass, gulping in the fresh air. Numbness spread over me and the edges of my vision dimmed again. The rushing sound in my head grew louder.

Beside me, Lacy scooted into the hollow space between the exposed roots of a partially collapsed tree, and pulled her legs to her chest, hugging herself and shivering. "M-Mr. Whiskers," I heard her say, her voice an uncertain whisper.

"All this for that . . . darned . . . cat." Mrs. Gibson's words seemed far away. "I should have stayed in the cellar instead of going up to get him. Darned cat."

From the road I heard a siren. A volunteer fireman's pickup squealed into the driveway as blackness slowly circled my vision. The blue-gray afternoon sky faded like a kaleidoscope closing. I felt Mrs. Gibson's fingers over mine, cool and trembling.

"You're a brave girl, Jenilee Lane," she said, but in my mind the voice was Mama's. Mama used to say that to me, but she was wrong.

I had never done a brave thing until that day. And I thought I never would again.

CHAPTER 2

Light pressed at the center of my vision like the headlamp of a train rushing into a tunnel. A single bright light, burning. I tried to close my eyes to make it go away.

"Jenilee. Come on, Jenilee." A voice drifted through the whirling noise in my head. "I need you to wake up and talk to me." The light shined in my eyes again, and I felt someone's fingers prying open my eyelids.

Confused, I raised my arm and shoved the hand away. "I'm . . ." The word scratched against my throat like sandpaper. A hand touched my face again, and I pulled back, trying to remember where I was and what was happening. "I'm . . . I'm all right." I blinked hard, my vision still blurry, clouding the wreckage of Mrs. Gibson's farm. Even through the fog, the awful reality of what had happened was impossible to ignore.

I tried to focus on the face that hovered over me, partially hidden beneath a Hindsville Volunteer Fire Department ball cap. The voice was familiar, but he had a thick white beard that made him look like . . .

He smiled. "Yeah, I know," he said. "I look like Santa Claus. I've got to get this beard shaved off."

"Doc Howard?" I started to laugh, but the movement made my head whirl. I rubbed the ache, feeling a swelling where I'd hit the wall. "I thought you closed down the vet clinic and went fishing for the rest of the month. Aren't you supposed to be resting after that heart surgery?"

Doc shrugged off my concern, leaning over to examine the bump on my head. "Naw, I'm fine now. I heard about the tornado on my weather radio, and I headed for town. I figure, I may be a horse doc, but I'm better than nothin'." He touched the lump on my head, and white-hot spears shot past my eyes. "You do have a nasty lump here. Something hit you in the head? Do you think you can sit up?" The words rumbled from somewhere deep in his barrel chest, taking me back to the days when the vet clinic was a haven for me, a place apart from Mama and Daddy where I felt protected from the mess at home. For just an instant, my mind settled on the idea that it was three years ago, before Mama died, before I left Doc Howard's to get a real job that would pay the bills at home.

I blinked hard, and the illusion went away. "Uhhhh." A groan rattled past my lips as he helped me sit up. My head reeled and white sparks zipped through the air in front of me. I stared dizzily at Mrs. Gibson, who was resting against a tree with a compress on her head. Lacy was curled in the hollow of the roots, watching me with a distant expression. I wondered what she was thinking.

Doc Howard took a compress from his bag. "This cold pack's for horses, but it'll do." He tried to put it on my head.

"I'm O.K.," I told him. "I just bumped my head."

Beside me, Mrs. Gibson nodded. "We'll be all right. You'd best get on to Poetry."

"Yes, ma'am." His voice turned grave. For the first time I heard the emergency radio in his truck—frantic voices, a constant stream of cries for doctors, ambulances, rescue dogs, and bulldozers.

"Is it bad?" I whispered as Doc leaned close, gathering his medical supplies.

He seemed not to hear, or he didn't want to answer. "You two ladies look after each other," he said, loudly enough for Mrs. Gibson to hear. "Neither of you needs to go to sleep. Go to sleep after a whack on the head, and you might not wake up, understand?"

I nodded.

Mrs. Gibson answered, "Yes."

He closed his vet bag. "Stay off the road. You may see more emergency vehicles coming from Hindsville. They've called in all available personnel from the surrounding towns. This is one of the few roads that isn't blocked with downed lines or flooded at the low-water crossings."

Mrs. Gibson laid her hand on his arm. "Have you heard anything about Weldon and Janet? Weldon would just be closing up the pharmacy, and Janet would be finishing up at the school for the day. They'd be picking up my grandbabies from the after-school care—Toby, Cheyenne, Christi, and Anna? Can you check on them? Will you send back word that they're all right? Oh, my Lord, they have to be. . . ."

Doc Howard patted her hand sympathetically. "I'll try, Mrs. Gibson." But the tone of his voice said more than the words. His eyes met mine for just an instant, and his expression went to the pit of my stomach like a razor. In all the years I'd worked with him at the vet clinic, I'd never seen him look so afraid.

Beside me, Mrs. Gibson put her hands over her face and began to cry.

Pulling my knees to my chest, I watched Doc Howard hurry to his pickup. The truck squealed from the driveway and disappeared over the hill. I stared at the spot where he had vanished, wondering what he would find. . . .

I don't know how long we sat there. Finally Mrs. Gib-

son stopped crying. Nearby, Lacy curled into the tree
roots and fell asleep. Mrs. Gibson prayed quietly, asking
God to protect her son, Weldon, and her daughter-in-
law, Janet, and their four kids, telling Him she couldn't
bear another death in her family. I supposed she was
talking about fifteen years ago, when her husband had a
heart attack on the tractor and died right there in the
field.

I didn't remember much about it, just lots of cars
parked up the road and people dressed in dark clothes
gathered on the Gibsons' lawn. Daddy caught us watching and sent us inside, saying it was none of our business. Mama was crying on the sofa, because both of my
grandparents had been buried just before that, and all
of that death was more than she could bear.

Mrs. Gibson stopped praying and looked at me. I
wondered if she was making sure I was awake, or if she
thought I should be praying, too.

I didn't bother to tell her that praying wouldn't do me
any good. God and I always seemed to have different
ideas about how things should be. And God always got
His way.

I met her eyes, deep and moist and violet, narrowed
by folds of wrinkled skin, red from weariness and tears.
I realized that I'd never been close enough to really see
her face.

I had the feeling she was thinking the same thing
about me. "You look like your mama," she said. "Your
mama and my daughter, Elaine, were friends growing
up. Your mama was such a pretty girl—big brown eyes
and long hair all the way down to her waist, red, not
blond like your hair, but you've got her eyes."

I shook my head. Mama never talked much about
what the farm was like when she was growing up. I think
she was afraid to point out that our farm was once the
finest in the county, that neighbors came to share dinners and buy cattle. After my daddy took over, the farm

went to ruin and Daddy started selling it off piece by piece to pay the bills. After that, neighbors didn't want much to do with us.

"Back when my Elaine was young, they had a path worn between your grandparents' old house and this one." Mrs. Gibson looked down the road toward the abandoned farmhouse where my grandparents had once lived. "Oh, Lord. Looks like the storm got that old house, and the hay barn, too."

I followed her gaze, looking at the decaying remains of the house. The front had collapsed in the storm, leaving only the two bedrooms behind the kitchen still standing. Out back, the ancient barn that had sheltered the first cutting of hay looked like a pile of matchsticks. The heavy bales of hay were gone as if they had never existed at all. I wondered how we would survive the loss of the hay, but I didn't want Mrs. Gibson to know that.

"Daddy just kept junk stored in that old house, anyway," I said. The words sounded hard, like something Daddy would say. "It needed to be dozed."

Mrs. Gibson gave me a hurt look, and I wondered why I had said it. I wondered why I felt the need to make her believe the old house meant nothing to me.

"I suppose you don't remember your grandparents living there."

I looked at the house, recalling an Easter Sunday, my blue Easter dress, my feet in tiny white Mary Janes, Grandpa's hands clasping mine as we pitched horseshoes into a pit. I heard him laughing and Grandma fussing about getting the dress dirty. Mother lit four candles on a birthday cake while my brothers and I ran on the lawn popping soap bubbles that seemed to float forever on the breeze. I remembered a soft gray kitten in my lap, purring as I fell asleep on the porch swing just as dusk was falling. . . .

"No, I don't remember," I said. Those memories were too quiet and warm and gentle to think about. It was like opening the door to a room full of beautiful things and knowing you could never go inside.

Mrs. Gibson sighed. "That's a shame. Your grandparents were good people. Your grandma and I were distant cousins somewheres down the line. She sure loved you and your mama." Mrs. Gibson didn't mention Daddy, of course. Everyone knew my grandparents never liked my father.

A pickup with a camper shell pulled into the driveway, and my train of thought slipped away.

"Mother!" Mrs. Gibson's son and daughter-in-law rushed from the cab.

Beside me, Mrs. Gibson raised her arms, hollering, "Weldon! Janet! Praise God!" The hatch on the camper shell opened, and Weldon's kids scampered out, four of them, their ages from twelve to five, all calling her name and crying at once.

They crowded around Mrs. Gibson, helping her to her feet. Lacy awakened and stood against the tree with her arms wrapped around her stomach, like she didn't belong with the rest of them.

I rose unsteadily, feeling as if I shouldn't be there either.

Mrs. Gibson stumbled backward, pushed off balance by the knot of grandchildren wiggling around her.

Weldon caught her from behind, making a quick, nervous laugh in his throat. "All right, now, all of you. You're going to knock Granny into the mud." He leaned around her shoulder and touched the compress on her forehead. "Mama, are you all right? What happened to your head? We tried to come quicker, but the low-water crossing was flooded, so we had to come around the long way."

Mrs. Gibson twisted clumsily to look at him, dragging the children with her. "I'm all right. Got a little bump on my head in the cellar. Tree fell on the old door, and Jenilee Lane come down with her tractor and pulled us out."

Weldon and Janet looked over their shoulders at me, and I could see in their eyes what they were thinking: *Jenilee Lane came and pulled you out?*

Mrs. Gibson laid her hands on each of the grandchildren, taking a head count. "The children are all here. Praise be!"

Weldon's wife tried to wipe the soot off Mrs. Gibson's face with a rag. "We had just picked them up from the after-school care before the storm hit. We were on the way home when the warning came over the weather radio. We stopped on the side of the road and hid under a cow crossing, but the tornado turned and didn't come our way."

Tears rimmed Mrs. Gibson's eyes. She wrapped her arms around the grandchildren and squeezed them so hard they squirmed like puppies with their heads caught in the fence. "Granny!" the boy, Toby, protested, his voice muffled by the overhang of her breasts. "I can't breathe under here."

Mrs. Gibson hung on and gave the back of his head a knuckle-rub that looked like it might have made a bald spot. "You hush up, Toby Ray. I'm praisin' the Lord and ringing the bells of heaven here, and I'll quit when I'm darned well ready."

Anna, the oldest, wiggled loose from the circle of Mrs. Gibson's fleshy arms, releasing the rest of the children. They scattered, looking for air. Only the littlest girl, Cheyenne, stayed with her arms around her grandma.

Mrs. Gibson reached down and picked her up. "Oh, that's my little girl." She held on tight as Cheyenne wrapped her arms and legs around as far as she could, which wasn't nearly all the way. There was plenty of Mrs. Gibson to hug.

"My little precious girl." Mrs. Gibson closed her eyes. She didn't see Weldon, Janet, and the rest of them turn to look at the house. She didn't notice their expressions of disbelief as they realized there was nothing left but rubble.

They straightened their faces and wiped their eyes quickly as Mrs. Gibson set Cheyenne down and cleared her throat. "How bad are things around at the neighbor places?"

Weldon gave Janet a guarded look. "It's bad, Mama," he admitted finally. "The radio said there were twelve tornadoes reported so far, all over the tristate area, some almost a mile wide, and on the ground for nearly an hour. The state's never seen anything like it. The one that hit Poetry came from Kansas City, halfway across the state."

I didn't hear what Mrs. Gibson said next, some kind of prayer, I think. *From Kansas City, halfway across the state,* repeated in my mind. *Daddy took Nate out of school this morning, and they were headed to the cattle auction in Kansas City.* . . .

My head reeled. I felt Weldon Gibson grab my arm. "Jenilee, are you all right?" He looked at me with the same concern he had always shown when I came into the pharmacy to fill Mama's prescriptions. *Jenilee, are you all right?* he'd say, and he'd look right at me, like he knew things at home were anything but *all right.*

"Weldon . . . I . . ." I clawed a hand against my forehead as my vision dimmed. "I've . . . got to get home. Daddy took Nate to Kansas City this morning to the cattle auction. They might be"—*in trouble, hurt, dead*—"trying to call." I pulled from Weldon's grasp, shaking my head to clear the darkening images. "I've got to get home." It was my voice, but it felt as if someone else were saying the words, as if I were standing outside somewhere, watching a movie too horrible to be true.

Weldon came after me with his hands out, like I was going to fall and he was going to catch me. "Jenilee, wait."

"I'm all right," I said, unhooking the winch line from

the fallen tree and climbing blindly toward the tractor. "I've got to go home to wait for Daddy and Nate. If you hear anything, will you let me know?"

Weldon nodded, regarding me with a mixture of pity and concern. "I'll let the sheriff know about your father and brother, and if I hear anything, I'll come tell you. The phone lines are down from St. Louis all the way to Kansas City, into Kansas and Oklahoma."

I pulled the choke on the tractor.

"Thanks for saving Mother and Lacy, Jenilee." Weldon shifted from one foot to the other, like he thought he ought to say something more.

I nodded, but I wanted to tell him I hadn't saved her, just helped her out of the cellar, and I couldn't even do that without knocking myself out cold. "She hit her head pretty bad," I told him as I watched Mrs. Gibson being helped into the car by her daughter-in-law. Lacy was standing beside the car, staring across the ruined field through glassy silver eyes. "I don't think Lacy's hurt, but she hasn't said much since we got out of the cellar."

"We're trying to call her mother in Tulsa," Weldon replied, glancing at Lacy as if there were more to it than that. "Don't worry. We'll take care of them. You let me know if you hear from your family."

"I will. The tornado didn't hit Springfield, did it? I think my brother, Drew, is still working there."

Weldon shook his head. "I haven't heard about any damage down that way, but the news is still real sketchy."

Strangely, I didn't feel relief, just numbness. "Oh," I heard myself say; then I started the tractor and backed it slowly onto the road. My head spun dizzily. I gripped the steering wheel hard to make my hands stop shaking as the tractor lurched toward home.

An impractical hope kindled inside me as I came closer. I pictured Daddy's truck in the driveway, he and

Nate surveying the damage to the hay barn and discussing how they would get some fat government check to keep us afloat next winter.

By the time I cleared the grove of trees and the house came into view, I had almost convinced myself that they were home. But, of course, they weren't. The driveway was empty, the one-story brick house growing dim in the waning afternoon sun. No yard light, which meant the power was out.

Bo sat motionless at the base of the tree, looking down the road in an eerie silence, as if he knew something.

A coldness came over me as I parked the tractor in the shed. The engine died before I could kill it. Out of gas. Daddy had taken the can to refill on the way back from Kansas City.

Climbing down, I stepped into the faded light as a gust of wind blew by, stroking the grass, rustling the papers that littered the lawn and covered the yard fence. Slowly, numbly, I picked up a scrap of paper, and another, and another.

Scraps of other people's lives slowly filled my arms— a newspaper clipping, a kid's math homework half-done, a wedding photograph in black-and-white, a torn page of photos from someone's scrapbook. *The Grand Canyon* it said in some kid's handwriting, next to pictures of a family standing on the edge.

I moved methodically through the yard, trying to bring some order to the world. In the back of my mind, I knew more papers would blow in. More pictures . . . more scraps . . .

The sound of a vehicle coming stopped my thoughts, and I looked into the distance, squinting against the twilight. A diesel engine, like Daddy's truck. I waited for the rattle of the cattle trailer behind it. I could almost hear it. . . .

The truck came around the bend in the road. Red, not

white like Daddy's. A Hindsville Fire Department truck racing away from Poetry with people in the back.

I leaned against the fence as it passed, clutched the armful of papers to my chest, and sank into the grass, suddenly exhausted. Something inside me started to crack. Closing my eyes, I hugged the bundle of papers and cried.

Evening dimmed the light around me, and the breeze stilled as high clouds flushed crimson and amber in the sunset—just as if it were any other evening, any *normal* evening. Just as if today were no different from any other day.

A vehicle came around the bend from Hindsville. A gas engine, not a diesel. Not Daddy's truck.

The car sped closer, then passed without slowing down. Bits of debris danced in its wake, spiraling like ghosts in the twilight. A torn paper brushed against my leg, and I laid my hand over it, looking at the even lines of handwriting—neat, careful cursive like my English teacher used to write, a poem or a song. I didn't try to read the words. They didn't matter now.

A police car passed with sirens wailing. After that, there was nothing. Nothing for as long as I sat there. Not a sound, not a voice, not a vehicle passing, or a light from a nearby farm. I heard the faint sound of Bo baying somewhere out in the pasture, telling me he had escaped his chain again, slipped under the yard fence, and run off.

The sound jolted me to life. I stood up and walked to the house, laid the pile of papers on the coffee table, lit a candle against the gathering darkness, tried the phone, cleaned the mess from the dinner that had never gotten eaten, walked from room to room looking at the pictures on the walls. Everything was just where it had been, just where it belonged.

How can there be such destruction less than a mile down the road while we still have pictures on our walls?

It seemed as if everything normal should cease to be.

I sank onto the sofa, staring at the torn papers and soiled photographs on the coffee table. Taking the picture of the newborn baby girl from my back pocket, I propped it near the candle. I stared into her cloudy blue eyes, wondering who she was and if she was all right. The candle burned lower, flickering as it drowned in a pool of melted wax. I closed my eyes, drifting.

Nate's voice awakened me. "Hey, Jenilee, are you sleepin'? Good God, girl, you don't do nothin' but sleep." I opened my eyes to see him standing in the doorway, his big grin beneath overgrown sandy blond hair, his Poetry Pirates ball cap pulled low in front, the brim curled. Nate was always smiling. When he smiled like that, he looked more like twelve than sixteen, like a little boy full of mischief. "Hey, Jenilee . . . hey, Jenilee . . ."

I laughed and felt my body jerk fitfully. Nate vanished like a puff of smoke, and I searched the flickering orb of light from the candle, hoping to find him in the melting shadows. The room smelled of burning wax and rain somewhere far away.

"Nate?" My voice crackled into the air like static on a radio. "Nate?"

Nate wasn't there. I was dreaming.

The events of the past day flooded my mind as I sat looking through the window at the empty driveway, knowing that if nothing were wrong, Daddy and Nate would have been home hours ago. My heart ripped down the middle, half hope, half dread, a thin, dark line in between.

I leaned closer to the candle, staring at the picture of the baby. Beside it lay the sheet of paper with the flawless cursive handwriting. I picked it up and started to read.

The top was torn away, so that only the lower part remained. The paper was old and yellowed, water-stained on one corner. The torn edge was white, like a fresh wound.

Touching it, I read the words.

. . . I do not know how to imagine my world, because I cannot imagine a world without you close to me. This terrible separation has been more than I can bear. I sometimes wonder if I can go on, rise and dress each day, cook, eat, work, when you are in a place beyond my imagining. Somewhere half a world away, cold or lost or hungry.

Yet love has no weight, or size, or substance. It does not know the barriers of time or space or distance, of life and death. Love travels on the wind. Love is greater than the trials and the suffering of this world. Love endures all things.

I imagine traveling on the wind like a puff of smoke, seeking you. I imagine floating around you, encircling you. You are not lost or cold or hungry. You are in my arms, and I in yours. We can never be far from one another.

Close your eyes, love.

Imagine.

You are home.

Tenth, November, 1944

I closed my eyes and imagined my little brother, laughing, teasing, driving a little too fast along the county road toward home. I listened to the ring of his laughter until I could believe that what was in my mind was real. I pictured him coming home, as if wanting could make it so.

I could not imagine the world any other way.

CHAPTER 3

Eudora Gibson

When an angel comes to you, it will wear the face of someone you know. I learned that from the old Mexican tinker who worked for Daddy when I was a little girl.

"An angel will wear the face of someone you know, so that you will not be afraid," he said in thick, foreign-sounding English. "So that you will listen . . ."

It was 1932, and I was just eight years old, a barefoot slip of a girl. I looked at that tinker and thought he must be very, very wise. There was a soft look in his tobacco brown eyes, a hardness in his coppery skin that made him seem ancient.

That night I dreamed about an angel with Grandma Benton's face. She smiled at me, and touched my face, and told me she loved me, and to take care of my mama.

When I told Mama about the dream and about what the tinker said, she took after me with a bar of soap. "Don't you be speakin' none of that voodoo nonsense of Ignacio's, you hear," she hollered. "Angels don't come to Missouri, and sure not to talk to regular folks like us."

Later on that day, we were told that Grandma Benton had passed away down in Little Rock. Mama was spooked, and she shook her finger in my face. "You're not to go tellin' anyone about that dream," she told me. "Especially not Brother Bartles down at the church. He wouldn't take kindly to such sinful nonsense."

"Yes, Mama," I said. "I'm sorry, Mama."

"Don't be sorry." She touched the side of my face and started to cry. "Just stay away from old Ignacio. He's talkin' out of his fool old head. Angels don't come to Missouri on a regular day and talk to ordinary folk."

After that, I never dreamed about angels again.

Not until I was seventy-eight years old, lying on the root cellar floor, and the tornado was howlin' overhead. My sister, Ivy, come to me as an angel, her face all filled with love and her body awash in light. She reached out a hand, and all I wanted to do was take it. She was trying to say something to me, but I couldn't make out the words.

Then Jenilee Lane's voice come through the darkness. Ivy darted off into the shadows and was gone.

All I wanted was to make Ivy come back. I wanted to lay there real quiet, so she would come out of the shadows again. There was so much I needed to say to her.

But it didn't happen that way. Jenilee Lane took my arm, hoisted me up like a sack of potatoes, and dragged me back to the world.

I'm not sure I was grateful to Jenilee at the time. The first thing I saw when I come out of the cellar was my house torn to bits, my things thrown everywhere, the stained-glass window that Olney brung all the way from New Orleans in 1944 smashed in the dirt.

"Oh, Olney, it looks like heaven." I still remembered saying that to him when he hung that window high in the eaves of the house we built with our own hands. The sun glittered through the colored glass dove and sent rainbows into the kitchen as the children ran and played, catching slivers of light like the shadows of butterflies. When I had hard times or bad days, I looked up at that window and it reminded me to be strong.

All of a sudden, it lay shattered in the dirt beside the root cellar. I wondered how God could let such a beautiful thing be destroyed.

Then Lacy touched my face, and suddenly that window didn't matter much. I closed my eyes and prayed that the rest of my babies were all right, and thanked God for my poor little Lacy.

When we brung her and the rest of the children home to Weldon's place, and their house was fine, I told myself I'd not dwell on the misery of what happened to my house. When Weldon left to go help folks in town, and the rest of us sat at the dinner table, I told myself again and again that I wouldn't let myself fall apart over losing my home.

But I couldn't look at the children. I couldn't bear the sadness in the eyes of Cheyenne, Christi, Toby, and Anna. I knew they were thinking of all the good times we had at the old farm, and how there would never be any more now. I knew they felt like something had been stole away from us. I felt that way too.

It don't pay to dwell on misery anyway, Eudora.

Janet popped up like she'd been shot from a gun as soon as the children finished eating. I reckon she couldn't take the quiet anymore. "Come on, kids, grab your things and we'll go to the spring to wash up. The power's out, so we need to conserve what little water is in the storage tank here in the house." She put on a brave little smile. "It'll be . . . an adventure."

The other children headed for their bedrooms, but Lacy didn't move, just sat staring at her plate. She didn't seem to notice when Janet touched her shoulder. "You too, Lacy. We'll go down and get all this soot washed off of you, and you'll feel so much better, all right?"

Lacy stood up without saying anything, walked to the door, and stood there staring out the screen into the dim, dusty evening.

Janet's lips trembled, and she pressed her knuckles to them, then turned and went to the door as the rest of the kids started to gather.

"You coming, Granny?" Christi called.

"No, the rest of you go on." My body groaned at the thought of traipsing down the path to the spring hole. "Just bring me back a bucket of water, and I'll wash up here."

"All right." Janet herded the kids out the door. "Toby, you get a bucket to bring some water for Granny. Mama Gibson, you just rest until we get back. Weldon said you needed to rest."

I didn't answer, because I had no intention of sitting there doing nothing while they were gone, and I knew Janet would fuss about it. Hard work is sometimes the only way to keep a soul going on, so I set to lighting candles and filling oil lamps around Janet's house as the evening grew dim. Then I made up the sofa bed, so she wouldn't go booting any of the kids out of their rooms on my account.

I sat down for just a minute to rest before they come back, and my eyes fell closed like lead weights. I felt Ivy's angel there in the room with me. I tried to see where she was, but all I could do was feel her close by.

The slamming of the porch door jerked me awake just as I finally caught sight of her.

"I brought some water for you, Granny." Toby cocked his head, looking at me. I realized I was sitting there on the sofa with my hands reaching into the air. I must have looked like a crazy old woman.

I grabbed Toby to give him a kiss before he could skitter by to his room. "I was just waitin' here for a boy to hug."

Toby giggled and wiggled away as the rest of them come in the door.

Janet frowned at the sofa bed. "Mama Gibson, you shouldn't have done that," she said. "The kids could have used their sleeping bags."

"No, now, it's all right," I said. "They need to be safe in their own beds tonight, and I'll be fine here. Don't imagine I'll sleep much, anyway."

Janet shooed the kids down the hall, then headed for the kitchen. I knew she had to be feeling pretty wore out, or else she would have argued with me more.

Lacy didn't follow the other kids to the bedrooms. Instead, she curled up on the other side of the sofa.

"Come here, sweet one," I whispered. If she heard me, she didn't show it. She just drew her legs up to her chest and hugged a pillow instead of me. Staring out the window, she looked like my sister, Ivy, her dark hair like the pitch of night, and her big gray eyes like the last shadows of the day. My heart ached, and I wished things were different between me and Lacy, the same way I'd always wished things were different between me and Ivy.

A mud swallow flew against the window, looking for a place to roost, and I startled upright. Lacy didn't move.

"Ssshhhh," I whispered, taking the quilt and wrapping it around her shoulders. "It's just an old mud bird. It'll go away in a minute. You're all right." But Lacy wasn't all right. She hadn't been all right since her good-for-nothing mother dropped her off at Weldon's two months ago with some excuse about how her and my son, Cass, were having problems and needed time to work things out.

Patting Lacy's back one more time, I swung my legs around, rocked once, twice, three times, then heaved myself to my feet. My body ached like I'd been on the old Case tractor plowing all day with no power steering. A groan yanked from my lips, and I reached out to catch the arm of the sofa bed to keep from toppling over.

"You all right, Mama?" Janet called from the kitchen.

"Yes. I'm all right." My head whirled and sparks flitted in front of my eyes. I took a deep breath, waiting for my eyes to clear. "I'll be there in a minute and help you get the dishes done."

"Don't worry about it, Mama." I knew Janet would say something like that. She didn't much like me in her kitchen.

My head cleared, and I walked to the kitchen, shuffling the way I do when my knees are like old plow handles and my joints are rusted shut. The living room tile was cool as ice against my feet. I had told Janet when they were building the house that tile would be darned uncomfortable. "Wish I had my house shoes. Don't suppose there's any knowing where they are."

Janet shook her head, scraping some drips of gravy off the gas stove. "No, Mama, I don't suppose there's any telling where your house shoes are now. We'll pick you up a new pair in a few days when the roads are cleared and we can get to someplace to shop."

"Good thing that stove is gas, else we wouldn't of been able to get supper cooked with the power out." I recalled that I was the one who convinced Weldon and Janet to put a gas stove in their new house instead of one of them fancy, flat-surface electric ones.

Janet stiffened a little. She didn't like being reminded about the stove, I guess. Sometimes I rubbed her the wrong way without even meaning to. I stood there for a minute trying to think of what would be good to say. "Lacy don't seem any better."

That rubbed her the wrong way too. Maybe she thought I meant it against her, because she'd been taking care of Lacy these past two months along with her own four youngest children.

"I know," she said.

"It's just hard, I reckon, all that's happened to her. She's had a hard life so far."

"I know."

"When it gets a little better, we can take Lacy up swimmin' at the state park on Lake of the Ozarks. We could just load up all the kids and go have a picnic one day."

Janet thumped the spoon against the frying pan, even though there wasn't anything stuck to it. She stopped for a minute and just stood there, her shoulders stiffening as she looked into the dishpan.

I put some plates in the sink, trying to think of what to say.

She dropped the spoon into the dried-up gravy in the frying pan and put the back of her wrist to her forehead, drawing in a long, ragged breath. "God, Mama Gibson, how can you talk like it's just another normal day? Do you even realize what happened today? There's no telling how bad things are in Poetry. There are no phones, no electricity, probably no way for help to even get here." She turned slowly and looked at me, her face a mask of weariness. "Things aren't normal and they're not going to be."

"I know that." I wondered what kind of an addlebrain she thought I was. *I'm old, not stupid,* I thought, but I said, "I've gone through enough bad things in my life to know that it don't help to sit and cry. You just have to do your best to go on like normal. That's the only way things get back in an even row."

Janet shook her head and put her hand over her eyes while the dishwater started to boil. I reached over and took the pan off the burner, then dumped the water in the sink and added some soap.

"We'll be all right." The picture of my shattered stained glass come into my mind, and tears started to seep from my eyes. "We'll be all right. What we need to do, soon as morning comes, is start cookin'. We'll get some of that beef out of the deep freeze—if the power don't come on pretty soon, it'll be ruined anyway—and we'll take a couple of big pots, and we'll start makin' chili. We'll take it down to the armory for the folks there. Folks must be hungry and cold, and hot food will taste good to them. Maybe Weldon can take a meal out to the little Lane girl." I felt bad for not offering to do it myself, but I was afraid that seeing my house again would be more than my heart could bear. "She ought to be checked on. She got a pretty good whack on the head pullin' me out of the cellar."

Janet stopped crying and looked at me like my ears had sprouted corn. I imagine because she'd been hearing me complain about the Lanes for fifteen years, and she couldn't get used to me showing concern.

"Well," I said, by way of explaining myself, "I just want to make sure that no-good father of hers don't come home and get cross with her for helping us. You know he don't allow that tractor off the place. One time I saw him drive right by on his tractor and leave two old ladies stuck in the ditch in the snow. If he'd been there during the tornado, we'd of died in the cellar probably."

"Mama. Don't talk like that."

"Well, it's true. But I ain't dead, so I want to cook chili in the morning and take it to the armory."

"Weldon said you need to rest. The only reason you're not at the hospital is because we can't get you there."

The way she talked to me like a child ruffled my feathers. "I'm not a cripple, and I'm fine. I ain't sittin' on no couch all day tomorrow when there's work to be done. We'll cook chili and we'll take it down to the armory and serve it up to the folks."

The muscles in the side of Janet's jaw twitched, but she smiled at me the way she might at an ill-behaved child. "You don't need to be at the armory, Mama. We can cook tomorrow if you want, and I'll take it down there."

"I'm goin' to the armory tomorrow if I have to load that chili in the wheelbarra' and push it there on foot." No one can accuse me of not having pluck. I've always had plenty of pluck. "There is no way on God's earth I would ever sit on the sofa all day wallowing in my own misery when there is work to be done." I stood back and looked her hard in the eye, so she'd know she might as well make plans to go to town. I wasn't going to back down. I couldn't.

There had to be a reason I didn't die in that cellar, and maybe this was it. Maybe there needed to be someone around after this storm who could help folks pull themselves up by their bootstraps and go on—somebody stubborn like me.

Janet sighed and shook her head while I finished the last of the dishes and set them on a towel. "I can't talk about all this right now," she muttered tiredly. "We all just need to get to bed."

I felt bad for arguing. Didn't seem like we should be arguing on a day when we'd been spared from death's door. "I thought I'd wait up for Weldon."

Her shoulders started to shake as she turned away. "There's no way to know when he'll be back. There's no way to know anything." She didn't say anything more, just walked off down the hall looking tired.

I stood alone in the kitchen, then walked outside to the bucket of water to clean up. Closing my eyes, I sat in a drift of moonlight and rubbed the cool, fresh water over my arms and legs. I took in a draft of air, smelling the mineral spring, thinking of how I used to love to visit the spring by moonlight.

I smiled at the memory, almost forgetting where I was, almost losing the terrible picture of the day. It didn't seem possible that such destruction could be real. Everything was so silent now. But even the quiet told me the night wasn't right. No katydids churring, no whippoorwills singing, no coyotes calling out to the heavy orange moon. Nothing was the way it should of been.

I went inside, slipped off my shoes, and climbed into the sofa bed beside little Lacy. In the moonlight her face looked peaceful, like sleep had taken her away from all that was. I closed my eyes and hoped it would take me away too.

Ivy's angel come sometime in the dark of midnight, sometime when my mind was drifting through dreams of the old days. She stretched out her hand to me and tried again to tell me something, but the wind started to blow, pulling me away.

In the darkness, breath come rushing into me like the swoosh from a passing train, howling on its way to someplace, the wheels thumping over the track in a rhythm. *Thump-thump, thump-thump, thump-thump.*

I thought about Olney, and where he might be on one of those trains, and when he might drive it back to the station here and come on home to me and the kids.

I sat up in the bed, trying to remember what was real. It was all such a blur. . . .

Those thoughts went through me in less than a minute, and then the clock struck nearby, and I realized it shouldn't be there so close to my bed, and I realized I wasn't in my bed. I was on a sleeper sofa, and the room around me was Weldon's living room, and Olney had been dead for fifteen years. The thumping of the train against the track was only my heart pounding and the howl of its passing just a memory. Only the breath was real.

I took in another long, slow draft of air and smelled the oil lamp burning atop the woodstove nearby. *Eudora, you're seventy-eight years old, and trains don't run through Poetry anymore, and a tornado come yesterday and blew your house away, and Ivy's been gone for sixty years.*

It was a lot to understand in the depth of night, just waking from a dream.

Beside me, Lacy stirred and made a soft little cough.

"Ssshhhh," I whispered. "It's all right, sweet one." I knew the sound each one of the grandchildren made when they coughed, and when they sighed in their dreams, and when they laughed. I worried about them, even when they didn't need it. But lately, Lacy needed it.

I rested my cheek atop her head and whispered to her, even though I knew she was sleeping. "All the babies are all right. Toby, Cheyenne, Christi, and Anna are asleep in their beds down the hall, and their older sisters are far away at college. Your auntie Elaine's in Michigan with her two girls, and you're right here with me." I didn't mention Lacy's father, my son Cass, and his wife. I wasn't sure what to say. They were living somewhere near Tulsa, last I knew.

When I had counted them all and I knew where they were sleeping, I let out a long, slow breath. "That's what really matters—that all of our babies made it through the storm. Compared to that, an old house don't mean much." I whispered the words like a prayer, then sent them to God on the oil-scented smoke from the lamp. I watched it float around the ceiling for a moment, then disappear.

I tried to close my eyes and sink again into the quiet darkness of sleep, but instead I lay thinking of my house. Something my papa used to say come into my mind: *When your heart wants to grow heavy, it is always best to remind yourself of other folks who have got it worse.*

"I wish I had my notebook to write that down," I whispered close to Lacy's ear. I often wrote them old memories in my notebooks, because sometime after my seventy-eighth birthday, I begun to notice I was getting forgetful, like my mama did when she got old. I didn't tell any of the kids about it, but the notebooks helped me keep my mind straight. Now even they got snatched up by the wind.

Somewhere there's a grandmother whose arms are empty tonight, I reminded myself, *and she's wishing all she lost* was *her house and some dime-store notebooks.*

Somewhere there's an old lady who's lost everything, and maybe her memory ain't just a little gone, but gone so completely she can't even remember what she's lost. . . .

My eyes drifted closed, and sleep must of come on me. It come in quiet, peaceful, like the moment I looked into the face of Ivy's angel and saw the door to heaven. The moment before Jenilee Lane come into the cellar, called my name, touched my hand, and pulled my soul back into my body . . .

A noise startled me awake, and I saw someone moving in the shadows of the lamplight. My mind fluttered around like a bird trapped in the barn loft, not quite sure how to find a way out, or whether it wanted one. "Weldon?" I whispered. "Is that you? Is everything all right in town? You been gone for hours."

"Things are bad, Mama." He sighed wearily. His shoulders sagged as he opened the old chest by the fireplace and started pulling out blankets. "I just came to get what blankets and medical supplies we've got here. We're still pulling survivors out of the collapsed houses and buildings in town. There should be some search dogs here in the morning, we hope. Nineteen tornadoes touched down all over the tristate area, so there's damage everywhere. Roads are closed, hospitals are jammed. Help is slow in coming. We're just doing the best we can to dig ourselves out and take care of the injured."

"It's that bad?" I tried to picture it in my head. "Dear Lord, Weldon, how can that be?"

Weldon was too tired to mince words. "The armory is about the only building left standing in town. Doc Howard and I set up a field hospital there, but a vet and a pharmacist aren't much of a substitute for a real doctor. We've got a couple of EMTs from the Hindsville Volunteer Fire Department, and we're doing the best we can to take care of folks until we can get them to a real hospital. The park out at the lake was full of campers here for the music festival. There's no telling how many people are hurt out there."

"My Lord," I whispered. I wanted to wrap Weldon in my arms and curl him in my lap like I did when he was a little boy, so I could protect him from all that was happening. "My Lord. I'll get my clothes on and come help."

"No, Mama," he snapped, starting toward the door with the blankets. "Just stay here, all right? It's black as pitch out there—no lights on anywhere in town and rubble everywhere. You just stay here and help Janet take care of the kids. You'd be in the hospital if we could get you there."

I felt my hackles rise. "Ain't nothing wrong with me." It's a terrible thing to have your own children talk to you like you're an infant. "I'm fine."

"Just stay here," he barked, heading toward the door. "There's nothing you can do in town, and . . ." He paused as a voice came over the radio on his belt. He pressed it to his ear, trying to make out the words, then clipped the radio back on his belt and turned toward the door in a hurry.

"Weldon, what's going on?" I tried to get out of bed to go after him, but my body was heavy as lead.

"One of the sheriff's deputies has found a medical doctor. At least that's what I think he said. The man was trying to beat it out on the backroads to the interstate as the storm came in, and his car got stuck in the mud. Been stranded at one of the flooded low-water crossings all night, somewhere out past Good Hope Road. The deputy's going to try to get through the crossing at Ataberry and bring the doctor back to town." He combed his hair from his face, his eyes flickering in the lamplight. "Pray they make it, Mama. We need a doctor. Now."

CHAPTER 4

The image of Nate hovered in the doorway as I drifted awake in the gray predawn light. Drew stood beside him, not smiling, just watching, his eyes not blue and sparkling like Nate's, but dark like Daddy's, brooding, sad, angry.

I blinked hard, and the images faded like smoke, weaving in and out of the faint glow from the windows.

I thought about the last time Drew came home, after he got out of the army four years ago. The year before Mama died.

He came while Daddy was gone hunting and Mama was at work, trying to make it through the day even though she was sick from chemo. Drew stayed just long enough to get the boxes of his stuff that were stored in the barn. No one would have seen him at all if I hadn't ditched school that day.

He greeted me as if I were someone he didn't know and didn't want to know, as if he hated me as much as he hated that house and Daddy.

"Hey, Jenilee," he said, standing in the doorway with

his ball cap pulled low over his eyes. He looked over his shoulder at his truck, wanting to be gone from there, as if staying in that house any longer would bring it all back. There was a girl sitting in his truck, staring across the pasture at my grandparents' old house.

Drew looked at the matted orange carpet between us, the ball cap shielding his face. "How's things?"

"O.K.," I said, then plopped on the couch and opened up a soda.

"You still in school?"

"Um-hmm."

"Doin' good?"

"O.K. I missed a lot last semester, but I'll still graduate next year, I guess. Mama had to have another surgery and chemo." I watched closely for his reaction, trying to gauge whether he cared. If he did, he didn't show it. He just crossed his arms over his chest and looked over his shoulder at the truck again. We stood there in silence.

Finally he said, "I heard Nate's been ditchin' school. That's darned stupid. Twelve-year-old kid shouldn't be ditchin' school. I'm gonna talk to him about it."

"I don't think it'll do any good. They kicked him out of middle school football for his grades, and he says he isn't going back."

Drew tipped his face upward and gave me a hard look through Daddy's dark eyes, so black you couldn't see anything in them. "Probably won't."

"I don't blame him." I don't know why I said it, maybe just to tick Drew off, because it hurt me that he didn't care at all about Mama, that he was five years older than me, a grown-up, yet I was the one stuck home taking care of Mama, when I was only seventeen. "He's making four-fifty an hour tax-free, helping put in sod for Shad Bell's daddy's construction company. Shad got him on there. Shad said he could get me on there filling out construction invoices in their office."

Drew's eyes flashed the way they used to when he was about to beat somebody up at school. "You stick with your job at the vet clinic with Doc Howard. You stay away from Shad Bell."

"Whatever." I swirled the liquid in the soda can and watched it through the hole.

"I mean it, Jenilee."

"At least Shad cares what's going on around here. At least he's trying to help me get a job that'll pay some more money." I knew that would cut deep, and I wanted it to. Drew and Shad had always hated each other. I wanted Drew to know how lousy I thought he was for running away and leaving Nate and me in the middle of Mama and Daddy's mess.

Drew took a step forward through the doorway and pointed his clenched fingers at me with a key braced under his thumb like the blade of a knife. "Shad Bell is a drug dealer. The only reason he ain't in jail is because his daddy's got the money to bail him out of trouble. You stay away from him and don't get any ideas about going to work for his daddy, either. You need to spend your time catching up in school."

I looked at him with my mouth hanging open. There was Drew, who graduated high school only by the grace of the football coaches, who had to join the army because he was one step from being hauled off to jail for fighting and drinking, telling me to be a good student.

"Geez, chill out." I didn't want to admit it, but something about what he said made me feel good. No one ever asked me about school anymore. When you're worried about doctor bills and electric bills, and how to pay for food, high school doesn't matter much.

The horn honked on the truck outside, and Drew took a step backward. "Gotta go," he said.

I nodded, feeling as if I were sinking into the matted sofa cushions and disappearing. He looked at me like he might say something more.

*Jenilee, pack your stuff and jump in the truck. We're
getting out of here. Don't worry. I'll take care of everything.* I wished he would say it. For just an instant, I
thought he might. Then he turned and left, and the
screen door slammed behind him.

I wondered if, as he was driving away, he thought
about turning around and coming back, or if he just
headed up the road, forgetting us as each mile passed,
letting us grow smaller and smaller, until we disappeared altogether.

Funny how after the fact, you always wish your last
words to someone were something better. Something
better than *Geez, chill out.* Afterward, I always wondered if I could have said something that would have
made him come back. . . .

A truck passed on the road, and my body snapped to
life. I pushed off the sofa and looked out the window,
hope fluttering in my throat. A thick morning fog hid
the road from view, so I listened.

It's not a diesel. It's not them.

The engine faded and everything grew painfully
quiet.

Lowering my head into my hands, I tried to think beyond the throbbing that started where I had hit my head
and pounded down my spine. A tangle of images flashed
through my mind, images of everything that had happened the day before. *Did it really happen, or was I
dreaming?*

I sat there, not wanting to know.

"Do something." Mama's voice was so real, I looked
up, expecting to see her in the room.

Instead, the hazy, unfocused blue eyes of the newborn
baby watched me from the picture on the coffee table.
Shivering, I turned the picture over.

I rushed to the kitchen and grabbed a grocery bag,
opened it, and held it next to the coffee table, then
swept the pile of papers into it. The old letter and the

picture of the baby fell in last. I closed the top so I wouldn't have to look at them, or wonder, or think. Hugging the bag to my chest, I went out the door and walked into a thick morning fog that shielded me from everything.

I couldn't see where I was going. It didn't matter. I let my feet move methodically beneath me, carrying me through the heavy gray stillness toward the light that was dawning somewhere beyond the shroud that covered Good Hope Road.

Bits of paper blew loose from the weeds on the side of the road, cavorted close by, then disappeared into the gray veil like spirits vanishing. A filmy child's nightgown, white with pink lace, caught a ride on the breeze, floating like a jellyfish in the ocean. Stopping, I watched it swim higher, twist in a swirl of wind, then drift downward and skitter along the road until the fog consumed it. Who did it belong to? A little girl probably only four or five. I wondered if it was her favorite.

I reached out to catch a picture as it tumbled by. I didn't look at it, just slipped it in the bag and reached for something else. I moved to pick up one scrap, then another, the action pulling me along like knots in a lifeline—grab one, grab the next—a greeting card, a little gold bracelet with *Amanda Lynne* engraved on it, a kindergarten graduation certificate for the little Taylor boy. I knew his parents. Nearby, I found his school picture. He was smiling all toothless in front, eyes twinkling as if he hadn't a care in the world. I added his picture to the others in the bag until I couldn't see the little baby with the blue eyes any longer.

I passed old man Jaans's place, about two miles up the road from ours. I could see his house at the end of the lane. For an instant it felt like a normal day. The old cracker-box house looked as it always had, paint peeling, screens flapping in the breeze, porch roof sagging where a post leaned cockeyed. I squinted through the fog, expecting to see old man Jaans doing what he normally did since his wife died—tending his small herd of scrawny cows, talking to his chickens, sipping whiskey from the flask he kept in his pocket. When he was sober enough he'd drive down to our house, set fresh milk or eggs on the post by the mailbox, then leave in a hurry in case Daddy was home. He was the only neighbor who bothered to stop anymore.

The cows bellowed and came to the fence looking for food, and the noise jolted me back to reality.

Today isn't a normal day. Nothing is normal.

Old man Jaans's pickup wasn't in the barn where he kept it. I didn't want to think about what that might mean or where he could be, so I started walking again.

The cows ran along the fence complaining until they reached the corner of their pasture, then stood quietly watching me walk away.

I continued toward town as the sun crested the horizon, conjuring the warmth of a Missouri July. The wispy fog withdrew into the valleys as I picked my way carefully through the debris on the road, passing farms that were not farms anymore. Where there had been homes, and barns, and families whose names I knew, there were now only piles of rubble and splintered timbers with windows and doors sticking out like broken appendages. Good Hope Road was deserted.

I descended into the valley along Judy Creek, where the fog grew thick again. I slowed my steps, moving carefully. I could hear the rushing water but I couldn't see it. If the bridge was flooded, I'd never be able to get to town.

The sound of something moving in the cedar brush beside the road caught my attention. I stopped, unsure of whether to move closer. "Hello?" I whispered.

A high-pitched bark answered, and Bo bounded through the weeds. "Oh, Bo." I sighed, slapping a hand over my racing heart and squatting down to pet him as he wiggled around my legs, limping on three feet. "Oh,

Bo, you big, stupid dog, where have you been all night?" I stroked my hands over his wiry blue-gray fur, feeling the comfort of something familiar. "What kind of trouble have you gotten yourself into now? It looks like you got yourself wrapped in barbed wire and took the hide off your leg." Bo whimpered, struggling to break free as I unwound the scrap of barbed wire from his leg. "Stop that!" I hollered, trying to examine the scratches. "Quit! Let me look at this!" Bo yelped and slipped out of my grasp, then started for home at a run. I cupped my hands around my mouth and hollered after him, but he didn't come back.

A voice answered from somewhere on the other side of the creek. "Helloooooooo." The word echoed in the heavy fog. "Who's back there?"

"Jenilee Lane," I called over the noise of the rushing water. "Who's there?"

"Caleb Baker." I saw him, a gray form in the morning mist, waving one arm on the far side of the water. His voice was familiar. He'd been one class ahead of me in high school, the chubby kid who made jokes all the time so people would laugh with him, not at him. He'd been away at college for the last few years. "Are you all right?" he called.

"Yes. Can I get across?" I stepped carefully into the mud at the water's edge.

He waded in on the other side, and for the first time I could see him clearly. His chest, arms, and face were covered with blood, and his jeans were torn. "It's not too deep, but it's fast. Hold on to that tree as you come across. I'll come out to get you."

"No, don't!" I called. "I can make it." He looked like he could barely support himself. "Don't come any farther. I'm all right." Closing the bag of pictures tightly, I slipped the paper handles over my arm and inched into the torrent of muddy water, clinging to the branches of the overhanging tree as the water whipped around my feet.

"I'm O.K. I'm O.K.," I said again and again, unsure whether I was trying to convince myself or him. "Don't come out for me."

I reached the end of the tree and saw Caleb close by. Bracing my feet against the pull of the current, I moved nearer to him, one step, two, three, until my fingers touched his and his hand closed around mine. He pulled me to the bank, and we stood dripping on the other side. I closed my eyes for a moment, catching my breath.

"You all right?" I felt him lean close to me, felt the warmth of his body banish the chill.

I nodded, opening my eyes. His arms and legs were covered with cuts and bruises, and one of his eyes was swollen. "Are you all right? Are you hurt bad?"

"I don't think so." He groaned and straightened slowly, so that he stood a head taller than me. "Last thing I remember is unloading cattle yesterday afternoon at the Gann place. Then I heard the tornado coming, and a minute later pieces of the barn were flying everywhere, and I went flying with it like Superman. I must have hit my head somewhere, because when I woke up, it was sometime in the middle of the night and I was pinned under some pieces of the barn wall. I had to wait until the sun came up to figure which way was out. When there was some light, I crawled through a hole and started toward town."

"Are you sure you're all right?" I leaned closer to look at the cuts on his face, thinking that there seemed to be far too much blood on him, considering that the cuts were minor.

He nodded, moving away. "Just cuts and bruises." He braced his hands on his knees, shaking his head. "I still can't quite get . . . get it straight in my mind, I guess. One minute, I'm delivering cattle from the auction in Kansas City, and the next minute, I'm pinned under the side of a barn and eight . . . maybe ten hours have gone by. I kept laying there in the dark, thinking. . . ."

I didn't hear the rest. "You were at the cattle auction in Kansas City?" Hope swelled like a tide within me. "Did you see a white diesel flatbed with a brown stock trailer? Did you see Nate and Daddy there? They were hauling a load of brindle cows. Please tell me you saw them, Caleb. They haven't come home." I met his eyes, realizing how strange it was for my hopes to be resting on Caleb Baker, who had never said a single word to me all the years we were in school together. I was as invisible to him as I was to the rest of them.

Caleb's face turned grim, and I felt the hope in my chest sinking like a breath exhaled. "I only saw them first thing in the morning, Jenilee. I know they were there, but it was a big auction, and I left right after lunch with Mr. Gann's first load of cattle. I'm sorry. I wish I had news for you."

I nodded, hugging the bag of pictures against myself, listening to the dull crinkling of the brown paper. Despair prickled hot in my throat, and I turned away, unable to talk. I started walking, clenching my fists against the bag and taking deep breaths, determined not to cry.

It won't help anything to cry. It won't help. They're out there somewhere, and they just can't get home yet. Nate's coming home. He's coming home.

I painted the image in my mind, trying to make it real, trying out a dozen stories about where Nate was, and what had happened to him, and why he wasn't back yet. All of them were logical, they made sense, they could happen, I told myself. I couldn't give up hope. It would be like quitting when Nate needed me most.

I heard Caleb walking beside me, saw the outline of him moving stiffly, rubbing his head. I didn't look at him or talk to him. I knew if I did, my resolve would crack. I didn't have the strength to do anything except keep walking as a cold numbness started where my clothes had been dampened by the water and spread over me. Even the numbness, even the cold were not enough to block out the terrible realities of the storm as we neared Poetry. Each step closer to town brought destruction that was more complete, disintegration of the houses more absolute, until finally we crossed the path of the beast on the final hill above Poetry.

I stood frozen in the road, my gaze sweeping a circle, my mind trying but failing to comprehend.

How can this be . . . ? How could this happen . . . ? I wanted to shout, but my lips were mute.

Nothing remained. What had once been a small subdivision was barren earth and streets strewn with bits of wood, brick, and stone. The houses had been lifted from their foundations, so that nothing remained but slabs with twisted conduits sticking out and cement stairs that led to nonexistent porches.

All the trees were gone, the trunks snapped like kindling. Climbing over a fallen tree in the road, I stood looking at the neighborhood, remembering a quiet circle of asphalt with perhaps eighteen or twenty homes and massive pecan and oak trees. Cars in the driveways, flowers in the flower beds, toys in the yards.

People. Families. The man who owned the feed store, the lady who worked at the bank, the second-grade teacher who just got married, the Andersons, the Jenkes, the Halls . . .

Staring at what was left of their homes, I tried to connect the image with the neighborhood I remembered, but it was impossible to comprehend that both were the same place.

Beside me, I heard Caleb whisper something. *There's nothing left,* I thought he said, but perhaps it was the voice in my own head. The numbness inside me separated me from the warmth of the day, from the scene around me.

A faint sound of sobbing pressed through the shell.

I turned to see a woman, motionless like a statue on the steps to a nonexistent porch, her head in her hands.

I wanted to go to her, to ask her what had happened and if I could help, but I couldn't force myself to step into that horrible place.

A half-grown cat emerged nearby. Mud-covered and missing a patch of hair along its back, it limped toward me. Squatting down, I touched it, the sensation of its fur weaving through me. Caleb picked it up and gently set it on top of the bag in my arms.

"Here, Jenilee, you know about animals."

The woman on the steps raised her head and looked at us.

"Mrs. Atherson?" I wasn't sure if I said her name or only thought it. She didn't react. My high school gym teacher just looked through me, then slowly put her hands over her face again, first covering her mouth, then sliding her fingers upward, shielding her eyes from the scene around her.

Caleb staggered backward, bumping into my shoulder. I glanced at him, noticing that his skin had gone pale, his face damp with a mixture of sweat and blood.

"Are you all right?"

He didn't seem to hear me at first. I asked again, touching his arm and shaking him.

He shook his head, reeling sideways, then nodded, blinking hard. "Uh-huh. We better get to town."

"Here, lean on me." I slipped under his shoulder, and we continued over the hill toward Poetry, his steps heavier, less steady than before.

In my arms, the muddy cat nestled into the folds of the bag and closed its eyes. My mind crawled into the warm space beside it and hid there. I hardly saw what was around us: the road littered with twigs, papers, bits of houses and cars, fallen trees, smashed cans of food, dented pots and pans, broken glass, the bases of shattered lightbulbs, toy animals with the stuffing hanging out, a mangled bicycle, a splintered baby crib.

Beside me, I heard Caleb gasp in a breath, and I looked up and saw what was left of Poetry.

Nothing remained of Main Street. Where buildings had stood for over a hundred years, there were now only crumbling brown sandstone frontispieces. The wooden walls, the heavy old doors, the blurry blue-tinted plate-glass windows were gone. Vanished, as if someone had dropped a bomb and vaporized anything that was not made of brick or stone.

It was not like anything I could have conjured in a dream. I tried again to connect the image in front of me with the picture of Poetry, where old men sat on benches along the main street, where kids Rollerbladed in the park, and cars lined the street by the café. The images would not meld, as if one could not possibly be the shadow of the other. I clutched tightly to the bundle in my arms, not wanting to see.

No one could have survived this. . . .

A helicopter flew overhead, seeming out of place, and suddenly everything came into focus in a rush of clarity. I saw movement in the streets below—emergency vehicles, trucks, cars, four-wheelers, tractors. Frenzied movement was everywhere. People were sifting through piles of rubble, working in human chains to clear away collapsed stones. Jess Carter was walking the streets of a devastated neighborhood on the west side of town with one of his hound dogs on a leash, sniffing through the piles. The dog zigzagged from one house to the next in eerie silence, Jess following heavily behind him.

A pickup truck rushed up the main street, rattled over loose bricks and chunks of stone, then turned into the driveway that led to the old armory building east of town.

Caleb's arm pressed heavily on my shoulders as we walked closer.

"There's nothing left but the armory," I whispered,

staring at the building that towered on the hill above the baseball fields. The armory parking lot was filled with people lying on cots, lawn chairs, and tarps. Here and there people moved through the maze, carrying blankets, water bottles, cups, various belongings.

Caleb slipped his arm from around my shoulders as we turned off the road and started up the hill. I watched him stumble on the uneven surface.

"We need to find a doctor," I said. "You need a doctor."

He shook his head, mopping the blood-soaked sweat from his forehead with his sleeve. "I'm just . . . tired. My feet are numb. I just need"—he blinked hard, seeming to shake off the fog—"something to eat. I've got to find out about my grandpa, whether or not he was in town yesterday when the tornado hit. He comes over here from Hindsville on Fridays for ministers' meetings at the . . . ummm . . . the Poetry Café. I need to . . . make sure he's all right."

"There's Doc Howard," I said, spotting Doc near the edge of the parking lot, wrapping a little girl's arm. Beside him, Mazelle Sibley, the old lady who used to run the school lunchroom, was holding a box full of bandages, patting the little girl on the head like a puppy. She frowned at me as we came closer, the same way she used to at school. I remembered how glad I was when she retired and went to work helping her son run his convenience store outside of town.

She noticed Caleb, set down the box, and hurried to his side, elbowing me out of the way. "Why, Caleb Baker, my lands, what has happened to you?" She gave me a narrow glance, like she thought I might have been the cause of it. "Lord, you look a sight! It near scared me to death when I caught sight of you just now! Land sakes! Look at that swollen eye."

Caleb mopped his forehead again. "My grandad. Have you heard anything about my grandad? Was he here in town when the tornado hit? It didn't hit over near Hindsville, did it?"

Mrs. Sibley patted his hand, then grimaced at the blood on her fingers and stepped away to wipe it on the edge of a towel. "No, he's all right, I'm sure. He came by our store on his way out of town yesterday, headed back to Hindsville just after lunch. I'm sure he's fine. You know, as he was leaving, he said, 'May the good Lord bring you the blessings you deserve today, Mazelle.' That's what he said, and I'm sure that's the reason I survived this terrible storm. Survived without a scratch out in the old icehouse, while the store was torn to bits. I'm sure it was because of Reverend Baker's special blessing that I survived. Why, it's—" Across the parking lot, someone cried out in pain, and Mazelle jumped, reaching up with trembling hands to cover her ears.

Part of me wanted to do the same, to block out the sounds around me—the low moans of pain, the high-pitched whimpering of children, the sobbing of men and women, the low murmur of rescue workers' voices, and somewhere in the distance the baying of Jess Carter's hound dog.

Maybe he found someone. Someone who survived.

I looked around the makeshift hospital, my head reeling. The scene was like something on the evening news. People were everywhere, bleeding, crying, hugging one another. I knew most of them—the beauty-shop lady, the first-grade teacher, the new preacher from the Church of Christ, his wife who sold Avon, Wallie Mitchum who ran the feed store.

He was by just yesterday complaining that we owed a seven-hundred-dollar feed bill.

I knew their names, but they were not the people I remembered from a day ago, a week ago.

They looked past me as if they didn't see me.

I stared at a woman, Bob Anderson's wife, I thought, clutching a baby blanket to her chest, her face turned skyward, her mouth opening in silent sobs, her body rocking back and forth in agony. I thought of the picture of the baby girl.

Was that her baby? Did they have their baby yet? I couldn't remember. I didn't want to know.

"Jenilee . . ." Doc Howard's voice startled me, and I realized he was standing beside us. He looked exhausted, blood-spattered, hollow-eyed. He was rubbing his hand over his heart, the way he used to before his heart attack. "Well, I have to say I'm glad to see you. Weldon Gibson said you'd gone back home after the tornado. I was worried. You took a nasty whack on the head yesterday."

I shrugged off Doc Howard's concern, the way I used to when I worked at the vet clinic. Doc always asked too many questions about home. "Are Mrs. Gibson and Lacy all right?"

Doc Howard nodded. "Weldon said his mother is resting. Lacy isn't talking, and he's concerned about that. We haven't been able to get out there to check on them this morning. It's taking all hands to care for the injured here. We finally located a medical doctor, a fellow who'd been out at the resort golfing before the storm. Sheriff's deputy brought him back here sometime after midnight." He reached up and parted my hair, looking at the goose egg where my head hit the wall of Mrs. Gibson's cellar. "You'd better come in here and get yourself looked at. That head wound is pretty swollen today. You should be checked for a concussion."

"I'm all right, but something's wrong with Caleb. He's sweating and he can hardly stand up. He wasn't that way earlier. He said his feet are numb."

Beside me, Caleb was bent over with his hands braced on his knees. Mrs. Sibley was fanning him with a towel, saying, "Oh, dear. Oh, dear. Take deep breaths, Caleb."

Caleb batted a hand at her and the towel. "I'm all right. I just need something to eat."

Dimly, I felt the cat move against my chest. "I found this cat at the top of the hill," I muttered, watching Caleb. "I don't know what's wrong. He was talking just fine when we found each other by Judy Creek, but something's wrong now. He said he was delivering cattle at the Ganns' place when the tornado came through, and he was trapped under a barn all night."

"What?" I felt Doc Howard's fingers go around my elbow. He took the cat from my hands and set it down. "You'd better come on in here and see the doctor. You're not making sense. Did you and Caleb come in here together? How did you two get here?"

"We . . . we walked," I said, balking as he tried to force me to move forward. I stepped back instead, breaking his hold on me.

Doc Howard looked surprised. "You shouldn't have walked here. There are power lines down everywhere, and flash flooding. The tornado came right through town, then zigzagged back and forth across the road for six miles out your way. Nineteen confirmed tornadoes yesterday afternoon, all through the tristate area." He wiped his eyes with his sleeve, shaking his head. "Never seen anything like it. It's like hell broke loose yesterday. Twenty-seven towns and cities were hit hard, including Kansas City and the theme park at Cato Creek. We've got Lord knows how many people missing at the lake. Everyone was gathered there for the big bluegrass music festival."

I shook my head mutely. *Why would something so terrible happen?*

Caleb stood up, and Mrs. Sibley put her hand on his arm, patting him with the towel wrapped around her hand. "You come on over here and let the doctor look at you, Caleb. Come on now. Your granddaddy would never forgive me if I didn't take care of you. Why, just yesterday, I was telling your grandfather I had kept you in my prayers after you were in that car accident last year, and—"

Doc Howard pulled me forward a few steps until we caught up with them. "Take Jenilee, too," he interrupted. "Have the doctor look at her. She got a nasty bump in the head yesterday."

"Oh, of course, Dr. Howard," Mrs. Sibley said sweetly, adjusting her glasses so that she could look down her nose at me, the way she always did, the way that said *white trash* without saying the words out loud. Under her breath, she muttered, "Come on, Jenilee," just the way she used to in the lunch line at school, when she could tell I didn't have any money. *Come on, Jenilee, go around the side and get a peanut-butter sandwich,* she'd say loud enough so that everyone would hear. *You know a peanut-butter sandwich is what we serve to those who have too many lunch charges. Haven't your parents filled out the forms for charity lunch yet?*

I stopped walking, and looked down at the concrete to keep from having to look at her. "I'm fine. Go ahead without me." I caught up with Doc Howard before he could walk away. "Have you heard anything about my father and Nate? Are they here? They were headed to the cattle sale in Kansas City yesterday. They never came home."

Doc Howard hooded his eyes. "There's not much news coming in. There's damage all over the area—hundreds of miles in both directions. The radio and TV stations are out. Every hospital for sixty miles is full, and most of the roads going anywhere north are either closed with rubble or flooded, so if your father and Nate are stopped somewhere along the way, they wouldn't be able to get in touch with you. We're hoping to have cell phone communication later today, and maybe some of the disaster relief agencies coming in. Right now, everyone's busy in areas that were hit harder than Poetry. It'll be a little easier to get information once we get some outside help. Thankfully, there haven't been any fatalities yet in Poetry."

I squinted against the sun, looking around the parking lot in disbelief. It was hard to imagine that ours was just a small disaster, that there was worse destruction elsewhere, and that Daddy, Nate, or Drew might be in the middle of it. Blood drained from my face and ran hot and bitter like acid through my body.

Doc Howard squeezed my shoulder. "I know it's hard to wait."

His kindness touched some soft spot inside me, and I felt myself start to crumble. Taking a deep breath, I closed my eyes and rebuilt the wall between the rest of them and me. When I looked at him again, he was watching the loading dock with a look of concern. I glanced over just in time to see Caleb stiffen and crash to the cement like a fallen tree, then thrash wildly on the concrete.

Doc Howard grabbed his bag from the little girl's cot and ran forward. I followed, my mind flashing back to all of the times Doc Howard and I had dealt with injured animals together.

"He's having a seizure!" I hollered, trying to reach Caleb. "Get his head! Hold his head!" I screamed, but Mrs. Sibley just stood frozen. Doc Howard pushed her out of the way and squatted on the ground, trying to protect Caleb's head. I slid into place beside him, helping to keep Caleb's head from hitting the concrete.

"It's all right, Caleb. Hang in there, son. It's all right." Doc Howard leaned close to Caleb's face, trying to keep his attention. "We're just going to try to keep you from hurting yourself until this thing is over. Try to be calm, son. Can you talk? Can you tell me what's wrong?" He glanced over his shoulder at Mrs. Sibley. "Where's Dr. Albright? Get Dr. Albright!" The words were barely out of his mouth when a man in a bloody lab coat ran out of the building to us.

"Head trauma?" he asked, his voice calm and emotionless, an odd contrast to Doc Howard and me. "Can anybody tell me what happened to him?" He tried to shine a flashlight into Caleb's eyes as the seizure slowed and Caleb's body relaxed.

I found my voice. "He was fine an hour ago . . . he seemed fine. He was caught in the tornado yesterday. He said he was knocked out and trapped under some boards, but he seemed fine." Caleb's face relaxed and he looked desperately at me. "He said he was fine, except that his feet were feeling numb, that he needed something to . . ." Something from the past clicked in my mind as Caleb's body started to stiffen again. I remembered running into him behind the bleachers at school years before, and him turning away, trying to hide a needle, making a face at me and saying, *It's insulin, all right . . . ?* "He's diabetic!" I exclaimed, leaning close to his face. "Come on, Caleb, stay with us. Am I right? Are you having a diabetic low?"

Caleb nodded, and the doctor in the lab coat jumped to his feet, "I need IV dextrose!" he shouted, running toward the armory. "Somebody get me IV dextrose!"

Caleb stiffened again, and Doc Howard held his head. "Hurry!" he called over his shoulder. "We need that IV!"

Frantically, I dumped the contents of the doc's medical bag, grabbed an IV needle, and tore open the package. Pinning Caleb's arm between my legs, I pressed a vein and slipped the IV in, then held it. "It's in. Where's the IV?" I hollered. "Where's the bag?"

"I've got it." Hands closed over mine, slipping the tube onto the IV needle, then taking Caleb's arm from me. "I've got it," the doctor said again, his eyes catching mine for just an instant. "Get me tape."

"Here you are, Dr. Albright." Mazelle Sibley elbowed me out of the way and held out a piece of tape. He handed her the IV bag, and she stood above Caleb with it pinched between her fingers.

I sank against the concrete and pulled the hair away

from my face, my entire body starting to shake. I realized everyone, including Dr. Albright, was staring at me.

"It's all right, Caleb. It's all right now," I heard Mazelle Sibley say as Caleb relaxed and started to open his eyes. She swiveled her head and glared at me. "Good Lord, *Jenilee Lane,* what in the *world* did you think you were doing? This isn't one of your animals you've dragged home from the woods. You're *lucky* you didn't *kill* him. Good Lord. For heaven's sake. Let's get him inside to a bed. *I'll* take charge of him."

I stood up and stumbled a few steps away, trying to catch my breath, a sense of panic spiraling through me. *You're lucky you didn't kill him. . . .* Old Mrs. Sibley was right. I couldn't believe what I had just done.

I picked up the tattered sack of pictures, watching as Doc Howard helped Dr. Albright carry Caleb inside while Mrs. Sibley mopped his forehead with a towel.

I followed them up the concrete steps onto the loading dock of the armory and stood there, wondering if I should go inside. The sounds from the dim interior were clear and horrible. Moans, sobs, voices I recognized, Caleb groaning as the doctor helped him onto a cot.

I stepped through the door and stared at the maze of army cots lining the walls of the huge, open room. Overhead, sunlight beamed through high glass-brick windows, lighting the scene like a setting from one of the old war movies Daddy liked to watch late at night.

"Jenilee Lane." I looked down to see old man Jaans, the neighbor whose cows had walked the fence with me, lying on a cot near the door. It seemed like days since I had passed by his place, but it must have been just an hour or two ago.

Old man Jaans shivered beneath his blanket, even though the day was already warm. I squatted down next to him, the bag crinkling in my lap. "Hi, Mr. Jaans." He held his hand out, and I slipped mine around it. It seemed strange to touch him, to be that close. When he had come to our place to bring milk and eggs for Mama, he always stayed outside the fence. Just like everyone else.

He coughed, wincing in pain, then drew in a slow, raspy breath. "Is your family all right?" The words were whispered so softly I could barely hear them.

"I don't know," I admitted. "Daddy and Nate were gone to the cattle sale when the tornado hit. They haven't made it back yet." I bit my lip. "The roads are blocked and all the phones are out. They're probably just stuck somewhere." As if saying it with conviction would make it so. "Our house made it through, and I saw this morning that your place looks all right."

His eyebrows rose, deepening the leathery furrows in his forehead. Shifting painfully, he put his other hand, cold and trembling, on my arm. "What about my cows? Did you see my cows?"

I had a sudden memory of my grandfather touching me that way, his fingers cold against my skin. My heart remembered for a moment how much I loved him, and I smiled at Mr. Jaans, patting his hand. "Your cows looked fine. They're hungry, though. They followed me down the fence."

"Oh, praise be!" He let his head fall against the pillow and closed his eyes. "I was on my way home when this thing hit, and I just knowed it had got my cows. Did you see my old white bull, Charlie? He's scared of storms, you know. Busts loose every time the weather's bad."

"No, I didn't see Charlie, but your cows looked fine." Amid all the suffering, I felt joy in this one small happy ending, and an unusual tenderness toward Mr. Jaans. "Don't worry about your bull. You know he always comes home. I'll go by and feed the cows and look for Charlie when I get home. I'll watch after them for a few days, all right?"

He smiled, and his hand fell from mine. I tucked my bag of pictures under his bed as his eyes fell closed.

"Watch these for me," I whispered, but he didn't answer.

I sat watching him sleep for a moment, wondering what to do next.

A vehicle roared up outside, horn blaring, and across the room Doc Howard and Dr. Albright left Caleb's cot and ran toward the door.

"We need help!" I heard someone holler outside amid a screech of brakes. "We've got three badly injured! We need help!"

A pair of emergency workers burst through the door carrying two little girls. Outside, I heard a woman screaming, "My daughters! My daughters!"

I ran out the door and down the steps to the pickup outside. A blond-haired woman was struggling to drag herself from the truck.

"Wait!" I pushed her back. "Wait, let me get some help!"

She grabbed the front of my T-shirt. "My daughters! I have to get to my daughters!"

"It's all right," I said, trying to calm her as I would a frightened animal. I smoothed her blood-streaked hair from her bruised face, and recognized her, though I couldn't remember her name. Her husband was a lawyer from Springfield, and they owned one of the fancy new weekend homes on the lake. Last year they'd sued Mr. Potts because they said his fence was five feet over their property line.

Now here she lay, as helpless as the rest of us. "It's all right; you have to be calm. We'll get you inside just as soon as we can." I felt guilty for every mean thing that had been said around town about her and her husband and their big new house. I felt like our meanness had somehow brought this terrible tragedy on their family.

Her eyes, bruised and nearly swollen closed, looked into mine, terrified, pleading. "My girls," she sobbed.

"I know." I cradled her face as the rescue workers

hurried from the building to bring her inside. "It'll be all right," I said, holding her hand as they lifted her and carried her up the steps. "It's going to be all right."

"Code blue! We've got a code blue on the little girl!" I heard Doc Howard scream as the rescuers laid the woman on the floor. She moaned in pain and struggled to see her daughter as Doc Howard prepared to begin CPR.

"She's not breathing!" Doc Howard tilted the little girl's head back as Dr. Albright turned from the older girl to the younger one, his movements careful, measured, calm compared to Doc Howard's.

I thought of how many times Doc Howard had dealt with animal emergencies at the vet clinic, and how he got nearly frantic every time. Doc didn't like to see anything die. It was one of the reasons I liked him so much. He cared about every living thing. Even me.

By contrast, Dr. Albright was cool, detached. He reminded me of the doctors who treated Mama in the big hospitals—the ones who never looked her in the eye once they realized she was a Medicaid case.

"I'm starting CPR," Doc Howard said.

The woman moaned and opened her eyes, trying to rise to get to her daughters. "Lie still, ma'am," I said, pressing against her shoulders. I looked into her eyes, and my mind flashed back to when Mama was in the hospital.

"My . . . girls . . ." Her voice was little more than a whisper through swollen, bloodied lips.

"They'll be all right." *Please let it be so.* "The doctors are doing everything they can."

"Oh, God," she moaned, sobbing as her eyes filled with tears.

"They'll be all right. Ssshhhh. Lie still."

Doc Howard paused to check the little girl's pulse. "Come on," he muttered.

Dr. Albright turned to the rescuer who had brought her in. "When did she stop breathing?"

"Just now. Just before we brought her inside."

Dr. Albright glanced at Doc Howard, muttering, "There's no defibrillator. Continue CPR. This one is the most critical. The other girl is breathing, but nonresponsive, probable internal injury, slow internal bleed, flail chest injury." He moved efficiently, checking the younger girl's injuries as Doc Howard continued CPR.

"Come on, breathe," Doc Howard coaxed.

"Probable rib fracture. Probably internal puncture, deflated lung," Dr. Albright assessed quickly.

"Oh, God!" the woman sobbed, her arms flailing and hitting Dr. Albright in the shoulder.

"Keep her still, or get her out of here!" he shouted, the first sign of emotion he had shown.

I wrapped my arms around her shoulders, half hugging her, half pinning her down, stroking her hair. "You have to be still so the doctors can work." I looked into her eyes. The soft green centers were barely visible in her swollen, bruised face. "What's your first name?" I asked, remembering how the recovery room nurses used to ask that of Mama when they wanted her to settle down and focus.

"Linda," she whispered, her lips drawing back from her teeth in a grimace of pain. "Linda Whittrock. The girls are Crystal and Jennifer. My husband . . ." She winced again, groaning deep in her throat. "Is my husband here?"

"I'm not sure, Linda." I didn't want to tell her that she and her girls had come in alone.

"We were on the lake," she said, looking sideways at her daughters. "The girls and I pulled the boat up to shore and ran for cover when we saw it coming . . . and . . . God, I don't know what happened. We ran into a shelter. I can't remember. . . . How did we get here? Is my husband here? James Whittrock? He was back at our lake house, I think."

"We'll find him." I put my other hand over hers, trying to pour warmth into her cold, damp fingers. "We'll find him."

"We have respiration. Heartbeat," I heard Doc Howard say.

Dr. Albright nodded, barely glancing up from his examination. "Call for LifeFlight ASAP. Tell them we've got two females, prox ages seven and nine, critical, multiple internal injuries on both, one with a deflated lung and respiratory arrest." He spoke with as little emotion as he might have used to order a cheeseburger at a drive-through.

One of the rescuers ran toward the door as Dr. Albright turned to examine the older sister again. The girl opened her eyes, deep and brown against her deathly pale face. She regarded the doctor with a strange calm.

"What's your name?" he asked, the faintest hint of emotion softening his voice as he touched her abdomen.

"Jennifer." She looked around drowsily, her eyes settling on Doc Howard. "Is . . . that . . . Santa?"

Dr. Albright moved his hand along her abdomen. "Tell me if this hurts, Jennifer."

She moaned and tried to curl into a ball as he pressed into her stomach.

"That's all," he said to her, then turned to the second rescuer. "Get me a helicopter. Now."

The rescuer nodded and headed to the door. Mazelle Sibley watched him hurry past, then looked back at the girls, staring at the scene like she was watching an episode of *ER* on television.

"Wait!" I called after the rescuer, but he was already out the door. Desperate, I turned to Mrs. Sibley. "The mother says her husband was at their lake house. Can you ask them to see if he's been brought in? Ask them to put it on the radio." *This might be his last chance to see his daughters. . . .*

The mother squeezed my hand.

Mrs. Sibley didn't move.

"Mrs. Sibley, please!" I pleaded.

The volume of my voice jolted her. She jumped, then widened her eyes at me, her nostrils flaring. "Jenilee Lane, you just—"

"Do what she says, Mazelle!" Doc Howard barked. "Just go ask them to put it on the radio!"

Mrs. Sibley gave me a scorching look, and my heart hammered in my chest. I'd spent most of my life ducking blows from people like her. "His . . . his name is James Whittrock."

She didn't answer, just spun around and waddled toward the door, her perfectly arranged gray-blue hair flouncing.

Dr. Howard shook his head as he smoothed pale strands of hair away from Crystal's sleeping face.

Linda clung more tightly to my hand and wept. "Oh, God," she said. "Please, God. I need my girls."

I turned away, not knowing what to say. *God doesn't listen to me. . . .*

I realized that Dr. Albright was looking at me, sitting back on his heels, his blue-gray gaze fixed on me, as if he'd suddenly realized I was there. His expression narrowed for just an instant, accenting the frown lines at the corners of his eyes. Was he going to tell me to leave?

Instead, he hung his stethoscope around his neck and used the back of his arm to mop the perspiration from his face, then smooth back the wispy strands of thinning hair that had fallen over his forehead. He glanced at the gold watch on his wrist, as if the time might matter, then moved to Linda Whittrock's side and began checking her injuries.

"What are her symptoms?"

I realized he was talking to me. "Umm . . . I think she has a broken leg, and something is wrong with her shoulder. Maybe her collarbone, or maybe a bruised rib. She's hurting every time she moves it." He caught my eyes, and I sat there, unsure of what else to say. There was a hard, emotionless look about him that reminded me of Daddy, maybe because he was about Daddy's age. It made me draw back. "I'm not a doctor. I don't know."

He nodded, turning back to his work. "I'm aware that you're not a doctor." He took a breath to say something more, but one of the rescuers rushed in the door.

"LifeFlight will be here in twenty minutes," he said. "The girl's father has been here in the parking lot all night, looking for them. He's on his way up the hill."

Mrs. Whittrock turned her eyes toward the door, her eyelids fluttering with pain, until finally there in the doorway stood a man with Jennifer's brown eyes.

He ran to his family and fell to his knees beside his daughters, kissing them gently, then hugging his wife and whispering, "I knew you were all right. I knew you were all right. Hi, Jennifer. Daddy's here. . . ."

Watching the father gently kiss the foreheads of his daughters, a sense of power and awe came over me. Despite all the terrible things happening around us, there in the long beams of sunlight filtering through the high windows, something strong and powerful and timeless was present. For a moment there was no destruction, no pain, no injured to be tended. The world was hushed, and there was only the love of a father for his children.

I wondered how that kind of love would feel.

Dr. Albright glanced at me, and for an instant, I thought he was thinking the same thing.

How would that feel . . . ?

CHAPTER 5

I held Mrs. Whittrock's hand as she lay on a cot in the corner. Outside, the whir of the helicopter blades accelerated, and her daughters were lifted away.

"Oh, dear God, they're gone," she whispered. "They're all alone."

"The doctors and nurses are with them, but there's no room for anyone else on the helicopter," I told her. "Just try to lie still, and we're going to get you to a hospital as soon as possible." I knew that would be little comfort to her. She wasn't worried about herself, just her daughters. "Crystal and Jennifer will get the care they need at the hospital in St. Louis." I glanced toward the doorway, where the girls' father stood with his hands wrapped white-knuckled around the doorframe. Ashen-faced, he looked at his wife, then out the door again, his gaze following the disappearing helicopter.

Dr. Albright stood beside him, staring out the door with a detached expression, his arms across his chest. Mazelle Sibley handed him a towel from her supply box, and he casually wiped the blood from his hands, then tossed the towel on the floor, turned, and walked to the table to pour himself a cup of water.

I watched him, wondering why he left the girls' father standing there alone, why he didn't offer comfort. They were his kind of people—rich weekenders who built big homes on the lake and came down from St. Louis and Kansas City to play golf or ski behind boats that cost more than most of the houses in Poetry. They were wearing clothes that came from high-dollar department stores, wristwatches that counted the minutes between glittering diamond studs, just like the one on Dr. Albright's arm. Big gold wedding bands that said, *I have it all*, just like the one on Dr. Albright's finger.

Why did he walk away from them and leave Doc Howard to dole out comforting words to the girls and their father?

I wondered what the Whittrocks would say if they knew Doc Howard was the town vet, not a doctor at all. *They'd probably sue, just the way they sued Mr. Potts for having his fence on their property.*

Guilt needled me. It wasn't right to think that way about these people now. They needed help, just like the rest of us. We were all the same now.

Doc Howard stood up, walked to the girls' father, and patted Mr. Whittrock on the shoulder. Doc leaned close and said something quiet that I couldn't hear, then straightened and frowned thoughtfully at the other doctor.

The roar of a vehicle arriving in front of the armory masked the fading sound of the helicopter. Mr. Whittrock and Doc Howard stepped back as tires skidded on the gravel outside.

I held my breath, wondering if more injured were arriving.

A teenager wearing a Poetry Pirates shirt rushed in, his face hidden beneath a ball cap.

I stood up and started toward the door. "Nate!" I heard myself say. He paused and looked at me, and I realized what some logical part of my mind already knew.

It wasn't Nate. It was one of the Warren boys. I wasn't sure which one. He and Nate were on the baseball team together.

"Where's the guy who's trying to follow the Life-Flight?" he asked breathlessly.

"That's me." James Whittrock stepped forward, looking hopeful. "My daughters just left on the helicopter—Crystal and Jennifer. They're taking them to St. Louis."

The Warren boy motioned toward his truck. "Well, come on, man. Sheriff told me you need a ride. I'm gonna take ya to the hospital in St. Louis."

Mr. Whittrock glanced uncertainly at Doc Howard.

Doc shook his head, looking grim. "Matt, the roads are impassable. There isn't any way to get to St. Louis."

Matt grinned, a smile that reminded me of Nate's. A smile that said, *Don't tell me the rules. I can do anything.* "I got four-wheel drive, a chain saw, and my four-wheeler in back, Doc. I'll get him there."

It sounded like something Nate would say. It was the kind of crazy thing Nate would try to do. Nate would do anything to help someone out.

Mr. Whittrock glanced at Doc, then at his wife. "I've got to try it. If there's any way I can get to that hospital . . ."

"Go." Linda bit her lip and nodded. "I'm all right." She raised a hand and waved him away. "Go, James. Please. Be with the girls."

Her husband nodded, rushed over to kiss her quickly, whispered something close to her ear, then ran out the door behind Matt. The engine roared, and the truck skidded away.

I looked at Mrs. Whittrock, watched the tears seep from the corners of her eyes and wet the fringes of her hair, heard the low sound of grief exhale from her like a painful breath. I felt her hand squeeze mine, and my mind traveled back to Mama, when she held my hand in the hospital and looked at me and cried.

"It's going to be all right," I whispered, the same thing I said to Mama back then.

I thought about all the times I had passed those fancy houses on the lake, and hated those people with their money and their brand-new cars and their attitudes. I realized now how wrong that was. It seemed back then that they were so different from us, but now I could see the thin line that separated us—just houses, cars, clothes. All things that could be swept away in an instant.

Mrs. Whittrock pulled her hand away, pressing her palms over her face and closing her eyes.

"I'm sorry," I whispered, but I doubt she knew why I said it.

I stood up and walked to Caleb's cot not far away.

He smiled at me, looking sheepish. "Sorry for all the drama."

I slid my hands into the pockets of my jeans. It felt strange to be there talking to him. Caleb, the class clown, the chubby kid who made fat jokes so people would like him, talking to Jenilee, the invisible one who never said anything, so they wouldn't notice her at all.

"It's all right," I said finally.

He had kind eyes, hazel with gold flecks in the middles. "Thanks for helping me. I really thought I'd make it all right. I haven't passed out like that since I lost all that weight after the car accident last December."

"You should be more careful the next time." *Geez, what a stupid thing to say. The next time . . . what?*

"I guess I should. Anyway, thanks." Self-consciously, he pulled the cuffs of his denim shirt over the burn scars on his lower arms.

"You're welcome." Silence fell between us. I turned away, so he wouldn't think I was looking at the scars. "You probably better get some rest."

"Oh, I'm all right. I'm going to get up in a minute and see what I can do to help."

"Well . . . take care . . ." I searched for something to say. What did you say to someone with whom you'd just shared some of the most horrible moments of your life, yet whom you didn't know at all? "I mean . . . be careful, all right?"

"I will. You too."

I wrapped my arms around myself and crossed the room to the door. Standing on the loading dock, I watched heat waves rise from the pavement of the parking lot as the morning sun began to warm up.

Just like any other morning.

I watched absently as Nolan Nelson, the high school principal, set up a makeshift soup line at the corner of the asphalt.

". . . beans and ham," Mr. Nelson's voice boomed through the still air, seeming out of place, too loud for this day of stifled sobs and hushed realities. People in the parking lot looked up as he stirred an enormous black kettle on the tailgate of his pickup and spoke with one of the sheriff's deputies.

Mr. Nelson's voice drifted over the murmur of other voices the same way it drifted through the halls at school. The familiarity was comforting. "Figured I'd better make use of all that firewood the storm delivered to my place," he said. "Not much else left. I had some beans down in the cellar, and everything that used to be in my smokehouse landed on my living room floor, so I scrounged up a ham, washed that old kettle in the front yard, and started cooking. I can't vouch for how it'll taste. I haven't cooked over an open fire since Boy Scouts in 1959." He filled a bowl and gave it to the sheriff's deputy, then filled two more and started handing them out.

I had never liked Mr. Nelson until that day. He and I were always crossways about school. He hassled me about being gone so much and talking about leaving school early. He told me that if I'd just apply myself, I could have the grades to get a scholarship to college, instead of barely scraping through high school.

"You're a smart girl, Jenilee," he'd say. "You like to read, you like to learn. You're interested in science, and you've learned so much working at the vet clinic. There's no reason why you couldn't pursue that, pick up your grades and aim for a scholarship. Med school. Vet school. Whatever appeals to you. You have the ability, but you have to put in effort."

I'd tell him I didn't have time to study because I was busy taking care of Mama and Nate, and working to help keep the farm going. I'd look at the floor and tell him I didn't give a crap about school, which wasn't really true, and I couldn't imagine what I would do with a scholarship—that I was going to have to quit the vet clinic to go to work writing invoices at Bell's construction company, because the money was better. He'd shake his head and look at me as if I were no better than dirt, and tell me there wasn't any future in that, and I should go to college, and blah-blah-blah.

I had to give Mr. Nelson credit for determination. He'd even suggested that we get a nurse to come out and look in on Mama, so that I could be in school more of the time. I told him we couldn't afford a nurse, and Daddy didn't want one around anyway, but Mr. Nelson insisted on talking to Daddy about it. I couldn't hear what was said when Daddy met him at the yard gate, but it ended with Daddy yelling, and Mr. Nelson leaving in a hurry. That was the end of that. The principal was not a big man, and, like everyone else in town, he knew Daddy's reputation. I think he was glad when I finally graduated, and the only Lane he had left to worry about was Nate.

Now, I watched Mr. Nelson serving food, holding hands, smiling and asking after people. I thought about him cooking on a campfire outside of his fallen-down house and taking the time to bring food when he could have been sifting through the mess trying to salvage his possessions, as people in town were now beginning to do. I couldn't help thinking that maybe I should have listened more to him and less to Daddy.

When Mr. Nelson had served all his beans, Mrs. Gibson arrived with her daughter-in-law and began dishing up chili from the trunk of Janet's car. From the backseat, Janet handed out blankets, towels, and coats. I felt guilty for not bringing things from our house. Old habits die hard, and I wasn't used to thinking about what other people needed. We Lanes were usually pretty busy just trying to get by.

Mr. Nelson walked over and gave Mrs. Gibson a hug. "Lordy, look at that fine batch of chili. I'll tell you what, if that chili would have come here first, I wouldn't have been able to give away my beans."

"Oh, Nolan, cut that out. It's just plain old chili, but it'll feed people." Mrs. Gibson backhanded him half-heartedly, and he ducked aside.

I crossed my arms over myself, wishing I could be like they were—part of things, close with other people, inclined to help when people needed it. I wished I wasn't standing there worrying about what Daddy would do if I went home and got things from the house and gave them away to people.

Mrs. Gibson saw me watching and scooped up two bowls of chili, then started toward me, limping just a little. "Oh, Jenilee Lane, it's good to see you here," she said, handing me one of the bowls. "I was sure worried about you last night."

"I'm all right."

She smiled again, a fluttery smile, like she had a butterfly caught in her teeth. "We got over to Weldon and Janet's all right. No damage over at their house."

I didn't know what to say. I wished she would walk off so I could go back into the armory and not have to remember yesterday. "I'm . . . um . . . sorry about your house."

She shrugged and set the other bowl of chili on the steps, then turned around to lean against the cement dock beside me. "Don't matter. I wouldn't care if I lost a hundred houses, so long as all the kids are all right. I've lost things in my life, and I've lost people. I've come to know it's the people that matter. Anyway, there are lots of folks worse off than me. It's good to remember that."

"Um-hmm," I said, looking at the chili and feeling a lump in my throat. I didn't think I could eat anything.

"How about your brothers? Have you heard any news?"

I shook my head, setting the chili on the armory steps. "I better get back in there with Doc," I said, feeling tears start to prickle. *It doesn't help anything to cry.*

She reached across the space between us and took my hand in hers, then covered it with her other hand. "You're a brave girl, Jenilee Lane," she said, just as she had the day before. "You done a brave thing saving me and Lacy yesterday. I want to thank you for that. Not everyone would of done it. Who'd of thought that—"

She stopped, and our eyes met for an instant. I looked at her gray hair, coming out of its bun in curly wisps, and her face, wrinkled from years in the sun, and her eyes, blue-violet behind her eyeglasses. Her breath seemed to be caught behind the overhang of her chest, hiding the rest of what she was going to say—the part she thought she maybe shouldn't say now, after everything that had happened. What she would have said a day ago, without a second thought.

Who would of thought one of you Lanes would help somebody out?

I pulled my hand out of hers and turned away, muttering, "I better go help in the armory. I'm not really hungry." Rushing up the steps, I left her.

I knew if she looked at me, really looked at me, she would see the truth—that I wasn't anything like her and

Mr. Nelson, Weldon and Doc Howard. I was only there because I was afraid to be anywhere else, because I didn't want to be alone. It hadn't occurred to me to bring blankets, or cook food, or search our cabinets for medicine and bandages.

But I imagine, deep down, she knew all of that about me, just like everyone else did. They knew we Lanes didn't do anything just to be charitable, and I was still Jenilee Lane, a grown-up version of the little girl they all whispered about behind their hands. *Poor little thing doesn't have any upbringing. Her mama's been sick since she was just little, that farm's falling in around their ears, and that father of hers, well, he's* . . . The descriptions would vary. They called him everything from a no-good drunk to a criminal.

I knew that as soon as these days passed, things would go back to the way they were before, and they would say those same words again. Words like that don't go away just because a tornado blows through town.

I heard Mrs. Gibson coming after me, her feet scrunching heavily in the gravel as she walked around to the steps. I knew she was right behind me with the two bowls of chili.

She caught up with me just inside the door. She looked past me instead of at me, and shifted her weight uncomfortably from one foot to the other. What she hadn't said hung between us. Both of us heard it.

She straightened her back and puffed out a determined sigh. "Jenilee Lane, you take a break and eat this food," she scolded, then turned to Doc Howard, who was standing nearby. "You too, Doc."

Doc Howard accepted a bowl, sinking wearily into a chair to eat. He looked pale and his hands were shaking as he lifted the spoon to his mouth.

Mrs. Gibson noticed it, too. "Doc, you need to get some rest. You're gonna give yourself another round of heart trouble."

Doc Howard rolled his gaze upward. "You been downtown talking to my wife." He smiled beneath his thick white mustache. "She send you up here to molly-coddle me?"

Mrs. Gibson huffed and braced her hands on her hips. "No, but I did see her downtown, when we took some chili to the sheriff's temporary station down there. She's pretty busy running the dispatch radio, but she's worried about you. A man who just got over a heart attack ought not to be doing this kind of work. Not for this many hours, anyhow."

Doc took a bite of chili and rolled it around in his mouth. "Not much choice about that. Anyway, I'm just helping out since they brought that Dr. Albright in here late last night. It's not so bad now that we've got a real doctor."

Mrs. Gibson glanced suspiciously around the room. "Don't see him here."

Doc shrugged, wiping a chili bean from his beard. "He went out the back door. Reckon he had to use the bushes. Why don't you go check, Eudora? He might be in some kind of trouble out there."

"Oh, Doc, you hush!" Mrs. Gibson flushed red. "Honestly!"

Mazelle Sibley piped in, from where she was carefully arranging bandages on the supply shelves. "Dr. Albright *has* been gone overlong. Maybe someone *should* check. . . ." She flushed, as if she'd suddenly realized what Doc had meant by *use the bushes*.

Doc Howard looked proud of himself. He always called Mazelle Sibley, Mrs. Gibson, and the rest of the garden club "the bossy biddy society." He liked to get the best of them when he could. "Mazelle, for heaven's sake, leave the man alone," he said. "Reckon he's entitled to a minute to himself. It's been a long morning. You been hanging on his coattails since the minute you got here."

Mazelle coughed indignantly, then threw her chin up and went back to arranging bandages. "Well, it only comes natural, my father having been the *doctor* in town for *sixty* years. You know I always was his best assistant."

Doc Howard rolled his eyes. "Yeah. I know. You told me that. Once or twice." He glanced sideways at me and winked, then went back to his chili.

Mrs. Gibson leaned over to look in my bowl. "You eat that chili, Jenilee Lane. You need something to eat. The sheriff told me you been savin' lives this mornin'."

Over by the medicine shelves, Mazelle coughed and smacked her teeth just loudly enough for us to hear.

Mrs. Gibson opened her mouth to say something, but the wail of a siren outside drowned her out as a car skidded up to the loading platform.

Doc set his chili on the floor and stood up as a highway patrolman rushed in carrying a mud-covered toddler bundled against his chest in a blanket.

"Doc! I got a little boy, probably around two years old." The highway patrolman unwrapped the blanket and tried to lay the naked, mud-covered toddler on the floor, but the baby screamed and hung on with all ten fingers and toes.

Doc Howard chuckled, relief lifting the corners of his thick white beard as he took a rag and wiped the dirt from the baby's eyes and mouth. "Can't be too much wrong with this one. He's stuck like a tick."

The patrolman smiled, and I was surprised by how good it felt to see someone smile.

"This one's a miracle," he said. "I was just driving along Highway Forty-two, and I looked over and saw a ball of mud moving in the ditch. No houses around or anything. I'm thinking I'm going to rescue a dog or something. I climb down the ditch and pick up this thing, and there it is, a little boy. He grabs aholt of me and he ain't lettin' go. Don't have no idea who he is, but

I put it out over the radio. You know someone's desperate to find this little guy."

Doc continued trying to check over the child while he clung to his rescuer. "See if he'll let you hold him, Jenilee, so I can get a good look at him. Mazelle, go see if you can find Dr. Albright."

I reached out tentatively, but the boy turned his face away and clung tighter to the patrolman's jacket.

Doc ruffled the baby's muddy hair and chuckled again. "I think you're stuck with him, Ray. He's adopted you whether you like it or not."

Ray chuckled. "Well, that'd be fine, except I've got to get back out in the car and drive those backroads. There's still people out there needing help."

No one answered. None of us wanted to consider the idea that there might still be injuries or fatalities.

Looking at the little boy, apparently still strong and healthy under that coating of mud, I felt my spirits rise. If something so tiny could survive the storm, then surely Nate was all right.

"O.K., Jenilee, you're going to have to take him and turn him around so I can get a better look at him," Doc ordered. "I'm amazed to say it, but as far as I can tell so far, all this little guy needs is a bath and his mama."

"Wow, that *is* somethin'," the patrolman said. Hugging the little boy against his chest, he rested his chin on the boy's head. He closed his eyes for just a moment, then began to pry loose the grip on his jacket. "Come on, little fella. Time to go now."

"Have you seen a white four-door Ford pickup with a brown stock trailer behind?" I asked, unwilling to miss the chance for outside information. "My brother and my father were headed to the cattle sale in Kansas City yesterday. They should have been on their way home when the tornado hit."

"I haven't seen it. But I've only been in this county. Could be they're stopped somewhere farther north. All the roads are blocked up there. No phones, so don't give up hope. A lot of people out there are still trying to get in touch with family." He looked at the boy in his arms again, seeming reluctant to give him up. "Just like this little guy. You know, there wasn't a house or an abandoned car anywhere near where I found him. Could be he's been wandering a while, maybe from one of the campgrounds or something. How he survived is just . . . well, a miracle."

I nodded, not knowing what to say.

He peeled the little boy loose and handed him to me. I held him clumsily as he squirmed in my arms and started crying, trying to get back to the patrolman. Mrs. Gibson was beside me quickly, taking him away. She held him while Doc finished checking him; then she picked up the blanket and nestled him to her chest. He stopped crying and burrowed against her like a kitten.

"There, that's better," she said, laying a hand over his hair and bouncing him gently up and down. Clinging to her flowered housedress, he sighed as his eyes started to close. She looked at me and winked. "Whenever you hold a little one, you bundle its face right here. Right against your heart, see? So he can hear it. It reminds him of his mama, and that's a comfort."

"Oh." I didn't know the first thing about holding babies, not human babies anyway. "It works with kittens, too," I said, because I knew about kittens, and puppies, and calves, and other orphaned baby creatures.

Mrs. Gibson smiled, her violet eyes twinkling. "Every living creature needs to hear the beating of another heart once in a while." Her words were quiet, almost as if she were only thinking them, not speaking at all. "Nothing God made on this earth is meant to go on its way alone."

I nodded without knowing why.

On his cot by the door, old June Jaans moaned in his sleep, then opened his eyes and looked drowsily at us. "Lordy, what you got there, Eudora?"

"You just—" Mrs. Gibson stopped as the hiss of air brakes filled the room. "What in the world . . . ?"

We walked to the door and looked out. In the parking lot, an enormous white motor home with glittering mirrored windows roared past the front of the armory, towing a matching enclosed trailer. Mrs. Gibson and I looked at each other in confusion, then watched the vehicle roll onto the baseball field down the hill. Shiny and freshly painted, it glittered in the noonday sun, a stark contrast to the dirt-covered, tumbledown town reflected in its windows.

June Jaans twisted in his bed, trying to see. "Well, what is it? Sounds like someone landed a plane out there."

Mrs. Gibson read the grandly scripted letters on the side of the motor home. "Lake Oaks Church Men's Relief Mission, St. Louis, Missouri." She shifted the toddler on her chest. "Well, praise be, finally help has come. And all the way from St. Louis."

We watched from the doorway as the air brakes let out another loud burst, startling the people on cots in the parking lot. Several sat up and shaded their eyes, looking at the vehicle as if they were encountering something from another planet.

The motor home door opened, and passengers began filing down the stairs—men in bright jogging suits, clean casual clothes, jeans and golf shirts, clean white sneakers and expensive loafers. They talked and stretched like participants on a Sunday-afternoon golf tour.

Mrs. Gibson watched them with her brows cocked doubtfully. The men below hardly looked prepared to save anybody, much less a whole town of tornado victims. In fact, they seemed unsure about how to operate the cargo hatches on their bus.

Mrs. Gibson crossed her eyes at me, and the expression made me giggle.

"I'm sorry," I said.

Covering her mouth, she chuckled, and we stood there for a while watching the men try to figure out how to open their truck and trailer. Finally Mrs. Gibson snorted. "Well, heck, I guess them fellas are badly in need of a woman to tell them what to do." She braced her hands on her hips. "Doc, you oughta come see this." She glanced over her shoulder. "Oh, look, Doc's fallen asleep."

Doc Howard was sitting in the lawn chair sound asleep with the bowl of chili about to spill onto the floor. I stepped over and took the bowl away, then went back to the doorway. "I think we better see if we can get Doc to go lie down somewhere quiet," I said. "He really doesn't look good."

Mrs. Gibson nodded. "I'll leave that to you. I'd better walk down there and get those St. Louis gents lined out. Looks like they just ain't gonna be able to function without some female instruction. Sometimes the Lord picks the strangest times to show a sense of humor." She moved to hand the little boy to me.

Mr. Jaans shifted and pulled his blanket back with a quivering hand. "Put that little boy in here with me, won't you, Eudora? I'll keep care of him."

Mrs. Gibson frowned over her shoulder at him, then looked at me, muttering, ". . . put this child in with that filthy old codger."

I felt sorry for Mr. Jaans. I leaned close to her, touched the baby's mud-streaked face, and whispered, "Right now, Mr. Jaans is cleaner than the little boy."

Mrs. Gibson set her lips in a hard line and tipped her chin up, the wrinkles around her mouth deepening. I remembered that frown. It was the same scowl she used to have when we walked past her house after getting off the school bus each day.

"We can't put the baby in bed by himself," I pointed out, "and I have to help Doc get somewhere to rest, and . . ." She didn't seem to be softening, and I couldn't imagine why she was being so gripey about it, except that she'd always had a hateful streak a foot wide. "The baby doesn't care *whose* heartbeat he hears."

She huffed and rolled her eyes. "He's a dirty old *drunk*." She said it loudly enough for Mr. Jaans to hear.

Anger welled up inside me, and I remembered all the times I'd heard her and those other old bats from the garden club whispering about me. "Yes, but he has a heartbeat. Even dirty old drunks have a heartbeat."

She rolled her eyes again, and I felt my temper boil over. For a change, I found the courage to say what was on my mind. "I'm going to give him that little boy the minute you leave, anyway. You may not like Mr. Jaans much, but he was the *only* one who *ever* came around and asked about my mama in all those years she was sick. He brought over fresh milk from his cows and vegetables from his garden all summer long. There's nothing wrong with his heart. It's better than a lot of people's around here."

She opened her mouth in astonishment. I realized I had struck a nerve, and I wasn't sorry. Inside me, there was that deep resentment of her and of all the rest of them who had treated us like we were less than everyone else.

Mrs. Gibson huffed a breath of air, her nostrils widening. "Well, all *right*," she said, then walked over to Mr. Janns's cot and pointed a finger at him. "Don't you roll over on this baby, June Jaans—you hear me?"

"Yes, m-ma'am," he said, stammering, face flushed. "I'll . . . I'll take good care of him. You can count on that, Eu-Eudora."

"All right, then." She laid the toddler in the bed, brushing the mud-covered strands of hair from his sleeping face before she pulled the cover over him. "If he wakes up, see if he can tell you his name. We need to find out who he is so we can get him back to his folks."

"Yes, m-ma'am," Mr. Jaans stammered again as she turned and headed for the door. He watched her walk away as if she were Miss America gliding down the red carpet.

I wondered how he could look at her with all that admiration when she treated him like dirt.

"I'll take good care of him, Eudora," he called after her, sounding almost giddy. "Don't you worry about a thing."

Mrs. Gibson threw her chin up and gave me a glare that could have fried an egg. I stared straight at her and smiled, the way Drew used to when she tried to look down on him. He just ignored her like he didn't care what she thought.

It felt good to stand up for myself. All these years I had been letting them say whatever they wanted to me and about me, and I never argued, because I didn't want anyone to come to our house and get into it with Daddy.

I felt a strange sense of freedom at not having to worry about Daddy now. On the heels of that lightness came a heavy slap of guilt that told me it was very wrong for me to be glad Daddy wasn't here.

CHAPTER 6

EUDORA

"Weldon!" I hollered, from the armory doorway. "Weldon, the doctor needs help in here! Weldon!"

He was too far away to hear, down in the baseball field with the church volunteers, setting up tents there and moving people into them from the parking lot. I turned and started into the armory, then stopped when I realized help wasn't needed after all. Flat on her rear, Jenilee Lane had her arms and legs wrapped around little ten-year-old Jimmy Ray Owens, who was spitting, scratching, struggling, and doing everything he could to keep his father and that city doctor from cutting off his pants leg so they could see where all the blood was coming from.

"He just slipped and fell. Fell right down on a broken windowpane," the boy's daddy said, white-faced. "We were just working to clean up what was left of our house, and Jimmy Ray fell off the cistern. There was blood everywhere."

The doctor nodded, pulling the cloth away from the

wound. "I'm going to need you to help hold him still. There is glass in the wound. I'll be administering Xylocaine first to ease the pain and reduce the blood loss; then I'll remove the foreign objects from the wound." He headed toward Jimmy Ray's leg with a syringe and a big set of tweezers, and the boy squealed and jerked like a trapped baby pig.

The doctor's hand slipped, and the boy screamed louder. "I said, hold him still!" the doctor hollered at Jenilee.

Jenilee wrapped her arms tighter around Jimmy Ray's shoulders and hands, holding him like a papoose. "We need you to be a big boy now, Jimmy Ray," she told him. "It's almost over. Just hold still. Hold still. Just a minute more. Just think, you'll have a story to tell when you get back to school. . . ." She kept right on talking, and all the while Jimmy Ray screamed at the top of his lungs and tried to get loose.

The doctor pulled the glass out of Jimmy Ray's leg, then quickly cleaned the wound.

When the antiseptic hit his leg, Jimmy Ray swiveled his head to the side and sank his teeth into Jenilee's shoulder through her T-shirt. She squeezed her eyes shut, but held on until the doctor finished the stitches and bandaged the wound; then she unclamped Jimmy Ray's teeth and handed him over to his father. She climbed to her feet, rubbing her arm with shaking fingers.

Jenilee glanced at me, and all of a sudden I realized I had just stood there and watched the whole thing. I hadn't lifted a finger to help; it all happened so fast, I couldn't think of anything to do except holler for Weldon. I just stood there, frozen and panicked, watching while little Jenilee piled in to help.

It's humbling to realize maybe you ain't as good as someone you've spent years looking down on.

I felt a hand on my shoulder and looked up to see

Weldon beside me. He followed my gaze to Jenilee, who stood next to the medicine shelf wiping blood off her hands.

"Someone down the hill told me you were hollering for me," Weldon said. "I guess they've gotten it taken care of."

I looked at my son, the son I'd always been so proud of, and I felt even more ashamed of myself. "Well, I gotta admit, I panicked. Doc Howard's dead asleep in the back room, and I couldn't rouse him, and Dr. Albright needed help right away. Next thing I knew, Jenilee was there," I said, still in awe of how she had seemed to know just what to do to calm Jimmy and hold him so that the doctor could work. "Weldon, I doubt if I ever been so wrong about anybody in my life as I been about little Jenilee," I admitted. "I never, ever thought that girl had so much pluck. She always seemed like such a mousy little thing, walking around town with her hair hanging over her face, hardly talking to anybody."

"Well, Mama, she hasn't had much of a chance." Weldon sighed and rubbed his eyes tiredly. "She's been taking care of her mother and her little brother since she was pretty small, and having to deal with her father ranting around drunk half the time. I think she's just learned to keep quiet and stay out of the way."

I nodded. "The only time I ever saw her act like she had any feelings was when the school bus hit that stray dog in front of my house. She run out there and tried to save that dog, and when he died, Lord, she just sat there in the road and cried." The picture of her in the road, probably only eight or ten years old, come into my head. "It's strange, now that I think about it—we all just stood there and let her cry."

Weldon shook his head, looking at the ground. "You're right, Mama. It's strange," he said sadly, then turned and walked outside.

I stood looking at Jenilee, realizing I never gave them

Lane kids a thought until that moment when I was trapped in the root cellar and Jenilee carried me out of there like a sack of potatoes. I never would of looked at her and guessed she'd be that strong. Never would of guessed I'd ever need her to come pull me out of my root cellar, either. It's an odd thing when life twists itself around to where the one person you thought you didn't need winds up being the one you need the most. Guess that just goes to show things don't happen by accident. You have a use for everyone you meet in your life, and God don't put in any extras.

I thought of Ivy's angel. *Was that what she was trying to tell me?*

A whimper come from June Jaans's bed beside the door. I looked over and saw him holding a toddler, trying to clean the mud off him with a towel. "June Jaans!" I spat, taking a few quick steps over there and reaching for the little boy. "What in land's name are you doing with a baby in your bed?"

June stopped what he was doing and looked at me with his mouth hanging open. "W-well . . . I . . . you give him to . . ." He paused, staring at me like I'd just sprouted a second head. "Eudora, don't you remember? You give him to me to keep care of—well, it couldn'ta been more than a couple hours ago."

My hands froze in the air between us, and my mind tried hard to bring that memory back. Breath choked in my throat, because I knew I should remember. "I remember," I snapped. "Course I remember." But I didn't. I got a snatch of it—a quick picture of a mud-covered little boy coming in with the highway patrolman. "The highway patrolman brung him in." I bent over the toddler, taking my eyes away from June's, because I was afraid he was seeing right through me. June Jaans had known me since I was seventeen years old. He knew it wasn't normal for me to forget.

"Um-hmm, that's right," he said. "The highway patrolman brung him in and Doc checked him out, said it was a miracle he was all right. You took him from the highway patrolman, and when you had to go down the hill, you put him in here with me. Sound asleep, he was, just wore out. He just now woke up, and I was trying to clean him up a bit. He don't like it much, though."

I nodded, and I had a feeling June knew that memory had gone right out of my head. That was why he retold the whole story of the little boy, so I would know what was going on. The worst thing was that I was grateful to him for it. Grateful to drunk old June Jaans! I didn't know how much worse than that things could get.

I took the towel and used it to clean the boy's tiny fingers while the little fella held on to my hand, silent and lost. "Sure I remember that," I said, trying to save my pride. "Wondered why nobody come for him, that's all."

"Oh . . . I understand," June said, his sun-freckled hand brushing mine as he lifted the blanket so I could clean the little boy's tummy. "He just now started to wake up and look around. I tried to get him to talk to me, but so far, nothin'. Suppose he's in shock, I guess. Poor little fella. Nobody come for him, and I sure am afraid of the worst. Afraid something might of happened to his folks, I mean."

A lump gathered in my throat, and I shook my head. "Well, that ain't so, and don't you even say it, either." I blinked back a tear that tried to wet my eye. "This little one didn't survive everything to end up alone now; you can bet on that. God wouldn't let it happen that way."

June frowned and smacked his lips, leaning back against his pillow. "Well, I'm beginnin' to wonder if God's payin' much attention here. He's probably busy in one of them big cities where all them fancy churches are," he barked, and the roughness of his voice, as much as what he said, sat me back on my heels.

"June Jaans, don't you say that!" I hollered louder than I meant to, and Annette Abshier, sitting with a

sprained ankle a few beds away, turned to look at us.
Lordy, I could imagine what she was thinking. *What's
Eudora doing over there talking to drunk old June Jaans?*

I lowered my voice because I didn't want to wind up
as fodder for garden club gossip. "Don't you say that,
June Jaans. Just because you're a heathen don't mean
this little boy is. God kept His hands around this little
fellow, just as sure as we're sittin' here, and He's going to
bring this boy's parents back to him. You just see to it
that he's taken care of in the meantime, you hear me?"

June caught my eyes again and twitched his lips into
a crooked smile, almost like he'd only made that com-
ment to bait me. "I hear ya," he said, smiling wider,
looking up at the ceiling and chuckling in his throat.
"You done put the fear of God back in me. I ain't
been scolded like that by a woman in a good many
years."

A disgusted snort come from me, and I stood up,
wishing he wasn't injured so I could pop him on that
smug smile. "Blanket's all wet. Looks like he ain't potty
trained. I'll go see if I can find a diaper." I shook a finger at him. "You just take good care of this little boy,
June Jaans. Don't let him fall out of bed."

"Yes, ma'am," he said, still smiling like an idiot.

I pulled the reins on my temper and took in a deep
draft of air as I walked away from his bedside. *I don't
know why you're getting yourself so crossways over dirty
old June Jaans, Eudora. He's just as sorry an individual
as he ever was.*

"Don't have the sense God gave a goat," I muttered
as I rifled through the pile of supplies by the door, looking for some diapers that would fit the baby. "Got more
lip than an old muley cow, and he's just as ugly. . . ."

"Excuse me?" A voice from behind startled me, and I
turned around to find that city doctor there.

I had to look at his name tag to remember his name.
"Oh, Dr. Albright, I'm sorry," I said, feeling like an

addle-brain. "I was just talking to myself. We old ladies do that sometimes."

He shrugged, looking as humorless as ever. As far as I could tell, Dr. Albright didn't have much personality, and what little he did have was pretty uppity and about as fake as that silly combed-over hair. *Wonder if he takes that off and puts it on the bedpost at night. . . .*

I realized I was staring at his hairline, and I flushed a little, ashamed. The truth was that, even if he was one of them rich fellas from out of town, we were lucky to have him here. Without him, there would still be no doctor at all, especially now that old Doc Howard had wore himself to a frazzle.

"Can I help you with anything?" I asked, glancing over his shoulder at little Jimmy Ray, who was being laid on a mattress on the floor by his father and Jenilee Lane. Mazelle Sibley was hovering behind them with a blanket, giving orders. "How's little Jimmy Ray's leg? He sure sounded in a lot of pain a while ago. Is he gonna be all right?"

The doctor continued rifling through the medicine shelf. "Are you a relative?"

"No, just a neighbor."

"Then you'll need to talk to his father for information." Grabbing a bottle off the shelf, he turned around and walked off without another word.

"Well . . ." I coughed, standing there shocked. It had been a long time since anyone had the nerve to treat me like that. "Just like one of them out-of-towners to act that way. Come here, and think they're better than the rest of us folks. Don't know how to be neighborly. Probably just roll people through on a conveyor belt in that big-city hospital."

"Excuse me, Mrs. Gibson?"

Caleb Baker was standing next to me holding a box.

I flushed again, because I knew he had heard me. He followed my line of vision to the doctor. "Sorry about that," I backpedaled. "That doctor just got my goat for a minute."

Caleb grinned, his hazel eyes twinkling. "Not the friendliest in the world, is he?"

His good-natured grin cheered me up. Caleb had a way of making folks laugh. "Caleb Baker, are you supposed to be out of bed? I heard from Mazelle that you gave everyone quite a fright earlier. Mazelle said you might of died if she hadn't got you right to Dr. Albright."

Caleb smiled a private little smile, glancing over his shoulder at Mazelle. "That's not exactly how it happened, but anyway, I'm fine now. Here's some supplies they brought in the motor home."

"Well, have you been able to contact your grandpa, so he'll know you're all right? I know he must be worried." I remembered the year before, when Caleb nearly died in a car accident, and his granddad held a special prayer vigil.

"I asked the sheriff to radio a message over to Hindsville." He set down the box of supplies and pulled off his long-sleeved shirt, using it to mop his forehead. "Getting hot, isn't it?"

I glanced at the scars on his arm, even though I was trying not to look. "It's good to have you here, Caleb." I couldn't express what was in my mind, the feeling that he was living proof it was possible to go through the worst of times and come out of it all right. "I mean, it's good to see you up and around and feeling well."

He blushed a little and hung his head, his light brown hair falling over his eyes. For just an instant, he reminded me of the shy little fat boy who used to sing in front of the choir box at his granddaddy's church in Hindsville.

"Thanks," he said finally.

He turned to leave, and I watched him walk out. Seeing Caleb Baker returned from the deathbed made me believe again that all things were possible.

That city doctor come back to the medicine shelf and

grabbed a roll of gauze, knocking over Mazelle's carefully arranged pile, then walked off.

He carried the bandage across the room to little Jimmy Ray's cot, where Mazelle had elbowed Jenilee and Jimmy's father out of the way and took over settling Jimmy Ray into bed. She was tucking a green army blanket tight around him, wrapping him up like a mummy. Dr. Albright didn't seem to like that. He pulled the blanket loose and draped it over Jimmy, then demonstrated something with the bandage on his own arm, giving some instructions I couldn't hear.

Mazelle watched what he did, nodding like she understood, then reached for the bandage.

Instead, the doctor turned and handed it to Jenilee. It was clear he'd been talking to her all along, and it was her he wanted to take care of Jimmy Ray. My mouth hung open, and across the room, Mazelle's did, too.

Mazelle stepped back, her eyes flaring the way they did last year when Annette Abshier's flower beds won the garden club's annual contest. Mazelle didn't take kindly to second place. She'd never had to. Her father being the town doctor, and her his only child, she'd been spoiled rotten all her life.

Mazelle spun on her heel and come across the room, looking around to see if anyone had noticed what went on. I turned quick to the shelf, so she wouldn't know I'd been watching, but she come across the room to me anyway.

"Well, can you *be-lieve* that!" she groused under her breath.

"Hmmm?" I tried to look busy. "Guess I must have missed something. I been busy trying to get these bandages stacked back on this shelf."

Her eyes flashed fire. "*I* already *had* those bandages stacked on the *shelf.* How in the *world* did they get *knocked* on the *floor?*"

A chuckle tickled somewhere below my ribs, and I

swallowed hard to make it go away. I didn't dare laugh. "The doctor done it . . . uhhh . . . by accident, I mean."

Mazelle pressed her lips together, tighter and tighter, and her face grew redder and redder, until she looked like an overripe persimmon starting to wrinkle up. "I don't know *why* I even *try* to help. Here I am, nearly killed by the storm yesterday, our store torn to bits, my house ruined, down here trying to help folks, and does *anyone* appreciate it? Does *anyone* ask about what *I've* been through? Of course not. People in this town are just as *backward* and *ungrateful* as they've always been." She huffed and braced her hands on her hips. "Since *no one* seems to *appreciate* my help around *here*, I guess I should drive out to the sheriff station at the lake, and see if I'm needed *there*. I heard this morning they might have as many as fifty people missing, or dead, or worse."

June Jaans calling across the room interrupted Mazelle's ranting. On purpose, I was sure. "You gonna bring those diapers here for this baby, Eudora?"

"I'm comin'." I hated to admit it, but right then I was grateful for June Jaans and his big mouth. "I better tend to this," I told Mazelle. She didn't answer, just huffed, turned around, and snatched her handbag off the shelf.

I grabbed a couple of diapers and scooted out of there. When I got to June's cot, I pulled back the cover and looked at the little boy, curled up as tight as he could get against June, looking up at me with big, worried brown eyes. "Poor little fella is a mess. Better get this diaper on him before the waterworks come on again," I said, loud enough for Mazelle to hear. From the corner of my eye, I could see her hovering in the doorway, hoping we'd try to stop her from leaving.

I couldn't help noticing a large bruise on June's chest and a pocket of swelling the size of my fist. "The doctor look at that?" come from my mouth. *Oh, Lord, what will Mazelle make of that? She'll think I've got something*

going on with this old fart. Why I even cared about that
bruise on his chest, I couldn't say. June Jaans's body was
fully pickled. If he did have an injury, it probably
couldn't be hurting him too much.

"Yeah, the doctor said I got some ribs bruised, where
I hit the steering wheel of my truck when the tornado
rolled it over. Got a twisted ankle, too, but the doctor
got it all wrapped for me. He said it'll be better in a day
or two. Least that's what I think he said. He don't take
too much time to explain things, that city doctor, I
mean. He just wrestles you around, asks you if it hurts
about the time you got tears runnin' down your face,
then mumbles what's wrong with ya as he's headed on
to the next person. He ain't very reassuring."

"He is a little odd," I agreed, noticing that Mazelle
was gone from the doorway. *Finally.* I couldn't help asking. "You were rolled over in your truck?" Taking the
sodden blanket off the little boy, I wiped him and laid
the clean diaper under him. I needed to find a notebook
and write down about the highway patrolman bringing
in the mud-covered toddler, so I wouldn't forget again.

"Yes, ma'am," June said, swishing his hand through
the air. "Caught right up like Dorothy and spun around
on the wind. I half expected to see the Wicked Witch of
the West come ridin' by on a broomstick with the monkey men trailin' behind her."

I laughed in spite of myself. My mind went back to
the year our whole high school class drove up to Kansas
City to see *The Wizard of Oz* on the big theater screen
at the Bijou, when it was brand-new. It was the first
color picture we ever saw.

June sighed and leaned back against his pillow, looking tired. "I don't suppose you remember that time that
all of us went to see Dorothy and Toto on the big screen
at the Bijou?" he asked.

I jerked back in surprise, afraid he had read my mind.
"No, I don't recall." I wasn't sure why I lied.

"Oh, Lordy, I do," he said, chuckling again. "All the gals hung on to the boys when the Wicked Witch come after little Dorothy with her monkey men, and y'all cried when Dorothy sung that song about way up high, bluebirds fly. Can't respeak the name of that just now."

I turned my face away and pretended to be busy with the diapering. "Can't either. Can't recall." *Somewhere over the rainbow.* Watching Dorothy sing that song, that day, when I was young like her, pretty like her, a dreamer like her, was one of the fondest memories of my life.

"Funny, I can't recall that. . . ." June whispered, lost in his thoughts.

I nudged his shoulder to get his attention, feeling odd, feeling a closeness I didn't want. "Look here." I motioned to the little boy. "Pay attention so you can change his diaper when he needs it again and I ain't here." My hands trembled as I worked the tapes loose. I couldn't imagine why. "You pull these here tapes free like this, and you stick them down good and tight on this belly band. See? Like this?"

June nodded. "Don't look too complicated."

"Good. Then, here are two more diapers if he needs a change. If you can't sit up to do it, call Jenilee or Weldon or someone else. Just about anybody can change a diaper."

"I reckon," he said, looking intently at me, trying to make me look back at him.

Instead, I focused out the door. "I've got to get to work down at the soup line. You take good care of this boy, June Jaans, until someone comes for him, you hear?"

"Um-hmm," he replied, and I felt something warm, his fingers touching mine, trembling like mine.

"What was the name of that song?" His voice was barely a whisper, like the swish of a door opening on a hot summer afternoon. "The song Dorothy sung about bluebirds, what was the name?"

I stood there for just a moment, looking into his blue eyes and seeing that towheaded teenager who had been the best player on our school baseball team, the clown, the one everyone said would leave Poetry and go far. For just an instant he was that boy, the boy who took my sister, Ivy, to the USO dance in Springfield one night and never brought her back. . . .

"I don't know," I said, and pulled my hand loose from his. "I can't recall the name of that silly old song. What does it matter, anyway?"

I walked away and didn't look back.

Lord, Eudora, what's wrong with you, standing around there talking with that dirty old drunk? He ain't worth giving the time of day to.

I didn't stop hurrying until I got to the motor home at the bottom of the hill, even though I wasn't sure what I was running from. The men at the motor home had finished setting up their soup line and begun handing out bottles of water and other necessities from their pull-behind trailer. Some of them were busy raising army tents in the ball field, then moving folks down the hill to shelter.

The sense of calm was as strange as the sight of the tent village on the baseball field. With all those green tents from the armory, it looked like soldiers had set up camp in our town.

The young preacher who was in charge of the operation walked by carrying a shovel, his lips twisted with worry.

"Brother Colville, can I help you with somethin'?" I asked.

He stopped and fidgeted with the shovel handle. "Mrs. Gibson, we're going to have to do something about . . . ummm . . . well . . . ummm . . . sanitation." His freckled face turned as red as his hair. "We've got over seventy-five people who don't have any homes to go to and no . . . well . . . no . . ."

"No outhouse," I finished.

"That's it exactly, ma'am," he said.

I started to laugh. The desperate look on that young city fella's face was just plain comical. I suppose he couldn't imagine what folks would do without running water and flush toilets. "Well, young fella," I said, laying a hand on his shoulder and getting close to him like I was going to tell him a secret, "don't take long to build an outhouse. You dig a hole in the ground, build a big box around it, and put a door on one side, then put a bench inside and cut a hole in it. Everything else pretty much takes care of itself."

Brother Colville grinned sheepishly at me. "Well, I figured out that much. I just wondered if there were any Porta-Johns anyplace near town that we could go get."

"Nope. I'm afraid we'll have to do it the old-fashioned way," I told him. "Only Porta-Johns around here belong to Bell's Construction Company, and they ain't willing to bring anything down. Sheriff asked yesterday could he use one of their dozers, and Walter Bell said he don't have a dozer in working order. I know that ain't true because I seen them working with a dozer at a construction site on Ataberry Road not two days ago." I shook my head, spitting air through my teeth in disgust, wondering how old man Bell and his worthless son, Shad, could be so selfish. "Some people are just a sorry sort."

Brother Colville nodded, looking disappointed. "I guess I'd better get back to work the old-fashioned way, then."

"Reckon."

Janet's car drove up in the parking lot, and I turned and headed up the hill. I saw Janet lean over and say something to Lacy in the passenger seat, then get out and walk into the armory carrying blankets.

Lacy stared right through me as I walked up to the car. For just a heartbeat, my mind told me it was Ivy sitting there. With her pale gray eyes and dark hair, she looked so much like Ivy.

"Hello, sweet one," I said, wishing just this once she would talk to me. "You didn't want to stay home with the other kids this time?" She didn't respond. "Lacy, honey . . ." Again, she didn't move. I laid my hand over hers on the doorframe.

"Look, there's Jenilee," I said as Jenilee Lane walked out the armory door for a breath of fresh air. I motioned to her. "Come here, Jenilee. Janet brung our little Lacy."

Jenilee came to the car door and leaned close to Lacy. Lacy raised her eyes, a little spark coming into them, but she didn't say anything.

I stood there watching, struck by how alike they were—two frightened little birds hiding in the grass together.

"You did a good job yesterday," Jenilee said. "You're a very brave girl."

You're a brave girl. I remembered saying that to Jenilee yesterday.

Lacy looked for a long time into Jenilee's eyes, then slowly reached up and touched the hay-colored strands of Jenilee's hair, bringing her closer. My heart stopped in my chest as Lacy moved her face close to Jenilee's cheek and whispered . . . something.

Jenilee nodded. Looking into Lacy's eyes, she took Lacy's face in her hands. "Yes, it was. But we're all right now. The tornado isn't going to come back. Don't worry."

A car horn blared nearby, and Mazelle's silver Chrysler roared across the parking lot, skidding to a stop in front of the armory door.

Jenilee stood up to look, then hurried toward the car.

Lacy ignored the racket and stared across the field like she was too far away to hear it.

CHAPTER 7

JENILEE

The driver laid on the horn as the silver car skidded to a halt. I rushed to the driver's-side door, my heart pounding. On the armory steps, Caleb set down the stack of blankets he was carrying and also ran toward the car.

The smoked window lowered, and I realized it was Mrs. Sibley inside. My stomach twisted into a knot. "Is . . . is something wrong?"

She leaned out, both hands clasped on the halfway-open window. Her urgency lit my nerves like a sparkler. "Well, of *course* something's wrong, *Jenilee*," she sneered, then looked over my shoulder as Caleb stopped behind me. "Caleb, is the sheriff back yet?"

Caleb glanced at me and shrugged his shoulders, so I answered the question. "No. The last I heard, he went down to the rescue center at the lake. Can I help . . ." *Can I help you?* What a stupid question. Of course not.

She rolled her eyes and slung her head sideways, causing her helmet of fluffy gray hair to bounce up, then settle into place again. "Well, *not* unless *you* have a way to get a fifty-gallon barrel off a *bull's head*." She turned to Caleb again, talking to him instead of me. "I was just on my way down to the rescue station at the lake—I was needed there, you see—and just as I came onto farm road Nine-thirty-five, right there in the road, there was a . . . oh . . . *ga-ra-cious!* There it is!" She pointed far down Main Street.

Caleb and I turned to look as a massive Charolais bull crashed through the remains of the pharmacy on the edge of town.

"What the . . . ?" Caleb muttered. "It's got a barrel stuck on its head."

Dr. Albright stepped out of the armory and walked down the steps, scowling as he approached the car. "Is something wrong out here? I heard a car horn."

I shaded my eyes, trying to get a better look at the big white bull as it crashed through town, its head and neck wedged inside a crushed fifty-gallon metal barrel. "How in the world . . . ?"

Mazelle leaned farther out the window, pointing down the hill, waving her finger. "That thing rammed right into my car on the county road! I'm lucky to be alive. It knocked me right into the guardrail of the bridge." She adjusted her glasses and peered at Dr. Albright, waving her finger at the dented fender and broken headlight on her car. "Call the sheriff. Tell him to bring a *rifle*. That *creature* is liable to kill someone! I'm lucky to be alive."

Dr. Albright glanced down the hill, but the bull had disappeared into what remained of the old sale barn. The muted sound of crashing and bellowing testified to the fact that he was still inside.

"Hurry, now!" Mazelle screeched. "They can get him while he's still trapped inside."

Dr. Albright shrugged, still confused about what was going on. "I'll go call the sheriff on the radio."

"No!" I heard myself say. "No. Don't call the sheriff.

That's Mr. Jaans's old bull, Charlie. He's a big pet. He's just scared."

"I'm sure the sheriff can handle it."

"We can't take a chance on someone shooting him. He's a pet," I insisted.

"He's a *menace!*" Mazelle waved her hand wildly out the window. "Call the sheriff!"

Dr. Albright shifted from one foot to the other. "We can't have a dangerous animal on the loose. We have a whole field full of injured people down there. What we *don't* need are any more injuries."

"*Ex-actly,*" Mrs. Sibley chimed in. "We don't need any more injuries." She climbed from the car and slammed the door. "For heaven's sake, I'll go in and call the sheriff *my-self.* This is a dangerous situation. Lord. I think I have *whiplash.*" She disappeared through the armory door, screaming, "June, that worthless bull of yours is crashing through town like a wild animal."

"No one is shooting that bull!" I hollered after her, then wondered whose voice that was. I had never, ever in my life raised my voice to anyone that way, especially not to Mrs. Sibley.

Dr. Albright glanced from me to the building and back, trying to decide what to do.

Caleb pointed down the hill. "Oh, shoot, here comes the sheriff. Someone else must have called him."

The sheriff's car skidded into the parking lot between the vet clinic and the sale barn. "Oh, no!" I gasped, and started running down the hill. Caleb followed, passing me before I reached the ditch.

As I crossed the road, the sheriff and his deputy started banging on the pipe fence, trying to keep Charlie from charging. The bull was trapped in the corner of one of the sale pens, pawing mud into the air and slinging his head and the barrel into the pipe fence.

"Don't shoot him!" I hollered, sliding to a halt beside Caleb.

The sheriff glanced over his shoulder at me. "I ain't sure what we're gonna do. Darnedest thing I ever seen. Don't know how in the world that bull got that bent-up barrel stuck on his head, but one thing's for sure: We can't let him get out of here, and we can't go in there with him. He's likely to kill somebody. There isn't a corral here that's still in one piece to lock him up in, either."

"Guess we could try to rope him or somethin'," the deputy suggested.

"Well, what in the world you gonna rope, Tom?" the sheriff scoffed, banging his nightstick against the iron fence to keep the bull from charging. "His horns are *inside* the *barrel.*"

"Well, I don't know. That's a problem. Guess we could—"

An idea came to me. "Wait, just keep him there for a minute." I hurried across the parking lot to what remained of the vet clinic, partially tumbled cement-block walls with the roof ripped off.

"Jenilee, what are you doing?" I heard Caleb call after me as I squeezed through the metal door, which was hanging ajar.

"Getting some . . . ouch . . . tranquilizers," I called back, scrambling across the debris toward Doc's medicine room. "Doc keeps all of that in the old refrigerator." I climbed through another collapsed doorway into the back room. The refrigerator was lying on its side with the door hanging open. Bottles of livestock medicine were everywhere, some shattered, some intact. I searched through them until I found a vial of Acepromozine and a syringe. One of Doc's vet kits lay nearby. I grabbed it and headed through the debris again.

"I found it," I said, shoving the vet kit out the door. "Here."

Caleb took the box and helped me through the door. "What are you going to do?"

"I'm going to tranquilize him." I took out a syringe and pulled a dose of Ace, then squirted a little from the tip to remove the air bubble.

"You're gonna what?" Caleb looked doubtfully at the syringe as he followed me toward the corral. "You going to throw that at him or something? Because you can't get in there with him. He's ramming those fences at a hundred miles an hour."

The sheriff reached out and caught my arm just as I was going to squeeze past his deputy into the corral. "What are you gonna do with that?"

"Tranquilize the bull," I replied, determined to go through with my plan.

"How the heck you gonna do that?" The sheriff stopped banging on the fence and looked at me as if I had gone completely out of my mind. "Minute he hears you in there, he's gonna charge."

"I'll be quiet," I said, jerking away.

"This ain't an episode of *Wild Kingdom,* Jenilee Lane. He'll charge as soon as you stick him with that needle."

"I'll be quick."

"You ain't gonna be able to do that."

"Watch me," I shot back. The sheriff just stood and gaped.

I moved slowly across the corral, thinking, *This ain't an episode of* Wild Kingdom. Holding the syringe ahead of me, I moved one careful step at a time through the mud as Charlie slung his head and rammed the fences with the fervor of an animal gone mad from hunger, thirst, and fear.

My heart stopped in my chest as I inched closer and felt the heat of the bull's body, smelled the scent of sweat and dirt. I heard the rattle of his breath as he paused for a moment, and then the deafening collision of metal against metal as he charged the fence again. I waited for him to stagger to his feet and pause again;

then I rushed forward the last few steps, stabbed him in the flank with the syringe, squeezed the plunger, and jumped out of the way with the needle still hanging loosely in Charlie's skin.

The bull bellowed, wheeled around, and charged toward the men, who scattered across the parking lot with Charlie roaring behind them.

The sheriff, beer belly and all, shinnied up the trunk of a tree with the grace of an acrobat. Charlie rammed the tree, then stumbled unsteadily backward as the tranquilizer began to take effect. In slow motion, he took another run at the tree, stumbled back, charged again, then fell to his knees and lay down, panting inside the barrel.

Ashen-faced, the sheriff climbed down from the tree. "If I told that story, no one would believe it. Come on, boys, let's see if we can get this thing off him. Maybe if we twist it around some and pull, his head might slide on out."

I moved forward and tried to help guide the barrel off the bull's neck as the men pulled. Slowly, inch by inch, the barrel worked loose until finally Charlie's head, bloodied and bruised, tumbled free. He laid his massive head on the ground and sighed, as if he knew his misadventure was finally over.

Caleb squatted down and rubbed the curly tuft of hair between Charlie's ears. "Poor fella. Been one heck of a day, hasn't it?"

Charlie rolled his eyes drunkenly at the sound of Caleb's voice, then pulled in a huge breath and let out a long snort, clearing his nose on Caleb's jeans.

"Yuck!" Caleb looked at me and curled his lip. I laughed, and everyone else laughed with me.

"I guess we can take it from here," the sheriff said finally. "We'll get some ropes on him before he wakes up."

I stood up and retrieved the vet box. "Be careful what you do with him. He's an escape artist. He gets loose from the Jaans place every time there's a storm." Kneeling down beside old Charlie, I stroked his bloodied coat. "I'm going to go ahead and suture this cut where the barrel was on his neck and give him a shot of penicillin. It'll be easier to do it before he wakes up." I pulled out a suturing packet. No one argued about whether I was capable of doing it or not. They just watched me clean Charlie's wound and put in an even row of stitches, then give him a dose of intramuscular penicillin just before he started to come back to life.

Caleb cleaned up the supplies and closed the vet box hastily. "Well, no wonder you were so good at dissecting frogs in science class," he joked as we started up the hill. "I didn't know you knew how to do that."

None of you knew anything about me, I thought, but I said, "Caleb, I worked for Doc Howard almost all the way through high school. Until I took the job writing invoices at Bell's Construction Company, that is."

"Yeah, I guess you did. I just never pictured you as the bull-wrestling type." He cracked a wry smile.

I smiled back. "Well, there are a lot of things you don't know about me." The wrong thing to say. It opened up too many doors to too many subjects.

"I guess that's true." He looked away, toward the armory. "You still dating Shad Bell?"

I tried to decide how to answer, wondering why he would ask about Shad and me. I pretended to focus on my footing as we crossed the ditch. "Shad's been gone out of town ever since"—*since he got caught selling drugs, and his daddy sent him to Wyoming to get him out of the state*—"since he went to Wyoming to work on his uncle's ranch. We've only seen each other a couple of times since he moved back to Poetry last month." That wasn't exactly true. I saw Shad every day at work in the construction company office. He wanted things to be the way they used to be when we were dating in high school, and I wasn't sure they could be.

"Why?" I asked Caleb.

"Well, I just figured, with you working for his daddy . . ." He paused, as if there were something else he didn't want to say, then finished with, "I just saw his truck pulling into the armory. I thought maybe Shad was here to give you a ride home." He slid his hands into the pockets of his jeans. "I wanted to make sure I had a chance to tell you . . . well, thanks . . . before you left."

You're welcome, Caleb. You're really welcome. "You don't have to say thanks. Anyway, I'm not going anywhere. I want to stay here, in case word comes about my father or my brothers."

The rumble of an engine rattled the late-afternoon stillness on the hill above us. I knew the sound even before we crested the hill and the truck came into view— red Dodge four-by-four, custom paint job, glass packs on the pipes. Shad's truck.

Caleb paused at the corner of the parking lot. "I'm going down and get something to eat at the motor home. You want to come along? Cold chili and dry corn bread ought to taste good after a full day of bull wrestling." He gave Shad's truck a narrow look. I couldn't blame him. Shad was one of those kids who'd liked to pick on Caleb back in school.

"No. I want to see if Shad has news about Daddy or my brothers. They might have contacted the construction office, looking for me."

Caleb paused a moment longer unsure.

"You go ahead," I said, starting toward Shad's truck. "I'll be just down the hill."

He turned and walked off, and I hurried to Shad's truck, hoping he would have news. On the heels of that thought came apprehension, murky and black, a sense of something bad about to happen.

Shad jumped out before the engine quit shuddering. "Where have *you* been?"

"What?" I stepped back, a habit from a past with him

that didn't seem so long ago now. He was already acting jealous and possessive, the way he used to when we were together back in high school.

He stopped about two feet away and threw his hands in the air. "I been lookin' all over the woods by your house, thinkin' something happened, that maybe you was outside when the tornado come through, and you was layin' in the woods dead. Where's Nate and your daddy?"

Tears pressed into my eyes, because I realized he didn't have any news. I swallowed hard. Shad hated it when I cried. "They never came back from the sale in Kansas City yesterday." *Was it just yesterday?* "Nobody has heard anything about them at all. I thought maybe you were coming with news."

"I haven't heard anything. I'm sure they're just holed up somewhere waitin'. There's a lot of roads flooded and blocked between here and Kansas City." Again, he threw his hands into the air, widening his eyes at me. "How are they supposed to let you know anything if you *ain't home*?"

I winced and looked away. I hated it when he talked to me like I was stupid. "The phones are out. They couldn't get in touch with me there, anyway."

"Well, at least *I* could of found you there." His voice echoed across the parking lot. By the soup kettles below, Mrs. Gibson stopped talking and looked our way.

"I'm all right. I couldn't just sit at the house alone." I wondered why I was explaining myself to him. Why I felt I had to.

"You look like crap. Did you get scratched up or somethin'?"

I wiped my face on the shoulder of my T-shirt. "I'm all right."

He pulled me into his arms. I wanted to push away from him, but I knew he would get mad and make a scene in front of everyone. I closed my eyes and tried to think.

I felt him release me, slip his arm around my shoulders, and guide me toward the truck. "Come on. I'll give ya a ride home."

An answer drummed in my head, growing louder until finally it found a voice. "No. I'm staying here."

He kicked a boot toe into the gravel, sending tiny stones across the parking lot. "What's wrong with you? You get knocked in the head or somethin'?"

Actually, yes. "I'm helping the doctor take care of people here. I can't leave."

"Jenilee, that's ignorant. What do you know about doctoring people?"

The way he said it cut deep—as if there were no possibility that I could do something so important. I wanted to tell him about everything that had happened today. I wanted to say, *I know more about taking care of people than you think. I've been doing it all my life.* Instead, I looked away and said, "Enough, I guess."

He just shook his head and said, "This is stupid. Get in the truck," like he knew I would do it.

For the first time in my life, I stood my ground. "I'm staying here. You could stay and help, too." Some part of me hoped he would say yes, even though I knew better. Shad only did what Shad wanted to do.

He started toward his truck, cussing under his breath. "I ain't got time. I gotta go check on the construction site down Ataberry Road. We got a dozer and a few other things still there. Daddy said to load the dozer up and take it home, so nobody gets ideas about using it."

He climbed in the truck and started the engine, rattling the ground beneath my feet. I stood watching him, thinking about what he had said. *Daddy said to load the dozer and take it home, so nobody gets ideas about using it.*

Had he even considered how much a dozer would help in town right now? Had he even thought about the fact that, even though his daddy told him to take the dozer home, it might not be the right thing to do?

Of course not, Jenilee. He always does exactly what his daddy says, just like you do. Even if it's wrong.

I crossed my arms over myself and watched him drive away, the truck roaring through the parking lot, scattering debris. I watched it turn onto Main Street, steering haphazardly around downed branches and piles of rubble, until it disappeared behind what was left of the sale barn.

Staring at the spot where it had left my sight, I thought about how much had changed in the space of one ordinary day. It was late afternoon again. Just twenty-four hours ago we were living in a different world. I was somebody different. How could so much change in so short a time?

"Amanda Lynne! Amanda Lynne!" a voice called from somewhere down the hill.

"Here, Mama."

The second voice was close, the high-pitched singsong of a child. I looked down to see a little red-haired girl, maybe five years old, sitting on the armory steps holding the injured cat I had found earlier in the day.

I had forgotten about the cat. "Are you taking care of the kitty?" I asked.

"It's *my* kitty," she said. "He blowed away in the storm. I don't know how he getted here."

I smiled, watching the cat nestle into her arms. "Well, it's good you got him back."

"I hope my grandpa comes here, too."

"Me too." A lump rose in my throat.

She glanced up as her mother crested the hill, looking frantic. "Amanda! I asked you not to wander off. You scared me to death!"

The little girl stood up, frowning guiltily at her mother. "I had to find Gray Kitty." Rubbing her face against the softness of the cat's fur, she smiled at me. "Anyways, I was talkin' to the doctor lady. That's all. I wasn't alone." She shifted the cat and put her hand in her mother's.

"Sorry," her mother said, smiling at me. "She's been fussing over this cat all day. She let him get out the door yesterday, and we couldn't find him when the tornado came. She felt so bad about it, she just cried and cried, and then this morning when we came here, all of a sudden, there was her cat. It was amazing. It was a miracle."

"That *is* amazing," I replied. *A miracle. Is there a place for miracles in the middle of something so terrible?* "I'm glad you got your cat back, Amanda Lynne."

Something about saying her name triggered a memory in me, and I raised a finger. "Don't leave yet. I think I have something else of yours." Excitement filled me, and I hurried into the armory and grabbed my forgotten bag of keepsakes from under Mr. Jaans's bed. He jerked in surprise and looked at me.

"Long story," I whispered, because the toddler in his arms was asleep again. I rushed out the door.

Amanda Lynne and her mother watched me questioningly as I unfolded the sack on the steps and dug through the photos until I found the little gold bracelet. Untangling it from the nest of papers, I read the engraving, *Amanda Lynne.* "This must be yours," I said, holding it out to her.

She covered her mouth with her hands. "My bracelet!" she gasped behind her fingers, then took it carefully, as if she couldn't believe it was really there. Holding it in front of herself with one hand, she danced in a circle, singing, "My bracelet! My bracelet!"

Her mother gaped at me in amazement. "Where in the world did you find that?"

"About three miles out on Good Hope Road, just lying by the ditch." I caught a dose of Amanda's joy and found myself smiling. The horrible feeling inside me vanished, and the joy of the moment replaced it.

Amanda's mother touched her trembling lips, then laid a hand over her heart. "Oh," she breathed, watching her daughter dance with the cat in one arm and the bracelet held out in front of her. "Her grandpa got her that bracelet. It's special to her. Thank you so much for returning it."

"You're welcome." *Of all the people I could have run into, I ran into Amanda Lynne, and I was the one who found her bracelet. Miracles do happen. Even here. Even now.*

Especially now.

"When everything's gone, little things matter a lot," Amanda's mother said. "We still haven't heard from her grandpa. He lives up toward Kansas City. We're keeping our fingers crossed and praying."

Perhaps the cat and the bracelet are the answer to a prayer. Maybe prayers do get answered. "Me too," I said finally, thinking of Nate and Daddy.

She seemed to know what I was thinking. "Good luck." She took Amanda's hand, the bracelet laced between their intertwined fingers as they started down the hill.

CHAPTER 8

The sun crept lower as I listened to the sound of cars coming and going, picking up bottled water and hot food from the soup line below. In the camp, propane lanterns and campfires flickered to life. The scene seemed almost peaceful, but as I shifted my gaze to our devastated town below, there was no peace.

How can all of this be happening? The question tapped a wellspring of grief inside me. *It isn't fair. It shouldn't happen. What did any of us do to deserve this?*

It's almost night again, and Nate and Daddy haven't come home. No word of Drew. It's almost night. More than twenty-four hours . . .

Unable to face the pain that came with that thought, I climbed the steps to the armory to find something, anything that needed to be done. Some immediate need to block out eventual realities.

"Well, I just wanted you to know." At the sound of Mrs. Sibley's voice, I stopped just outside the door. "I *thought* you should be told. Well . . . because there could come a *lawsuit* out of it later, or something *worse* even."

"Mrs. . . . . uhhh . . . Sibley, is it?" It was Dr. Albright's voice.

"Why, *yes*. *Mazelle* Sibley. Don't you remember? I told you this morning that for years my father was the only doctor in this town, rest his soul. So I do know what you are going through, Dr. Albright. I do know how ordinary folk will come around thinking they know more about doctoring than the doctor, and that is why I feel it is so important that I . . . well . . . I inform you of this matter. You being from out of town, you wouldn't know."

"Mrs. Sibley, I'm tired, and I'm hungry. I'm not interested in making friends here or sharing the town gossip. If I hadn't stayed a half hour too long on the golf course and then tried to take the back roads to the interstate, I wouldn't even *be* here. But as bad as things were today, it is a good thing that I was here."

"Yes, truly. Oh, you don't know how true that is," Mrs. Sibley rushed on. "And that is *exactly* why I wanted to make *sure* you *knew* that—"

"That what? If you have something to say to me, just come out with it."

I took a step closer to the door and saw Dr. Albright throw up his hands and pace a few steps away. Mrs. Sibley followed him, twitching her nose like a mouse looking for a piece of cheese.

"That *Jenilee Lane* hasn't a *scrap* of medical training." She made a *tsk-tsk* sound under her breath, as if she hated having to tell him that. "I fear you've been misled. She shouldn't be giving medical aid to people. Well, my word, she barely even graduated high school. She might kill someone!"

I stepped back from the door, feeling as if something hard and cold had slammed into my stomach. I wondered what Dr. Albright must be thinking about me now.

Mrs. Sibley clicked air through her teeth again. "Well, I can *imagine* what *she's* told you about herself, but the *truth* is that there isn't a *one* of those *Lanes* who has more than a *high school* education, and that is *only* because the school pushed them through out of a sense of *charity*. The Lanes are the worst *white trash* in the county."

I didn't wait to hear Dr. Albright's answer. I spun around with the sack still clutched in my arms and ran away.

. . . those Lanes are the worst white trash *in the county*.

It wasn't anything I hadn't heard before. Why did it hurt so much now? Why did it make my stomach churn to think that she had said it to Dr. Albright?

Sitting on one of the empty picnic tables in the fading sunlight, I faced the answers to my own questions. It hurt because inside me there was the hope that things would be different now. It hurt because Dr. Albright looked at me with respect. Because, together with him, I had helped people. I had hoped they would begin to see me differently.

Now, one by one, they would all go back to the way they used to be, and so would I.

Footsteps crunched on last year's leaves, and I looked up to see Mrs. Gibson coming. I wiped my eyes as she sat on the bench beside me.

"What's in there?" She motioned to the paper bag in my lap.

Without thinking, I pulled it away. I was used to Daddy grabbing things out of my hands and looking them over as if everything belonged to him. If I acted like the things mattered to me, then he would tell me how stupid that was, or throw them in the trash.

"Pictures and things I found in our yard and on the county road," I said, hoping she couldn't tell I'd been crying. "Just things I thought someone might want back, but I don't know who they belong to." I pulled a school picture from the bag. "This one is the little Taylor boy. Are they here anywhere? I found his kindergarten graduation certificate, too."

Mrs. Gibson took the picture. "The Taylors come in for some bottled water earlier today, but they're gone now. I think they're camping out in the root cellar on their place. But if they come in tomorrow, I'll tell them it's here. It'll probably make them real happy to have it returned." She handed the picture back to me.

"It probably would," I agreed, and put the picture back in the sack. I sat staring into the bag for a moment, looking at the shadowy images of acquaintances, neighbors, strangers. Where were they now? What were they thinking?

Mrs. Gibson leaned closer and peered into the bag. "You didn't happen to find any notebooks around anywhere, did you? Nothing fancy. Just little spiral notebooks?" She scratched the pleated lines below her bottom lip, looking worried. "It's not a big matter, really. Just sometimes I write things down in notebooks, and, of course, they've come up lost with everything else in the storm."

I met her eyes for a moment over the top of the sack. There was desperation there, something more that she didn't want to say. "I haven't found any notebooks yet," I said. "I'll look for them as soon as I get home." Reaching into the bag, I took the piece of the old letter and held it out to her. "I found this. Is it yours?"

She glanced at the letter and shook her head. "No. Doesn't look familiar."

We sat in silence for a moment. Gazing at the letter, I wondered who had written it, and whether I would ever be able to return it to its owner. Someone wanted it back as badly as Mrs. Gibson wanted her notebooks. Someone had saved it for fifty years, and now in the blink of an eye, it was torn in half and stolen away on the wind.

The unfairness of that seemed monumental.

The fallen look on Mrs. Gibson's face echoed my thoughts. Her lips started to quiver, and a tear traced the wrinkles on her cheek as she looked at the haphazard village of tents nearby.

I felt something inside me buckle like a dam holding back too much water, and the horror of the past day rushed over me, loud and fast and relentless like the storm itself. Images flashed through my mind like a black-and-white movie running too fast—Daddy and Nate driving away in the morning, stew pot boiling, tornado disappearing into the sky, papers falling, Lacy beating against the cellar screen, the picture of the baby with the blue eyes, the father kissing his injured daughters. . . .

Those Lanes are the worst white trash *in the county.* . . .

The images, those words, whirled in my mind, punching holes somewhere inside me like puzzle pieces nailed to my soul. In the quiet of the evening, everything that had happened came back, and there was no buzz of activity, no urgent need for survival to keep it away.

Mrs. Gibson laid her hand over mine and squeezed my fingers. "Oh, honey, I didn't mean to make you cry. I'm just a foolish old lady. Don't pay any mind to me."

"It's not you . . ." I said, sobbing, but I couldn't explain what was wrong.

I felt her arms slip around me. She pulled me close and stroked my hair, the way Mama used to when I was little. I couldn't remember the last time anyone had done that to me, the last time anyone acted like they cared. Loneliness, desperation, sadness made me cling to her like a child.

We rocked back and forth in a well of sorrow, clinging to each other as we had on her cellar steps, trying to find a path back to the light.

"Oh, honey, you're just tired," she said finally, when I'd cried myself out. "Come on up the hill, and we'll find you a place to sleep. You're just all worn out. Things will look better in the morning."

I leaned on her, numbly following her up the hill to the armory, to a pallet near Mr. Jaans's bed.

"There, now, you rest," she soothed. "You just rest."

I closed my eyes, too tired to argue, my head throbbing where I'd hit the wall of the cellar. The images in my mind grew dimmer, more scattered, blurred.

"Is she all right?" I dimly heard Dr. Albright's voice.

"She's just tired." Mrs. Gibson's reply seemed far away. "She got a terrible whack on the head yesterday in my cellar."

I felt someone's fingers touch the wound on my head. "This should have been looked at. . . ."

Pain spiraled from the touch of his fingers, and I rolled over, throwing my arm over my head to keep them away. "Leave me alone," I whispered, drifting away from them, back to that quiet, dark place where there was silence. . . .

My pictures were there, all of my pictures, fluttering slightly in the breeze, as if they hadn't quite forgotten the freedom of sailing the winds. . . .

There was a candle burning above me when I awoke. I watched the flame spreading and coming into focus, spreading and coming into focus, as if someone were passing a prism between me and the light. I closed my eyes for a long moment, drifting.

Somewhere nearby, I heard the sound of someone crying. A woman. It sounded like Mama.

I closed my eyes, then opened them again, trying to remember where I was.

The room was dark and silent, save for the spill of moonlight from high windows overhead. In the light, a woman in a white sweater sat on her knees, her body curled around a tiny child. She wrapped the little one in her arms, rocking back and forth, crying.

"Oh, God, thank you, God. Thank you, God," she said, her voice a mere whisper between her and heaven. "Oh, God, thank you, God. . . ."

I tried to rise, to keep my eyes open, but they fell heavily closed, and my mind started drifting again. A good wind blew me into a calm, quiet place. I floated, like the pink-and-white nightgown caught in the breeze, pictures and papers dancing all around me. . . .

The first rays of dawn were drifting through the open doorway when I awoke again. The electric lights were flickering overhead, and the generator was humming, masking the sounds of people still sleeping around me.

Rolling over, I remembered in a rush where I was. I pushed myself to a sitting position, feeling weak and dizzy.

A hand touched my shoulder and I jumped, turning to see June Jaans on a cot beside me.

"Ssshhhh," he said. "It's all right. It's barely even mornin'. Go back to sleep a while."

I shook my head, feeling lost. "What happened?"

He smiled in understanding. "You just fell out. That new doctor says you got a nasty bump on your head, and you ought to of been resting yesterday."

"No, I mean what happened last night? I heard someone crying." I pointed to the center of the floor. "Right there."

He smiled. "That little boy's mama come and found him. Lordy, was she happy to see him! They'd lost him from the music festival during the storm, and they'd been lookin' for him everywhere. That highway patrolman found him miles down the road, if you can believe that. Nobody knows how he got there, or how he could of wandered that far." He smiled, moving his hand to hold mine.

His eyes, clear and blue against his weathered, aged face, met mine, and I knew we were both wondering how such a beautiful thing could happen in the middle of such ugliness.

"I remember," I whispered. "I saw her there. Right there with the little boy in her arms."

He nodded. "She come in the door and asked the doc,

had they seen a two-year-old boy, that they had been lookin' everywhere and checkin' everywhere around by the lake. . . ." He chuckled down in his throat. "Lord, that was somethin'. That baby heard his mama's voice, and wasn't no answer needed from the doctor. That baby like to have wiggled out of my arms, and he started callin,' 'Mama! Mama!' She come runnin' over here, and she scooped him up. She fell down on her knees right over there, huggin' that baby and crying." He smiled and moved his hand as if drawing the picture, the wrinkles around his eyes growing moist. "There was a big pool of moonlight all around her, just around her and that baby. Everything got quiet, and she sat there rocking him. Sat there for the longest time, like she didn't care if she ever did anything else again." Laying his head back against the pillow, he sighed and closed his eyes.

"I saw." A long moment of silence stretched between us. He held my hand, his fingers cold around mine.

"That's the way Geneva used to rock our grandbaby, Seth." His words were little more than a sigh, memories finding a voice that came from somewhere deep inside him. "We was in such a hurry when we raised our own children, Abbey and Carl. Then Abbey got stricken with the polio, and she was gone, and Carl grew up, and he started traveling with the army. But when he brought that grandbaby home to Geneva, she rocked him every minute she could. She said she didn't care if she ever did anything else. She said everything else would keep, but the baby wouldn't." He smiled. "Lordy, she loved those babies."

Releasing my hand, he pulled the covers up around his shoulders against the morning chill. I stood up, wondering where his son and grandson were now. I had never seen anyone visit at his place since his wife died six or seven years ago. In my earliest memories, I could recall my grandparents inviting him and his wife to Sunday dinners. I dimly remembered his wife's funeral taking place, and Mama wanting to go look in on him later that day. Daddy said she shouldn't take any food because that worthless old man wouldn't bother to bring back the dishes.

Mr. Jaans stirred on the bed, and I looked away guiltily, feeling that he could hear the ugliness in my mind.

"You remember this," he said quietly, sounding exhausted, near sleep. "That part of you that wants to care for other folks is like fresh milk. You might as well pour it out as you go along the path. It don't . . . keep in a bucket . . . very long." Letting out a long, slow breath, he relaxed into sleep.

I thought of the jars of fresh milk he brought when Mama was sick. He would set them by the yard gate and drive away. He didn't bother to come to the house, and we didn't bother to come out most of the time. We would go out after he left and bring in the glass jars of milk with the cream still floating on top. Mama said the fresh milk healed her more than anything that came from the pharmacy. Now I knew why. It wasn't the milk; it was the fact that someone cared enough to bring it.

"Well, you're looking fine and fit." Mrs. Gibson stepped in the doorway and smiled at me. "They're serving breakfast at the relief mission trailer. You come on down and get something to eat. There ain't so much to do today. Quite a few people been taken on to hospitals overnight. They even had to take in poor old Doc Howard, but just as a precaution because he was having some pains in his heart."

"Is he all right?" I climbed to my feet, wondering why Doc would have left without saying anything to me. "Someone should have gotten me up. Well . . . I mean, I just wish I could have told him good-bye and to take care of himself."

She patted me knowingly on the shoulder. "He said to let you sleep. He said just tell you he's all right, and he's only going to the hospital to keep Mrs. Howard from having a heart attack of her own."

"All right." I looked around the room, feeling strangely alone now that Doc Howard was gone.

Mrs. Gibson seemed to understand. She wrapped an arm around my shoulders. "The mission men are taking care of cooking the meals and handing out bottled water. They called the church over in Hindsville and had reinforcements come in last night. Now they got two trailers and a corn-dog stand down there. Looks a little like the county fair has come to town."

She gave Mr. Jaans a quick glance as we turned to leave. "I don't guess he'll be wanting anything right now." The look on her face was softer than the day before, as if even dirty old June Jaans had come to matter a little to her.

"Sounds like he was up most of the night," I said as we walked out the door. "The little boy's mother came last night."

"I heard." She smiled. "Weldon couldn't wait to tell me when I got to the armory this morning. I wondered why Weldon never come home last night, but now I understand. What with Doc Howard gone, Weldon would be needed here more than ever." She paused, raising a finger in the air. "Oh, by the way, the Taylors came here for bottled water first thing this morning, and I give them back the school picture of Justin, and his little kindergarten graduation certificate. Lordy, was Justin thrilled to get that back! He thought without it he was going to have to go to kindergarten all over again, and he was mighty concerned about that. His mama said that picture was the only one they had from his kindergarten year. She said to tell you thank you so much."

"I'm glad you gave it back to them," I said, thinking about it as we took bowls of oatmeal and a biscuit from the soup line and sat down at one of the old stone picnic tables. Tasting a spoonful of the oatmeal, I thought about the pictures still in my bag, perhaps a hundred or so, and the hundreds more that the storm had scattered.

Papers rattled on a bulletin board the rescue mission men had set up near the head of the serving line. It proudly proclaimed their sponsoring churches and held little folded pockets containing religious tracts, and a larger one holding a dozen or so tiny Bibles. People were reading the papers and leafing through the Bibles.

An idea came to me as I watched the pages flutter, and my heart started beating faster. "Do you think they would have some paper and a pencil in there?" I asked, grabbing a few last bites of oatmeal, then setting my bowl aside, the food half-eaten.

"I suppose they would. Why?"

"I have an idea," I said, taking a bite of my biscuit, then grabbing it and the bowl. "I'll be back in a minute."

I tossed the paper bowl in the trash can on my way to the motor home. Caleb was coming out the door with a tray of biscuits in his hands. "You look like a woman on a mission." He stopped, the tray suspended between us.

"I was wondering if I could get a pencil, and . . . ummm . . . some paper and Scotch tape."

He cocked an eyebrow. "Sure. Go on in the bus. Ben's in there. He ought to be able to find what you need."

"Thanks," I said, then hurried away like I had one of Daddy's hounds nipping at me.

I stepped into the motor home and waited a moment for my eyes to adjust to the dim interior. In the kitchen, a nice-looking dark-haired man was busy putting biscuits on a tray.

"Ummm . . . hello?" I said.

He started, then set the biscuits down and wiped his hands. "Sorry. I didn't see you come in."

"Are you Ben?" I asked.

He smiled, his bright blue eyes catching the light from the window. He stuck his hand out and shook mine. "Ben Bowman. Can I help you with something?"

"Caleb told me you might be able to get me a pencil and some paper, and maybe a roll of Scotch tape."

He seemed relieved that I hadn't asked for something more difficult. "That shouldn't be too hard." He started opening drawers, fumbling around. "There's got to be something like that here. You'll have to excuse me. I'm one of the extra hands who just came over from the church in Hindsville. I don't know my way around in here." Finally, he produced a black marker and some fliers for a church revival. "All right to write on the backs of these? Oh, and here's some tape."

"Sure. Thanks." I took the things he offered, the vision growing in my mind.

"No problem."

I thanked him again, then ran to the armory, an idea blooming in my mind, becoming something real, something urgent. In the armory, I found my bag of pictures near the pallet where I had slept. My hands trembled as I sorted through them, selecting three and quickly taping them to the paper. Beside them, I wrote in big block letters:

PICTURES AND MEMENTOS FOUND
SEE IN THE ARMORY BUILDING

I hurried down the hill again and pinned the paper to the bulletin board, then headed back to the armory.

CHAPTER 9

EUDORA

I shook my head, watching Jenilee disappear up the hill to the armory.

What in the world is that girl up to now? I thought, looking across the way at the paper she'd tacked to the bulletin board. It was too far away for me to read it.

Between me and the bulletin board, I saw Dr. Albright sitting at a picnic table, bent wearily over a bowl of oatmeal. He set down his spoon and watched Jenilee walk up the hill. Stroking the outline of his bottom lip with his thumb, he narrowed his eyes like he was thinking about something.

Like he was thinking about *her*.

I wasn't sure I liked the look of it. I'd come to care about Jenilee in the last few days, and that city fellow looking at her stirred an uneasy brew inside me. The last thing a backward little country girl like Jenilee needed was some rich city fellow who was old enough to be her daddy making eyes at her.

I walked to his table, thinking that maybe I ought to say something, or at least let him know I'd seen him

watching. He didn't even look up when I got to his table.
His gaze was still on Jenilee.

I noticed the diamond wedding ring on that hand he
was rubbing back and forth across his lip. *Doubt if his
wife would like the way he's lookin' at Jenilee.*

"Hey there, Doc."

"Hmmm?" he muttered. He must not of been embarrassed about his gawking because he didn't stop.

"I had a question I wanted to ask ya."

Jenilee disappeared into the armory, and the doctor
glanced at me, then down at his cereal bowl. For just a second, I thought he knew what I was thinking about him.

He cleared his throat, picking up his spoon, suddenly
all business. "It's been a long night. Unless this question
is about a patient, I'd appreciate your asking someone
else."

Well, his manners ain't any better this morning. He
didn't ask me to sit down, so I helped myself. I braced
my elbows on the table and stared across at him. If it
bothered him, he didn't show it.

I took a breath and started right into what was trou-
bling me. "Doc, I was just wondering . . ."

His cool blue-gray eyes were slightly narrow, icy, impatient. He had the look of a man who didn't let anyone
push him, who controlled every situation. He had the
better-than-thou look of someone who wouldn't possibly be gawking after a young girl in a way that wasn't
seemly, and wouldn't stand well for being accused of it,
neither.

I begun to think I had read too much into it. I lost my
nerve and decided I'd better take a little more round-
about course. "I . . . uhhhh . . . I was wondering. I wanted
to ask you about . . . about . . ." *Think of something, Eudora.* "Well, first, I wanted to thank you for helping us
here. You come when we sure enough had a desperate
need."

He tipped his chin back like he was suspicious of the

compliment. "As I'm sure you know, I came here completely by accident."

"Nothing in this life happens by accident."

There was a flicker of something in his pale eyes, something I couldn't quite read. Some bit of emotion that made me think he wasn't the rock he pretended to be.

"You were the answer to some pretty desperate prayers." I pressed on to see if I could break through that steel shell around him. Why I wanted to, I couldn't say.

He just shrugged and went back to his bowl of oatmeal. "I suppose you could look at it like that." He put a bite in his mouth, swallowed, then added coolly, "Or you could just say I turned on the wrong back road leaving the golf course, got my car stuck in the mud, and happened to be trapped there when the deputy came by. You could say that I wouldn't even have been here that day, except that I had two surgeries canceled, the golf course in St. Louis was too wet, so I drove out here to play a round of golf." The corner of his lips twitched—a smile? a frown?—hard to say. It was gone quick.

"I don't know why you'd want to describe it like that," I said quietly. "I don't know why you'd want to call it other than a string of miracles."

"I don't believe in miracles," he told me flatly, trying his best to finish the oatmeal so he could get away from me. "Not modern ones, anyway."

"I seen two just yesterday," I said, thinking about the emptiness that must be inside him for him to say that.

"I saw good medicine and some luck under bad circumstances. There weren't any magic roots and berries, angels, faith healing, magic potions, or miracles." He shook his head, letting out a heavy, frustrated sigh. "It's all just medicine. Science and biology, that's all."

"There's more to folks than that."

He stopped with the spoon suspended in midair, his

lips pressed in a thin, tight smirk. "I don't have time for more than that."

"That's a shame."

Silence fell between us as he finished his bowl of cereal and took a swallow of coffee. He glanced at me, then away, then back, like he was wondering why I was still there. "Something else you wanted?"

The question in my mind found quiet words. "You a man of faith, Doc?"

He tore the top off a packet of sugar and dumped it in his coffee. "I'm a member of the board at Grace Life Church in St. Louis." He paused to stir the coffee, then added, "If that's what you mean."

"That ain't what I mean." I had a feeling he knew it wasn't.

"Mrs. . . . Gibson, is it?" He smacked his tongue against his front teeth irritably. "I don't know why it was you felt compelled to sit down here and probe into my background, but I don't need it, and I don't have time for it. I don't need any amateur backcountry psychology, grandmotherly wisdom, life coaching, or faith counseling. I'm not looking to build relationships, make friends, or gather hero-doctor stories for my scrapbook here."

"I didn't say you were."

"I have a perfectly good life back in St. Louis—wife, house and two cars, kids that go to dance class, private school, and all that other jazz, the whole thing. You can rest at ease. I'm a happy man."

"I didn't say you weren't."

I noticed that his hands shook as he raised the coffee cup to his lips, took a sip, then looked toward the motor home. "The damned coffee is cold," he muttered under his breath, then stood up and walked away without another word.

I watched him as he downed the rest of the cold coffee like a shot of whiskey, threw the cup in the trash can with a vengeance, and stalked off toward the armory.

If you're happy, then why do you look at Jenilee like that? What is it you want from her?

I chewed the end of my thumbnail, trying to figure it all out and wondering why I cared. It really wasn't any of my business. Like he said, he wasn't looking to make any friendships in our little town. He only come to play golf on the exact wrong day, at the exact wrong time, and took the exact wrong road home. All by accident.

Except God don't create accidents. We only think there are accidents because we don't know what God has in mind.

And when you're a nosy old busybody, you don't like to let even God keep secrets. You do all you can to figure it out, and have a hand in the outcome.

Brother Colville come out of the motor home to wash out a kettle. He was there alone, so I took advantage of the opportunity.

"Morning, Brother Colville," I said, walking over to him.

"Good morning, Mrs. Gibson. You're here early this morning." He paused in what he was doing and stood up, bracing his hands on his back and stretching stiffly. "How are you this morning?"

I started to smile, then didn't. "Better than you, looks like." It didn't seem right to smile, with all that was going on.

Brother Colville nodded. "Long day yesterday."

"Um-hmm. Well, we sure appreciate it, Brother Colville. We surely do. We appreciate you and all your crew coming all the way from St. Louis, and you calling in all the extra help from the church over to Hindsville. And, my goodness, we surely do appreciate that Dr. Albright. He come when there was a desperate need. When lives were at stake, and he saved the situation. Little Jimmy Ray come within just an inch of cutting an artery in his leg and bleeding to death. Probably would have if Dr. Albright hadn't been here yesterday."

Brother Colville nodded. "He's a fine doctor. You

couldn't ask for someone more qualified. Dr. Albright is one step away from becoming the next chief of surgery at All Shores Hospital."

"Is he, though? Well, that *is* something." *Must be personality don't count for much in the medical profession.*

"A fine community man, too. On the board at our fellow church, Grace Life in Blakely Heights."

"That *is* impressive." Interesting that he didn't add more personal compliments, like *good friend, loving father, man of faith*—all those things preachers usually said when they bragged someone up.

Brother Colville seemed to be searching for something else to say. I wondered if he knew what I was thinking, if he knew his compliments rung pretty hollow.

"Has a heart for charity, too."

"He does?" It slipped out a little more honest than I meant it to.

"Why, sure." Brother Colville went back to rinsing the pot, like he wanted our conversation to be over. "Didn't you know that he was the one who put out the radio call that brought our relief van to Poetry? We were all set to head to a relief center in Marshall."

Good thing the preacher was busy rinsing out his kettle, because my mouth dropped open and I gaped like a cow trying to cough up a cud. All them unkind thoughts I had been chewin' about Dr. Albright went right down my gullet, and I got a bellyful of shut-my-mouth guilt.

"Oh, well . . . yes. I . . . certainly, I . . ." It ain't good to lie to the preacher, so I made an excuse instead. "Oh, my, look at the time. I'd better get back up the hill and . . . and see what needs to be done up there."

Brother Colville nodded, and I scooted out of there like I had brimstone on my tail. I walked up the hill thinking about my conversation with Dr. Albright, trying to piece together the puzzle and wondering why I cared to. In a day or two, he'd be gone and we'd probably never cross paths again.

*You shouldn't be such a busybody, Eudora. You ought
to stay out of things that aren't your business.*

I sat down on the armory steps, thinking about it.
*Maybe you ought to apologize to Dr. Albright for getting
into his business down there at the picnic table.*

Mazelle Sibley's car pulled into the parking lot and
come to a stop near where I sat, like that thought had
brung her there. She climbed out carrying a tray of
candy bars and cheese crackers.

"Well, good morning, Eudora," she chirped like a
spring robin.

"You back again this mornin'?" The words come out
of my mouth before I could stop them. Luckily she was
busy knocking her car door shut with her rear end, and
she didn't hear me.

I looked toward town instead of at her, hoping she
would pass on by me and go into the armory.

Instead she plunked her tray down and sat on the
step next to me, her body deflating with a huge sigh. "It
sure is hard to take in," she said, looking at what was left
of Main Street. "Sometimes my mind just wants to forget it all happened. I forget it for a minute, sometimes,
and then I look and it's all real again. I wonder how
we're going to get through it all."

"Um-hmm," I muttered, wishing she would get up
and leave. The last person I wanted to talk to right then
was Mazelle. I could tell by the singsong in her voice she
was ferreting around for gossip.

"So I see that Janet isn't here with you again this
morning."

I couldn't imagine what that had to do with anything,
but I knew Mazelle was aiming at something. She always was. "She went on home after she dropped me off
this morning. She needed to get Lacy back to the
house." Why in the world, today of all days, couldn't
Mazelle lay off looking for gossip?

"Well, I can understand that. Yes, I surely can. Poor

little child, left on the doorstep by her folks, and now having to go through this storm." She folded her hands in her lap, sticking her nose my way like a weasel sniffin' at the chicken house door. "I wondered why *you* didn't stay home *with* Janet today, Eudora. You look completely exhausted."

"Um-hmm."

"Well, I would think you would want to get settled in at Weldon and Janet's house. You will be staying *there* now, won't you? Now that you don't have a place of your own, I mean. It's a terrible shame about your house. It truly is."

"I reckon." Truth was, I hadn't let myself think about where I would stay after the worst was over. When I kept busy, my mind stayed convinced that I was going to go home to my own house eventually.

"Do you think you'll move in with Weldon and Janet for good? I mean, I'm sure they and the kids must want you to, what with poor little Lacy living there now, needing help and all. Surely you're not thinking of rebuilding the old place . . . well, at our age, I mean. It just doesn't seem practical."

"I really hadn't given it a good think." *I can't even make myself go back and look at the old place.* It was more than my heart could bear to think of all my life's work, all the things I thought were solid and would last longer than I did in this world, blown everywhere like so much trash. Below in town, I could see people sorting through what was left of their homes. I wondered how they got the strength to do it.

"I'm going to move in with Benjamin and Patty," Mazelle prattled. "They have been wanting me to move in with them in the worst way these last few years, but I've always said I didn't want to be a burden to my children." Which wasn't true. Mazelle was nothing but a burden to her children. She called around, seemed like daily, telling her kids, and anyone else who would listen, about who in town had died, and who was arrested, whose teenage daughter was pregnant, and who was getting divorced and why. Then she'd add on her own aches and pains.

Mazelle Sibley spread misery like cake frosting. It was no wonder she was enjoying hanging around the armory stacking bandages, wallowing in the sadness and grief, gathering horrible stories she could tell around town and to visiting newspaper reporters.

Looking up, I noticed Dr. Albright stepping out the door behind us. He stood on the stoop for a minute, not seeming to notice we were there. Bending his head forward, he rubbed his eyes, looking tired.

I hated the fact that he was going to see me there with Mazelle. Now he really would think I was an old busybody.

"Eudora . . ." Mazelle's voice scratched the surface of my mind, and I glanced sideways, realizing she was still talking, and she hadn't noticed the doctor standing in the doorway. "I said, did you hear about that little Anderson baby? Pulled right out of her crib by the wind. Just ten minutes after her mama put her down for a nap. Her mama was right in the next room when the tornado came through, and she couldn't get to the baby."

She sighed, shaking her head and making a sorrowful *tsk-tsk* with her teeth. "It's just the most terrible thing. So sad. A newspaper reporter came around earlier and asked me about it. I could hardly tell him the story for crying, myself. It's just the saddest thing. A newborn baby. They still haven't found her. Just can't imagine why something like that would happen to good *church-going* folks, and meanwhile, the houses of people like . . . well, the *Lanes*, for instance, left standing without a scratch." She crossed her arms. "And can you *believe* that *Jenilee Lane*, running around here pretending she's Florence Nightingale? Well, it's just a fortunate thing she didn't *kill somebody*. I can't imagine *what* she was *thinking*."

My dander rose when she mentioned Jenilee's name that way, like it was a dirty word to spit out. I realized I had said it that way in the past myself. "I imagine she was thinking that people needed help."

Mazelle tipped her chin up, and clicked her tongue against her teeth again. "Don't imagine you can blame that *Lane* girl for not knowing any better. That family is all so *backward*, and it's no wonder, given the way their daddy is. Wouldn't be the worst thing in the world if *he* never came back. Do you know, just the other day he and that *Shad Bell* came into my store drunker than Cooter Brown and darned near picked a fight with some poor truck driver who was just trying to get gas. They . . ."

Behind us, the doctor let out a long breath, so that Mazelle noticed he was there.

I realized I'd got myself interested in the gossip about Jenilee's daddy, and I felt a pinch of shame, because I knew in the past I would of joined right in.

Mazelle shifted on the step beside me, holding up her tray. "Oh, Doctor. I didn't notice you were there. Would you care for a candy bar or some cheese crackers? I salvaged these things from my store, thinking folks might be tired of chili and oatmeal." The doctor didn't reply, just glanced at her, gave a quick sideways jerk of his chin in answer, and then folded his arms across his chest, looking at the tent village below.

Mazelle went on talking to him. "I was just telling Eudora how horrible it is about the Anderson baby. Blown right out of her crib by the tornado and just two weeks old, and no sign of her yet, and her mother looking everywhere around town, completely out of her mind with grief. It's made me ill worrying about her and the baby and the poor father. I've been crying and crying all day long."

The doctor didn't answer and neither did I. A flicker of emotion crossed his face; then he closed his eyes tight and jerked his head quickly back and forth, shaking it off.

". . . heard there were six children missing from a day care in Shale City," Mazelle was droning on, sounding like one of those terrible talk show hosts on TV. "The police said they might never be found, I heard. Can you imagine that? That a person could just be swept up in a tornado and never be seen again? That a family could lose their *children*? Just in the blinking of an eye? *Gone?*"

Without saying a word, Dr. Albright turned on his heel and walked down the steps, and along the side of the building, disappearing around the corner like he couldn't take one more word of Mazelle's mean-spirited prattling.

"Well!" Mazelle made an offended cough in her throat. "He's an odd sort."

"He ain't the only one," I muttered, and walked off, too.

I heard Mazelle huff and mutter something, but I didn't turn around and say I was sorry. On any normal day, I would of put up with her and done my best to be cordial because we were in the garden club and the ladies' Bible class and various other groups together. None of that seemed to matter now.

I'm not sure why I walked around the corner of the armory after Dr. Albright. I didn't want him to think I was like Mazelle, though oftentimes in the past I had showed a pretty wicked tongue myself.

Olney used to tell me that once I latched on to an opinion, I held on like I was Moses and it come straight from a burning bush. It wasn't a good way to be, and it wasn't only them Lane kids that had been damaged by my gossiping. I had done damage to myself. All that mean-spiritedness took a lot of the laughter out of me over the years. I had pretty much let myself become a mean old lady.

I slowed my steps as I reached the corner, wondering

if the doctor might be just around the edge of the wall, and if he might not appreciate me following him. I took one last, careful step, cleared the corner, and just stood there staring.

There, squatted down in the long grass by the wall, was the doctor, his head in his hands, his shoulders round and trembling.

I stood still for a long moment, trying to decide whether to say something or just slip away. I wondered what had brought him to that point, crouched alone in the grass with his head in his hands.

Not a sound came from him, not a word or a sigh or a sob, just the quaking across his shoulders that said he was feeling something powerful.

He looked for all the world like a broken man.

I waited to see if he would notice I was there and look at me. Finally I stepped back around the corner and left him to himself. I didn't figure I'd know what to say to him, anyway.

Mazelle was gone from the step and headed toward the camp down the hill. Parked next to her sedan was Janet's car. The front seat was empty, the passenger-side door hanging open, and the seat belt bell chiming.

I scratched my head, climbing the steps to the armory. My eyes took a minute to adjust to the dim light inside. Jenilee was on her knees in the light from the door, her bag of pictures spilled out on the floor. She didn't even notice I was there, she was so busy turning the pictures right side up and laying them on the floor.

What in the world is she up to?

A small sound from nearby stopped me before I could ask the question.

I heard Lacy before I saw her. The softest whisper, just a little coo like baby kittens make.

"Oh," she whispered.

I turned my head and saw her there beside June's bed. The old coot was propped up on his pillow, his blue eyes fixed on Lacy, who was watching his hands intently. Wrapped around those old hands was a loop of red string, and he was showing her how to make a cat's cradle.

How in the world can that be? I thought. How could drunk, dirty old June Jaans be sitting there showing my granddaughter how to make a cat's cradle, and how could it be that Lacy, who hadn't said a word to me in two days, was talking to him?

"Oh," she whispered again as he moved his hands and changed the string.

"Sure enough like magic, ain't it?" June smiled at her. "See here, this middle part looks like a little kitty's ears."

Lacy nodded.

"Sure does, doesn't it?" June smiled, his teeth surprisingly even and white. I remembered that smile. I remembered a young fella who used to smile like that when he got a home run for our school baseball team.

"Now, look at this. Watch this." I didn't hear June's voice. I heard the boy's, saw him smile underneath a mop of sandy blond hair. "Looks like a cup and saucer now, see?"

"Oh." Lacy's voice wasn't much more than a breath sprinkled with sound.

"Would you like to learn how to do that?" June smiled at her again, and that long-ago time and place come flooding back to me. I remembered that young blond-headed June Jaans doing parlor tricks in the hall at school, making a little primrose appear out of nowhere, handing it to me, and saying, *It's just a little trick. Would you like to learn how?*

I remembered shaking my head and stepping back, thinking that maybe he was doing some sort of sinful thing. He was new to our school, moved in with his family from New Orleans, where folks said his mama used to sing jazz in nightclubs. They didn't go to church, and nobody in town was sure what to think.

"Here, lean close now and put this string on your fingers like this," he said to Lacy. *Here, hold your hand out, now you put the flower here like this,* I remembered. I remembered him touching my hand, talking to me in that strange, foreign-sounding way of his, the words slow, drawn out, with just a dash of his mama's French accent and a strange rhythm that sounded like the blues music that made people dance in heathen ways I had only heard about.

"See now, move your hand this way," he said to Lacy, cupping his hands around her small fingers and helping her twist the thread into a basket. "Now spread your fingers out like this. There, that's it, and the thread goes this way, and that way. See? Like weaving a blanket."

Lacy looked at him, a spark in her eyes.

June nodded, tipping his head to look at her face, hidden under a shield of dark hair. "There, now, see you got a little bit of a smile under there, after all."

I remembered him saying that to my sister, Ivy. Little Ivy, who looked so much like Lacy, they could have been twins. Ivy Grace. So plain and shy with her dark hair and big gray eyes always looking up so that there was a rim of white around the bottom. She moved through the world quietly, soft like a shadow, so that most people never really noticed she was there.

I always wondered why June Jaans noticed her—why from that first day he come to our school, he picked Ivy out of the crowd. I wondered why he come around and teased her with those little tricks of his, and said things like, *Well, look at that, Ivy's got a smile in there after all. A real pretty smile, and a nickel behind her ear. Now will ya look at that. . . .*

Maybe I was jealous. I suppose I was. But I was also worried for Ivy. June Jaans was popular with the girls. He had a smooth way of talking and a million parlor tricks up his sleeve. I couldn't figure why he paid attention to Ivy, or why, when he finally asked me to a social, he said we ought to take Ivy along too. I figured he felt sorry for her, so I asked Mama to let her come along.

I never figured anything bad would come of it. . . .

"See, now you got a little magic of your own." June's voice was soft. I looked at him, and it was more than I could bear, seeing him with my Lacy, who looked so much like my sister all those years ago.

A sick feeling started in my belly and gurgled hot and sour into my throat. I walked to the bed and took Lacy's arm, getting her to her feet. I glared at June with fire in my eye. "*Where* is Janet?" I heard the words spit from my mouth like venom. "How in the world could she leave this child here alone like this?"

June opened his mouth mutely, like he didn't understand what I'd said.

Lacy slumped against me, the string dangling from her hand, all the life gone out of her. Finally she opened her fingers, and the string fell to the bed, a little pool of red against the white sheet.

"Don't . . . don't know," June stammered out finally. "The little girl just wandered in here by herself. I didn't know who she belonged to."

"Well, she *belongs* to me," I said, wishing I would have told him that about Ivy all those years ago. *You can't have her. She belongs to me. Leave her alone before something bad happens.*

"One of your grandchildren?" I heard him ask.

"Cass's daughter," I bit out. I wondered how he could look at her and not notice how much she looked like Ivy. Maybe he'd forgotten all about Ivy, but I hadn't. That long-ago summer still festered in me like an old sore waiting to be scratched open.

He moved his hands back to his chest and pulled his blanket higher, giving me a surprised, hurt look.

I felt guilty, even though I didn't want to. "She's had a hard time lately. I better go find Janet and get Lacy home. She needs rest and quiet."

June breathed a long, slow sigh, a sad sound, like a groaning from somewhere deep inside him. Reaching up, he put the red string in Lacy's hands. "Here, sweetness, you take this with you. You practice cup and saucer, and sometime later I'll show you how to go all the way on and make cat's cradle."

Lacy didn't reply, just turned toward the door.

"We got string at home," I heard myself say. I took Lacy's hand and led her out of there without taking a look back at June, or saying a word to Jenilee, who was sitting on the floor looking at me with her mouth hanging open.

Janet was coming up the hill outside as I walked Lacy down the steps. She crossed the parking lot quickly, her arms swinging stiffly at her sides. I could tell before she got to us that she was mad.

"What in the *world* are you doing taking Lacy in *there*?" she snapped.

I gritted my teeth. It's a good thing about old age that your temper gets as dull as all the rest of your wits. Ofttimes, it forgets to wake up, when in the past it would of come claws-out like a wet cat. "I found her inside, sitting there playing cat's cradle with old June Jaans, of all people."

"Oh, good Lord," Janet muttered. "I left her in the car." Leaning down, she took Lacy's face gently in her hands. Lacy looked right through her. "Lacy, honey, I told you to stay in the car. You can't wander off like that. Next time you better stay home with the other kids, all right? It'll be best that way."

Lacy stared off across the field.

Janet closed her eyes and pulled her eyebrows together in the middle. She blinked hard and stood up, turning away from Lacy and wiping her eyes.

"Mama, I really want you to come on home, now that you're finished helping with breakfast here, all right? You're trying to do too much," she said, her back turned toward me and Lacy, and her arms wrapped around herself. "Weldon will be here. He promised if we were needed here, he'd get word to us."

"All right. All of a sudden I feel like the life's gone out of me, anyway. Guess it's all catching up with me." I put my arm around her shoulders. "Let's go home and have a little rest, then go down to the creek where it's quiet. It would be good to sit down there, don't you think?"

Janet nodded, sniffing as she turned toward the car and my hand fell away from her. "Um-hmm. It would."

"Lacy, you can dangle your feet in the water. It'll feel good," I said, but Lacy didn't answer.

Janet opened the car door, helped Lacy in, then buckled her seat belt like she was a baby. I opened my door and climbed in, my joints creaking like old hinges as I pulled my legs around.

I laid my head against the seat, watching Lacy in the side mirror as we pulled away. "Sometimes a little quiet is what a soul needs," I whispered as my eyes closed.

In the darkness of my mind, I saw Ivy's angel, her face a mirror of Lacy's. She was trying to talk to me again, but just like with Lacy, I couldn't hear what she was saying.

CHAPTER 10

JENILEE

Around me, people sat up in their bunks, or stood and came over to watch as I taped pictures to the wall.

"Oh!" a woman said behind me. "Oh, goodness, that's my wedding picture." I turned to see the school librarian reaching for the picture in my hand. She stopped and picked up one from the floor. "And here's the day we brought my son Kyle home from the hospital. That's my granddad holding him. I thought for sure this picture was lost for good." She cupped her fingers around mine for a moment, then slowly took the picture, looking at it through tear-filled eyes. "You don't know what this means to me. This was the last picture we ever took of Granddad. It was such a happy day. Thank you for bringing it back. The picture, I mean."

"You're welcome."

I turned back to the photographs, taping them carefully to the wall, bringing back a time and a world that right now seemed lost, a Kodacolor dream that had evaporated, leaving behind only gray reality. The pictures were evidence of the lives we had come from, and to which we would someday return.

As people came closer, surveying the pictures, I taped up the last photograph—the newborn baby girl with the cloudy blue eyes.

Only the old letter remained on the floor where the pile of pictures had been. Unfolding it, I stared at it for a moment, thinking that it didn't belong on the wall, that it was meant to be private, shared only between two people, two lovers of long ago.

Finally I taped it to the wall with all of the others, wondering if those lovers would ever find it there. I imagined where they might be as I read the last words of the letter.

> *You are not lost or cold or hungry. You are in my arms, and I in yours. We can never be far from one another.*
> *Close your eyes, love.*
> *Imagine.*
> *You are home.*

When I turned around, Drew was standing in the doorway, as if the words had brought him there.

I stared at him for a long moment, afraid to believe. He looked different, older, more like my father, with his dark hair and eyes, and the high cheekbones that made his face look stern. He was wearing a National Guard uniform.

I took a step forward, afraid he would disappear like a mirage. "Drew?" I whispered.

He nodded, and suddenly I realized he was real. He was here. He stretched out his arms, and I knew he was going to say what I had hoped for him to say all those years ago when he left. *Don't worry about a thing, Jenilee. I'll take care of everything.*

I no longer needed for him to say it. I didn't need to be rescued.

The idea of it stopped me where I stood. I didn't want to be dragged back to the place I had been six years ago, six months ago, two days ago. I didn't want that world to return.

Drew turned his hands palms up, then lowered them to his sides, disappointed by my reaction. "It's me."

I stood close enough to touch him, but I didn't close the last inches between us. I wasn't sure why. For years I had been hoping he would come back. Now he had, and I didn't know what to say. "I know it's you," I said. "Are you all right? I was . . . umm . . . worried about you."

He nodded, wiping the back of his sleeve across his forehead. "My guard reserve unit was called up to help with rescue efforts right after the tornado. I couldn't get here until this morning when a relief unit came to take over our sector. I went out to the house, and it was empty. I looked all around the sheds, the fields, the neighbors' places. I couldn't figure out where you might be. Finally I came into town and started asking around. I heard you were helping the doctors here at the armory. I heard you saved old lady Gibson's life."

I looked away from him, embarrassed to hear it described that way. "I pulled her out of the cellar. Everyone made a bigger deal of it than it was."

"That's not how people around town tell it. They say you were a regular hero—saved her and her granddaughter and helped the doctor here yesterday when things were pretty bad."

I started to tell him I was only here because I couldn't stand the silence at home, because I was afraid to be there alone any longer, but then I didn't say it. Drew was finally looking at me with something other than pity and guilt, and it felt good.

"Mrs. Gibson's a nice lady." I wanted to turn the subject away from me. "She's been up here taking care of people and making sure all the food got handed out, even though her home place is wrecked. Not everybody would do that."

Drew nodded. It probably wasn't coincidental that he thought of Daddy at that point. "I talked to the hospital before I left for Poetry this morning. The doctors took Daddy in for surgery again. Nate's doing better today, though. They think he ought to be ready to leave as soon as they get his leg in a cast."

I took in a quick breath of air, and the room seemed to spin around me. "You've seen Daddy and Nate?" I gasped, trying to process what he had said. "Are they all right? Where are they?"

He frowned, looking confused. "You mean you didn't know? The hospital didn't get in touch with you?"

"No." Did he have any idea what the last two days had been like in Poetry? "We haven't had much communication here. Mostly it's emergency only." Reaching out, I touched his arm, trying to connect, through him, to Nate. "How's Nate? Is he all right? What happened?" I realized how it sounded, and quickly added, "Is Daddy all right?"

Drew took a deep breath and hesitated.

A veil of tears crowded my eyes. I could tell he was going to say things that would be hard to hear. "Drew, *tell me*." I wasn't sure what I wanted him to say. How did I want things to be after this moment? So many needs and desires, strengths and weaknesses were at war inside me.

Drew grabbed my shoulders, not tenderly but roughly. "Daddy's pretty busted up." His raven eyes searched mine, as if he needed to know what I was thinking. "They were in the truck on Highway Seventy-one almost to the Hindsville exit when the tornado came through. It rolled the truck several times and broke the trailer free, then threw the truck off an embankment. It was a bad crash. The highway patrol said they were lucky to be alive. They've been taken south to the hospital in Springfield because all the hospitals up north toward Kansas City are full and some of them have tornado damage, also."

"Nate's all right?" I heard myself whisper.

"Nate's darned lucky. It could have been a lot worse. He's shattered some bones in his leg, and they had to put a plate in there to hold them together. He asked about you."

I pictured Nate in a hospital bed somewhere, smiling beneath that mop of blond hair, asking about me. A warm feeling washed through me. "I knew Nate was all right. I saw him in a dream the night after the tornado." *I saw you too, Drew.* But I couldn't make myself say it. So many old resentments were battling inside me. I didn't want him to know how glad I was that he'd come home.

Drew smiled a little, not a real smile like Nate's. Drew never smiled like that. There was a closed, apprehensive look behind Drew's smiles. He never smiled with his eyes.

"What did the doctors say about Daddy?" I was almost afraid to ask. There was a load of worry and guilt and fear wrapped in the question, and Drew knew it. Blood throbbed in my ears as I waited for him to answer. The rushing grew louder and louder, as if my body wanted to drown out whatever Drew had to say.

"Daddy's in bad shape." He looked at the floor to hide the thoughts behind his dark eyes. "He's bleeding inside. They did surgery yesterday to try to stop the bleeding, but so far they haven't gotten it under control. They took him in again this morning. He was conscious for a little while, but not since then. He's been on oxygen and they've been giving him blood transfusions. They say he lost a lot of blood before he and Nate were found. They said he would have been dead if Nate hadn't finally dragged himself out of the pickup and gone for help. The truck was half-buried in some debris down in a creek bottom, and they could have stayed there for days. Nate tore his leg up good trying to get it loose from under the seat."

I shivered, imagining Nate leaving Daddy behind, breaking free, crawling away to get help, to save Daddy's life. A flush of shame went through me, hot and bitter, because some part of me had been enjoying the freedom from Daddy and all his craziness these last few days. *What kind of a person would think such things?*

Drew's arms went around me, strong and solid and warm. I leaned into him, listening to the steady beat of his heart.

"I know," he whispered, and I had a feeling he understood. I knew he was just as confused, and lost, and afraid of the world as I was.

I couldn't remember Drew ever putting his arms around me like that before, or speaking with his voice strangled by emotion. Drew was always loud and solid, a little threatening. He was an island with no approachable harbor.

I wrapped my arms around him and hung on because I didn't know what else to do. The world was spinning again. We were powerless to stop it, with no way of knowing where we would land.

"I want to see Nate," I choked out, needing to be with Nate, to touch him, to hold his hand the way I used to when he had the flu or the chicken pox. Even though he was sixteen, he still got lonely and scared when he was sick. *He must be scared right now.*

Drew released me and I stepped back. "Drew, can you take me there?" I stood there, afraid he would say no, afraid he would walk away from Nate and me again. "I . . . I don't have a car or anything."

Drew ran his thumb and forefinger wearily along the crest of his dark brows. "We can try. Just don't get your hopes up, all right? A lot of roads are flooded, and the guard may have closed some of the bridges I took. It was pretty hairy getting here."

I nodded, unable to push words past the lump in my throat. *Nate's all right*, was all I could think. *Nate's all right, and you're here, Drew.* Tears crowded my eyes, and I turned away, so Drew wouldn't see how much I needed him.

On his cot nearby, Mr. Jaans held his hand out to me, and I moved forward until my fingers touched his.

"You just remember you done a good thing today. This day. Right now." I didn't know if he was talking about the pictures on the wall, or about Drew and me. "It don't do any good to dwell on whatever come before. A bad past is like gristle. You can chew on it forever and starve yourself to death, or you can spit it out and see what else is on the table. You just go on from here, Jenilee, and you'll be all right."

I nodded, but all I could say was, "When I get back home, I'll look after your cows."

"Tell my cows I'm comin' home soon." He gave my hand a squeeze, then let his fingers fall away. "Keep an eye out for my bull, too, all right? The sheriff come in a while ago and said Charlie got away from them again. Keep an eye out for him, will ya? He don't mean to hurt anybody."

"I will."

"Sure hope that bull makes it home. My wife and I raised that little cuss on a bottle just before she passed on. . . ." He trailed off, then relaxed against the pillow and closed his eyes. "I told Tom he better not let them trigger-happy deputies shoot my bull."

"I'm sure he'll show up at home," I said. "He always does."

Mr. Jaans let out a long sigh. "Ya know, I think I'd just as soon lose the house as lose that old bull. Don't know what I'd do without him showing up at my window bellering in the mornings." His lips curved upward with the thought. "Guess that goes to show it's the small things you miss. It's not houses, or cars, or furniture that ya want back. It's the way someone smiled or the sound of a voice, or a silly old bull bellering at the window."

Drew came back to the doorway, and I turned to follow him out, looking at the wall of pictures as I walked away.

Drew followed my gaze. "Who put those up there?"

"I did," I said. "I wanted people to be able to find them."

"It's a good idea."

"I'm going to gather all that I can and bring them here." The idea lit in me like a flame in a dark room.

"It's a good idea," he repeated.

Dr. Albright was coming in the doorway as we were going out. He was dirty and blood-spattered, red-eyed, wrinkled, and tired now like the rest of us. He looked sad.

He stepped back so that we could pass through the door, and he regarded me with something strangely like admiration. "The pictures are a good idea." The slightest smile creased his lips. "Sometimes small things like that help patients as much as the medical care does."

"Thanks." I met his gaze for a moment, wondering if he really meant it, wondering why he would care about someone like me. "I'm going to bring more when I can. It's like getting a little bit of our lives back." I didn't know why I felt the need to explain to him. Maybe I was afraid he would tell me I couldn't clutter up his hospital.

He nodded, glancing at Drew, as if he suddenly realized I was leaving. "Do you have a place to stay? There's room here in the armory, or in the tents."

His kindness made me stammer. Why did he seem different all of a sudden? "M-my brother's here. We're going to the hospital in Springfield. My father and my younger brother are there. They were caught in their truck during the tornado."

Dr. Albright met my gaze with a thoughtful look I didn't understand, as if he had something more he wanted to say. Instead he said, "Take care," stiffened his shoulders, and walked past me, rubbing the back of his neck.

I followed Drew to his pickup at the edge of the parking lot and climbed in the passenger side as Drew turned the key and the engine roared to life, shutting out the sounds of the campground below.

We headed out of town, passing what was left of the convenience store and the Dairy Queen, then driving slowly past neighborhoods where little remained but piles of boards and overturned appliances. People were sifting through the rubble now, picking up bits of clothing and personal mementos. Not much remained.

It's the small things you miss.

Looking at Drew, I thought about all the small things I had forgotten about him. He was the one who made me do my homework when Mama was too tired to care, and stuck up for me when Daddy got mean, and did my chores when I forgot, so I wouldn't get punished. He made sure nobody at school made fun of my clothes. He woke me up in the mornings and fixed oatmeal and irritably told me to eat it before the bus came.

Drew had been my protector. He had been a rock because the rest of us needed him to be. He was a mother and father, protector to Nate and me when Drew was no more than a child himself. He had done a million little things right, and one big thing wrong. He saw a way out, and he took it.

For me, that one big thing had eclipsed all the rest. Now I realized how much the rest had mattered. Drew was the reason we had survived at all. He took care of the place when Daddy was off hunting or drinking. He cooked the meals when Mama was too sick or tired or lost in her own sadness to do it. He was the one who finally stood up to Daddy and said, "You're not taking that belt to anybody else in this family again. I swear to God, if you do, I'll go to the sheriff and I'll tell him *everything*."

I was ten, and I wondered what *everything* meant. I crouched by the sofa near Nate, frozen, my heart hammering like a caged bird in my chest as I watched this clash of Titans in our living room. Drew was seventeen then, a lineman on the football team, and he made even Daddy look small.

Daddy looked Drew in the eye for a minute, staggered a step backward as if Drew had hit him, then turned and left. Drew waited until he was gone, then moved to the couch and sat down with his head in his hands.

I watched him, amazed at what he had done, afraid we would pay for it later.

"You hadn't oughta done that," Nate said, which was interesting considering that Nate was the one about to get a whipping. Nate took a lot of whippings. He was stubborn, and he didn't seem to ever learn. "Now he'll be ticked off."

Drew didn't look up, just combed his fingers roughly into his dark hair and sat there, hunched over, his forearms pressed against his ears as if he didn't want to hear anything. "I'm sick of his crap. He isn't gonna do that anymore."

Nate shrugged, then stood up and headed for the door. "Heck, it don't hurt."

"I'm not takin' any more of his crap." Drew's fingers trembled where he held his hair, the muscles in his arms twitching in steely coils. Staring at the floor, he repeated, "I'm not takin' any more of his crap. This is the end of it."

I don't know if Mama ever knew what happened that day. She was at work, and by the time she came home,

Daddy was gone and everything was like normal. None of us ever told her about the fight. We were too afraid to talk about it.

Daddy stayed gone for a week, and Mama was worried about that. In spite of all the ways he was bad, she loved Daddy. She couldn't see much beyond that. She would have done anything, been anyone, to banish that part of him that drank too much, and got mean, and set off the house like a powder keg.

It wasn't much of a way to live a life, but you can get used to anything.

Drew glanced at me from the driver's seat, his dark brows lowered in concern. I realized I was crying again.

"You all right?"

"Yes." I pulled the visor down and looked in the mirror, wiping my eyes. My face looked pale, tired, filthy—older than just a few days ago.

A picture fell from the top of the visor, and I picked it up, looking into the dark eyes of a little boy, perhaps four or five years old, and a little girl a year or so younger with long dark hair.

"Those are my kids," Drew said. "That's Alex on the left and Amber on the right. That picture's six months or so old. Their mama's supposed to send me a new one."

"They don't live with you?" I don't know why that didn't surprise me. It had always been hard for me to picture any of us married, or having kids, or raising families. It was as if the old images were forever burned into my mind, and I couldn't see us as anything else or anything better.

Drew frowned, watching the road, his face stiff. "Naw. She moved back to a house near her folks a couple months ago. We been havin' some problems, and she said she needed some time to think."

"That's too bad." I didn't know what else to say. "Did Mama know you got married and had kids?"

Drew sighed. "We're not married. That's one of the

problems with Darla and me. She doesn't like it that we're not married."

"How come you don't just get married then?"

He thought about that for a minute, then sighed again. "Don't know. I guess I'm worried that if we do, it'll all turn bad. Guess it seems like I don't know how to make a right life."

I understood what he meant. I hadn't thought about anything beyond getting by for the next two years until Nate was eighteen and out of school. Beyond that, I didn't know what kind of a picture to paint. "Were things good when they were there with you? The family stuff, I mean?"

He squinted, thinking about it. "Yeah, I guess you'd have to say so. We had some problems—she talks too much, I don't talk enough, Alex likes to climb on things, and Amber don't want to poop in the pot. You know, that kind of thing."

I chuckled. It was hard for me to imagine Drew worrying about a toddler's potty habits. "Sounds pretty normal."

Drew shrugged. "I guess. I never took a belt and knocked the crap out of my kid with it. I can tell you that."

My heart skipped, and an old, sick, nervous feeling washed through me, as if I were remembering not the past, but the way the past *felt*. "You wouldn't do that, Drew. You're a good person."

He tapped his thumbs rhythmically on the steering wheel. "But that's the thing. I'm never quite sure. All that stuff's inside me, and I always wonder if someday I'll just lose it."

"You never lost it before." I thought of all the arguments in our house. "Even with everything that happened, you always kept it together."

He shook his head, his chest deflating with a long, slow breath. "I've been closer than I want to be, Jenilee. I've been closer than you've ever seen."

I swallowed hard, that familiar, fearful feeling churning in my stomach. The expression on Drew's face was ominous, dangerous, angry. He looked like Daddy.

I reminded myself that he wasn't Daddy, that Daddy was far away in a hospital bed.

Drew stared at the road ahead, his dark eyes burning a hole somewhere in the distance. "There's a lot that you don't know, Jenilee. Daddy came home from Vietnam really messed up, and he's still messed up. There's a lot that happened before you were old enough to remember it, and a lot that you just plain weren't there to see. You don't know the trouble there was between me and him before I left for the army."

"I heard more than you think." *I heard everything.* That old resentment crept into my mind. The one that said, *If you thought things were that bad, why did you go away and leave Nate and me in the middle of it?*

Drew sat shaking his head, and I had a feeling there really were things I didn't know. When he spoke, his voice was low and emotionless. "I was ready to kill him. I really was. I'd have done it if it hadn't been for Coach Ellis. He kept up with me that summer after I graduated, when I was just runnin' the streets getting into trouble. He came to get me out of jail one night, and he signed for me. He took me out to the football field, and he turned on the lights, and we sat there on the bench. He told me sooner or later the fights and the stuff at home were going to land me in prison or dead. He looked me right in the eye and told me I had to get myself out of here. Then he took me to Shawnee the next day and I signed up for the army." He paused for a moment, then added, "I never could get along with Daddy like you could. I figured that would get you by after I was gone. You always find a way to get along with people."

Because there is no me. There has been only what other people tell me to be. "I just never had the guts to stand up for anything," I said, disappointed in myself. "I never even thought about it until a few days ago."

"Sometimes it's best not to dwell on it too much." He said it as if that would fix everything.

Just don't dwell on it too much . . . Was that possible?

Drew's cell phone rang in his pocket. He pulled it out and answered, looking surprised and worried. "Darla? Is everything all right with the kids? I can't hear you very well . . . what?" He paused, bracing the phone on his shoulder and covering his other ear with his hand. "The connection's really bad. What?" He listened, his brows drawing together in the center. "What do you mean, the hospital called you about Daddy?"

I heard the echo of a voice coming through the phone, the cadence hurried, seeming nervous, but I couldn't understand the words.

"So he's out of surgery now?" A pause, and then, "He's stable now?"

I held my breath, watching Drew nod as he listened to the answer to the question. He was silent for a moment after the voice on the other end stopped; then he asked, "What are they doing calling you? How'd they get your phone number?"

He was silent, his jaw clenching; then he slammed his hand against the steering wheel. "Why did you do that? I told you not to go down there."

Words echoed through the phone again, hurried, the pitch higher.

Drew's jaw clenched. When he answered, his voice was low, almost a growl. "Because it isn't any of your business, Darla. It doesn't have anything to do with you."

The voice rose on the other end.

Drew's reply echoed through the cab of the truck, ringing in my ears. "Yeah, you're right about that. I can't *tell* you *anything*." He didn't wait for an answer, just gritted his teeth and added, "Go home, Darla. I told you before, my family isn't any of your business." And he disconnected the phone, tossing it hard onto the floor-board of the truck.

I picked it up and set it on the seat, my fingers trembling, a black sense of the past churning inside me. Wrapping my arms around my stomach, I turned away from Drew, laid my head against the seat, and stared out the window, not knowing what to say.

CHAPTER 11

Silence hung over us like a cloud as we left Poetry behind, traveling the backroads south, toward the hospital in Springfield. My thoughts tangled in a web of questions, I watched the miles pass as Drew piloted the truck through muddy low-water crossings and over country bridges where streams of thick brown water crashed against the cement guardrails. Closer to the interstate, the roads were clogged with wrecked cars, construction equipment clearing debris, and sightseers gawking at ruined homes.

Everywhere, the destruction was unimaginable—cars overturned in ditches, trees stripped, power lines hanging from broken poles, entire neighborhoods vanished.

We reached the interstate, and Drew exhaled a long breath through pursed lips, visibly relaxing in the seat beside me. "I think we'll be all right now," he said. "I came through here this morning. About a mile from here, a tornado went right across the interstate. There are wrecked cars stacked up two and three deep everywhere. The whole road is closed. A mile south of here you hit the line where the tornado left the ground, and just like that, everything's normal." He pointed ahead. "Up there, see. You can see where it changes."

I gazed ahead to where the earth turned from black to green. The metal farm buildings beside the road were barely damaged, just a few sheets of tin lifted from the edges of the roofs.

"It's hard to believe," I muttered, but my thoughts weren't really on the tornado damage. My mind was spinning with questions. *Will Daddy be awake when we get there? What news will the doctors and nurses have about Daddy, about Nate? Will we be able to take Nate home? What will happen afterward . . . ?*

The sign beside the road said, SPRINGFIELD 15 MILES. I knew from going for Mama's cancer treatments that the hospital was only ten. *Ten more miles . . . What then?*

Drew's hands tensed on the steering wheel, as if he were thinking the same thing. "I hope Darla's gone when we get there," he muttered. "I'm not in the mood to deal with her crap."

The knot in my stomach pulled tighter. *Drew's ex on top of everything else . . .* "It doesn't sound like things are too good between you and her," I probed, even though I knew it was probably a subject better left alone. Drew and I had enough problems of our own to deal with. Still, what he'd said to her bothered me. *I told you before, my family is none of your business. . . .* Did that mean they had talked about us before?

"No, they're not," he answered flatly, the profile of his face hard, his jaw set in a stubborn line.

I waited to see if he would say anything more. He glanced sideways and saw me watching him as we pulled off the exit to the hospital.

"She's always in my business, that's all," he grumbled, looking over his shoulder to weave into traffic on the access road. "Always trying to get in my head, acting like I'm one of her social work cases, or something. I don't need that crap."

"Is that why you don't want her to know about us?" I wanted to swallow the words as soon as they were out. Yet I wanted to know the answer.

"She knows about y'all."

"But she doesn't *know about* us, does she? She doesn't know how things were with Mama and Daddy and us?" The pain of his rejection stabbed the old wound inside me.

"She doesn't need to. She needs to learn to stay out of my business."

"But when you're married, people expect—"

"We're *not married*." He stopped me, cutting a hard look in my direction.

"Well, you have kids together."

"You sound like her." Drew pulled the truck into the parking lot of the hospital, threw it in park, and got out, clearly anxious to end the conversation. He stood with one hand on the door, scanning the parking lot, probably looking for Darla's car.

I peered through the mud-spattered windshield, gazing at Vista Ridge Hospital. It loomed twelve stories high, its dark granite surfaces and mirrored windows reflecting broken images of Springfield that looked like the work of the tornado itself. I glanced over my shoulder to make sure it was only a mirage.

Nearby, a news crew was interviewing a doctor outside the emergency room. I heard the drone of their voices through the open window, but not the words, and I wondered if that doctor had treated Daddy or Nate. I wondered if he had dealt with the kind of chaos after the storm that we had seen in Poetry.

Everything that had happened in the Poetry armory seemed unreal now. The undisturbed city street behind me made it seem as if the tornado couldn't possibly have happened just an hour's drive north in Poetry. My mind grasped the idea that I was going inside to see Mama after one of her cancer treatments.

"I guess we'd better go in," Drew said, following my line of vision to the news crew. "Check on Daddy first, see if he's awake."

I nodded, my stomach rolling over. I tried to picture Daddy in a hospital bed, pale and weak, helpless the way Mama had been after her cancer treatments.

"Drew?" His name rasped against my throat like sandpaper.

He stopped with the car door halfway closed.

I don't want to go inside. "What do you think Daddy will say?" *Will he ask what happened at home?* "I . . . I mean, how do you think he'll be?"

Drew squinted at our reflection in the hospital windows. "We'll just have to see. He'll be pretty weak, if he's awake at all." I could see in him the same thing I felt inside, that thin white line between duty and fear. He closed the door and walked to the sidewalk without waiting to see if I was following.

I slid from the truck and hurried after him, following through the doors and into the building. The air inside was strong with the smell of antiseptic and thick with the odor of people and bedding.

I looked up and down the halls as Drew went to the desk and asked for Daddy's room number. Around us, both sides of the corridors were lined with beds filled with people. I wondered if all of the other hospitals were as overwhelmed as Vista Ridge.

"God," I whispered. How long would it be before things were even close to normal?

A little boy stirred on his bed nearby in the hallway, whimpered, and turned over in his sleep. Stepping closer, I laid a hand on his arm and looked at his head, where his hair had been shaved away and a long gash had been closed with sutures. He sniffled quietly, his cheeks and lashes wet with tears as he muttered drowsily.

"Ssshhhh," I whispered. "It's all right. Just rest for

now." The straight blond hair clinging to his forehead made me think of Nate when he was younger.

The boy quieted and I stood watching him breathe. I wondered where his mother was, and why he was lying in the hallway all alone with no one to comfort him.

A nurse passing with a clipboard stopped, and I stepped away, realizing I wasn't supposed to be there.

"He was moving around and talking in his sleep," I told her.

She nodded, a flash of sadness crossing her face. She wiped it away as if she were erasing a blackboard, looked at the boy's chart, and took his pulse. "Probably having a nightmare. It's common. It'll get better with time. It just takes time . . . and prayer. Lots of prayer." She hung the chart again and walked away.

Looking at the chart, I read the words, *Male, 10 years prox,* and below that his name, *John Doe.*

Tears prickled in my eyes, and I turned away, trying not to think of what it meant, that after nearly forty-eight hours he was still alone and no one knew his name.

Drew stepped away from the information desk and gave me a look of concern. "You all right?"

"It's just sad to see so many people hurting." I ran my hands up and down my arms, smoothing away the goose bumps. "Seems like it's too big of a mess for anybody to take care of, like things will never be all right again, I mean."

Drew put a hand on my shoulder, and we started toward the elevator. "If you'd seen how bad this place was a couple days ago, you'd think this *was* all right."

"I guess so." I thought about how bad Poetry was a couple days ago, and how things were slowly coming back to some kind of order. "I just feel sorry for people having it so bad. That little boy over there in the bed has had surgery on his head, and they haven't even figured out who he is yet."

"That's too bad."

"I wish I could do something to help."

Drew laughed softly under his breath as we stepped onto the elevator. "Guess you haven't changed much. You always did want to rescue every lost critter that got dumped on Good Hope Road. Remember when you found that litter of kittens in the culvert outside, and you hid them in the barn and sneaked milk out to feed them with an eyedropper?"

"Oh, my gosh, I had forgotten all about that." I had forgotten a lot about those days before Drew left and Mama got so sick. "I kept those kittens for weeks, remember? I used to get you up at night, because I was afraid to sneak out to the barn by myself and feed them."

Drew rolled his eyes and smiled. "I remember."

For a minute I forgot where we were, caught up in the warmth of the memory. "We used to sit out there in the barn for a long time, remember, and listen to the crickets chirp and the coyotes howl." My eyes started to close, and I could smell the damp summer air again, feel the cool mist as it rose from the dew-covered pastures, see stars glittering through the gaps in the old tin barn. "That was so . . . peaceful." At that moment, everything in me wanted to go back to one of those secret summer nights, when I was safe in the barn with Drew.

"It was." His eyes were like mine, and I could tell he was thinking the same thing I was.

The elevator chimed, and the doors swung open. The summer mist, and the coyotes, the stars, the rhythmic sounds of the insects rushed out the door like air being sucked into a vacuum.

Drew let out a quick breath and stepped into all that was left—the sterile corridor of the hospital. "Until Daddy found the damned things and drowned them all."

Of course, the conversation had come back around to Daddy. Everything always did.

I realized I had never known what happened to those kittens. *Drew told me they ran away....*

He pushed open the ICU door, and we stepped into the nurses' station. Behind glass panels up and down the hallway, patients lay connected to masses of wires and tubes. Around them, medical staff moved purposefully and loved ones stood by bedsides with worried faces.

I followed Drew down the hall, hearing the breath moving in and out of my body, my heart beating slowly, in time with the beeping machines.

Come on, Jenilee, get your head together. I heard Mama's voice in my mind. She sounded impatient. I knew she expected me to go in there and take care of Daddy.

I wished we had gone to see Nate first. Seeing Nate, alive and smiling, making jokes and laughing, would make everything else easier. It always did.

"There's Daddy," I heard Drew say. He motioned through the doorway of an ICU cubicle, and both of us stood in the entrance, watching a nurse move efficiently around a stone-still body covered lightly with a sheet and wrapped in a tangle of machines, tubes, and wires, like a bull trapped in a barbed-wire fence.

I glanced at Drew, but he didn't seem to remember I was there. His face was hard, his gaze far away and his eyes glassy.

I realized it took all he had to stand there in the doorway. He didn't have the strength to help me cross the threshold.

The nurse finished what she was doing and stopped to talk to us.

"You can go on in and speak to him for a few minutes, if you want to. He probably won't wake up at this point. He was responsive for about an hour earlier today, but he was in a lot of pain and became combative with the IV and tubes, so he is pretty heavily sedated now. We brought your brother down to see him and they were able to talk for a few minutes, but he has since become weaker. His pulse rate dropped and we've had to put him back on the oxygen mask."

Drew nodded, and the nurse slipped through the door.

"I'll leave you alone now. Only a few minutes, though, all right?" She laid her hand on my arm as she passed. "Things look a little more encouraging today, overall. They think they've halted the internal bleeding, but he's still very weak. Don't stay long."

Drew nodded again, but she was already gone.

We stood a moment longer in the doorway. Finally I stepped into the room. Three steps forward, and I stood at the foot of Daddy's bed.

I squinted at the bed, trying to see Daddy in the swollen, bruised face with the tube coming from the nose. I listened to the slow rise and fall of his breathing, tried to imagine his voice. I couldn't see anything left of the hard, angry man I remembered. Silent and pale against the wrinkled white sheet, he was just another lost creature, like those kittens, at the mercy of forces stronger than he was.

I slipped my hand into his without thinking. "Daddy?"

The figure in the bed didn't answer. The room was silent except for the rhythmic sound of the pulse oximeter and the steady beep of the EKG.

"Daddy?" I said again. "Daddy, it's us. Jenilee and Drew. We're here."

Again, no movement from the bed.

I exhaled the breath I had been holding in rhythm with the gush of the machine. "I guess he's asleep again."

Drew nodded, standing at the foot of the bed like a reflection of Daddy watching his own body.

"Let's go see Nate," I said. "The nurse said they were

trying to keep Daddy under for a while. It probably isn't good for us to be here talking to him."

Drew nodded, turning his shoulder toward me and stepping to the door. He slumped against the doorframe for a moment.

I turned to follow him. Just before I slid my hand free, Daddy's fingers squeezed mine. I looked at his face, but there was nothing—no movement, no flutter of eyelids. Laying his hand against the sheets, I turned and followed Drew out the door.

We left ICU and wound through the corridors to Nate's room. My fingers burned in that hot circle of Daddy's life. I knew that he would wake up. He would wake up and he would take over our lives, like he always had.

I didn't tell Drew. I didn't want him to know how I felt inside. It was wrong of me to think that way about Daddy when he lay near death in a hospital bed. He needed us now.

We came to the room that was Nate's, and Drew pushed open the door. There was only a small walkway in between rows of beds. Nate was sitting up, his leg raised on a stack of pillows, encased in a cast that ran from his ankle to his hip.

The other boys in the room looked up as the door swished closed behind us. Disappointment that we weren't there for them registered on their faces. Nate's lips lifted into an easy smile, the smile I remembered except for the swollen black-and-blue eye above it.

"Nice shiner, huh?" he quipped.

All the love I had for him filled me, and I rushed forward, grabbed him in my arms, and drank in the scent and the feel of him.

"Oh, God," I heard myself whisper, my voice shuddering with tears that I couldn't keep away. "Oh, Nate, thank God."

Nate held on to me for a minute, then started trying

to wiggle out of my grip. "You're gonna give me broke ribs to go with my broke leg," he complained, chuckling in that silly way of his. "Geez, Jenilee, turn loose already."

I forced myself to let go. Gingerly touching the bruise on his face, I sat back, looking at him.

He rolled his eyes, blushing and looking twelve, not sixteen. "Geez, cut that out already." Pushing my hand away, he looked around the room, which was filled with boys his age, most of them in casts of one kind or another.

Nate glanced at Drew with a cool expression. "Hey, Drew."

"Hey, Nate." Drew's expression was a mirror of Nate's—as if they didn't know each other at all. "How's your leg? You look a little better than when I saw you this morning."

Nate rapped his knuckles against the cast. "Yeah. Don't hurt so much now. Guess I better stay away from metal detectors for a while. They stuck a piece of number-five pipe in there and screwed the whole thing back together with toggle bolts."

Nate grinned at me, and I chuckled, sniffing and wiping my eyes.

Drew maintained his serious expression. "Did they say you can get out of here today?"

"Shoot, they can't wait to get rid of me." Nate grinned, but kept his gaze on me, as if I had asked the question.

Drew didn't react.

For just an instant, Nate looked a little hurt by that. His gaze wavered toward Drew, and his grin fell. He turned back to me, his blue eyes intense, questioning, desperate. "Did you see Daddy? Did you find out anything new? Darla's been trying all day to get information, but they won't hardly tell us anything."

Drew stiffened at the mention of Darla's name.

"We didn't find out anything new," I said, before the conversation could turn to Drew and Darla. "The nurse said he was a little better, but that's about all we know. He was sleeping when we were there." *His fingers closed around mine. He squeezed my hand.* "He didn't wake up."

"Y'all should of come earlier. Darla said maybe Daddy would have been calmer if someone he knew was with him." He glared narrowly at Drew, as if that were Drew's fault. Nate had learned to blame Drew for a lot of things. He'd learned that from me.

Drew shrugged, looking out the window, his eyes hard. "Darla's not a nurse. She doesn't know." His eyes said the rest as he glared narrowly at Nate. *She doesn't know Daddy.*

Nate straightened in the bed and leaned forward, ready to fight right there in the hospital room. My body tensed and my stomach squeezed into a knot, just the way it always did when chaos was about to break loose in our family. I sat there, as usual, feeling small and powerless.

"Daddy said you probably wouldn't come at all," Nate goaded.

"Daddy's full of crap," Drew shot back. "I told him before I left this morning that I was coming back as soon as I found Jenilee. He was awake when I said it. He knew I was coming back."

"That ain't what he told me. He said—"

"Stop it!" I heard myself hiss, the words beating in my head like a drum. The other boys in the room turned to look at me. "Just stop it, both of you."

Drew and Nate fell silent, staring at me openmouthed. "We're not going to do this. We're all finally together. Do you know how many people wish they could have their families together right now?" Bold with anger, I flailed a hand toward the door. "There's a little boy downstairs with stitches in his head and John Doe on his tag, because they haven't *found* his family yet."

Bracing his hands on the bed frame, Drew let out a long breath, his head sagging forward. "Jenilee's right."

Nate crossed his arms over his chest and sank back against the pillows, like a pouting boy. "Sorry, Jen. He just ticks me off."

"No, Nate, you *want* to get ticked off," I spat. "You're *trying* to pick a fight. It isn't anything Drew did."

"It's *everything* Drew does."

"Just shut up about it! Hush about Daddy, and hush about Darla. You're just trying to make Drew mad." Nate looked hurt, as if he thought I was choosing Drew over him. For so long, it had been just me and Nate, clinging to each other to keep from being swept under.

I leaned close, putting my forehead against his. "I'm sorry, Nate," I whispered. "I don't want to fight. I'm so sick of fighting."

Nate shrugged away from me, then rubbed his eyes with the pads of his fingers. "I didn't mean to start anything. I'm just uptight about Daddy. He ain't doin' good. He said he was really hurting, and I told the nurse that, and she wouldn't give him anything else. He got mad and started pullin' on those IV things."

"He's sleeping now," I said. "It's all right." *When will it ever be all right? What would the picture of all right look like?*

Nate nodded, wiping his eyes impatiently, turning toward the window because he didn't want Drew to see him crying. "I just keep thinking that if I'd of gotten out of the truck sooner and gone for help . . . If I wouldn't of sat there and waited for help . . . then Daddy . . . I should of gone for help sooner. By the time I got him here, his belly was so full of blood, he couldn't breathe anymore, and . . ." He slammed a fist into the mattress, turning onto his side so that his back was to us. "It hurt too bad to get my leg out from under the seat, so I just sat there. I should of gotten out. . . ."

"Ssshhhh," I whispered, laying my hand on his arm. "You did the best you could."

"No, I didn't." His words were hoarse, barely audible. "Daddy knows it and I know it."

I wondered if Daddy had laid the blame on Nate, or if that was all in Nate's mind. "That's not true." I felt Drew's hand on my shoulder, his fingers trembling, as close as he dared come to touching Nate.

Nate shook his head violently against the pillow, as if he were trapped in the throes of a bad dream. "He tried to get me to go sooner, but I wouldn't do it. I told him somebody would come get us out . . . and . . . and then he passed out, and I kept waiting. I should of yanked my leg out from under the seat and gone for help before I did."

"Ssshhhh," I whispered again. "You saved Daddy's life. You did everything you could."

Nate sank against the sheets. "That's what Darla said." He choked. "She was wrong, too."

Drew's shoulders softened, and he turned toward the door, rubbing his forehead. "We should get Nate out of here," he said quietly. "I'll go see about the paperwork and check on Daddy one more time."

"All right." I turned back to Nate, feeling the air touch my shoulder when Drew's hand fell away. I shivered, even though the room was warm. Someone coughed in another bed, and I realized again that we were surrounded by people.

"You'll feel better once we get you home." I talked to Nate the way I did when he was a little boy and had the flu, or strep throat, or a stomach virus. Those were the only times Nate slowed down long enough to need affection. "The electric is still out, so no TV, but you can lie in your own bed. That'll feel good, right?"

He didn't answer, just wiped his face on the sheet and stared out the window, as if nothing I could say would help this time.

"Drew will be back in a minute, and we'll go. The roads are probably in better shape by now."

"I want to stay here with Daddy."

My heart lurched. "You can't stay here, Nate. The hospital needs the bed."

"Someone needs to stay here with Daddy."

Scrubbing my fingernails against my forehead, I tried to think of the right thing to say. "We can't stay with Daddy. He's still in ICU. They only let us in for a minute or two. The nurse said they gave him medication to keep him under until they see how he's doing. The roads will be clear tomorrow, and Drew or I can come back. You can't stay, Nate. You're not in any shape for it. You need to get home and rest."

Nate let out a long sigh, his shoulders going slack. "Will they call us if Daddy wakes up?"

"I'm sure they will. We'll tell them to. It'll be all right, Nate."

I looked at my hands and wished I had the power to heal the injury inside Nate.

Just press a bandage to it. Press hard. Hold it long enough, and the blood will stop flowing. Dr. Albright had said that to me when we were working in the armory. I doubted if even he knew how to bandage what was wrong with Nate.

CHAPTER 12

EUDORA

Cheyenne tugged at my sleeve. I didn't realize it until she pulled pretty hard. I looked away from the creek, where Toby was still jumpin' in the shallows and Anna was following him around like a thirteen-year-old mother hen, reminding him he was only seven and couldn't swim.

Cheyenne looked up at me with her little face too sober. "Did Daddy die in the tornado?" she asked.

The question stole my tongue.

Sitting alongside me, Christi clucked her lips. "Geez, Cheyenne. You're such a baby. What a dumb question."

I shook a finger at Christi. "You watch your tone, young lady. A nine-year-old girl ought not have such a smart mouth. Your little sister's just worried about her daddy. That's understandable." I gathered Cheyenne in my arms and hugged her close, rocking her under my chin. "Your daddy's fine, Sissy. He's just been busy in town doin' all he can to help folks, that's all. That's why he hasn't been home."

Cheyenne puffed a breath through her nose. "He oughta come home."

"Oh, he will." I noticed that Anna and Toby had stopped playing and come to the shore, so they could hear the answer to the question, too.

I thought for a minute before I said anything. I didn't want to tell them that their daddy was helping to dig through the rubble, and, yes, it was dangerous. "He was home for a little while that first night, and then he was gone again early in the morning." *I asked him not to go. I'm ashamed of it, but I did.* I kissed the top of Cheyenne's damp hair. "He kissed you just like that."

Cheyenne wiggled loose and craned her neck to look at me, her lips twisted to one side. "I didn't *feel* anything."

Anna piped up, her tone sweeter than her younger sister's. "You were asleep, silly. Daddy left early this morning before you got up."

"Did *you* see him?" Cheyenne asked her sister, sounding doubtful.

"Yes, I saw him." Anna met my eyes and winked, like she was keeping a secret.

Cheyenne puffed out another sigh and leaned against me, burrowing under my chin. She looked down the creek at Lacy, who was writing on a piece of shale with a wet finger and watching the letters slowly fade. By herself, like she usually was.

"Is Lacy's daddy ever coming home?" Cheyenne asked, too quiet for Lacy to hear.

"Hush." I couldn't bear to think about Cass, or what the future might bring.

"Of course Lacy's daddy's comin' back," Anna said, with the certainty of a thirteen-year-old. "Uncle Cass just has to get things worked out. That's all."

"How come Uncle Cass don't ever come around?" Toby piped up, his brown eyes so innocent as he asked such a complicated question.

Because he went against his mama's wishes and married that bar waitress. Because she don't want him to come around here, that's why. She don't want him to be close to his family, and now look what's happened. Poor Lacy's so upset about being left with strangers, she won't hardly talk. If only Cass had listened all them years ago when he wanted to run off with that girl ...

I gazed at Lacy, her face reflecting the sun's glow on the water, her dark hair swirling on the afternoon breeze, and guilt heaped on me. If Cass hadn't done what he did, we wouldn't have Lacy.

The sound of a truck pulling into the driveway rattled the afternoon quiet. The four kids hopped to their feet and scampered up the hill.

"Daddy!" I heard them scream. "Daddy's home! Daddy's home!"

Praise God, I thought. *Praise God*.

Down the creek bank, Lacy watched the other kids go, her soft eyes filled with a silent yearning that broke my heart.

"Come on, Lacy," I said, standing up. "Let's go up and see Uncle Weldon." I stretched a hand out to her, even though I knew she wouldn't take it.

She stood up and wrapped her arms around herself, all the comfort she wanted. She followed me up the hill like a shadow, stopping when we got close to the knot of kids clamoring around Weldon like hungry pups.

I held out my hand again. "Come on, love. It's all right. Come see Uncle Weldon for a minute."

Lacy stared at Weldon, her brows knotting in thought. I wondered if she was thinking about how much Weldon looked like her daddy. Cass was younger, but they both looked like their father. Same straw brown hair, same hazel-green eyes. Sometimes I wondered if Lacy looked at Weldon and thought he was her daddy. Sometimes she would almost go to him.

She turned away, as usual. Stepping back to the fork in the walkway, she took the path to the house instead of the one to the driveway.

I walked on over to Weldon.

He was patting the kids on their heads, watching Lacy go. "She's still not any better?" It was a question that didn't really beg an answer. He knew the answer just by looking at her.

"A little, maybe," I lied. "She did talk today, to old June Jaans of all people, if you can believe that. He was showing her cat's cradle."

Weldon rubbed the unshaven stubble on his chin. "That's a little something, anyway. We'll get her to a doctor next week, when things are back to normal. It's been a traumatic forty-eight hours."

Just forty-eight hours? Only that long? "How are things in town?"

"Better now." He rolled his head back and forth, stretching his neck. "There's been a National Guard unit come in to help with the search and rescue at the lake. They've taken charge out there. The guard transports have carried all the serious injury cases to hospitals. Just bumps, bruises, sprained ankles, that kind of thing, are left at the armory. And some old folks who can't go home without someone to take care of them. And, of course, there are still people in the tents who don't have homes to go to."

"Still a lot of people camped out there in the tents?" I asked. "I should probably go down there and help with handing out suppers."

Weldon frowned, looking at his feet, trying to come up with the words to say something he knew I wouldn't like. I could always tell when he was working up the guts to do that. Mamas know.

"Actually, Mama, I was thinking we'd go on out to your house and see what can be salvaged."

"I don't want to go there!" I blurted out, my voice a hoarse cry from the pocket of grief deep inside me.

"Mama, it has to be done. There's rain brewing over there to the west. We need to finish going through things out there, salvage what we can before it gets rained on."

Tears crowded my eyes. "I can't, Weldon. I just can't. I can't even think about it."

"Mama . . ." He set a hand on my shoulder, and I pushed it away.

"No!" My voice echoed through the yard. The kids backed away, staring at me like they seen a two-headed chicken. "I won't go there! I just won't." My mind hunted for an excuse, a way to escape the idea of seeing my house. I couldn't bear it now. I didn't know when I would be able to. "I promised I would go to the armory to help with the suppers." *Sorry, Lord, I know that's a lie, but my heart can't bear to see that house.* "I was hoping you'd drive me up there, or if you don't need your truck for a while, I can drive myself. You can stay here and rest."

Weldon slapped the heels of his hands against his jeans, frustrated.

"Don't argue with your mama, Weldon," I pleaded. "Sometimes hard work is the only way to keep a body and soul going on. Sometimes your only comfort is in realizing other folks got it worse."

Weldon nodded. "I'll drive you up there."

"I can drive myself. I won't be away long. You rest."

He was too exhausted to argue. "All right, Mama." He pulled the keys from his pocket and handed them to me.

"I'll be all right, Weldon." I smoothed a hand over his cheek, like I always had when he was a little boy.

"I know you will be, Mama. You always are. You're stronger than any of us."

I wondered how he could think so.

He turned away from me and gathered the kids around him. "I want all of you to run and get the travel trailer cleaned out. The Andersons are going to come stay until . . . well, for a little while, anyway. They need a quiet place to stay."

My breath caught in my throat. "Weldon, did they . . ."

Did they find their baby? I didn't want to say it in front of the kids. I didn't want them to know the baby girl was still missing.

Weldon shook his head. "No, and reporters have started to come around asking about it."

"Oh, Lord," I whispered.

Weldon nodded, then turned and walked to the house as the kids scampered off toward the travel trailer out back.

I climbed into the pickup. At the bottom of the patio steps, Lacy still stood watching me. I knew she wanted me to take her along, but I shook my head at her and put the truck into reverse.

No. She's better off here. There's nothing good for her at the armory. Nothing good at all.

I tried to put out of my mind the sparkle she showed when June Jaans did his parlor tricks. I wanted to ignore the picture of his hands joined to Lacy's with that red string, but the image needled me. It brought back all them feelings from the past, when it was Ivy he charmed with his tricks.

You're not gonna think about this, Eudora. Not now, I told myself; then I said a silent prayer that when I got to the armory, June would be gone.

By the time I pulled into the parking lot, I had myself convinced that's how things would be. They weren't serving supper yet down the hill, so I parked the truck by the armory building and went inside.

The building had emptied out some since I left that morning. Just a few folks resting on cots around the outer walls. Folks like June Jaans, sitting propped up on some pillows, diggin' through papers in a cardboard box. I stopped in the doorway and glanced heavenward.

Is this a test, Lord? Is this a punishment? Why can't he be gone? Why do I have to be reminded, now of all times? Why?

I gave myself a mental slap. *It don't profit to feel sorry*

*for yourself, Eudora. Just go on down the hill and find
something to do down there.* I turned to leave.

Wonder what June's got in that box. . . .

A rustle of papers caught my ear, and I shuffled
around to see pictures taped to the wall, all sorts of pictures. I realized that was what Jenilee had been up to
that morning. She was putting those pictures up where
people could find them.

What in the world would give her such an idea?

But I already knew what gave her that idea. It come
from a kind heart and a gentle spirit, one that could forgive the very people who had whispered behind their
hands about her all her life. One that could want them
folks to have back these lost bits of their lives.

Shame fell over me like a shadow. *I ain't as good as
she is. I ain't.*

"It's something to see, ain't it?" June's voice made me
jump like a guilty soul. I turned around, my anger taken
away by the wall of pictures, by the act of grace it rep-
resented. But when I looked at June, fear come into me.
Fear of talking to him without that shield.

"I reckon," I muttered, feeling like the ground was
shifting under my feet.

June swiveled his head to look at the pictures. "People been comin' all day, just one or two at a time, lookin'
at the pictures, takin' some that belong to them. Caleb
Baker found out what Jenilee was doing, and he started
going around town telling folks, and asking them to
gather up any more pictures and personal things they
found that didn't belong to them. Pretty soon, folks
started bringing in pictures and things they'd picked up.
Dr. Albright's been telling folks to pile them next to the
door there." He motioned to a pile of boxes and bags by
the door.

"Well, he ain't the sentimental type," I muttered, taking a step closer to see what June had in his lap.

June shrugged. "Could be he figures putting them up

ought to wait until Jenilee comes back, being as she started it."

I peered over June's shoulder, trying to see into the box, but I couldn't without getting closer.

"Drew come to get Jenilee this noon. He was gonna take her to the hospital. Turns out her little brother and her father got caught in the tornado in their truck. Her daddy's in a pretty bad way, but the boy's all right. Just got a broke leg and some bumps, sounds like."

"Well, thank God for that." On the heels of that thought followed the not-so-holy idea that it would be better if Jenilee's daddy never came home.

June shuffled the contents of the box. "She couldn't wait to get to the hospital to see her little brother. Left in a hurry. Don't know when she'll be back, so I thought I'd start sorting through these things people brought in, pull the wet ones apart to dry, maybe get some more hung up."

I realized I was standing so close to him, I could feel his breath on my arm. I jerked back. "Well, there ain't any way you can do that," I yelped like a stung dog.

June swiveled toward me, looking surprised.

"I guess I'll have to help ya," I heard myself say. "You can't even get up out of bed." *What am I doing? Oh, heavens, why I am I getting myself tangled up with that old drunk? What if one of the ladies comes in . . . ?*

June smiled that even white smile. "That'd be fine, Eudora. That would be just fine."

I stepped back, waving a finger at the floor by his bed, my insides buckling. "You . . . you put them pictures there when you get them pulled apart. We'll sort 'em into groups, if we can find ones that go together. If we know who the pictures go to, we'll set them aside with the person's name on them."

June's face was flushed. "That'll be good, Eudora. It'll be good." He held up a handful of pictures, and his blue eyes met mine. "It's a start."

I knew he wasn't talking about the pictures. I grabbed the stack and turned around in a hurry.

It's a start. . . .

I got tape from the shelf and tore pieces with a vengeance, sticking pictures on the wall. Behind me, I heard June humming under his breath, the deep, warm baritone of his voice bringing back the past.

Somewhere over the rainbow, bluebirds fly . . .

I finished hanging the batch of pictures and stood with my hands braced against the wall, trying to fight the tide of memories swelling inside me.

I heard the shuffle of shoes near the doorway, and looked up to see Dr. Albright there. I was glad to see anyone, even him.

"I see you've decided to hang some more of the pictures," he said flatly.

I took a deep breath, swallowing the tremor in my voice. "Someone's got to."

"I suppose so." He stood looking at the wall with his hands in the pockets of his stained lab coat.

I waited for him to move on, but he didn't. Just stood there. What was he thinking?

"Reckon it wouldn't hurt you to help," I heard myself bark. "You could get them pictures from June for me."

I pretended not to notice that he gaped at me. Suppose he wasn't used to getting ordered around like that. Then he turned around and walked over to Mr. Jaans.

Well, I'll be darned. You just never know about folks, I thought.

He set them pictures on the table between us. "Any particular system you have going here?" He kept his gaze fixed on the pictures, and so did I.

"No, not that I know of. I don't think Jenilee had a real plan. I think she just set out to do a good thing the best way she knew."

He nodded. "You heard she found her family, I guess.

The roads are open again, so she and her brother left for the hospital."

I nodded, pressing a picture of the kindergarten stick-horse rodeo onto three loops of tape. "Heard that." What he said made me wonder again about how I caught him watching her that morning. "Reckon now that the roads are clear, you'll be headed back home to St. Louis, bein' as you were just here by *accident*, anyway. Reckon you're anxious to get back to your own family."

He paused a minute, a picture suspended in his hands, inches from the wall. He jerked his head sideways a fraction, shaking off some emotion before he answered. "No, not yet. I still have something to do here."

"I see," I said, but I didn't see at all.

CHAPTER 13

JENILEE

Nate sat silently in the backseat as we wound through the maze of roads heading home. Drew waited until Nate had fallen asleep to say anything.

"Those nurses shouldn't have taken him down to see Daddy," he said. "It didn't do him any good."

"I'm sure they thought they were helping. They don't know how Daddy can be." Rolling down my window, I let the warm summer breeze stroke the side of my face, lifting the damp strands of hair from my neck.

"No, I guess they don't."

We fell silent, neither of us knowing what to say next. It didn't seem right to say things against Daddy when he was lying near death in a hospital bed. No matter how bad he had been to us sometimes, there was still some part of us that cared about him.

I swallowed hard and asked the other question that had been on my mind all day. "Is that why you didn't want Darla to be at the hospital? Because she doesn't know how Daddy can be?"

Drew stared grimly ahead as we turned onto Good Hope Road. "That's part of it."

The tone of his voice said, *Don't ask anything more*, but I did anyway. "Does she know anything about . . . us? About how things were, I mean."

"I don't know." The muscles of his jaw twitched, and his eyes were hard and narrow.

I pressed on, in spite of the ominous undercurrent from him. I wasn't sure why. "Didn't you ever talk about it?"

"Not really."

"Well . . . didn't you ever want to?"

"Leave it alone, Jenilee," he bit out, whipping the truck into our driveway so fast that Nate jerked and woke up in the backseat. "There's a whole lot to it you don't understand. Just leave it alone."

"Wh-what?" Nate muttered, groggy from painkillers.

"Nothing." Drew opened his door and got out of the truck, done with the conversation. He jerked the back door open and reached in to help Nate down.

Nate shrugged away Drew's hand. "I can get out myself."

Drew grabbed him anyway. "No, you can't. They said no crutches until tomorrow morning, and you've got to keep the leg propped up." He hauled Nate out of the backseat like Nate was still the eight-year-old brother he'd left behind. "Come on, I'll help you to bed."

Nate moaned in his throat. "Owwww. I don't think I'm gonna live that long."

"Hang in there, Bubby," Drew said as I slipped under Nate's other arm, and together we helped him toward the house.

Bubby. Nate was in too much pain to notice the nickname. That was what Drew used to call him when he was little, back when Nate thought the sun rose and set at Drew's feet. *Bubby* was a name from a world that didn't exist anymore.

Drew didn't even seem to realize he'd said it.

"Hang in there," he said again, as we helped Nate up the porch steps.

"I'm all right," Nate panted, his eyes clamped against the pain. "I'll make it." His head rolled backward, then sagged.

"Just a few more steps, Bubby." Drew grimaced, as if he felt the pain, too. "See, there's your room. We're almost there. Hang in there with us."

Nate's head sagged against mine, the dampness of his tears wetting my hair. "It's all right, Nate. We're here. Look. Here's your bed."

We helped Nate onto the bed. He drew in a breath, coming back to life as we lifted the long cast and propped it up on a stack of blankets. Finally he laid his head back, closing his eyes, while tears streamed from beneath the fringe of his sandy brown lashes onto his suntanned skin.

"I'll go out and get the medicine from the car," Drew said as I covered Nate with a blanket.

"Ssshhhh," I whispered, dabbing Nate's cheeks. "We'll get you another dose of pain medicine. That'll help."

Nate turned his face away from me and raised his arm, laying it across his eyes. "Tell him not to call me that again." His voice trembled as he spoke.

I knew it wasn't the pain that had made him cry.

I sat on the side of the bed, stroking my hand up and down his arm. "Ssshhhh," I whispered. "Ssshhhh."

Drew came back with a pain pill and a glass of water. Nate was almost asleep, but he sat up and took the medicine, then lay back and closed his eyes. I stayed with him, my hand on his chest as his breaths grew long and slow. Drew waited in the doorway.

Finally I stood up and walked out of the room with Drew. He crossed the living room and went out the door to the front porch, as if he couldn't stand to be in that house. I stood uncertainly by the sofa, old feelings dripping over me like thick black ink. I understood why, once he had broken free, Drew didn't want to come back to this place.

I followed him onto the porch.

He didn't turn around, just stood with his hands braced on the railing, looking past Mama's oleander bush, toward the hay fields. "Looks like the electric is still out, but there's plenty of water in the storage tank, so it ought to feed into the house all right. Go ahead in and get something to eat and a shower, if you want to. I'll go out and feed Daddy's cows."

I wondered why he wanted to get away from me. "I promised old man Jaans I'd feed his cows and look for that old white bull of his," I said. "He's been running loose again, getting into trouble ever since the storm."

"I'll go on down there and take a look around, then come back through our pasture and feed Daddy's cattle. I'll be back after a while." He pushed off the porch rail and hurried down the steps and across the lawn, without looking back.

Just like before. A note of panic went through me. *Just like the last time he left.*

I walked to the yard fence and closed the gate behind him as he climbed into his truck. Even though I knew he was coming back, deep within me was the fear that he would leave Good Hope Road behind again.

My hand touched a piece of paper tangled in the rusty wire of the gate. I pulled it free and stood looking at it. The handwriting was different, not lacy and feminine like that of the first letter, but the paper was familiar, old, yellowed by time.

It felt crisp and brittle in my hands as I unfolded it and read the words, whispering them into the silent air.

My Dearest,

> *Today, as we prepare for the fiftieth anniversary of the day we wed, I have read again a letter you wrote*

long ago. The words took me back to that time when there was so much pain, and anger, and sadness in me. You wrote to me that day and told me your love would never leave me, that love can travel on the wind. I doubt if I told you then, or since, or could ever tell you what that letter meant to me. Oh, I know I have left these little love notes almost daily, but I have never said the things that are deepest in my heart. Perhaps I cannot still, so I will leave this note in the trunk with my old uniform, where you will find it someday when I am gone.

When you read this, know that your love sustained me through the darkest hours of my life. You were the breath in my lungs and the blood in my veins. Without you I would have surely bled until I died. You led me forward, a single step in faith, and then another, and another, until I had walked far from the shadows of the past. Had I not suffered the loss of everything I thought would matter, I would have missed everything that truly mattered in my life.

I am, my darling, so thankful for the many happy days we have shared together, but looking back, I am thankful also for the dark ones. These were the times when I understood the strength of faith and love, when this was all we had to cling to, and it was enough. Faith is a stalwart ship, carrying us through the gale, not destroyed by the ocean, but strengthened by it. Even the fiercest of life's trials are no match for her sails. Trials pass like a storm. The day rises anew, and we rise with the day.

We have been truly and richly blessed.

The letter ended there, as if he had never finished it, or didn't know how to, or didn't want to. Had he left it for her? Had she found it, or had it been waiting hidden somewhere when the tornado came, and she wasn't supposed to find it yet?

I read the letter again, whispering the words into the still afternoon air. *You led me forward, a single step in faith, and then another, and another, until I had walked far from the shadows of the past.* Was it possible to walk, one step at a time, away from the past until it didn't matter anymore?

Somewhere in the distance thunder rumbled, like the growl of something old, and black, and ugly. I folded the letter and hurried into the house. Dropping the letter on the table, I checked on Nate, then went to the bathroom, slipped off my clothes, washed up, and put on clean jeans and a T-shirt.

I stood in the doorway of Nate's bedroom, watching him sleep. Leaning against the doorframe, I looked at his clothes strewn all over the room, his baseball cleats hung on the bedpost, his football trophies covered with the collection of dirty, ragged ball caps he would never throw away.

Every inch of the room whispered of Nate and his silly, disorganized, seat-of-the-pants way of living. Nate never brooded or got angry like Drew. He never got afraid and quiet like me. He never tried to think things out ahead of time, or to plan for what might happen, or to try to steer clear of trouble. Nate dove in headfirst without checking to see how deep the water was. No rules, no fear, no worries.

Even Daddy's rages didn't seem to bother him. He'd stand there while Daddy hollered and carried on, told him how stupid and worthless all of us were. Nate could turn it all off. He'd shrug and say, "He's just drunk," like that explained everything. I always wondered how Nate could do that. I wished I could be like him.

The rumble of a diesel engine coming up the road rattled the edges of my consciousness. *Shad's truck.* Tires squealed, rattling the glass in the front door as I slipped my shoes on and went outside.

Shad's truck was shuddering to a halt in our driveway

with a flatbed trailer carrying a bulldozer fishtailing behind it. Shad threw the door open, climbed out, then slammed it shut so hard it hit the side of the truck and bounced open again.

Something inside me tightened into a knot. He looked just like he used to back in high school, jealous and possessive, angry most of the time. I'd thought he was different since he came back from Montana. He'd been quieter, less rowdy, less interested in running around drinking with his friends, easier to talk to.

Now he had that wild look in his eye again as he stopped on the other side of the yard fence. "You could let me know where you're gonna be! I went back to the armory to pick you up, and they said you weren't there no more."

"I'm sorry." What was I apologizing for? Just as in the past, I felt I was to blame for every argument between us. *Just like Mama and Daddy . . .*

Something pink blew by and I picked it up. A napkin from somebody's wedding last June. *Steve and Jenny, two hearts, one love . . .*

Shad glanced at the napkin in my hands. "Just leave that stuff in the ditch. It'll blow away in a day or two."

"I don't want it to blow away," I said. "I'm picking up pictures and other things to take to the armory, so that people can come and find some of what they lost."

"Doubt if anybody gives a rat about that stuff when the whole town's been tore up." He grabbed playfully at the scrap of pink tissue, and I held it away.

"It matters if it's all you've got left." I folded the napkin and stuck it in my pocket.

Shad let out a sarcastic laugh. "You're ignorant sometimes. You sure you didn't get knocked in the head yesterday?"

Heat boiled on the back of my neck and spilled into my face, but I didn't say anything. He knew I wouldn't.

"Let's go to my place. My electric's out of Hindsville, so it's still on." He started toward the truck.

"I can't."

Surprised, he stopped with one hand on the truck door, turned back, and looked at me. He crossed the distance between us. "You know, that's the second time I come to get you and you didn't want to go. You're not actin' normal, Jenilee. You sure you're all right?"

I didn't feel normal anymore. I wasn't sure what I felt. I knew there wasn't any way I could explain it to Shad.

"Drew's here," I said finally, looking up the road toward Mr. Jaans's place. If Drew came home and found Shad, there would probably be a fight. Shad and Drew had hated each other for as long as I could remember. If Drew found out that Shad was back, and that we were seeing each other again, he'd probably have a fit. "We just brought Nate home from the hospital."

Shad's eyes burned like the coils on a stove. "I'll come check on ya tomorrow."

I crossed my arms over myself. "It's probably not a good idea. I'll call when they get the phones back on, in a day or two, all right?"

"I'll stop by *tomorrow*," he said, turning and walking toward his truck, punching a fist into his hand. "Tell Drew I said hi." Then he climbed into the seat, squealed the tires, and threw gravel against the fence as he left our driveway.

Tell Drew I said hi. I knew what he meant by that. He wanted to start trouble with Drew.

Thunder growled again in the distance. The gathering storm was coming closer. Everything left outside tonight would get drenched.

I ran to the tractor shed, grabbed an empty feed sack, and started picking up mementos among the debris. I hurried across the yard, out the gate, and into the ditch, where more papers had blown in since the day before.

Drew's truck topped the hill and rattled slowly up the road, drowning out the faraway thunder. He pulled up beside me, put the truck in park, and leaned out the window. "You look better. Did you get something to eat?"

I shook my head. "I'm not hungry right now," I said, not wanting to go back to the house. "It sounds like rain's coming. I want to pick up as much of this stuff as I can, just in case. All these papers and pictures will be ruined if it rains tonight."

Drew turned the truck off, climbed out, and started walking with me, picking things up and looking at them as he talked. "Nate all right?"

"Sound asleep," I answered. "I imagine he'll stay that way for a while, after taking that pain pill."

Drew dropped a bunch of papers into my bag. "Some fences got knocked down at old man Jaans's place. I ran his cows back in and put the wire up the best I could. Looks like his house is still all right. The wind knocked over that old garage of his and made a mess, kind of scattered things around. It blew open the doors to this house, too, and made a mess inside."

"That's too bad, but at least he's still got his house. I feel really sorry for Mrs. Gibson."

Drew looked up the road toward the Gibson place. "Yeah. Place sure is torn up."

"She says she doesn't care about the place being ruined," I said, trying to blot out the horror of those moments after the storm. "She says all that matters is that her grandkids and her kids are all right, and she wouldn't care if she lost ten houses as long as she doesn't lose them."

Drew shrugged. "It's just a house."

"I guess. But she's spent almost her whole life there. It's got to be hard for her to lose everything."

I thought of our own house. The things that had happened there defined who we were. In some ways, I wished the tornado would come back and take the house away—so that all the old definitions would be gone.

But I didn't imagine that Mrs. Gibson felt that way

about her house. Her home and her yard had been filled with the sounds of people—dinners on Sunday afternoons, Easter egg hunts with bunches of grand-kids, church socials on Sunday, old ladies coming by for tea and cribbage. Even from a half mile down the road, we could hear their laughter drifting on the warm Missouri wind, reminders that just a stone's throw away, life was good.

Drew's eyes met mine for a moment before he bent and untangled a picture of a high school cheerleader from the weeds. "Well, all I can say is that when I heard about the storm, I didn't call to see whether it got the house or not. All I thought about was where were Darla and the kids, and were they all right. Not much else mattered. I guess that's pretty much how Mrs. Gibson feels."

I nodded, surprised. I had never thought of Drew as caring about someone that way. He always seemed so hard, so far out of reach. *If you love them that much, why are you fighting?*

I didn't have the courage to ask. Instead, I made small talk as we came closer to the Gibson farm. "Mrs. Gibson asked me to look around her place for some notebooks of hers. She was really worried about losing them."

"All right," Drew said, but squinted doubtfully at what was left of the house. "It's going to take a miracle to find anything here." He picked up a soggy wad of old newspaper, then dropped it in the ditch again. "Did she say what the notebooks looked like?"

"Just plain spiral notebooks, I think. Sounded like she had things written in them, stories or something." A sense of guilt came over me. We didn't deserve to have our house right down the road with pictures still on the walls while Mrs. Gibson's house was in shreds.

Pink tinsel glittered near my feet. Tears prickled in my throat, because I could remember the tinsel wrapped around Mrs. Gibson's porch railing at Easter time. But there wouldn't be any more Easter egg hunts here.

It was hard to imagine not having Mrs. Gibson down the road anymore. She had always been there, a constant in an unpredictable world. We never knew what would await us at home as we stepped off the school bus and walked down that gravel road, but we knew Mrs. Gibson would be sitting on her porch. She'd watch the bus as if she expected her kids to still be getting off.

At Easter, her place would be alive with lilies. At Halloween the porch would be lined with pumpkins. At Thanksgiving she'd set a big wooden turkey by the door. At Christmas she would wind pine garlands and red ribbons around the porch railings. The Gibson place was the same year after year. It looked the same. It sounded the same.

And now, suddenly, it lay in ruins, without a word to say. Not a sound. Not a whisper. Not the tinkling of the wind chime, or the squeaking of the screen door, or the swish of sheets on the clothesline. Not even the low flutter of leaves on the old trees.

I never realized how I loved the flutter of cottonwood leaves. Looking at the twisted remains of the stumps, I felt tears spill onto my cheeks.

"Jenilee, you all right?"

I nodded, wiping my eyes impatiently. "I was just thinking about how quiet it is. Nothing sounds the way I remember."

"Hard to get used to the quiet," he agreed, squinting at what was left of the trees in the orchard. "I remember thinking that when Darla and the kids moved out. Seemed like I missed the sound of them as much as anything."

Then why did you let them go? I reached across the space between us and laid my hand on his arm. *Is it just Daddy you want to keep separate from them, or is it all of us?* "I'd like to meet them someday."

"It's hard to picture how it could happen. Anytime soon, at least." The words were little more than a sigh.

"It's pretty much of a mess. It's not . . . like things are supposed to be. Guess we Lanes don't do the family thing too well." He turned and headed off across the yard, looking beaten.

I watched him go, wondering what he was thinking. Drew could remember how it was when Grandma and Grandpa were alive better than any of us could. He knew what a normal life felt like, what it was like to be taken care of and not be afraid. Maybe that was why he, of the three of us, had the hardest time living with the way things turned out.

Drew and I searched the area around Mrs. Gibson's place without talking. Drew dug out her old wooden feed bin from under the fallen-down barn, and we started filling it with items that could still be used—a few dishes, some old picture frames, a toy horse model with only three legs, some pots, pans, and other cooking stuff, a photo album, a recipe box, some quilts, anything that we thought she might want. It was strange to be digging through the bits and pieces of her life—seeing all the things that were once in her house.

Walking by on the way home from the school bus, I had always wondered what was inside.

Drew closed the feed bin as the sun descended and the air turned still. "I don't think there are any notebooks here, Jenilee. I found some old-time pictures of the Poetry baseball team, and one of a parade in front of Poetry School. They're probably hers." He put them in the feed sack, then stood up and wiped his forehead with his sleeve. "Getting too dark to look anymore. I think we better head on home."

"Look at this," I said, clearing dirt from the twisted framework of a stained-glass window. "The dove is still in one piece. I bet the rest of it could be fixed. Can we carry it home?"

Drew shrugged. "Guess so." He looked at the caved-in cellar door. "Any point in pulling that cellar door out of there? We could put her stuff down here so it won't get wet if it rains."

I shivered, remembering. "No. There isn't anything down there." The dark, damp feeling of that place came over me, and I turned away, in a hurry to be gone. "Let's just close the lid on that old feed box. It'll keep the rainwater off."

"All right," Drew said, then closed the feed box before lifting the heavy stained-glass window frame. "You sure you want to take this home?"

"Um-hmm. It ought to be fixed. It's too pretty to leave in the dirt." I remembered that window in the peak of the house, how it glittered in the afternoon sunlight, making the dove seem to come to life. I wanted to be like that dove, white and pretty, wings spread, high above everything.

Distant thunder rumbled as we started toward home. I shivered as a cool puff of breeze fluttered down the gravel road.

Drew squinted at the churning black clouds on the horizon. "Rain's coming."

I ducked my head, trying to ignore the clouds. "I hope not." I was thinking of all the pictures and belongings that were still lying everywhere, and of all the people in Poetry staying in tents.

"Looks like it might already be coming down over south of Poetry. We better step it up."

We hurried home as thunder growled and lightning whipped the sky. Drew put the stained-glass window in the garage, then ran out to pull his truck into the driveway and close up the barn.

I went inside to check on Nate.

"Nate," I whispered at the door to his room, "are you hungry? I'm going to warm up some canned chili."

Nate shook his head and pulled the covers up, murmuring something before he drifted back to sleep.

I closed the door to his room, walked through the

house, and lit the oil lamps we always used when the power was out. The house was already getting dark as the storm blotted the last of the evening sun.

Heavy drops of rain began pelting the windows as Drew came in the front door and fought the wind to pull the screen shut behind him. He set the feed sack full of papers on the floor and came across the room dripping.

Pulling his cell phone and keys out of his pocket, he set them on the table. "I'm gonna go clean up."

"I'll put some chili on," I said, shivering in the gust of cool air, then jumping as lightning lit the windows and thunder boomed so loud it seemed to rattle the house to its foundations.

Drew frowned at me. "You're nervous as a cat."

I nodded, rubbing my hands up and down my arms. "It's just the storm." *I'm glad you're here, Drew.* "It just seems . . . strange to be back here in a storm again."

Drew looked around the room, as if he were seeing it for the first time, the way a stranger would have seen it—the paneling with holes in it, the threadbare curtains, the stained orange shag carpeting, the windows with bushes grown so high that little light came through, the torn recliner, the couch so faded the forest print barely showed anymore.

There were empty spots on the walls where pictures used to hang. I wondered if Drew noticed that Daddy had taken down all the photographs of him.

His body stiffened. He shook his head as he disappeared down the hall, muttering, "Home sweet home."

CHAPTER 14

Drew's cell phone rang on the table. I wiped my hands on a kitchen towel, grabbed it, and pressed the button, worried that the noise would wake up Nate.

"Hello," I said, suddenly realizing that I shouldn't be answering Drew's phone at all. "Just a minute. I'll get Drew." What if it was the hospital? What if they were calling about Daddy? "Is this the hospital?"

"No," said a woman's voice. "Is this Drew's sister?"

I stopped in the hall. "Yes, this is Jenilee. Who's this?"

A pause followed, during which she seemed to decide what to say. "This is Drew's . . . This is Darla. Has Drew told you about me, about us?"

"Yes." Breath fluttered in my chest. I knew Drew wouldn't like my talking to her. I tried to think of something harmless to say. "Nate said you sat with him in the hospital yesterday." *Drew was wrong to be mad about that.* "I just . . . I wanted to say thank you. That was nice."

"That's . . . that's why I was calling, really." I could tell by the tone of her voice there was more to it than that. "I stopped by the hospital this evening, and they said you'd taken Nate home. I just wanted to check on him.

Nate and I got to know each other a little bit yesterday. I was just thinking about . . ." She stopped again, then finished quickly with, "I was just thinking about Nate. Could you tell him I asked about your father, but they wouldn't give me any new information because I'm not family?"

But you are family. You have Drew's children. "I will. I'd let you talk to him, but he's sleeping now."

"That's all right. I don't want to tick Drew off. I just . . ." She paused, and the sound of a child's voice drifted through the line in the background. I heard the word *Daddy.* Darla covered the phone and whispered something, then came back on, her voice choked. "Anyway, I just wanted to check on Nate. Tell him I'm thinking about him. I wasn't trying to make any trouble between him and Drew. I was just trying to help. I guess I should . . . let you go."

I didn't want her to go. "I can hear the kids. They're really cute." *I want you to know that Drew's not like Daddy. He's nothing like Daddy.* "Drew showed me a picture."

"*Drew* showed you a picture?"

"Yes . . . ummm . . . he did. Why do you sound so surprised?"

She gave a quick, sarcastic laugh, her voice turning bitter. "Well, you just wouldn't know Drew gave a crap about his kids. He hasn't sent a dime to support them in two months. I'm having to go to court to sue him for child support. He walked away from them like they don't matter at all."

Anger and disbelief boiled inside me. *He walked away from us, too.*

I didn't say it. I knew it would only cause more problems. "He said his kids were the first thing he thought about after the tornado."

"Funny he would say that," she bit out.

I stood silent for a moment, gazing out the window as

lightning gashed the night, illuminating the yard, over-grown with Mama's dead flower vines. *How can I explain this place to her?* "It's hard," I said. I could hear her crying softly on the other end of the phone. "It's hard to explain to anyone else, to anyone who didn't grow up here. From here, it's hard to picture . . . it's like . . ." I tried to form my feelings into words. Drew's words came out. "It's like we don't know how to make a right kind of life."

Silence answered the other end of the line. Finally she whispered, "He's never said that. He never talks about any of that."

"He said it this morning."

"Why can't he say it to *me*?" she pleaded. "If he feels that way, why can't he say it?"

The lock clicked in the bathroom door and I jumped, catching a quick breath. "He's coming out of the bath-room. Do you want to talk to him?"

"No," she rushed out, sounding as nervous as I was. "We'll just fight."

"O.K. I should go." *If he sees me here on the phone, he'll be mad. If he knew what I said . . .*

"Will you let me know how Nate is? How things are?"

"O.K. Bye." I hung up the phone and set it on the table like a hot coal. *Why did I promise that? It's Drew's place to talk to Darla.*

The bathroom door opened, and I stepped back to the stove, my hands trembling as I dished up bowls of chili. I glanced over my shoulder, making sure the phone was back in place.

Drew came across the living room, and I looked guiltily into the chili pot, feeling like he would see right through me, wondering why that filled me with dread. Was I afraid that if we pushed him too much, if we asked too much, he would leave again?

Would he?

"When did you learn to cook?" He looked over my shoulder into the pot.

"A long time ago." *Eight years ago, when you left us and Mama was too sick to cook.* Did he have any idea what the last seven years had been like? Old resentments crept to the surface like sludge rising from the river bottom. I set the bowls on the counter and tried to concentrate on getting glasses from the cabinet.

My hands started to shake, and the dishes rattled. A glass fell from the shelf and shattered.

I braced my hands on the counter. "Drew," I heard myself whisper, my voice a million sharp pieces. "How can you leave people behind the way you do?" *How could you leave us and never look back? How can you leave your own children behind?*

Part of me was afraid to know the answer—afraid he would say something like, *Life ain't easy, Jenilee. Anybody tell you it was supposed to be?*

I heard Drew set spoons on the table and pull out a chair. "I told you, I was in a lot of trouble when I left here." His voice was flat, emotionless. I couldn't tell what he was thinking. "It was a long time ago."

I picked up pieces of glass, tossing them into the trash, anger making me bold. "You're doing it again now. You're leaving your kids."

He cleared his throat indignantly. "Where's that coming from?"

"*Darla* called," I blurted, hurling bits of glass into the trash can. "She said you haven't paid child support or seen your kids in two months."

He slammed his hand on the table, and a spoon clattered to the floor. The legs of his chair squealed on the linoleum as he stood up. "Darla called to give you her sob story, and you took her word for it, is that it?" His voice roared through the house like thunder.

For the first time in my life, I wasn't shaken by it. I didn't care. "Darla called to check on *Nate*. We *talked*. That's *all*."

"And you just took her word for it?" he boomed, pacing the kitchen behind me. "Drew's a jerk, and Darla didn't do anything wrong."

I spun around, glaring at him. "How am I supposed to know, Drew? You don't want to talk about it. All I know about you is what I can remember from before *you left.*"

Drew reached past me, jerked open the silverware drawer and grabbed a clean spoon, then shoved the drawer closed. "You believe what you want to believe."

"I don't want to believe it. I want you to tell me it isn't true about you and your kids."

"*Darla* brought all of it on. *She* took the kids and *she* moved out. It was *her* choice." He sat down and huddled over his supper. "There, how's that?"

I realized I had no idea where the truth really lay. "I don't know," I said more calmly. "How is it?"

He shook his head, not looking at me as I sat down beside him. "It stinks."

"Well, at least you and Darla agree on something." I stirred the chili around in my bowl, my anger spent. "She didn't sound very happy either."

Drew stopped eating and looked at me, surprised. I could tell he wanted to know if that was true. He was too proud to ask. I didn't say.

We sat in silence for a long time while Drew ate and I stirred the contents of my bowl back and forth.

"Better eat that," Drew grumbled finally, his idea of a peacemaking gesture.

It made me think of the mornings when I was little, and he made oatmeal for us, then slapped it down on the table with a big huff like we were too much trouble. *Better eat that*, he'd say. *Mama forgot to give me any lunch money for today. Guess I'll try to make us a sandwich or somethin'.* He would always figure something out so that Nate and I didn't have to go without lunch. After he went away to the army, I realized how hard that could be sometimes.

Maybe he did the best he could. Maybe that's what all of us are doing.

Drew finished his chili quickly, as if he couldn't wait to be away from the table, and me. He put his bowl in the sink, then grabbed the dustpan and brush and swept up the broken glass on the counter and floor. "My old bed still back there?"

"It's still there. Daddy lays his guns and stuff on there when he cleans them, so check before you lay down."

"Good night, Jenilee." There was a false calm in his voice, a pleasantness that was transparent. He grabbed his cell phone from the table as he passed.

"Drew?" I watched him, standing at the entrance to the hallway, seeming out of place in his National Guard uniform.

"Hmmm?" He didn't turn around.

"Thanks for coming back."

"You're welcome, Jenilee. I should have done it sooner. I'm sorry." And he walked slowly down the hall to the door at the end, opened it, and disappeared inside.

I heard the faint beep of him dialing his cell phone, then the low cadence of his voice, his words hushed, intimate. I hoped he was talking to Darla.

I put the dishes in the sink and went to Nate's room. He stirred, and I leaned over him, touching his forehead. In the dim lamplight, he looked younger, more like the little boy he used to be.

He opened his eyes and smiled at me.

"Hi, there," I whispered. "How you feeling?"

He blinked drowsily, thinking about it. "Better. My leg hurts again."

I checked the time, then got a pain pill from the table by the bed. "Here. The doctor said you should take one of these every four hours. He thought you'd be feeling a lot better by tomorrow. Here's some water."

Nate sat up against the pillows and took the glass of

water from my hand. "Thanks, Jen." He swallowed the pill, then laid back. "Sorry I'm not good for much right now."

"It's all right." I chuckled, tousling his sandy hair. "I'm just glad you're back."

"Me too." His eyelids drifted lower.

"I love you, you know," I whispered.

I expected him to roll his eyes and get embarrassed like he always did these days when I told him that. Instead he opened one blue eye and smiled on one side. "Thanks for taking care of me." His smile said, *I love you, too*, even if he wouldn't say it out loud.

"That's all right."

He slipped his hand into mine, and I sat looking at the cuts and bruises on his fingers as he closed his eyes again. "You gonna sit here awhile?"

"Yeah," I whispered. "I'm gonna sit here awhile."

"Good."

I curled up in the chair beside his bed like I had so many nights after Mama died, when he was all I had left to hold on to.

My mind began to drift, and I let my eyes fall closed, thinking of what a long, strange day it had been.

A thunderclap startled me just as I was drifting into sleep. I jerked upright and jumped to my feet. My heart hammering, I stood in the center of the dark room, a sense of panic rushing through my body like an electrical current.

"You took my kids away!" A voice boomed through the house. Daddy's voice. Breath caught in my throat. I rushed out the door and closed it behind me, so Nate wouldn't hear.

I stood in the hallway, my gaze darting around in the flickering lamplight, my mind trying to make sense of what was happening. *Was I dreaming? Did I dream it?*

"You took the kids, Darla!" I realized it was Drew's voice. "You took everything, and you left. I came home from work and everything was gone! You're the one with all the psychology classes. You tell me how I'm supposed to feel about that!"

He paused, then growled, "Talking about it's not going to do any good. You didn't want to talk about it when you let your father hire that jerk of a lawyer to keep me away from my kids, Darla!" His voice started to crack as he said her name. "I call your parents' house, and they won't give me your number. I can hear Alex and Amber there half the time, and they won't even let me talk to my own kids." The sentence was punctuated by the sound of the phone beeping, then clattering against the wall.

I realized I was standing outside Drew's room with my hand on the doorknob. I was afraid to go in.

"Drew?" I whispered. He didn't answer. I turned and walked away.

In the living room, I curled up in a corner of the couch, wrapped a blanket around myself, and waited for morning to come.

"Jenilee? Jen . . . wake up."

I startled awake.

Drew was leaning over the coffee table, looking at me with an unreadable expression. "You were talking in your sleep."

"I was? What did I say?"

"I couldn't quite tell. It's morning, anyway." He walked to the kitchen and set two bowls on the table. "Milk's gone sour, so all we have is instant oatmeal with water."

I stood up, rubbing my eyes, trying to remember what had really happened the night before, and what I had dreamed. "That sounds fine."

"I gave Nate some oatmeal. He was pretty hungry." Drew sat down and started eating. "He said his leg was still hurting, so I gave him a pain pill."

I glanced up, surprised that Drew had tended to Nate, and that Nate had let him. "Oh . . . well . . . good. That's good. But you could have woken me up. I would have done it."

"It's all right. We got it taken care of." For just an instant, there was a pleased look on his face.

I wondered if something good had happened between him and Nate. "Can I borrow your truck for a little while to go to the armory?" Maybe if I left them alone together, they would talk things out. "I want to hang the pictures we gathered yesterday and tell Mr. Jaans his cows are all right."

Drew looked suspicious. "I can take that stuff down there for you, and tell Jaans about his cows."

"Oh, I know," I said. "But I wanted to do it myself. He . . . might be upset about his bull still being gone."

Drew frowned one-sidedly, like he knew I was scheming to leave him there alone with Nate. "Jaans knows that bull will come home." He paused to eat a bite of oatmeal, then pointed the spoon at me. "That bull does this every time there's a storm. I remember after that big flood on Caddo Creek, Charlie disappeared for a week. All of a sudden one day he walks right into the sale barn café. I thought Jaans was going to kiss him right there." A rare grin lit his face. "Oh, Lord, old Mrs. Abshier was mad. She went to cussin' Jaans and chasin' after him and that bull with a kitchen broom in her hand and a fire in her eye."

"I never heard that story." I was struck by how good it was to see Drew smile.

He took another bite of his oatmeal, squinting thoughtfully. "Guess you were in school. I ditched that day so I could make some money working at the sale barn." He looked down at his bowl and shook his head. "I remember old Mrs. Abshier ran halfway down the street waving that broom with that bull bellowing and Jaans hollering behind him."

Picturing the scene, I laughed with Drew.

He reached into his pocket and pulled out his keys and cell phone. "You better take my cell phone, too. So you can come get us if the hospital calls about Daddy. I called around four a.m., and there was no change."

"All right." I picked up the keys and the phone, wondering how we could have been laughing about Jaans's old bull just a moment before. "What if Darla calls?"

The grim look on Drew's face said as much as his words. "Darla won't be calling." He stood up, tossing a napkin on top of his bowl. "I'm going out and feed the cows. I'll be back in a minute."

I hurried through getting dressed and saying good-bye to Nate, so I could get out of the house before Drew came back and changed his mind about letting me have his truck.

"I'll just be gone for a little while," I promised Nate. "Drew's here if you need anything."

"Great," Nate grumbled.

"Nate, don't be that way," I pleaded. "Drew's trying his best. Don't be so hard on him. He's your brother. Hating him won't do either of you any good."

"That's what Darla said." Nate picked irritably at the loose strings on his comforter. "You know, I heard him hollering at her last night on the phone."

"I heard it, too."

"I told him this morning when he came in here—I told him I heard him, I mean. I told him he shouldn't be such a jerk to Darla. Darla's nice."

I swallowed hard. "Geez, Nate, what did he say?" I wondered how I could have slept through Drew and Nate talking just down the hall.

"He said he didn't blame Darla." Nate squinted up at me, his blue eyes reflecting the morning light from the window. "He said Darla was only doing what Mama should of done years ago."

The words rolled like molten lead in the pit of my stomach. "Oh, Nate," I breathed. "What did you tell him?"

Nate shrugged, pulling a string loose and dropping it over the side of his bed. "I told him it wasn't the same thing. He isn't Daddy and Darla isn't Mama."

Love filled me in a rush, and I reached out and hugged him.

He gave me a hooded glance, twisting his lips to one side to ward off a smile, then lay back against his pillow, letting out a long sigh. "That medicine makes me tired."

"I'll be back soon," I said, turning to leave. "Be good."

"Um-hmm." He closed his eyes, grinning.

I left him there, grabbed Drew's keys and cell phone, took the bag of pictures by the door, and went to the truck. In the pasture, I could see Drew feeding and checking the cows as I left. Bo was jumping up and down, yapping at Drew's heels, finally home from his wanderings.

Driving down Good Hope Road, I watched Mrs. Gibson's place pass, watched the twisted-metal orchard, watched the path of the tornado as it zigzagged back and forth across the road. Nothing but bare dirt and ruined trees where it hit. Everything almost normal where it didn't. Even now, after seeing it again and again, I still found it hard to believe.

The storm overnight had filled the ditches with dirty water. Bits of paper were floating beside shreds of wood and pieces of insulation. I looked at the bag of pictures and papers in the seat beside me. *This is probably all that is left. After last night's rainstorm, everything else will be ruined.*

A shiver went through me as I topped the hill and saw Poetry. With the frenzy of activity slowed, it looked more desolate than ever, like a bombed-out city after the war is over. Even the armory was quiet. The wail of emergency vehicles was gone from the air, no sign of the soup line except for two men washing out a kettle. Cars were parked in the armory lot, but there were no people in sight.

I shouldn't have come here, I thought as I got out of the car. *It's too sad, being here now.*

Taking the bag of pictures from the seat, I walked slowly up the steps, hearing the hum of voices inside. Not hushed whispers of grief, but people talking, laughing.

I stepped into the doorway, a breath of wonder filling my lungs, stopping me beneath the ancient stone arch. The walls of the armory were filled with pictures, hundreds and hundreds of pictures, as far and as high as the eye could see.

Groups of people moved along the fringes of the room, gazing at the walls. Friends, neighbors, strangers. Bits of their conversations drifted on the air.

". . . Wandalene's wedding picture. Lordy, look at that hair! Must be a foot high . . ."

". . . Gann family reunion. Remember Uncle Bubba with his guitar?"

"That's Malena's birthday party. Right there. See that one? That's right before she hit Papa in the head with the piñata stick."

". . . that trip we took out to Yellowstone in 'fifty-four."

". . . my old yellow T-bird . . ."

". . . that Farmall tractor with the narrow front. Remember . . ."

Laughter rang in the center of the room, and I noticed for the first time that there was a row of lawn chairs there now. The garden club ladies were carefully peeling apart pictures and laying them on the floor to dry. On his cot nearby, Mr. Jaans was helping them, while Caleb Baker shuttled pictures back and forth between them and Mrs. Gibson, who was handing them up the ladder to . . . to Dr. Albright?

I stared at him, atop the ladder, cheerfully taping larger pictures up high.

"You listen to me, Brady." A woman's voice nearby caught my attention. I watched as she took the picture of the newborn baby girl with the sky blue eyes from the wall. She turned to the sheriff's deputy. I recognized her. Melanie Anderson, whose newborn girl had been swept from her crib by the tornado.

"This is her. This is my baby." She swallowed hard, wiping her eyes. "I know she's out there somewhere. A mother's heart just knows, Brady. I know she's out there somewhere."

The deputy, Brady Farrel, looked worried. "It's been two days. . . ."

"Don't say that! Don't you say that." Melanie leaned closer to him, her eyes filled with fire. "*My baby girl* is out there. *My baby girl* is coming home." She clutched the picture to her chest and started toward the door with the sheriff's deputy following. "If this picture can make it through the tornado, so can she."

CHAPTER 15

EUDORA

I noticed little Jenilee standing there as I handed a stack of pictures up the ladder to Dr. Albright. "Well, good mornin', Jenilee," I said, but she didn't hear me. She just stared at the Taylor family, who were chuckling together over some pictures from last year's Halloween carnival. Caleb Baker was helping them take down some of the higher ones.

"Good mornin', Jenilee," I repeated, walking closer to her.

"I can't believe all the pictures . . ." she muttered, but I wasn't sure she was talking to me. She seemed in a daze, staring at the wall with them big brown eyes glittering. A tear spilled over and traced a line down her cheek. She didn't seem to notice.

"Well, don't cry about it," I said. "You done a good thing here." I slipped in beside her and squeezed her shoulders, even though I knew she wouldn't like it. I wanted to hug somethin', and she was the only thing close enough.

"It's . . . wonderful," she whispered, loud enough so

that only I could hear. "It's just the way I dreamed about it."

"Well, that must have been a good dream." I give her another squeeze, and to my surprise, she laid her head on my shoulder like it was the most natural thing in the world. "It's a help to folks. They come in, and they look for their pictures, and they read that old letter, and when they go out, they feel some hope."

"It's perfect," she breathed, watching the old letter twitter in the breeze like a leaf barely clinging to a tree.

"Yes, it is," I agreed, laying my head on top of hers. Right then at that moment, she felt like one of my own. "It's perfect."

She stood there with me for a minute, quiet and still. I didn't move. I didn't want to break the spell.

A car door banged outside, and she jerked upright. She moved away from me as Caleb come by and offered to take the bag out of her hands.

"All right," she said, and let him take the bag away to June's bed to dump it out for sorting.

"No one came for the old letter?" she asked.

"Nobody yet," I said. "But it brought comfort to a lot of folks, so maybe it's meant to be here for a while. It's easy to get to dwelling on what you've lost. All the physical things, I mean. Sometimes folks forget that what really matters is the love you got in you, and there's not a storm in the world that can blow that away. I think that's what the letter says."

"I think so too," she whispered, running her hands up and down her arms like she had a chill, even though the morning was already warm. Her gaze traveled along the wall until it reached the ladder, and she saw Dr. Albright.

The look on her face made me chuckle. "Must be some kind of divine grace in this wall," I said. "It's even got Dr. Always Right up on the ladder hanging pictures."

Jenilee smiled, a little dimple forming where her cheeks blushed pink. "How did you get him to do that?"

I shrugged, not quite sure myself. "He just come up yesterday when I was getting started on this, and I put him to work. He come back this morning with a ladder, ready to help again."

She looked around the room, her sandy brows knotting in the center. "Doc Howard's still not back?"

"Still in the hospital, but just as a precaution. Mrs. Howard said they weren't takin' no chances."

Jenilee looked worried. "I hope he's all right."

"Anyhow, Dr. Always Right—oh, heck, I mean Albright—is lookin' after things for now, though there ain't much to do since they carried everyone off to the hospitals."

"That's good," she muttered, but I could tell she wasn't really listening to me. "Are there more pictures? I can't stay long, because I have to get back to go with Nate and Drew to the hospital, but I could start hanging some pictures up on the back wall. Maybe we could stand some pieces of plywood or something up in here to give us more space."

"I think that's a fine idea," I told her. I thought about asking after her daddy, but I didn't know how she'd feel about that, and I didn't want to upset her. "There's bags by the door. We been just dumpin' things out on the floor, and tryin' to sort out things that belong together, and pull apart the ones that are wet so they can dry. If we know who they go to, sometimes we just keep them in a pile to pass along, but mostly it's all shuffled like cards. You just have to hang things up and let folks come look."

I clapped my hands together, startling her. "Well, I guess we ought to get to work," I said. "Why don't you go over there and see if the ladies have some more pictures sorted for Dr. Albright to hang up high on the wall?"

"All right." Jenilee combed her blond hair back from her face, looking happy to have something to do. When she smiled like that, the littlest twist of her lips, she looked so sweet I wanted to hug her again.

She got away before I had the chance. She hurried over to the garden club ladies, and in a minute she was back with a stack of pictures and other things. She walked to the bottom of the ladder and stood there holding them, not sure what to do.

"Doc!" I hollered as I went along the wall filling spaces where people had pulled off pictures and taken them home. "There's another stack of pictures for ya."

The doc turned and looked over his shoulder. He stopped dead in his tracks and stared at Jenilee for a moment.

She climbed the bottom two steps of the ladder and held the pictures up, fidgeting while she waited for him to come down to get them.

I paused in what I was doing and stood there watching the two of them, wondering again what in the world that city doctor could be thinking, and why he looked at her that way.

He smiled and sat on the step a few rungs above her, like he thought to be there for a minute or two. He didn't take the papers from her hands. "How are you this morning, Jenilee?"

"Fine." She pushed the stack of papers upward. "Here. These are ready to be hung up."

He nodded and leaned down a little, tryin' to get her to look at him. "You know, you started a good thing here. People come in looking shell-shocked. The pictures give them a sense that things will eventually get back to some kind of order."

I took a step closer, so he would know I was listening. I felt pretty protective of Jenilee, and if that city doctor had in mind to flirt with a girl half his age, I wanted him to know this was a good, Christian town and we didn't let that kind of thing go on. A few years back, we run a basketball coach out of town for doing that same thing. If I ever got that doctor alone again, I thought maybe I'd tell him what we done to that coach.

"Thanks," Jenilee said, and ducked her head. "Well, here are some more pictures." And she tried again to give him the bundle.

He pretended to be busy finding the end of the tape. He knew if he took the pictures, she would scoot out of there. "I may not have said it yesterday," he told her, his voice so soft I could barely hear it, "but I want to thank you for your help. You did a good job."

She looked up, gaping at him, like she didn't know what to say. "Well . . . I . . . ummm . . . thanks."

"You have a natural talent for healing," he said. "I've seen med students who couldn't have done as well as you did."

Jenilee smiled a little, seeming to relax. "Thanks," she said. "But it was stuff anybody could do."

The doctor shook his head, pointing a finger at her. "Don't sell yourself short," he said, then put his hands over hers and slowly took the bundle of pictures from her fingers. "Some people have an inborn gift for medicine. It's something that can't be learned. It just happens. You have a way of keeping people calm in a crisis, of making them believe you can help."

Jenilee wrinkled her forehead, almost like she thought he was making fun of her, or like she couldn't believe someone would say such a thing about her. She looked at him for a long minute, wondering whether or not to believe him.

"I spent a lot of years working at the vet clinic," she told him. "Then when Mama got sick, I spent most of my time taking care of her." She paused thoughtfully, looking up at him. "I guess that's where I learned it."

Dr. Albright smiled. "A gift like that comes from the

heart. You can't learn it. You have a gift, Jenilee. You should do something with it."

Jenilee shrugged. "I guess I'd better get some more pictures." Shaking off the compliment like a dog shaking off water, she stepped down the ladder.

"Jenilee, why don't you go over and help Caleb and June sort that bag of pictures you brung in?" I suggested, thinking it might be good to get her away from that city doctor, since I couldn't tell quite what he was up to.

"All right," she said, then walked over and sat on the floor beside Caleb, who was holding up an old, yellowed picture, showing it to June.

I watched them laughing together, the town drunk, the chubby class clown, and the girl nobody ever noticed, and I thought what a strange grouping they made.

I reminded myself that everything was different now, and I needed to forget my old ways of thinking.

Everything's changed, and all the things you thought were so ain't so anymore, Eudora, I reminded myself. *It's the Lord's way of showing who is really leading this wagon train. In your life, you been a little stubborn about turning over the reins. . . .*

I walked closer to see what they were talking about. Caleb wrapped his arm around his belly, laughing as he held up an old black-and-white picture. "Look at this old picture of the Poetry baseball team. Look, there's Mr. Jaans with his baseball pants pulled up to his armpits."

Beside him, Jenilee giggled. "I think these pictures are probably yours, Mrs. Gibson. Drew and I found them near your house."

June let out a little cough, snatching the picture from Caleb. "I'll have you young folks know I was the finest pitcher the Poetry baseball team ever seen. Ninety-mile-per-hour fastball. At least."

He set down the picture and held up another one. "Now here, if you'll look at this old picture of the 1940

Poetry Watermelon Festival Parade, I think you'll see someone you recognize here in the queen's court. This one right here, don't that lady-in-waiting look a little like Miss Eudora . . . ? Well, it wasn't Gibson, then; it was Miss Eudora Crawford. And now, if you'll look beside her, Jenilee, you might recognize the Watermelon Queen here, or the handsome Watermelon King. Those are your grandparents."

Jenilee leaned closer to look at the picture, a little gasp passing her lips and her eyes widening. "Those are my grandparents? I barely remember what they looked like, and not so young, anyway. We didn't have any pictures. Daddy wouldn't let—" She stopped, realizing what she was saying.

June didn't notice. He just went on yammering about the past. "And this lady-in-waiting here. This is your grandma's sister, Bernice. She'd be your great-aunt. She married a Vongortler and lived in Hindsville. You know, you still got some kin over there, I think."

Jenilee sat back, blinking like she couldn't take it all in. "I didn't know my grandma had any sisters. Mama never said anything."

"Oh, sure she did. Lordy, your grandma was from a family of five or six kids. Can't quite remember for sure." He glanced at Caleb. "Caleb, you ask your granddad about it. He's the preacher over there to Hindsville. He'll know the whereabouts of Bernice Vongortler's kids and grandkids. Jenilee might want to look them up someday. Family's important, even long-lost family."

Jenilee sat staring at the picture, her brown eyes getting wider and wider. I felt bad that I hadn't thought to tell her she might still have kinfolk over Hindsville way. I guess it hadn't occurred to me that she didn't know any of her mama's family.

June went on pointing out people. "And look here in the contestants' row, with the big scowl on her face. That is Mazelle Sibley, mad because she didn't get picked for the Watermelon Court. And look right here, the Watermelon Princess with the pretty gray eyes and the dark hair, that's Iv—"

I had snatched the picture out of his hand before I realized what I was doing. "Stop that!" I hissed. *How dare he say Ivy's name!*

Jenilee and Caleb gaped at me in surprise, but I didn't care. They might not of known what was going on, but June knew.

"Nobody wants to hear that old business," I snapped, tossing the pictures on the side of the pile. "And them ain't my pictures. I wouldn't have them pictures."

June lowered his chin, looking hurt. I didn't care. Silence lay over us like a thick, musty old blanket.

Jenilee pushed it aside finally. "I found another letter," she said quietly, reaching into the pile and taking out a piece of paper. "I guess I'll go hang it up with the first one."

She stood up and walked to the wall.

Caleb hopped to his feet, ready to be out of there. "I guess I better go see if . . . they need any help down at the motor home."

I glared at June. "You got no right to say her name," I spat; then I walked away to where Jenilee stood by the wall.

I squinted at the writing on the ancient paper as she hung it up. "What does the letter say? I ain't got my reading glasses on."

Jenilee paused for a minute, her eyes meeting mine, filled with meaning. "It says you have to leave the past behind to start a new life."

I turned away from the letter, bitterness welling up inside me. If she'd understood all that had happened in the past, she wouldn't of said that.

"Do you think that's possible?" she whispered, her face desperate for an answer. "I mean, do you think a person can walk away from everything that's happened before and be somebody new? Somebody different?"

I looked into those clear, soft eyes of hers, and something inside me sank. I knew what she was asking and why she was asking it. I wished I could say, *Oh, yes, certainly I believe that. I think a body can leave behind all the bad in their past and turn off from it, like they were turning down a new road.* I wished I could say that. But I knew better. I knew that the past had pecked away at me all my life, and I never got away from it.

Every time I thinned the iris bulbs by the fence, I thought of my poor sister, Ivy, because she loved irises. Every time I thought of her, I looked down the road at June Jaans's place, and I hated him more because he was responsible for Ivy dying. Every time I looked at that oak tree in the yard, I remembered how Cass used to have a tree fort up there, and how he stood by that very tree and cursed me because I couldn't accept the girl he was gonna marry. He hadn't been home in years, because I made it plain I didn't like that no-good, barwaitress wife of his. That was why my granddaughter Lacy looked at me like a stranger now.

The past had been with me all my life, following me like a shadow, attached to my body and to the ground around me, so that I never got away from it.

I looked at Jenilee and thought all of that in a second or two. I wanted to tell her that the past is like a ball of twine. It starts small, and keeps unwinding, until the trail reaches to places you can't even see anymore. All the things that have happened before are all wound around you like puppet strings.

"You don't leave it behind," I said quietly. "You just do your best to manage with it and go on."

Jenilee nodded, looking out the window. I knew I had told her what she had expected to hear. She looked sad, but not surprised.

"People should." June's voice come from his cot in a rustle of sheets.

When I looked over my shoulder, he was sitting up.

"People should learn to leave the past behind," he said again, and I knew he was talking to me. "You can't plow a clean row while you're turned around looking where at you've been." He shook a finger at me, his blue eyes hard with determination, filled with sparks, like those of the boy he used to be. "You spent enough hours on the tractor to know that, Eudora."

He give me one last, hard look, then turned to Jenilee and held up a piece of paper. "Here's another letter, Jenilee. It was stuck to the back of one of them old pictures. Go hang it on the wall by the other two. It might do *folks* some good." He looked at me when he said *folks*.

Jenilee, of course, didn't know his meaning. Only June and I knew that long-ago part of our past. Only he and I felt those wounds that were still so fresh.

Jenilee moved to his bedside and reached for the letter. June put his hand over hers lightly, not holding her there, but she didn't pull back. Instead, she looked at him like a child might look at a grandparent—like he was old, and wise, and important.

"Don't let anyone tell you that you can't become somethin' new. You're like one of them spring calves, all tangled up inside your mama, and tryin' hard to get out and find your feet. You got a long ways to go in your life. You find your feet, and then look where you want to go, and start runnin'. Don't look back."

Jenilee nodded, sighing. "I don't know where I want to go." She pulled her hand away from June's, looking embarrassed by all his sentimental rambling.

June smiled, groaning under his breath as he lay back down. "You'll figure it out. Just keep goin' in a straight row, and don't look back, all right?"

"All right," she said, then walked across the room and hung the letter up with the other two. She run her hands up and down her arms, reading the words to herself; then she turned toward the door. "I better get home so we can go to the hospital," she said, but the look on her face told me she was about to cry, and she didn't want us to see it.

The look on her face stayed with me for a long time after she left. I wondered about her while I hung pictures on the wall. As the morning wore on, the crowd around the wall grew larger, folks wandering in one or two at a time, looking at the pictures, talking about what the pictures made them remember.

I wished Jenilee could of been there to see it. I wondered what she would find at the hospital—if that father of hers would be awake, and if she would be glad about that. I wondered if she was afraid he wouldn't recover, or afraid he would.

I thought again about what might of gone on in that house with the bushes grown over the windows to make Jenilee so quiet and shy and afraid of everybody.

Mazelle Sibley come in at noontime with one of her sandwich trays. She looked at the picture wall with narrow eyes. I reckon she didn't like it because it was Jenilee's idea.

"Well, I've just been down giving sandwiches to the sheriff's crew. Poor Mrs. Anderson is there with them, still hoping to find her baby. I gave her a sandwich and a Pepsi-Cola, thought a little food might be a comfort."

"Uh-huh," I answered, pretending to be busy. I was hoping she'd move on.

"Did you hear there are *reporters* in town asking about the *baby*? They're going to broadcast the story on the *news*. I told them what I knew, of course. Told them what a shame it was that the poor mother had to come in here and see her baby girl's picture *hanging* on the *wall* of the *armory*. Honestly, I can't imagine what that *Jenilee Lane* could be thinking, putting that picture up there. Doesn't she have any sense? How horrible for poor Mrs. Anderson."

"Jenilee didn't know who the picture belonged to," I

said flatly. "No reason she would know it was the Anderson baby."

Mazelle tipped her chin up, making a *tsk-tsk* sound. "Don't imagine you can expect—"

A string of curse words outside the door cut her off.

"Oh, my word!" She gasped, stepping out of the way just in time to keep from being run over by Shad Bell, of all people.

He let out another string of curse words as he bumped into the doorframe and stumbled through the door. He stopped just inside, his fists wadded up at his sides like he was spoiling for a fight. He walked past us and said something to June.

June raised his hands into the air, palms-up, looking confused.

I hurried over to see what was going on. "Shad Bell, you leave June alone," I said. "This is a hospital. You ain't supposed to be in here."

Shad turned to face me, stumbling against June's bed so that I thought he might fall right down on top of the man. "Where's Jenilee?" His words were slurred. He turned his face toward me, and I saw that he was half-covered in blood, dripping from a fresh gash in his forehead.

I grabbed his arm to keep him from falling. "My Lord, Shad, what in the world kind of idiot thing have you done to yourself?"

Behind me, Mazelle said, "Oh, my!" again, then scooted over to where the garden club ladies were sitting.

Shad drifted to one side, then righted himself again and looked at me, his eyes cloudy with liquor. "I'm trying to find Jenilee," he slurred, the words barely understandable.

My mind put two and two together, and I realized I was right about the two of them. Jenilee was mixed up with him again. I didn't like that idea at all. The only thing a boy like Shad Bell could bring to Jenilee was trouble.

"Well, she ain't here." I held on to his arm to keep

him upright. In the bed, June raised his hands up like he was going to catch Shad if he fell. Fat chance of that. I knew if Shad fell on that bed, June would be squished flatter than a fritter.

I pulled Shad's arm and got him to step away. The blood from his hand dripped on my arm, and I looked at that cut in his forehead. "Good gravy, what did you do to yourself, Shad Bell?" I asked again.

Shad wiped the blood away with the greasy, wadded-up T-shirt he had in his other hand. "I run my truck into the ditch outside of town." His eyes started to close, and I give him a quick shake to wake him up. He jerked, and went on talking, the words mixed together like garble on a radio. "I was bringin' the dozer . . . into town . . . to see Jen . . . Jenilee."

"Well, you're too drunk to be drivin' any truck with any dozer trailer on the back," I snapped, giving him another shake as he tried to close his eyes again. I glanced over my shoulder to where Dr. Albright was in the corner talking to some folks about the pictures. "Doctor!" I hollered, getting the feeling that any moment Shad Bell was going to topple like a ruined silo. "Doctor! Someone's hurt over here."

Shad shook his arm, trying to break my hold on him. "I don't need no doctor."

"Yes, you do," I barked at him. "Stand still. Doctor!"

Dr. Albright started over from the other side of the room. Seeing the blood, he got in a hurry.

"I don't need no doctor!" Shad hollered, breaking my hold on his arm and staggering backward. June gave Shad a push in the rear end, sending him back to me.

"Be still!" I said, grabbing his arm again.

"I don't need no doctor!" he wailed, like a kid about to get a shot. "I gotta go get the truck outa the ditch . . . and the dozer."

"You ain't in no shape to drive no dozer!"

"I can drive my dozer if I want. I'm gonna help folks

clean up." He tried again to get shed of me, but I hung on like a hound on a coon.

"Let me go!" he bellowed.

"I ain't lettin' go!"

"I'm gonna go help folks."

"You ain't in shape to help nobody."

The doctor hurried up beside me and grabbed Shad's arm, moving him toward an empty cot with strength that was surprising, considering that Shad was a big boy. "Calm down, son," he said, sounding much nicer than I did. "Sit down and let's have a look."

Shad struggled to get away as Dr. Albright tried to put him onto the bed. Pushing the doctor off his feet, Shad stumbled three steps, whirled around twice like a dizzy ballet dancer, and fell smack on the floor.

I stood there lookin' at him as the doctor climbed back to his feet. "Well, that was darned stupid," I said to Shad as he lay looking up at me, his eyes fluttering, on the verge of going under. "Now you're stuck on the floor."

He reached up a hand like he was gonna get up, then let it fall, groaned, and lay there, helpless. Something about him all of a sudden reminded me of a little boy needin' his mama. I walked over and got a pillow while the doc started examining that cut.

"Here you go, you idiot," I said, slipping the pillow under his head. "Lordy, Shad, haven't you got a lick of sense in your whole body?"

He groaned, and his eyes fluttered back in his head as the doctor spread the wound apart to look at it.

"Just be still, son," the doctor said. "All you need is a few stitches, and twelve hours or so to sleep it off."

Shad blinked hard, focusing his gaze on me. "I gotta get the dozer and help folks," he choked out, his voice almost gone.

"You can't help nobody right now," I whispered, stroking his dark hair away from the wound and the blood, trying to keep him calm while the doctor went for his medical kit. "Just go on and go to sleep."

"Can you . . ." I had to lean close to hear Shad's voice. His eyes were closed and he was drifting off. "Can you tell Jenilee I come here . . . to help . . ."

He fell away, and I stayed there for a minute as the doc came back and cleaned the wound, then stitched it up. I looked at Shad and felt sorry for the mixed-up boy that he was.

I didn't imagine he'd learn anything from this experience, or that he'd ever learn. His mama and daddy had him late in life after tryin' for years to get a baby, and they'd pretty well spoiled him rotten.

Whatever's going on between him and Jenilee Lane, I told myself, *you're gonna find a way to put a stop to it, Eudora. This critter is the last thing she needs to be mixed up with. You're a pretty stubborn old woman, and most of the time you can find a way to get done what needs doing.*

The doctor shook his head as he bandaged the wound. "Is this Jenilee Lane's husband?" he asked.

"Oh, Lordy, no!" I choked on the thought. "Don't even say such a thing. This here is just about the worst example of a young fella in the whole county."

"I see."

I opened my mouth to ask why he had such a powerful interest in Jenilee. Then I realized someone was over my shoulder. I looked up and saw Nolan Nelson, the school principal, leaning over me to get a look at Shad.

"Looks like he didn't come out of the tornado too well," he said, looking more concerned than Shad deserved.

"He ain't hurt from the tornado," I said, standing up. "He's drunker than a skunk, and he run his truck into the ditch pullin' the bulldozer trailer. Whacked himself in the head in the process."

Nolan grimaced. "Well, he's going to have a double

headache when he wakes up and his daddy hears about that. His daddy will be hotter than popcorn in a fire. Maybe Shad will learn something."

I laughed out the side of my mouth. "Not likely, I'd say. He come here looking for Jenilee Lane. You know anything about that?" I figured if anyone would know what was going on, it would be the principal. Nolan was like a daddy to the young people in town. He practically worked miracles with those kids, but even he hadn't been able to do anything with Shad Bell.

"Well, can't say I know anything about Jenilee and Shad," Nolan answered, "other than that they used to date before Shad's daddy sent him off to Montana a couple of years ago."

"I think there's something going on between them, and that would be a bad thing for Jenilee. She don't need to hook up with a lowbrow like this one."

Nolan squinted, looking concerned, but I could tell he wanted to be careful of what he said to me. "Well, I wouldn't jump to too many conclusions. Jenilee's a smart girl."

"Smart girls been known to get with ignorant men." I crossed my arms over my chest and let him know I wasn't backing down. "Happens all the time. It don't need to happen with her."

He raised a brow at me, I imagine because he was surprised to hear me asking after Jenilee. I'm sure he remembered I'd been to the school a time or two complaining about that big brother of hers and how he hot-rodded up and down my road and run over my chickens.

"You sure are taking an interest in Jenilee." He smiled a little at me, like he'd caught me in a joke.

"Well, you know she pulled me out of my cellar and saved my life, and Lacy's too," I told him.

Nolan nodded. "That doesn't surprise me. Jenilee's had to be a pretty tough cookie, given her home situation and the way her father is."

I nodded, feeling a heaviness inside me. It was guilt. "I feel pretty bad, thinkin' about that now," I admitted. "We folks in this town are usually pretty good, Christian people, but we all pretty well sat by and let that man treat Maggie and the kids any way he pleased. Instead of steppin' in to give them some help, we all just turned our heads and pretended like we couldn't see it." I looked Nolan hard in the eye, because I knew he done the same thing. He tried a couple of times talking to Jenilee's daddy, but when things got ugly, he backed off like the rest of us. "It ain't a right thing to do, to let something like that go on, a man treatin' his wife and kids so bad, cuttin' them off from everyone and everything."

I think that's why God stuck me and Lacy in the cellar, and the only person around to pull us out was little Jenilee Lane. He wanted to show me I done a wrong thing by turning my head all these years.

Nolan nodded, bracing his hands on his hips and looking down at his shoes, his shoulders bent forward. He looked whipped. "I know you're right, Eudora. These days we've got so many that come from dysfunctional families. It's sad to say it, but kids like Jenilee and her brothers just kind of fall through the cracks. If they're passing school and they don't show up with bruises, they get left alone. It isn't right, but that's the way it happens."

"Well, that is just a terrible shame." I felt sad and angry and helpless all at once.

"Yes, it is. Jenilee's probably one of the smartest students we've had, but she's never had any encouragement at home. She's had to live with a mother who was dealing with depression and then terminal cancer, and a father who came home from Vietnam with mental problems and probably a drug and alcohol addiction. I really always hoped she'd leave Poetry and go on with her education."

"She needs to do somethin'," I said. "Somethin' better than get together with that lowbrow on the floor. That ain't no kind of future."

All of a sudden, I realized Dr. Albright was standing there with us, listening to every word we said.

Rubbing my forehead with the pads of my fingers, I tried to ignore him and think about how I was going to do something about Jenilee. No matter what idea I thought of, it seemed like there were a hundred other problems I couldn't find a cure for. She was so far from any kind of decent life.

Lord, please send a miracle, I prayed. *We need you to send a miracle; that's all there is to it. This problem is bigger than I can fix on my own. You gotta send something to change it all.*

Beside me, the old letters rustled in the breeze.

I looked at the new one Jenilee had hung there. It matched the other two, the paper old and yellowed, the handwriting the same neat cursive as the very first letter Jenilee had found. It was the wife's handwriting, this time written not to her husband, but to her daughter. I leaned close so I could read the words.

My Dearest Daughter,

> *I know that the time will come in your life when all will seem hopeless. I do not know if I will be there when your darkest hour comes upon you.*
> *If I am not, this is the advice I would have given you.*
> *I would have told you about those painful days I sat near this very cradle in this attic room, pleading for a miracle to save the infant son we had so long yearned for. I would have talked about the days after, when I closed myself away, angry with God, angry with everyone. If I were telling you the story, I would knock lightly on the wall to describe for you the knock at the door, just a faint, uncertain sound as I sat here alone, blinded by my own tears.*

I would have told you that I hadn't the strength to answer, hadn't the strength to care who was knocking. I would say that I still do not know what powers drew me to rise from my mourning chair, descend the stairs, and answer the door. I would tell you there was a miracle on the other side. You were on the other side, just a babe in the arms of a mother who could not keep you.

There is so much more to your story, my dear one, but that is not what I wish to tell you here.

Today, I wish to give you this simple advice.

Do not pray for miracles. Only God can know what miracles He will send.

Pray for the strength to open the door when the knock comes. The sound is ever so soft. Listen well.

Mama

CHAPTER 16

JENILEE

Drew started making plans for how to handle things at the hospital before we were even halfway there. "When we get there, you go on in to see Daddy," he'd said to me. "Nate's supposed to go have his cast checked; then we'll come up to ICU and I'll take him in to see Daddy." I wondered why he wanted to be the one to go with Nate. Was it just because he would be better able to help Nate maneuver through the maze of doors and elevators at the hospital?

"All right." Did Drew dread going into Daddy's room alone, just as I did? Or was he afraid I would be too emotional and might upset Nate?

In the backseat, Nate stared out the window, not seeming to hear our conversation.

"Nate, Drew's going to take you down to have your cast checked, then bring you up to ICU," I reiterated in a louder voice. "Is that all right?"

"I guess," Nate muttered, cutting a quick glare toward Drew's back, then turning his gaze out the window again.

I rubbed my eyebrows, disappointment prickling in my throat. Their time together this morning hadn't smoothed the waters. Nate still looked at Drew with all the bitterness that had been building over the past eight years.

"Be careful on your crutches," I said. "You're still pretty unsteady. If you need help, ask Drew, all right?" I thought of the way Nate had insisted on dragging himself into the backseat of the pickup without help, even though the cast was heavy. Nate was in pain and covered with perspiration by the time he got in. "If you hurt your leg, you'll be back in the hospital again."

Nate didn't answer.

"You know that, right?" I pushed. "The doctor said you have to be really careful these first few days."

"I know," he conceded finally. "I'll be careful."

The conversation ended there. We drove the rest of the way to the hospital in silence. None of us spoke as we entered the lobby and parted ways.

Nate was feeling better when he came back from the visit with his doctor and we met up in the ICU waiting room. His smile lifted my spirits as he told me the doctor said he was amazed by his progress. Nate's smile faded when he asked me, "How's Daddy?"

I paused, not sure what to say. Daddy had looked worse when I went in, ghostly pale, his face sunken at the cheeks and temples, the bones jutting out, skeleton-like. He hadn't responded when I talked to him or touched his hand. I hadn't stayed long. Unable to bear the deathlike specter, I had gone back to the waiting room long before Drew and Nate arrived.

Behind Nate, Drew's gaze caught mine, searching for hidden meanings as I replied, "The nurse said he's about the same today." *How much more should I tell him?* I didn't want Nate to go in unprepared for how bad Daddy looked. "He looks pale today, but I guess that's normal after so much surgery."

Drew's eyes flickered with worry as he turned to take Nate to Daddy's room. I held Drew's gaze for a moment and shook my head, so that he at least might be prepared.

They left, and I stared into the bright afternoon outside, wishing I could feel the warmth of the sunshine, smell the summer air, experience something that wasn't sterilized and artificial. I tried not to think about Daddy in his cubicle of wires, machines, and stark white walls. Closing my eyes, I pictured the clouds floating by and tried to be somewhere else.

My mind snapped back to reality when I heard Nate come in the door on his crutches. He made his way carelessly across the room and sat heavily beside me on the couch. Dropping the crutches, he sagged forward, exhausted, his head in his hands.

I reached over and rubbed his shoulder. "You shouldn't have come," I said. "You should have stayed home and rested your leg. We could have waited until tomorrow to have your cast checked."

"It's not my leg," he muttered. "I just wish Daddy would of woke up. I wanted to be here when he woke up. I wanted to tell him I was sorry."

"Nate, you don't have anything to be sorry for." I leaned over so I could see his face. "You have to get past feeling like this is your fault."

Drew walked in the door and sat down on the other side of Nate.

Nate didn't seem to notice. He hunched over farther, lacing his fingers behind his head, looking defeated. "I can't help how I feel about it. When I look at him in the bed like that . . ." He shook his head, his hands gripped so tightly the knuckles were turning white. "I just want him to wake up. I want to tell him he was right. I should of gotten out of there and gone for help."

Drew laid his hand on Nate's shoulder, his fingers touching mine. His voice was steady, comforting. "Nate, the doctor said it was a miracle you got out of that car and made it up the embankment at all. He said even if you'd done it sooner, Daddy's injuries would still be what they are."

Nate shook his head. "Daddy said—"

"Daddy doesn't always say the nicest things," Drew interrupted. "You know that, Nate. We've all got to face the fact that we may not ever get what we want from Daddy. We've got to face the fact that he might not wake up at all."

Nate jerked away from us, heaving himself to his feet and grabbing his crutches. "Don't you say that!" he hollered. "Don't you say that about Daddy."

I stood up, reaching for Nate, afraid he would fall. "You heard the doctors, Nate. They said it could go either way. They said we have to be prepared, in case—"

"Stop it!" He turned away and started unsteadily toward the door on his crutches.

"Nate, wait!" I hurried after him as he hobbled into the hall. "Stop! You're going to hurt your leg!"

Drew caught up to us as Nate hit the elevator button and the doors opened.

"Nate, take it easy," he said.

Nate shrugged his hand away and barreled into the elevator. The two of us followed.

"Nate, please settle down," I pleaded.

Drew tried again. "I wasn't trying to get you upset, Nate. I just want you to be ready, if—"

"Shut up!" Nate spat. "Just shut up." He jerked away, falling against the wall.

Drew raised his hands palms-out, afraid to get close to Nate again. "Nate, you're just worn out. It's time to go home."

"I'm not going home with you!" Nate screamed, stumbling as he tried to get his crutches under himself before the elevator reached the ground floor. "Darla's coming to get me. I'm going to her house so I can be close by when Daddy wakes up."

Drew's voice rose to match the volume of Nate's. "What are you talking about, Nate? Darla's not here, and Darla's not gonna be here!" He threw his hands in the air, his face red and drawn with anger.

Nate's crutch slipped on the tile and he fell against the wall again. "She's coming. I called her house and left a message on her machine while I was in the doctor's office by myself. I'm gonna stay here and wait for her to get me."

"You are not!" Drew roared. "I'm sick of hearing you talk about Darla!"

Nate's eyes, white-rimmed around the bright blue centers, flashed daggers. "Darla understands! Darla knows how you are!"

"Nate!" I gasped, but I could tell by the look on Nate's face that he was beyond reason, saying the worst things he could think of to bait Drew.

Drew waved me away. He punched the stop button on the console, and the elevator jerked to a halt; then he advanced menacingly toward Nate. "Whatever you think you know, you don't know! Darla lies. She'd say anything to make me look bad."

"Darla's not lying! Darla knows how you are. You ran out on her and your kids just like you ran out on us." Hopping on one foot, Nate raised his crutch and swung it, aiming for Drew's head.

Drew dodged the blow, and the crutch skimmed past him, crashing against the elevator wall and taking Nate with it. Nate hit the railing hard and landed in a crumpled heap in the corner.

Drew started toward him, and Nate swung blindly with his fist. Drew caught Nate's arm in midair, leaning over, his face only inches from Nate's.

"Go ahead!" Nate screamed, his eyes glittering and his lips trembling. "Go ahead and do it! Do it! Prove you're just like Daddy! That's what you want. You want to prove you're just like him, so you have an excuse to run out on everybody!"

"Stop it, Nate!" I fell to my knees beside Nate. "Stop it! This is wrong!"

"I don't care!" Tears brimmed in Nate's eyes. "I don't care about him."

"Yes, you do, Nate," I pleaded. "Yes, you do. We both do."

"No, I don't! He ran out on us. He ran out on Mama. Mama died because he left!"

I sucked in a startled breath, the air rushing cold into my body. I'd never, ever seen Nate so filled with anger, so vengeful. I swallowed hard, trying to sound calm. "Nate, Mama died because she had cancer."

Nate tried to jerk his arm out of Drew's grasp, but Drew held on. "He'll do it again." Nate glared at Drew, sobbing, tears running down his face. "He'll leave again." He swung at Drew with his other arm, knocking me off balance so that I toppled to the floor, too. Drew caught Nate's other wrist, and they hovered in a stalemate. Nate tried to jerk away, and the muscles in Drew's arms tightened, holding him still.

Drew stared into Nate's defiant face, the anger in his own eyes softening, becoming a mirror of Nate's pain. He loosened his grip on Nate's arms one finger at a time. "No fists," he said, his voice quieter. "No more. We're not going to do this anymore, little brother. I'm not going anywhere. When you're ready to talk, you let me know. You want to know something about me, you ask—not Darla, not Jenilee—you ask me." His gaze locked with Nate's. "I don't have all the answers you'd like to hear. I don't know all the answers, Nate. I took a long time finding my way back here, and I didn't take all the right steps these last years, but I'm here now, and I'm not going anywhere. That's the way it's gonna be. We're going to have to take it a step at a time, but you're not going to hit me and I'm not going to hit you." He released one of Nate's arms, and then the other. "All right?"

Nate answered with only the slightest nod.

Drew braced his elbows on his knees and sagged forward, letting out a long sigh. "Let's go home now, O.K.?"

Nate nodded again, and Drew helped him up. I climbed to my feet and grabbed the crutches, handing them to Nate, my fingers shaking, my ears ringing with what had been said.

What do we say now?

Drew punched the elevator button, then leaned forward, bracing an arm above the console and resting his forehead there as he caught his breath.

Nate moved forward a couple of steps on his crutches, then stood hanging loosely between them with his head bowed forward, looking exhausted.

The door opened, and Nate limped into the lobby. Drew and I followed, anxious to be free of the silence, hoping to be free of the words.

I looked around the lobby and watched the people moving about their routines, not noticing as we passed. Even that seemed strange.

Drew stepped ahead and held the door open for Nate. For a change, Nate didn't give him a dirty look as he passed by. He hung his head, instead, as if he felt guilty. He moved to the truck as fast as the crutches would carry him, opened the door, and tried to lift himself into the backseat without help.

"Just a minute," I said, catching up with him, taking the crutches and helping hoist his cast in as he slid backward across the seat.

Behind me on the sidewalk, Drew had stopped.

Nate groaned as I set his foot on the seat. Laying his head back, he closed his eyes. "I'm sorry, Jenilee," he whispered.

"It's all right," I reached across the seat and gave his hand a squeeze. "I guess you needed to say all that. Maybe Drew needed to hear it. He needed the chance to prove it wasn't true."

"I wanted to make him mad." Nate squeezed the bridge of his nose, wincing in pain. "Why didn't he hit me when he had the chance?"

"Because that's what Daddy would have done," I said. "You said yourself, he isn't Daddy." I glanced over my shoulder. Drew was still standing on the sidewalk a few feet away, and a dark-haired woman was trotting across the parking lot toward him, her arms swinging at her sides, her face drawn with worry.

"I know." Nate sucked in a long, trembling breath, tears squeezing below his lashes again and tracing a trail down his cheeks. "I'm sorry."

"You should tell Drew that." I slipped away from the door and let the wind push it closed as the woman skidded to a halt beside Drew.

"How's Nate?" she breathed. "Is everything all right? I had a phone call on my machine. He said he needed me to come get him right away."

Drew crossed his arms over his chest, leaning away from her. "Nate's fine, Darla," he answered flatly. "He's just worn out. He shouldn't have called you."

Darla, I thought, taking a step closer. I stopped halfway between them and the truck, unsure whether I should come closer. All of the softness in Drew was suddenly gone.

I watched Darla nervously push strands of dark hair out of her face and tuck them in a hair clip. She looked like the little girl in Drew's picture, same dark hair, full lips, and deep olive skin, but her eyes were light brown, not dark like the little girl's. She looked friendly, sort of proper and carefully dressed in a short-sleeved business suit. She looked scared to death.

She seemed to search for something to say in the face of Drew's ominous silence. "Well . . . is there anything I can do . . . ? For Nate, I mean."

"No," Drew shot back. "He's fine."

She glanced toward the truck, barely seeming to

notice I was there. "Well . . . do you want me to talk to him?"

Drew's eyes narrowed. "I said, he's fine. He's not one of your social work cases, Darla."

She stiffened visibly. "I know that."

They stood there for a minute, each of them looking past the other, their lips set in tight, straight lines.

She softened first, raising her hands palms up into the space between them. "Drew, we need to talk. . . ." She ducked her head, biting her lips, trying to find words.

For a moment, he watched her as she looked down at the sidewalk. He leaned closer and started to unbind his arms, regarded her tenderly, as if it were natural for him to do that.

She raised her chin, and he raised the mask again. "You know what, Darla . . ." He turned and started toward the truck. "If you want to talk to me, you tear up that paper that says I can't come within a hundred feet of my own kids." He climbed in and slammed the door.

I stood a few feet from her, yet a world away, not knowing what to do. Behind me, Drew started the engine and shifted the truck into drive.

Darla hugged her purse in front of herself. Her gaze met mine.

I'm sorry. I mouthed the silent words, then turned and climbed into the truck.

She stood there, hugging her purse, watching us go.

CHAPTER 17

Drew leaned forward to look down the hill toward the armory as we pulled into Poetry. "What in the world's going on there?" He slowed the truck as we passed. "How come there are news crews at the armory?"

"I don't know . . ." I muttered. "With all the tornado damage up toward Kansas City, I can't imagine why they would want to come here. Seems like there would be better stories in other places. Pull in, all right?"

Drew threw the truck in reverse, backed along the shoulder, and pulled into the driveway.

Nate jerked in the backseat and sat up. "What . . . the . . . ?" He blinked drowsily. "What's going on? Where are we?"

"We're back in Poetry." I pointed to the armory. "Drew and I wanted to see what's going on with the news crews."

"Nate, you better stay here," Drew said. An uneasy feeling churned in my stomach as I climbed the steps behind him and stood trying to see past the crowd in the doorway.

I caught a glimpse of the sheriff, Mrs. Gibson, and Dr. Albright in front of the picture wall. The Andersons stood beside them, supporting a bundle of blankets in their arms. Cameras flashed and the bundle moved, the blanket falling away to reveal a tiny face.

All at once I knew. "Oh, Drew!" I gasped. "Oh, Drew, she's got her baby! She's got her baby back!" I rushed through the crowd, needing to see, to touch the tiny blue-eyed girl whose picture had come to me on the wind.

Mrs. Anderson held the baby up as I pushed past the circle of bodies. Her eyes, red-rimmed, exhausted, filled with joy, met mine. "We got her back. We found her," she whispered, as I touched the side of the baby's face. "It was the picture. The picture helped us find her."

"So you say the baby had been taken into the hospital in Joplin?" I heard a reporter ask from somewhere in the crowd.

"Yes, that's right," the sheriff replied. "The baby was brought to the hospital in the hours after the storm by a man who hasn't been identified yet. The rescuer is still unconscious and can't provide details. The hospital staff assumed that the baby was his daughter, until late today, when they saw the baby's picture being circulated on the news. Of course, we took the Andersons to be reunited with their baby girl right away." The sheriff sidestepped to put his arms over the Andersons' shoulders. "We're going to let these folks have some time with their baby now. I'd be grateful if you people wouldn't follow. This family deserves some privacy."

Mrs. Anderson met my eyes and mouthed, *Thank you,* just before the sheriff led her away.

The room fell into a strange silence, everyone watching the Andersons until they had disappeared through the doorway.

"Where did all the pictures come from?" one of the reporters asked finally.

"From everywhere," Mrs. Gibson answered. "All sorts of folks carried them in here, and a number of folks worked to get them hung up." She closed the space between us and caught my hand, pulling me close.

"It was all a project of the Poetry garden club," said a familiar voice, rising above the crowd. Mazelle Sibley pushed her way to the front and sidled up beside Mrs. Gibson. "When the call went out for help in sorting and hanging the pictures, *all* of us left behind our *own* damaged homes and came here to *give* of *ourselves*. After *days* of feeding the hungry and caring for the sick, well, it was a pure pleasure to—"

"It was all the idea of our Jenilee Lane, here," Mrs. Gibson butted in, tipping her chin up and bumping her hip out, so she knocked Mrs. Sibley off balance. "*She's* the one responsible for the picture walls, and for finding the photo of the Anderson baby, and for savin' my life, and my granddaughter's life after the tornado. She's no less than a hero." She glanced at Dr. Albright, and he smiled at her, then leaned closer to me and Mrs. Gibson as a battery of flashbulbs snapped.

Dr. Albright muttered close to my ear, "Smile for the camera, Jenilee. You're a hero."

I felt blood prickle into my face. "I'm not a hero," I said.

Mrs. Gibson hugged me, laughing and crying at the same time. "That's what heroes always say."

Beside her, Mazelle Sibley huffed an irritated sigh and walked a few steps away.

I wrapped my arms around Mrs. Gibson and hugged her while the flashbulbs popped, then faded away. Finally, the reporters left us and moved around the room snapping pictures and doing interviews with some of the garden club ladies.

Mrs. Gibson straightened and held my face in her hands. "Oh, now look. I've made you cry." She pulled a hankie from her dress pocket and dabbed my cheeks. "Lands, what a day this has been! What a day!" She put an arm over my shoulder. "And speaking of things like that, there's some folks over here I think you'll like to meet."

"Who?"

She gave me a sly sideways look. "It's a surprise." She led me toward the back corner of the building, where Caleb was standing beside a family looking at the picture wall. They turned to greet us as we came closer. I recognized the husband.

He smiled and stuck his hand out to shake mine. "We've already met, down in the motor home. Ben Bowman."

"I remember," I said, still wondering why Mrs. Gibson had brought me there. "Who knew all this would come from a few sheets of paper and a roll of tape?"

"Pretty amazing." He smiled, and nodded toward his wife. "This is Kate. Caleb tells us you and Kate are second or third cousins, something like that."

Kate smiled, shifting the baby in her arms to one side so she could shake my hand. Her brown eyes were warm and friendly. "Your grandmother and my grandmother were sisters."

Kate released my hand, and I stood there not knowing what to say. It was hard to imagine Nate, Drew, and me as part of a family. All of our lives it had been just Mama, Daddy, and us. "We didn't have much to do with Mama's family." As soon as the words came out, I realized they didn't sound good. "But, I mean, we would have . . . if we'd known."

Kate gave an embarrassed laugh. "Oh, us too. We've always lived away from Hindsville, and we just moved back a little over a year ago. I do remember meeting your grandmother one time at a family reunion a long, long time ago."

A blond-haired toddler pulled at her pants leg. "Mama," he pestered. "Mama, Mama, Mama, Mama."

Kate rolled her eyes, laying her hand on top of his head. "This is Joshua."

I smiled at him, and he ducked behind his mother's leg. "Hi, Joshua." He peeked out, then disappeared again.

"And this is Rose." Kate jiggled the baby girl in her arms. At the sound of her name, the baby started to fuss. Kate frowned. "And I've just reminded her that she's hungry."

"We'd better go," Ben said, picking up Joshua as the little boy tried to shinny up Kate's leg.

Kate nodded, touching my arm. "We won't keep you, Jenilee. But, listen, after things get back to normal, we'd love to have you come out to the farm sometime to visit. There are some old pictures of Grandma and her sisters there. You might like copies of those."

"I'd like that," I said, still trying to imagine myself as part of a family that included so many people. I wondered what Daddy would say if he knew I was standing there talking to them. Then I wondered if things would ever get back to the kind of normal Kate was talking about. Normal for us wasn't the same as normal for other people.

"It's really nice to have met you," Kate said. "If there's ever anything we can do, please feel that you can call, all right? We're not far away."

"All right." I glanced at Caleb. The way Kate said those last words made me wonder if he had been telling her about us, and maybe she felt sorry for us.

"Take care," Ben said, and they headed toward the door. As they left, Drew and Nate were coming in. I thought about trying to introduce them, but I wasn't sure what kind of a mood Drew was in. He hadn't said anything all the way home from the hospital.

Mrs. Gibson clapped her hands together, looking pleased with herself for having made the family connections for me. "Oh, say, it looks like Drew's brought your little brother in. Poor thing, looks like they've got him in a cast from toe to hip."

"They had to put a plate in his leg to fix it," I told her as we crossed the room to where Drew was helping Nate into a lawn chair next to Mr. Jaans's bed.

". . . and ain't all this somethin'?" We caught the tail end of what Mr. Jaans was saying. "I been alive a long time, but I ain't ever seen a day as good as this one—all them folks coming in and picking up their pictures, and then the Andersons getting their baby back. It's enough to put the faith right back in ya, that's for sure."

Mrs. Gibson turned her face aside and acted like she didn't hear him, so I answered, "It's wonderful, isn't it?"

"It's somethin' else," Nate agreed, looking around at the pictures.

Mr. Jaans smiled. "I have to say it's done me good to be part of it. Sorting through all those pictures today, giving folks back a little piece of their memories, that was the best feeling I've had in a long time. Feels good to have the chance to do for other folks."

"Well, it's all due to Jenilee," Mrs. Gibson snapped, as if she thought he was trying to take credit.

Mr. Jaans didn't seem bothered. "I'd say a bunch of people had a hand in it." He chuckled, glancing at Drew and me with a mischievous twinkle in his eyes. "And you, probably both hands, Eudora."

Mrs. Gibson coughed, her mouth dropping open. "You hush up, June Jaans." The corners of her lips turned upward. She wheeled around and hurried away so he wouldn't see her smile.

Mr. Jaans winked at me. "I think I'm getting to her."

"I don't know why you bother. She's so mean to you all the time." I knew what it felt like to be on Mrs. Gibson's bad side. I didn't understand why she could change her mind about me and not about Mr. Jaans.

"There's a lot of history to it," he said, then lay back against his pillow. I could tell he didn't intend to reveal any more, at least not in front of Drew and Nate.

Drew cleared his throat and changed the subject.

"Looked like your cows were all in pretty good shape yesterday, June. A few skin cuts, a little hide knocked off here and there, and I fixed some fence where your old bull got out."

"I do appreciate that. Ain't seen old Charlie, have ya? I hear he went wandering by what's left of Mazelle Sibley's grocery, near scared her to death. She had a bucket in her hand and Charlie was hungry. Chased her plumb down the block and into the Willamses' pasture. She finally got shed of him by runnin' through a bog. Charlie don't like mud much." He laughed, then winced, grabbing his ribs. "Lands! I'd of paid money to see that...."

My mind drifted away from the conversation, and I looked toward the doorway. Outside on the stoop, I could see Mrs. Gibson's shoulder. Her hands were moving and I could hear her talking to someone. I left Drew and Nate and walked over to see who was out there with her.

Weldon, Janet, and Dr. Albright were standing with her on the steps. They stopped talking when they saw me, and they gave each other strange, secretive looks that made me wonder if they had been talking about me. The bushes rustled behind them and Lacy emerged. She walked up the steps and slipped her hand into mine as an uncomfortable silence fell over us.

Weldon finally broke the stalemate. "Well, we wanted to see the pictures," he said, then gave the others one last, unreadable glance.

Lacy squeezed my hand. I tried to ignore the rest of them and focus on her as Weldon and Janet went into the building and Dr. Albright headed toward the motor home.

Mrs. Gibson stayed on the stoop, watching Lacy and me.

"How are you today, Lacy?" I asked, smoothing the dark hair away from her face. Her gray eyes met mine, and for just an instant I pictured those eyes looking at me from the darkness behind the ventilation screen in Mrs. Gibson's cellar. She seemed as lost now as she was then.

Lacy shrugged her shoulders.

"You look pretty," I said. "I like these flowered overalls. Can I borrow them someday? I think they would look good on me."

Lacy grinned, her eyes shining for only a moment before she did something that I could remember doing all my life. She ducked her head and hid the smile. Behind me, Mrs. Gibson sighed heavily, her disappointment like a cloud in the air. I suppose it was hard for her to understand why Lacy stayed closed within herself. Mrs. Gibson didn't know what it was like to feel the way Lacy felt—small and helpless and afraid of everything.

When you're afraid of everything, the thing you are most afraid of is happiness. You're afraid to step into even a little piece of it, because you know that as soon as you do, someone will slam the door, and you'll be trapped in the darkness again, remembering how the light felt.

It's easier never to know the light at all.

Lacy pulled her hand away and looked past me toward the door. Standing up, I glanced at Mrs. Gibson, who had turned her back to us, her shoulders trembling with withheld tears.

Lacy slipped past me and into the armory, and I let her go. I didn't want her to see her grandmother crying and know she was the cause of it.

I stood beside Mrs. Gibson, not knowing how to comfort her.

"She'll be all right," I told her. "Sometimes it's just hard to understand things when you're a kid."

Looking up at the sky, she dabbed her eyes with her hankie. "I don't want her life to be hard. I don't want her to hurt this way."

"I don't think my mama wanted me to, either." I

thought of the times Mama cried and told me she didn't want my life to be the way it was. "Sometimes it just happens."

"It's my fault." Mrs. Gibson wiped her eyes again, unfolded the hankie, and blew her nose like a foghorn. "I been a mean, stubborn old lady, and I drove her father away because I didn't like that gal he married, and that's why I don't know Lacy enough to be a help to her. I'm just one more stranger she don't know and don't like. The only thing she likes about me is my old cat, Mr. Whiskers."

I wasn't sure what to say to all that. As far as I could tell, a lot of it was true. Mrs. Gibson could be a mean old lady. Once she got her mind made up about somebody, it took something like a tornado to change it. "Sometimes things like that take time."

"I ain't got time!" she wailed, wadding the hankie in her fist and punching it into her pocket, her back turned to me. "I'm an old lady, and I'm losin' my memory, and I can't leave my life with all this meanness in it. God ain't gonna let me. He's gonna keep sending me back until I straighten out all this mess and keep the promises I made. That's what that angel come to tell me. I gotta set things right this time, get shed of all this meanness in me. God done turned me back from heaven once, and . . ." She paused. Gasping in a breath, she turned and pressed her fingers to her mouth, shocked by what she had said to me.

I stood looking at her, as dumbfounded as she was. We gaped at each other, both wondering what to say now. She had sounded crazy. Even she knew that.

Except the part about her losing her memory. That explained a lot of things—like why she would sometimes ask me the same question two or three times in a day, or why she sometimes looked at me for an instant the way she used to before the tornado, or why she kept forgetting Dr. Albright's name.

Was that why she was so desperate to find the notebooks? Because she couldn't remember things without writing them down? I could tell by looking at her that she didn't want me to know.

Silence stretched like a tightrope between us. "I don't think you want to be mean to people," I said finally. "It's just a . . . well, sort of a habit, I guess. People can change habits, if they want to."

"I been formin' this habit a long time." She sighed. "It's turnin' out to be a hard one to break."

"You could start by being nicer to Mr. Jaans. All he wants is for you to treat him with a little kindness."

Pressing a hand to her chest, she craned her neck back, as if she couldn't believe I had said that. "That . . . that goes way back." She coughed.

"Maybe so." I felt strangely bold. "But if you're trying to make God happy, that would be a good way. Mr. Jaans isn't a bad person. He's just trying to get by the best way he can, like everybody else."

Flaring her nostrils and widening her eyes, she peered around my shoulder to make sure no one was listening. "He done some *bad things* in the past."

"Everyone has. You just said you had. A bad past is like gristle. You can either starve to death chewing on it, or you can spit it out and see what else is on the table."

Mrs. Gibson blinked at me, coughing softly, as if that piece of gristle was stuck in her throat.

Finally, she pointed a finger indignantly toward the door. "*That man* turned my head and talked about marriage, and all the while he was sparkin' my baby sister, Ivy. He run off with her when she was just fifteen. Said he was gonna take us to a USO dance. He sneaked Ivy out of there and never brought her home. Come to find out, he'd got her pregnant, and they had to get married, and it was the shame of the county. The only reason he was sparkin' me was because I was old enough that Mama would let me date, and then Ivy could come along with us. That was the only way he could see Ivy, and he knew it. Once he and Ivy run off, everyone in the whole county knew it, too."

"Oh . . ." I murmured, wondering what kind of quicksand I had stepped into.

"So you can see why I ain't friendly with him."

"Uh . . . uh-huh."

"And you can see why I ain't gonna go makin' nice with him, actin' like nothing ever happened. He talked Ivy into getting married too young, and she shouldn't of been having babies, and she died trying to birth that baby. *His* baby. It was a terrible thing. He had the funeral for her and the baby—buried them right in the casket together, and didn't give my family one single say in the funeral or anything. Then he went off to the war, and by the time he come home again, he brought a new wife with him, and bought that place right down the road from us. He went right on like our Ivy never existed at all, and we had to watch it year in and year out. I ain't ever gonna forgive him for it."

I looked at the tents shuddering in the breeze below, not knowing what to say. Mr. Jaans had shown such kindness to me and Mama. I couldn't imagine that he would do the cruel things Mrs. Gibson was talking about.

"Maybe he really loved Ivy," I said, thinking of the words from the old letter I had found in our yard and how much that old couple must have loved each other. "Maybe he moved back here because he wanted to be close to her. Maybe he did what most people do." *What my mama did.* "Maybe he just did the best he could to go on when his life wasn't what he thought it was going to be."

She shook her head, hugging her arms around herself as a whippoorwill started singing somewhere close by. Finally I turned away, leaving her there, and went inside to get Drew and Nate.

Lacy was sitting beside Mr. Jaans's bed with a red string around her fingers, learning how to make a cat's cradle. "Then . . . I do this . . . one?" she said, as if it were the most normal thing in the world to be talking to him.

"That's right, precious." Mr. Jaans smiled at her, his aged, trembling hands guiding hers. "All right, see. That's cup and saucer. Right. See? You've got it. Hook your thumb in there like this now."

Lacy's lips lifted into a smile. For a minute she forgot to be afraid.

I motioned to Drew, and he helped Nate to his feet. Mr. Jaans gave us a quick wink, then went back to helping Lacy.

Mrs. Gibson came in the door. I motioned for her to stop, then pointed at Lacy and Mr. Jaans.

"Ssshhhh. Listen," I whispered.

Mrs. Gibson crossed her arms, narrowing her eyes at them, but she didn't say anything or step closer, or stop them from weaving the string.

"This one looks like . . . a kitty cat," Lacy said.

Mrs. Gibson's eyes widened and she glanced at me, then back at Lacy and Mr. Jaans. Mrs. Gibson's arms fell to her sides, and she leaned against the wall.

"Let's go, Jenilee," Drew whispered from the doorway.

I turned and followed them.

In the doorway, I stopped and looked back at all the pictures taped to the walls. They fluttered in the breeze from the doorway, whispering in the still air, a thousand stories, countless memories, now patched together like an enormous, murmuring quilt.

CHAPTER 18

I watched Lacy and June Jaans weave that string, him helping her move her hands this way and that, and her talkin' to him like she was a normal little girl. Her big eyes sparkled with joy as he praised how quick she was learning cat's cradle.

Why? I thought. *Why can't I get her to light up like that?* Lacy tangled the string and gave a frustrated groan, then smiled a little at him. He grinned back, his teeth looking straight and white against the gray stubble of beard grown over his thin face. I remembered how I used to like his smile. I remembered how, when that boy grinned at me, something went warm and soft and fluttery inside me. I didn't want to remember it, but I did. I guess, in a way, I always had.

"Come on, Dora," he would say to me back then. "How about a smile from the prettiest girl in school?" I'd giggle and blush and feel lighter than air.

Nobody else ever made me feel like that—not even Olney, though I loved him dearly and we made a good life together. That wild, fluttery feeling only comes with a powerful dose of first love. What made it all the worse was that June give me a first dose of heartbreak, too, and he was the one who took my sister away from me.

Lord, Eudora, what are you doin', standing here thinking about all this now? You got a hate for him that's as big and black and solid as the cloud that carried that tornado.

I heard Jenilee's voice in my head. *You could start by being nicer to Mr. Jaans. All he wants is for you to treat him with a little kindness.*

I could still see her looking at me with those big, doe brown eyes and telling me how to forgive. I wondered if God would really ask something so hard from me. I wondered if, the same way He made Jenilee the one to pull me from the cellar, He was going to make old June Jaans the one to pull Lacy from the pit she was in.

Thick silver hair fell over June's forehead as he bent forward to help Lacy with her cat's cradle. In the blink of an eye, I saw the young boy I knew all those years back. It come on me so quick and powerful that I moved a step closer, seeing a ghost. June drew back like a startled mule, and looked at my face like he couldn't imagine what I was thinking.

I'm sure he couldn't. I was thinking that, considering he'd kept himself pickled for the last six years since his wife died, he was still a pretty good-lookin' man.

Lordy, Eudora, what in the world is wrong with you? There had to be something wrong with me if I was thinking that way about June Jaans. Jenilee Lane must of put some kind of hex on me.

June turned back to Lacy. He helped her move the string again, then leaned close. "There, now, show your grandma." He pointed at me and patted Lacy's arm. "You done made it all the way to cat's cradle this time. Now all you got to do is go catch that old cat and put him in there for a nice little catnap."

Lacy made a little sound in her throat, something that

might of been the beginning of a laugh, and she held up the cat's cradle. "Granny . . . do you think . . . Mr. Whiskers will fit?" It was the first thing she had said to me since right after the tornado.

I come closer and sat down in the chair beside the cot, moving real careful, like I was trying not to startle some wild creature. I didn't want that smile to flit away. I wanted to call Weldon and Janet over, but I was afraid that would ruin things.

"I think he might like it fine. Maybe soon we can get out to the house and see if we can get him to come on up for a nap. Weldon said Mr. Whiskers had been eatin' the food he's been leavin' at the old home place, but that little cat is sure keepin' himself hid around there. Maybe if he catches sight of you, he'll come on up. You and that old cat are pretty good friends."

The smile drifted off Lacy's face, and she dropped her fingers from the cat's cradle, then unwound it, and started the loop again.

"There you go. That's the way," June said. "It's a pretty fun game, ain't it? Makes your brain and your hands work together. That's good for ya." He glanced at me and winked one blue eye. "Back in your grandma's and my day, why, we kids knew how to have fun with little things we could find around. We didn't need no five-hundred-dollar TV video game to have fun." He tapped a finger on Lacy's forehead, and the corners of her mouth lifted upward. "I told my grandson exactly that the last time I saw him when they were out to visit two summers ago. He lives in Germany, because his daddy's in the army, and that's a long, long way off, so I don't get to see him much." June looked sad, and right then I felt sad for him. I'd always had a mess of grandkids around me.

Lacy nodded, frowning as she dropped a finger and messed up her string. "I don't see my mama much. She lives in Tulsa, and that's a long, long way off, too."

June sniffed, then reached up and scratched his nose. "I

know, child, and that's a hard thing, ain't it? But I think that's why we got friends and neighbors—so it's like we got a whole great big family around us all the time."

"Oh," Lacy whispered, frustrated because the string was knotted up. She set it on the bed, then stood up and wandered off, looking at the pictures on the wall.

June sighed, watchin' her go. "She's got a hard row to hoe, don't she?"

"Her mother ain't any good."

June lay back against his bed. "Lacy don't know that. All she knows is that's the only mama she's got. Every critter wants to be loved by its mama. Maybe her mama will come around."

"I doubt that." Talking to him about Lacy's mama give me a double dose of bad medicine.

"You never know. Sometimes you have to be patient. You're awful hard on people, Eudora."

I opened my mouth to answer, but then that city doctor come in the door and walked over to us. I stood there looking at him, trying to recall his name. *Always Right . . . no, not Always Right, Albright. Dr. Albright.* I was going to have to jot that down somewhere so I could jog my memory.

"How are you feeling tonight, June?"

"Oh, fair to middlin', I reckon," June answered. "A little better now that all the excitement's died down. This is some hospital you're runnin' here, Doc. I feel like I'm on *Wheel of Fortune.*"

Dr. Albright chuckled. "Well, fortunately we don't have too many patients left. Mostly just pictures and a few curious reporters now." He pointed a finger at me. "To change the subject, I was thinking about what we were talking about earlier."

My mind was as blank as a summer sky. Panic scampered through me, because I couldn't recall talking to him earlier. I remembered the newspaper reporters and the cameras. . . .

"About Jenilee," he said, wheeling a hand in front of himself, trying to crank up my memory like an old tractor engine. "I had asked you earlier about whether she'd be interested in the summer internship program through the Vista Ridge hospital system. The purpose of the program is to help disadvantaged kids pursue a college education, particularly careers in medicine."

I nodded slowly, recalling standing on the steps with Weldon and Dr. Albright, talking about whether Jenilee would think about leaving Poetry if she got the chance. "Well, Doc, I don't know. Her family ain't got any money to help her."

The doctor nodded. "The program is designed to help kids work their way through school on a combination of work-study credits and grants. I understand that Jenilee's grades aren't outstanding, but I have friends on the board of directors, and I could write a recommendation for her. Given everything that's happened here, she deserves a chance, if she's interested. She's a remarkable young woman, and she has a God-given gift with people." There was a flicker of something in his eye that made me wonder again why he was so interested in Jenilee.

I wasn't sure it would be a good idea to send her off somewhere alone. I didn't know exactly what Dr. Albright had in mind.

June piped up before I got a chance to answer. "I think that would be a wonderful thing for Jenilee. Why, she's been rescuin' sick critters for as long as I can recall. She could darned near have a vet degree already, I think. She's a smart girl, and good-hearted. I just think that would be a fine thing for her."

"Hush, June!" I snapped. I was trying to get my thoughts clear, and all his talking was muddying up the waters. "I just don't know what to say about that. I don't even know if she'd think about going. Poetry ain't got much in the way of good things to offer her, but she's been here all her life. She's mixed up with that Shad Bell. I got a feeling she's thinking to settle in with him and go that route in life."

June shook his head. "Well, that'd be a pure shame."

"I ain't sayin' it's a good thing. I'm just sayin' that's what I think she's got in mind. She's come out of her shell a lot these last days, but it's a long way from here to some college."

"Ain't for anybody else to say," June barked. "It's *her choice.* I think you ought to talk to her about it, Doc. See what she says." He crossed his arms over his chest, glaring at me. I reckon he didn't figure I had Jenilee's best interests in mind, given the way I'd felt about her in the past.

"That's true enough," I agreed. "But, Doc, I guess I'll just come right out and ask what's been bothering me for a while now. I'm wondering why it is that you have such a big interest in Jenilee."

The doc drew back, surprised by the question, and put out that I would ask. I guess he thought nobody noticed the strange way he looked at her. "I . . ." He stopped for a minute, like he was thinking about how to answer. "I think she's a young lady with great potential. She's obviously very intelligent, she's calm in a crisis, and she has a natural talent for medicine. She clearly already has quite a bit of medical knowledge. I've worked with med students who couldn't have handled a triage situation as well as she did."

I thought for a minute about what he said. It still didn't explain the way he looked at her.

June piped up like he had some say in it. "I—I guess we'd just have to talk to her about it. I'll ask her if you want. She don't know you very well yet, Doc."

Dr. Albright nodded. "Let me know what she says. I'll probably be heading back to Kansas City tomorrow afternoon. I can leave my card and the name of the director of the internship program. Jenilee can call if she has questions."

I looked from one man to the other, and wondered what in the world they thought they were talking about. It was just like a couple of men to cook up a rainbow stew and forget all the practical details.

"*I'll* talk to her," I told them. "And it may not be tomorrow. She's got her little brother with a broke leg to take care of, and their farm, and her father still in the hospital in bad shape." *And if that sidewinder comes home, she'll stay right there and take care of him. She'll never leave Poetry if he comes home. You can bet on that.* "She ain't gonna be ready to even think about the kind of things you two are talkin' about. You gotta give her some time."

"There ain't time." June glared hard at me. "You heard that Shad fella in here earlier hollering for her." He pointed a finger at me, and give me a stare that made me step back. "Eudora, you know and I know, if that girl don't get out of here now, she never will. She'll end up settlin' down with someone who don't deserve her, and spending her whole miserable life here in Poetry."

"The internship program starts in four weeks," Dr. Albright added. "If she didn't start with this group, she would have to wait a year. From what you're both saying, she can't afford the delay."

"She can't." June nodded his head hard, then sucked in a breath and groaned, lying back against the pillow and rubbing his ribs.

"Lay still, you old fool," I grumbled at him, trying to get my mind to think. "But, June, she ain't gonna be willing to do anything until she knows about her daddy, and she ain't gonna leave that little brother of hers. She ain't gonna do it. You know that."

"There has to be a way." June closed his eyes. "We just gotta think. We gotta think of a way to make things work out. If she stays here, it'll be one more wrong thing on top of a bunch of other wrong things we let go on right down the road all these years."

I let out a long breath and rubbed my eyes as they started to sting. "I wish I had the answer, but I don't."

I met June's gaze, and I couldn't believe the two of us were sitting there talking like friends. If we didn't share much else, we shared a load of guilt because we had turned our backs on them three little Lane kids down the road. We should of helped their mama years ago, when she started showin' up in town with bruises and scrapes she couldn't explain. We should of helped her get out, make some other kind of life. A better life.

I, more than anyone, should of done it, because I promised I would. But it seemed too hard a thing to do then, and it seemed too hard a thing to do now.

Wanting something impossible don't make it possible. My mama used to say that to me. My mama was a practical woman, and she didn't believe in dreaming big.

I sighed, looking at the doctor and then at June, two strange partners for me to have. "I'll talk to her about it tomorrow. I'll ask after her father and her brother, and if it seems like she's willing to listen at all, I'll talk to her about it. If Doc Howard's back by then, maybe he can help me. I ain't got no idea what she'll say."

"I think she might surprise you." Dr. Albright turned to leave, drumming the tips of his fingers against each other. He looked like a man who was used to getting what he wanted. "If there's anything I can do to help, or if she has any questions, please let me know."

"I'll ask her," I said, getting that strange feeling from him again, almost like he thought he had some special right to Jenilee and we were getting in the way of it. "I don't think she'll talk to you about it. She don't talk much to people she don't know."

"We'll see," the doc said, then walked out the door into the night.

I let my face fall into my hand. It felt like someone

was beating a rug clean in my forehead. "It don't seem very possible, June. I almost hate to even bring it up with her. I'm afraid I'm gonna open a door, and it's gonna get slammed right back in her face."

"Have a little faith, Eudora," June said. The scratchy-old-man sound was gone, and I heard the soft, smooth voice of that boy from New Orleans. Just a hint of Cajun lilt. "We'll find a way. It'll be a right thing we can do together. We ain't done too many right things together in the past, have we?"

"No, we ain't." I sighed. "We pretty much been bad to each other."

"Reckon now's as good a time as any to start changing things."

I felt the warmth of his hand covering my fingers where they rested on his bed. I didn't move away, and his fingers tightened around mine, trembling at first like one of them poplar leaves in the wind, then turning steady, warm, solid.

We sat that way for the longest time. Finally I heard Weldon and Janet coming back across the room, ready to go home. June give my fingers a last squeeze.

I felt something strange come into my cheeks, and all of a sudden I knew I was blushing for the first time in probably thirty years. I turned the other way in a hurry, got up, and started a stiff-legged hobble toward the door.

"Good night, Eudora," the old coot called after me.

"Night, June." I rushed on out that door like I had a hound on my tail.

Later on, as I lay on Weldon's sleeper sofa, with Lacy curled up next to me, I wondered what in the world had come over me.

Jenilee must have hexed you with her fairy dust, Eudora. You ain't actin' like yourself.

I thought about June and Ivy, and how afraid they must of been, running off like that, young teenagers

256 256 • Lisa Wingate

getting married in some strange town in the dark of night, expecting a baby. I thought about June working hard those last few months of high school, trying to finish up his schooling, trying to support Ivy. I remembered him so tired from working at the sawmill that he could hardly keep his eyes open in school while the rest of us were laughing and talking about dances and such.

I thought about him watching the baseball team finish up the season without him, and him realizing that he wasn't gonna be going away to A&M college to play baseball.

I realized how sad he must of been, and how much he give up to be with Ivy, and how much he must of loved her. It must of broken his heart to put her in the ground holding his baby, the only baby he ever ended up having.

When he married again, it was to a young widow with two small babies of her own, and she couldn't have any more after that. He loved her anyway, and he loved those children, and if I hadn't of hated him so much, I would of seen that he was a good husband and father. His wife was a good woman, but she wasn't my sister, Ivy.

I wondered now if he ever thought about that baby who died with Ivy—that tiny part of him that never had a chance at life.

Sleep come to me finally, and I dreamed of Ivy and that little girl who would have been June's. She had Ivy's long hair, dark and curly, and June's sky blue eyes. When she smiled, she looked like June.

She and Ivy were picking wildflowers, somewhere far away, and they were happy. Ivy paused long enough to look across the field at me. She tried to say something, but, as always, I couldn't hear the words.

They faded like the mist as the rattling of pots pulled me out of my dreams, and Lacy stirred in the bed beside me.

"Ssshhhh," I whispered, pulling the quilt over her.

"You all right, Mama Gibson?" I heard Janet holler from the kitchen.

"Yes, I'm all right."

Lacy opened her eyes and rolled over on the pillow to look at me.

"Good morning, sweet one," I whispered.

She didn't answer, except with the littlest bit of a smile. At least that was something.

"I see you still got your red string." I touched her little hand. The red string had been wrapped around her fingers all night while she slept. "Maybe later today we can go back and see Mr. Jaans and he can show you some more tricks with the string. I recall he knows quite a few. Would you like that?"

Lacy smiled wider and nodded. I saw a hint of the brightness she had showed June—just a small portion, but it was my portion. It was enough to fill me.

Squealing come from bedrooms down the hall as the rest of the kids woke up and started a fight about something. "Here, you kids stop that!" I shouted. I climbed from the bed and limped down the hall with my legs creaking and crackling.

"Toby's been in here stealing my Easter candy, Granny!" Christi hollered. "I woke up and there he was in *my basket*!"

"Heaven's sake, what's this about Easter candy?" I walked into the girls' room, where Christi and Cheyenne had Toby pinned on the bed.

In the corner, Anna pulled her pillow over her head and grumbled, "Tell them to be quiet. I'm sleeping."

I looked around the room, and joy filled me like water running into a cup. It felt like such a normal day. Such a wonderful day. "Lands, Christi, that candy's been in that basket for four months. If it ain't rotten, somebody ought to eat it."

"Well, he didn't *ask*."

Under the pile, Toby squealed and tried to say something with his mouth full of jelly beans.

A chuckle wound its way up from deep inside me. It was good to know that storm or no storm, children were still children. "I hear some little ones got too much grouchiness and not enough love this mornin'." I stretched my arms open wide. "I think they need some hugs from their granny to take away all that orneriness."

The girls squealed and ran from the bed, and Toby got to his feet and followed them, dropping a handful of jelly beans in the Easter basket on the way. I wrapped my arms around the three of them and squeezed hard. In her bed, Anna lifted her pillow and rolled her eyes; then she smiled and pointed to the doorway behind me.

Over my shoulder, I saw Lacy. I opened my arms again, and she come into the circle with the rest of them.

I held on to them for a few moments after they started to squirm and tried to get away. "Well, let's get dressed," I said finally. "Today's a new day."

I went to the living room and slipped on my clothes, then hobbled into the kitchen, still trying to get the oil back into my joints.

Janet shook her head at me as I come in. "Mama, you're trying to do too much. You've got yourself all sore and crippled up."

"I'll be all right." Normally I would of gotten irritated with her mollycoddling, but for some reason, it didn't even bother me now.

You're awful hard on people, Eudora, I heard June's voice say in my head, and I knew I didn't want to be that way—just one more stubborn, grumpy old lady in a world with too many grumpy old ladies already.

I poured water from the jug into glasses, then sat down and took a big swallow as Janet set out the breakfast plates. "You think I can borrow your car for a little while? I got a couple of errands to run this morning; then maybe later we can drive over to Hindsville and get some groceries at Shorty's, if there's anything left in the store."

Janet looked relieved to be talking about normal things for once. "That sounds fine, Mama. The keys are on the mantel."

The kids come rushing in, and we ate breakfast listening to them chatter about going fishing down at the creek. Lacy got a piece of toast and a cup of water, and for once she sat down with the rest of them.

I smiled at her. "I told Lacy later on I'd take her to the armory to see June. You kids might want to come along and see all the pictures. There's some old ones there from when I was in the Watermelon court at the Poetry Fair. Don't know where they come from, but them old pictures are quite a sight." Laughter rumbled in my throat. "Lordy, that was some day! Me and some girl-friends and cousins got elected as the Watermelon Court, and Mazelle Sibley was hoppin' mad she didn't get picked. If ya look real close in the pictures, you can see her scowlin' in the contestants' row."

The kids giggled.

"Can we see later, Gran?" Anna asked. "I didn't know they had pictures way back when you were young." She grinned at me with a wicked twinkle in her eye.

"You just watch yourself, young lady." I wagged a finger at her. "You ain't had your hug yet this mornin'."

Toby and Cheyenne started into a chant. "Anna needs a Granny hug. Anna needs a Granny hug. Anna needs . . ."

I stood up and kissed Anna on top of the head, then mussed her hair up for good measure and went to put my dishes away. "I'll be back after a while."

As I walked out to the car, I thought about June. I wondered what he would do now. He was too busted up to go home by himself, and he didn't have any family close by to take care of him. Far away in Germany, his son and daughter-in-law probably didn't even know what had happened in Poetry.

Reckon he'll make out. He always does, I told myself. *Ain't got time to worry about June's problems now, anyway. I got Jenilee to worry about, and that's a big enough problem all by itself.*

I climbed into the car and headed off to find Jenilee Lane, so I could finally live up to the promise I made so many years ago.

CHAPTER 19

JENILEE

I left the house while Drew and Nate were still sleeping. I woke feeling the need to be alone and think. I
didn't ask Drew if I could borrow his truck. I just got up
and left.

I ended up at the armory, more from habit than anything else. I figured it would be nearly empty so early in
the morning, except for Mr. Jaans and a few other people who were still sleeping there. I wanted to go inside
and sit and look at the pictures and be still for a while.
So many conflicting emotions were at war within me. So
many questions about what the day would bring.

I turned off the key and sat in the truck, watching the
sky brighten over the misty purple hills.

*If God can make a sunrise like that, why can't He play
my life like a movie on the morning sky, show me what is
supposed to happen now? Am I crazy for thinking our
lives can be different—Nate's, mine, Daddy's?*

I need a sign. I need to know what's right. . . .

The sound of a car door startled me from my
thoughts, and I realized the Gibsons' car had pulled

alongside mine, and Mrs. Gibson was hobbling toward me. The look on her face said she had something to tell me. I climbed from the truck and met her at the bottom of the armory steps. My mind conjured the idea that she had somehow gotten word about Daddy, and she was going to say, *Jenilee, word has come in about your daddy. He's awake and he's ready to come home. He'll need you to take care of him, of course. Everything will go back to just the way it used to be....*

My stomach rolled, and my heart pounded like a hammer trying to drive a nail inside me.

"Jenilee, are you all right, child?" Her voice seemed far away.

"Yes," I heard myself say, a small choked sound that lacked conviction. "I ... just didn't get much sleep last night. I ... better ... I better go home. Drew's going to be wondering about his truck." I wanted to get in the truck and drive—so far and fast that reality couldn't catch me.

"I have a little something I want to talk with you about." Mrs. Gibson took my arm and pulled me close, as if she didn't want anyone else to hear. "Can ya spare a minute to sit here on the steps with me?"

"I really should go. It's light already."

"It'll only take a minute." She lowered herself to the steps, and I collapsed beside her. "You know I ain't a person to mince words, so I'm gonna say some things straight out. I don't want to hurt your feelings, so if I do, just try to bear with me a minute, all right?"

"All right." I looked at my hands in my lap, trying to imagine what she might say.

She took a deep breath and let the air out slowly, thoughtfully. "I'm worried about what's going to happen to you when all of this is over. June, Doc ... uhhh ... Doc Albright, we're all worried. We talked about it some the other night."

I remembered seeing the three of them talking, and blood prickled hot into my face. "I'll be all right," I said, like I didn't know what she meant, but of course I did. "Things will just . . ." I swallowed hard, my eyes burning. "It'll be the same as always, I guess."

Mrs. Gibson huffed a breath of air and smacked her lips. "Well, that ain't good enough. It ain't good enough for things to go back the way they always been, is it?"

I shook my head, staring at my hands in my lap. "No." It was the one thing I hadn't been willing to admit, even to myself.

"Doc Albright thinks you ought to sign up for this program in St. Louis where they let young folks work in hospitals and take college classes in medicine and such. He thinks you got a lot of talent for doctorin' folks."

I sat very still, trying to grasp what she was saying, trying to imagine myself doing what she was describing— leaving Poetry, leaving everything, going to college, working in some hospital somewhere, someplace where no one knew me. *Someplace where no one knew . . .*

"We couldn't afford something like that." I let out the breath I had been holding and wiped my eyes, impatient with myself. What was I doing, pretending something like that could happen?

"Doc Albright says he knows the people that run the program. He says he can get you in. You can get scholarships and work-study to pay for it. He says the program is for kids whose families don't have much money. He says he thinks you would be good at it. It starts in four weeks."

My heart fluttered in my throat, and panic spun through me. *Four weeks.* "I . . . I have to take care of Nate and Daddy." I felt like a person being swept out to sea, grabbing for a rope. "I couldn't go in four weeks." *Or ever.* "Maybe . . . maybe I could go later in the year. Next semester or something."

I could feel Mrs. Gibson watching me. "Doc says they only take a new class once a year."

"I . . . I could go next year."

She slapped a hand against the concrete. "You know you won't go next year. If you don't do it now, it'll be too late. You're only gonna be at this point once in your life, where you have this chance." She took my hand in both of hers and leaned close to me, watching my eyes. "There ain't any future in staying here tryin' to hold that farm together for your daddy. He's a grown man. It's time he took care of himself." She met my eyes, her gaze glittering with determination. "There ain't any future in getting with that Shad Bell either, Jenilee Lane, and you know it. I know it feels like the easy thing to do, but if you do what's easy, you're gonna end up in the same place as your mama."

Was that what I had been doing? Was I staying in Poetry because I was needed, or because I needed to stay—because I didn't have the courage to leave?

My mind whirled with possibilities, like pictures in the wind. I imagined what it would be like to leave everything behind, to become somebody new. I wondered if it would really be possible to be a doctor, like I had pretended to be years ago while caring for calves and puppies and kittens before I was old enough to understand the reality of the world I was living in.

My heart started to open that door again. *It's a mistake,* part of me said. *It'll only end up hurting.*

"I can't," I heard myself tell her.

"But if you could, would you? If something could be worked out, would you go? Would you want to?"

Tears blurred my vision, and I stood up, throwing my hands into the air, afraid to say yes, afraid to say no. "I . . . I can't," I sobbed.

"Jenilee Lane!" Mrs. Gibson's voice was stern. I jerked upward, looking at her, thinking of all the times Mama said my name that way.

Mrs. Gibson came at me with her hands on her hips. "You stop that kind of talk! I know you think I'm a pretty horrible person, but, by God, I never in my life went around sayin' 'I can't.' I never let people walk all over me, neither. I always had enough pluck to stand up for myself, and it's time you showed some pluck of your own. If you ever want any kind of a life, you gotta get yer back up and make it for yourself, and you ain't gonna do it by hanging around here lettin' that no-good daddy of yours run your life, and pretending that's all right. Doc Albright is offering you a chance, and that chance probably ain't gonna come along again."

I knew she was right, that if I didn't take it now, this chance, *my chance,* would probably pass me by. The idea was almost too painful to consider. The life that only days ago I had planned for myself now seemed terribly wrong, impossibly small.

Yet, in the end, all the facts remained the same, especially the most important one. "I can't leave Nate." I felt the air go out of me as I said it. In the end, that one reality outweighed all the fantasies about what I might do. "I just can't. He's only sixteen, and he still has two more years of high school left. Coach says that if he'll just buckle down on his grades, he can have a scholarship to Missouri State for baseball. If I leave now, he'll drop out and he'll go to work for Shad's daddy full-time, and that will be the end of it."

"I ain't askin' about the practicalities of it right now. Right now what I'm askin' is, if you had the chance, would you go try this work-study program that doctor has in mind?"

Turning away from her, I stood for the longest time, and watched the sun light the Poetry sky on fire, and tried to think. Below, the church workers began emerging from the motor home, and a few people wandered from their tents, stretching and talking to one another as they watched the day come into being.

"There ain't gonna come some point in your life when you get to start all over." I heard Mr. Jaans's voice float from the doorway like a quiet breeze. I turned around, and he was standing on one foot, his hands braced on the back of a chair for support.

His cloudy blue eyes looked into mine. The noise in my head, everything around me, faded away, and I saw only his eyes reflecting the morning sky as he spoke. "Life don't come around but once, Jenilee. It don't come with do-overs. This, right now, *this* is your life. Every minute you got, every talent you got, those are your God-gifts. He give them to you for a *reason*." He raised a quivering hand, pointing a finger at me. "You think hard about what He'd want you to do with them gifts. You think hard about what *you* want to do."

"I want to go," I whispered, the words coming from somewhere deep inside me, some hidden place I barely knew.

He nodded, his eyes falling closed, then opening slowly, meeting mine again. "Then it's time to find a way."

"How?"

"One step, then another," he answered, and smiled. "We been seeing miracles all week long, haven't we?" He turned and disappeared into the darkness of the armory, pushing the chair ahead of himself.

I felt Mrs. Gibson's hand over mine, her fingers cool and trembling. "We'll find a way," she said. She swept a hand toward the ball field below us. "A long time ago, I sat with your grandma on that very field, and we watched you in a little blue dress hunting Easter eggs. Your granddaddy had just passed away the week before, and I think your grandma knew that she wasn't going to be far behind him."

She paused, and I felt her watching me. "She asked me to promise that Olney and I would help the four of you get out. She said the week before, your mama had a big bruise on her, and she'd miscarried a baby, and she didn't have a good explanation for where that bruise come from or how she fell down and lost the baby. Your grandma knew the four of you needed to get out. She didn't want to see you left alone in this world. She knew what kind of life that would be. I promised her that Olney and I would look after your mama and you kids—that we'd help your mama find a way. I stood on this very field that day, and looked at your mama and you, and I made that promise, one friend to another."

I met her gaze, trying to understand what she was saying. In all of my life, Mrs. Gibson had never so much as looked my way, much less tried to help Mama and us kids, or treated us like family.

She turned her face from me, as if she knew what I was thinking. "I meant that promise when I said it. I truly did, child. Then your grandma passed away, and two weeks after that, Olney had a heart attack and fell off the tractor in the field."

I remembered all the dark cars at her house down the road, and the low murmur of many voices, and Mama wanting to take a casserole down there, and Daddy saying she shouldn't. The images painted themselves in my mind, clear and stark, drawn with the innocent lines of childhood memory, not understood at the time.

Breath shuddered into Mrs. Gibson's lungs and trembled through her body as she remembered. "Oh, God forgive me, I was so covered up with grief. I was so covered up with my own grief that I couldn't think about anyone or anything else. I hid myself away, and I forgot that promise. That's one of the worst things I ever done. I turned my back."

We stood silent for a long moment, neither of us knowing what to say. Gazing at the ball field below, I remembered my blue dress. I remembered my grandmother, and how calm and gentle the world we shared with her and my grandfather was.

"It doesn't matter now," I said softly. "I guess we just go forward from here."

Mrs. Gibson wiped her eyes and reached across the space between us, her arms slipping around me, hugging me close. I held on, thinking of that instant in the cellar when my hand slipped through the darkness and touched hers, and everything changed.

"Who'd of thought it?" She released me and stepped back, took her hankie from her pocket, dabbed at her eyes and blew her nose. "Who'd of ever thought I'd be standing here with you—old Eudora Gibson and little Jenilee Lane, leanin' on one another? Who'd of ever thought something good would come out of all this tragedy? I thought this storm was gonna be the end of me. I didn't see how I'd go on from here, old as I am, and with my house gone, and my memory failing, and my old things and my notebooks thrown to the wind. I thought it was the end of everything."

"Me, too," I whispered, remembering those moments after the tornado, when I wished that everything about me had been swept away in that storm. What I didn't realize then was that it had.

"Little did we know, it was just the beginning of something new." She gazed across the ball field, as if she could see the future.

I looked too, and wondered what she saw. For me the vision was still cloudy, like something from a book of fairy tales. I wished I could see as clearly as she did, feel as positive as she did that everything was going to work out according to some plan that was larger than we were.

"I do wish I hadn't lost my notebooks," she said, sighing. Her shoulders slumped forward and she held her hands in front of herself. "I doubt if these old hands will ever write all them things down again. I guess I couldn't, really. . . ."

"You can't remember, can you?" I put words to the question that had been creeping through the back of my mind for days. "That's why you keep the notebooks."

She slumped against the steps, her head nodding forward. "That's why I keep the notebooks. That's the truth of it. I'm better here these last few days since the tornado, but the truth of it is I'm worried that I'm losing track of things."

"Have you told anybody? Did you go see a doctor about it?"

"I didn't want anybody to know. I don't want anybody thinking I'm a burden. My mama got dementia when she got old, and she withered away for years with everyone having to take care of her." She drummed her fist angrily in her lap. "I don't want to be like that. I ain't gonna be like that."

I reached over to comfort her, then pulled my hand away, not knowing whether that would make things harder or easier. "Then you should see a doctor about it. These days there are tests they can run, medicines and hormones, special diets, and things that help. I read about them when I was sitting in the hospital with Mama."

She didn't answer. I wondered if she heard.

"You should get help," I pressed. "You just said that if I wanted any kind of life, I was going to have to get my back up and make it for myself. You said you had pluck, whatever that means. Well, it doesn't take much pluck to sit around waiting to lose your mind, just because you don't want to admit to anyone that you've got a problem, does it? If you're going to sit around and do nothing, you might as well have died in that cellar."

Her jaw hardened, and she raised her chin. "Reckon I need to pull myself out of the pity pit and get on with life, don't I?"

"Yes, I think you do." I punctuated the words with a nod, feeling good.

"Reckon we both do." She gave me a sly, sideways grin. "Reckon it's time we Good Hope Road gals got ourselves together and showed the world why God saved us from that tornado."

"Yes, I think it is." The generator roared to life behind

the armory, and I realized how long we had stood there talking. Drew and Nate would be wondering where I was. "I have to go now," I said finally. "There's a lot to do."

"Yes, there is." She patted me on the shoulder and started up the steps. "The first thing I gotta do is right inside this building."

She disappeared through the doorway.

Caleb Baker came out as she was going in. "Thought I never would get that generator started." He smiled, but didn't meet my eyes.

I wondered if he had heard the conversation between Mrs. Gibson and me, and if he had been in on the talk with Dr. Albright the night before. "You know what she was talking to me about, don't you?"

He nodded, pretending to be busy finding the end of a roll of gauze in his hands. "Yes, I knew. I heard them talking about it last night."

"What do you think about it? Her idea, I mean. What would you do if it was you?"

"It's not me."

"But if it were."

He focused on the roll of gauze, wrapping it around the scars on his forearm. He seemed to realize what he was doing suddenly, and flushed. "Sorry." He turned his shoulder to me so I couldn't see his arm. "Sometimes these things smart in the morning and I have to keep the air off them for a while. They're not a pleasant thing to look at."

"It doesn't bother me, Caleb." I sidestepped and held the end of the gauze for him, then waited while he wrapped one arm, then the other. "So if it were you, what would you do? About Dr. Albright's offer, I mean."

"I'd go." He stuck his hands in his pockets. "You know, if you're worried about moving to a big city like St. Louis alone, I'll be going back to college there this fall. I had to take last year off after my car wreck. I could help you get settled, show you around, things like that."

"You don't have to do that, Caleb," I said. "I'll be all right."

"I want to." He rushed the words out, then seemed embarrassed. "It's going to be a little strange, going back to college after the year off, and with the scars, and now after the tornado. I guess I liked the idea that you'd be there."

A lump caught in my throat. In all my life, I couldn't remember anybody but Nate acting like they wanted me around. "Maybe I will be," I said. I couldn't make any promises. Not yet. "It'll depend on what happens with Daddy, and with Nate."

He nodded soberly. "Well, listen. Don't be a stranger, either way. When the phones get back on, I'll call and give you my number. You can give me a ring if . . . well, if you need anything. If there's anything I can do to help. I still owe you one, you know."

He smiled into my eyes and a warm feeling washed through me. "You don't owe me anything, Caleb."

"Yes, I do." Still grinning, he turned and started toward the motor home. "No good-byes. Just 'see ya later,' all right?"

"All right, see you later."

I climbed into the truck and left the armory behind with no idea of what was to come next.

On the way home, I tried to think of what I would say to Drew and Nate—what kind of plans should be made, what kind of plans *could* be made, when we still didn't know about Daddy.

In my mind, I began planning a future in which Daddy came home from the hospital in one piece, and I said something like, *Nate and I are leaving, Daddy, and there isn't a thing you can do about it. We're moving out. Nate is going to finish high school and go to college on a baseball scholarship, and I'm going to college. Drew's going home to his son and his daughter, and he's going to be a good father. He's going to make a life. We're all going to finally do the things that normal people do.*

I pictured myself saying that to him. I played it like a movie script in my mind.

Shad and Nate were sitting on our porch when I drove up to the house. The two of them were laughing and drinking beer, the way they had these last few weeks since Shad came home.

I ran across the yard and grabbed the beer out of Nate's hand. "Your pain medicine says no alcohol. Geez, Nate, don't you have a brain in your head? Do you want to end up back in the hospital?"

Nate blinked at me, his reactions slow, his eyes dulled by the combination of beer and medication. "I'm all right. Shad gave me some of my pain pills for my leg." He chuckled, closing his fist and rapping his knuckles hard against the cast. "Heck, it doesn't hurt one little bit now. This stuff is great." Rolling his head against the back of the chair, he closed his eyes, still smiling. "I feel good."

Anger flamed inside me, and I turned on Shad, throwing the beer past him so that it clattered down the steps and landed on the lawn. "Good Lord, Shad, what in the world do you think you're doing! How many of those did you give him? What's wrong with him?"

Shad rolled his eyes at me the same way he did when I nagged him about turning in his time sheets at the construction office. "Settle down, Jenilee. It ain't gonna hurt him. That stuff is like baby aspirin. One pill didn't do him any good, so I gave him two. It'll just mellow him out a little."

"My God, Shad!" I gasped. "Don't you have any sense? He trusts you. How could you do that to him?"

Shad blinked at me through a haze of alcohol. "Aw, don't go into one of them woman-fits on me. He said his leg was throbbin', so I gave him some of his pills. It ain't gonna hurt him."

"Where's Drew?" I demanded, slapping the side of Nate's face to wake him up. "Nate, are you all right? Where's Drew?"

Nate opened one eye and shrugged toward the road. "He took the tractor and went on out to feed the cows and check on Mr. Jaans's place. I don't know when he's comin' back." He chuckled, raising his head and looking at Shad. "Shad and I were just talkin' about work, that's all."

Shad chuckled, pulling a pack of cigarettes and a lighter from his pocket. "How about a smoke, Nater?"

I turned around, furious, grabbing the lighter and knocking the cigarettes to the ground.

Shad rolled his eyes again, finishing his beer and tossing the can onto the lawn. "Jenilee, lighten up. He's fine. You know I'd never do anything to hurt our little Nater."

"Yeah, Jenilee, lighten up," Nate chimed in, slurring the words. "Little Nater's just fine. Just . . . fine . . ." He took a deep breath, his head sagging as he drifted into sleep.

Somewhere across the field, the tractor rumbled to life. I leaned out to look around the bushes, to see if Drew was coming up the road toward home. I could only imagine what would happen if he found out what Shad had done to Nate.

Shad glanced in that direction, and then back at me. "Nate and I been talkin' about how we're gonna work things when your daddy comes home." He suddenly seemed remarkably sober, his eyes hard and narrow beneath his ball cap. "Nate says them hospital people think that if your daddy makes it, he ain't gonna be in too good of shape. Nate says he don't have insurance on the hay barn or the hay that got ruined, and without that hay, he's pretty sure your daddy's gonna have to let the place go back to the bank. I was thinkin' if you and I went ahead and got married, I could probably get my dad to buy this place out, so your daddy wouldn't lose everything."

"What are you talking about?" I said, my mind spinning.

Shad threw a hand into the air and let it slap hard against his thigh. "This has always been your thing, makin' lots of plans. So here I am, makin' plans." He climbed to his feet and moved across the porch so that he stood towering over me. "We been getting along good these past couple months. How come all of a sudden you act like you don't know what I'm talking about?"

Because I'm leaving. I'm leaving here. I'm leaving all of it behind, and I'm taking Nate with me. Somehow.

"You'd better go before Drew gets back."

Shad leaned unsteadily against the porch post, crossing his arms over his chest. "Well, I ain't goin' until I get an answer. What's goin' on, because I thought we were getting back together."

"Shad, *please.*"

"It's a pretty simple question, ain't it, Jenilee? It's yes or no, ain't it? Are we getting back together? Yes or no?"

"No," I whispered. "It's no."

CHAPTER 20

S had pushed away from the porch railing and staggered backward down the steps onto the lawn.

"Everything's changed . . . everything's different," I explained, following him down the steps. "I want to do something with my life. I want to go to school, make something of myself."

Shad threw his head back and laughed ruefully. "Where did you get an ignorant idea like that? Who you been talking to, anyway?"

"It's not an ignorant idea." *Is it?* I felt my footing crumble, felt myself sliding back to that place where the doors were closed.

Shad laughed so loud that Nate stirred on the chair behind us, then drifted into sleep again. "How are you going to go off to some school? Where you gonna get the money for that?"

I paused, suddenly unsure of myself. Was I out of my mind? Was I crazy thinking that, just because Mrs. Gibson and Mr. Jaans said things would work out, they really would?

The rumble of the tractor grew louder again, and I glanced over my shoulder. "Oh, Lord, Drew's coming through the pasture." My heart leaped into my throat and fluttered like a swallow trapped in the chimney. "You've got to go before he gets here."

Shad glared toward the pasture. "Let him come on home. He and I got some things to talk about."

The tractor stopped. I glanced around the oleander bush and saw Drew opening the gate to the barnyard. "Shad, please. Just go. There isn't anything else for you here. It's over."

He took a step toward me, then backed off, raising his hands in the air. "All right. I'll leave." The anger seemed to fade, and he looked like a hurt boy again. "You ain't making sense, though, Jenilee. I'm gonna go to the woods for a few days; then I'll be back." He rammed his hands into his pockets and walked out the gate.

I stood silently, watching as Shad got in his truck and sped away.

"What's wrong, Jenilee?" Drew came around the corner of the house and stopped to look at me.

I tucked the lighter in my pocket, my hands shaking. "Nothing," I replied.

On the porch, Nate woke up and roared like a suffering lion. "Owww, my leg's asleep!" he hollered. "Hey, come get me off this chair. I gotta go to the bathroom."

"Can you look after Nate for a few minutes?" I asked, my mind spinning. What if thinking about college really was a crazy idea? "I need to go take a walk and clear my head."

Drew looked suspicious. "You're not going to run off with my truck again, are you? I've got to be able to find you if the hospital calls about Daddy."

"I'll just be down at Mrs. Gibson's," I said, as an excuse. "I want to see if I can find her notebooks."

Drew nodded as Nate howled again. "You sure you want to leave me here with him?" he grumbled. "I might kill him."

"Just do the best you can to ignore him." Questions

crowded my mind. "He got his hands on a couple of beers and I think he took an extra pain pill. He's pretty well out of it. Keep an eye on him, all right? Don't let him have any of that pain medicine from the hospital until after I get back."

Drew rolled his eyes and looked toward Nate. "I ought to leave him sitting there with his leg asleep. He doesn't need any beer; and he's too young for it, anyway."

"I know," I said, feeling sad, realizing how wrong everything about our lives was for Nate. Nate couldn't even imagine a life with all the normal rules in it.

I walked away, my throat a giant lump of emotions I was afraid to share. What was Nate going to say when I told him I was thinking about going away to school? Would he think I was running out on him?

My head cleared as I walked down the road, looking at all of the debris that had blown into the ditch overnight—papers, bits of clothing, more pictures, wrappers and empty food boxes. Fluffy scraps of foam insulation clung to the tops of the weeds like cotton candy. In the strangest way, it was beautiful.

Mrs. Gibson's farm was just as it had been before, except that someone, probably Weldon, had come and gotten the old grain box where Drew and I had stored the salvaged items. I wondered if Weldon had found her notebooks. Would she tell him about losing her memory, and see the doctor about it, as she promised?

Picking my way slowly through the tangle of wood, nails, barn metal, glass, insulation, and twisted pipes, I looked for Mrs. Gibson's memory books. I moved slowly around the house and barn, crawled into the fallen section of the house roof that rested off-kilter against the side of the barn. Here and there, I gathered her belongings—a few old pictures, some recipes, a doll with a handmade dress, a faded movie program from *The Wizard of Oz*. Picking up an old bucket beside the house, I put the things inside and stood staring around the place, thinking of those first, terrible moments after the tornado.

I heard the roar in my ears, felt the hailstones falling, heard water gurgling from the pipes where the well house had been.

Lacy's voice called to me from the cellar. I turned and saw her hands pressed against the screen, her eyes wide, gray, filled with fear in the darkness below.

The cellar door that had barred her escape was gone now. A branch had fallen from the power line above and knocked the door into the cellar, so that only a dark hole remained with the end of the branch sticking out where the door had been.

I moved closer to it without knowing why. Somewhere in the darkness below, I heard the mewing of the cat. My mind spun with a mixture of memory and reality that was hard to comprehend.

Reaching into my pocket, I pulled out the cigarette lighter and struck it, then started slowly down the steps, moving carefully around the branch. Breath caught in my throat as I descended from the sunlight into the darkness, into the memory of that day, of those moments when there was nothing around me but darkness and my own fear.

I stood in the nest of branches at the bottom of the cellar steps and looked around in the flickering yellow light. Water seeped through my shoes, cool and dark. I smelled it, remembering the scent from that day when I had crawled across the floor toward Mrs. Gibson.

I realized now how afraid I had been, how terrified of everything around me. Afraid to talk, afraid to do, afraid to leave, afraid to stay, afraid to be. Afraid to save someone else. Afraid to confront the darkness and save myself.

As I stood there, I realized I didn't want to be afraid anymore. In these strange, uncertain days after the tornado, I had come to believe that I didn't have to be.

The flame flickered out, and I felt the darkness close like something solid around me. There was no fear in me. No voices telling me what to do or who to be. Only silence.

Striking the flame again, I held it out and looked around. The walls of the cellar were lined with long dust-covered shelves that sagged in the middle under the weight of dozens of mayonnaise and pickle jars, the labels carefully scrubbed off. I supposed that at one time they had been filled with canned goods, but they were nothing but forgotten containers now.

I turned slowly as the light glittered against the collection of jars. The glass distorted the light as I moved, bending and changing the image of the flame.

In the corner, the light reflected against the cat's eyes, orange and glowing, hiding beneath the legs of a small table. The cat hissed as I came closer, then it slipped away into the shadows again.

Something caught my eye on the tabletop. I stepped closer to be sure, but in my mind, I already knew what it was. *The notebooks. They must have been there all along.* Along with the other things Mrs. Gibson had forgotten, she had forgotten taking her notebooks to the cellar before the tornado.

What would she say when I told her where I had found them? Would she be so glad to have them back that she wouldn't be upset about forgetting what she had done?

Holding the light in front of me, I moved carefully through the water, took the notebooks, and carried them up the stairs just as we had carried each other after the tornado. At the top, I stood in the uneven shadow of the stark trees and looked at the notebooks. Just ordinary spiral-bound, like the ones I had used in school, ten of them, the pages rippled and worn on the edges, as if she leafed through them often.

You never really know about people, I thought. All the

time that I thought she was living a perfect life down the road, she was hiding, just as I was. Afraid, just as I was.

Maybe everyone is, in some way or other. . . .

The sound of Drew's truck chased away my thoughts. I saw him coming fast with Nate in the backseat. Scrambling over the rubble, I hurried to the road as the truck slid to a halt where Mrs. Gibson's gate used to be.

Panic rushed through me where only a moment before there had been peace. *Oh, God, please, God, don't let it be Nate.*

"What's wrong?" I hollered, crawling over the remains of the toppled well house to reach the ditch. "Is Nate all right?"

"Get in!" Drew called, throwing open the passenger door as I jumped over the stagnant water in the ditch and reached the road. "It's Daddy. He's awake, and they need us at the hospital."

I climbed into the truck and shut the door, stacking Mrs. Gibson's notebooks on the seat between us. "What's wrong? What did they say about Daddy?"

"It was a receptionist on the phone. She told me she was calling for Dr. Garland in ICU, and they needed us at the hospital as soon as possible. She said it would be best to bring all the family members."

I clutched the base of my neck, swallowing the lump in my throat. "Is Daddy worse?" I whispered, my soul hiding in a dark corner of the shell that was my body.

"I don't know."

"Is he better?"

"I don't know. She—she couldn't say. She didn't know the details. She just said we should come." He tightened his grip on the steering wheel, his fingers kneading nervously. "She said Dr. Garland had to go into surgery, so he couldn't talk to us. Things are still pretty crazy at the hospital, she said. I told her we ought to be able to get there in about an hour now that the highway is open."

"Daddy's not in surgery, though?" I glanced at Nate, asleep in the backseat.

"No. Daddy's not in surgery," Drew answered, impatient with me for asking questions he couldn't answer. He glanced over his shoulder at Nate. "What's wrong with Nate? How many of those pain pills did he take this morning? I could hardly get him awake long enough to take him to the truck. What was he doing out on the porch drinking beer, anyway?"

I sighed, smoothing a finger over my eyebrows. "Shad came by. He gave Nate two of the pain pills because his leg was hurting."

Drew slammed a hand into the steering wheel, and the truck swerved, fishtailing on the gravel. "Oh, great! That's just great, Jenilee."

"Drew, be careful!" I screamed as the truck slid wildly around a corner, the rear tires careening off the shoulder and spinning out.

Drew ignored me. Letting the truck slow slightly, he turned toward me and pointed a finger. "The next time I see that Shad Bell, I'm going to kill him. You keep him away from Nate."

I nodded. It was my fault that Shad was coming around in the first place.

"And I'll tell you something else." Drew turned his attention to the road again, but kept his finger pointed at me. "When this is all over, I'm taking you and Nate back to Springfield with me. If Nate's drinking beer and popping pills with Shad Bell, he's about *that* close to some real trouble." He held his thumb and forefinger an inch apart. "And if you're still thinking about getting back together with Shad, so are you."

"Drew, I . . ." I stood on the line between fear and anger, unsure of which way to let my emotions fall. "Daddy will never let you take Nate away, Drew, and Nate won't want to go, either. Nate won't just walk out on Daddy. He won't. Nate's nothing if not loyal. Even to Daddy."

Drew glanced at me narrowly. "Nate's still a minor. I'll go to court if I have to."

"He's *sixteen*, Drew. You can't force him."

Drew glanced at our little brother in the backseat, and then at me, his dark eyes softening. "One way or another, I'm going to make it all work. I did the wrong thing when I left the two of you here alone. But Mama was sick, and I knew if I took you away, there would be no one to take care of her. I told myself it was best that way, but the truth was, I knew it was wrong."

He turned his attention back to the road, shaking his head, the hardness melting from his profile so that he didn't look so much like Daddy. "You know, Jenilee, I stood in the door that day, and I came so close to telling you to hop in the truck, we'd go by the school and get Nate, and we'd be out of there. But Darla was pregnant, and I was just out of the army. I didn't have a house or a job, and I didn't see how I could handle anything more."

I nodded, closing my eyes and thinking of that day, and how much I had wanted him to rescue us. I wondered what our lives would have been if he had. My mind couldn't paint the picture. I could not imagine what I would have become without the years of hardship, Mama's death, the tornado, all that had happened afterward.

I laid my hand on Drew's arm, and took a breath. "Drew, I want to tell you something. There are a lot of details to it that I don't know yet, but Dr. Albright, you know, the doctor who helped us at the armory? He thinks he can get me into this internship program where I could work in a hospital and start on a college degree in something to do with medicine. I know it seems like a crazy dream, but I was thinking . . . well, I was thinking maybe it would work. Maybe I could do it." I stared straight ahead, afraid to move, afraid to say anything more.

Drew rolled up his window so that the truck was quiet. The minutes ticked by in painful silence as he stared at the road ahead. Finally, he said, "I think it's a good idea. It would be a good thing for you."

I found myself nodding before he finished. "I know. It sounds perfect. I don't know any of the details yet, but it sounds like . . . well . . . like the answer to a prayer."

Drew quirked a brow to hear me talking about prayers, then nodded like he agreed. "Well, then we'll make it work out somehow. Somehow it'll be all right."

I nodded, but inside I was thinking, *Will it?* In all our plans, there was one thing left to consider—the one thing neither of us wanted to think about. The one person who held sway over our lives, and always had. Daddy.

I looked at Drew, now softened, weary, worried. If Daddy was recovering, if we reached the hospital and we had to face him, would we still have the strength to break free?

The questions spun through my mind like the cloud of dust billowing around the truck as we stopped at the highway intersection before pulling onto the interstate. Drew stepped on the accelerator and we sped toward Oklahoma City, toward something we didn't know or understand, and couldn't be ready for.

In the backseat, Nate slept, unaware. He awoke an hour later as we pulled into the hospital parking lot. Gripping his head, he leaned against the window. "I feel sick." He groaned.

"Yeah, no kidding." Drew jerked the back door open so that Nate almost fell out. "You ever take anything from Shad Bell again, I'm gonna make you more than sick, Bubby. You just keep that in mind. And you aren't legal for beer, either. Remember that."

Nate blinked at him, then bent over the storm drain and threw up.

Drew waved me away as I moved to help Nate. "You

just remember this the next time you think about popping pills and getting drunk." He stepped away and left Nate standing on his good leg, clinging to the side of the truck. Drew reached into the back of the truck and pulled out Nate's crutches. "And, here, you can use your crutches to get into the hospital. I'm not going to carry you. You're a big man drinking with Shad Bell. You figure out how to get yourself in the door."

Nate took the crutches and turned to me, utterly miserable, looking for help. Then he glanced at Drew and stood straighter, bracing the crutches under his arms and starting up the walkway.

"Jerk," he muttered, but there was a look of respect in him, as if he knew that what Drew did he did out of love.

Drew glanced over his shoulder, and Nate gave him a sarcastic smile, then continued limping toward the hospital doors.

"Sorry, Jen," he muttered sheepishly. "I didn't mean to get so wasted."

"You shouldn't be getting *wasted* at all," I snapped, my nerves on edge. "Drew's right. You're too young to be drinking."

Nate knitted his brows indignantly. "Daddy doesn't care. He says as long as I don't go through too much of his beer—"

"Well, Daddy's wrong," I interrupted. "Daddy's so messed up himself that he doesn't know what's right anymore."

To my surprise, Nate didn't argue. He glanced at Drew. Had Drew told him the same thing? I wondered what Nate was thinking, but as usual, he didn't say. "What did the hospital tell you about Daddy?" he asked.

"They just told us we should come." I held the hospital doors open so that Nate could get through with his crutches.

A flurry of activity in the lobby caught my eye. Two

dark-haired children, a boy and a girl, ran across the room toward Drew.

"Daddy!" they cried, their voices echoing through the granite enclosure.

Drew blinked in surprise, then bent down on one knee and scooped them into his arms. Closing his eyes, he buried his face between them and held on, whispering, "Hi, babies. How are my babies? Oh, God, I've missed you two." His voice was choked with tears.

Darla came across the lobby as we stopped behind Drew. She and Drew looked at each other for a moment, uncertain; then he stood up, still holding the children. He reached for her, and she fell into his arms, completing the circle.

"Thanks, Darla," he said against her hair. "Thanks for bringing the kids."

"I'm sorry." Her voice was thick with emotion. "Drew, I didn't know. I didn't know you were calling my parents' house looking for us. I thought you were running out on the kids. That's why I filed the legal papers. It was wrong, Drew. The kids need their father. I need you. What I did was wrong. I'm sorry."

Drew kissed the tops of the kids' heads. "We were both wrong," he said. "It's so good to see you guys."

Darla pushed away finally, wiping her eyes. "They need you upstairs, Drew. Your father's awake, but there are problems. I'm going to send the kids home with my brother. I want to stay with you, all right?" Her brown eyes were wide and uncertain, afraid he would say no.

He nodded. "Thanks for bringing the kids."

"They miss their daddy. We need you, Drew. All of us." She looked at the children, her eyes filled with love. Touching the side of Drew's face, she met his gaze. "When all this is over, we'll go home and talk, all right? We need some time, and the kids need time with their daddy."

Drew nodded, too emotional to talk, then closed his eyes and hugged the kids to him again.

Darla stepped back and turned to us. "Hi, Nate. You look better."

Nate nodded toward his cast. "Up on crutches now."

Darla smiled. "You just behave yourself and do what the doctors say. Don't be trying to get out of bed like you were that first day after the surgery."

Nate looked sheepishly toward his feet. "Yes, ma'am."

Drew set the kids down, resting a hand on each of their heads. "And these two are Frog and Toad. I mean, Alex and Amber."

The kids giggled, clinging to Drew's legs as Darla's brother came from the other side of the lobby and told Darla he was going to take them home. Drew kissed them good-bye, reluctant to let them go; then we turned and walked to the elevator, none of us saying anything as the elevator climbed slowly to ICU. I watched the lights change on the console, watched each floor passing, and wondered what we would find when the elevator stopped.

I felt my body go numb as the doors opened. Drew glanced at me and nodded; then he took a deep breath, stepped from the elevator, and held open the door. We asked about Daddy at the reception desk, and the nurse led us to the ICU waiting room, rather than letting us go in to see Daddy. As she turned to leave, we stood just inside the room, waiting for her to give us some clue as to what was happening, but her expression was unreadable.

"Dr. Garland will be here in just a minute. He's in with your father now. He asked that you wait for him in the waiting room."

We moved to the comfortless vinyl chairs around the edges of the room, all of us silent, not knowing what to say or what to hope for. Darla laid her hand over Drew's. He didn't move to hold her hand, but didn't pull away either.

Beside me, Nate tapped his knuckles against his cast,

looking worried. He glanced at me and his lips twitched upward at the sides, a false attempt at a smile.

I turned to stare out the window as the minutes crept by.

Drew jerked upright when the doctor entered. Nate leaned forward, sitting on the edge of his seat.

I closed, then opened my eyes, and watched as the doctor scooted the magazines out of the way and sat on the edge of the coffee table, facing us. Setting a chart on the table, he introduced himself, gave his title, shook Drew's hand. I barely heard what he was saying. I looked at his hands and pictured him holding Daddy's life in them.

He paused, taking a deep breath, seeming to think about what to say. I met his eyes. Dark blue. Compassionate.

"The situation is this," he said slowly. "Our immediate concern was the bleeding from your father's kidneys and the damage to his liver. During the last surgery, we were able to stop the bleeding and remove the damaged portion of his liver, but this morning's ultrasound detected multiple blood clots in his inferior vena cava. The danger, of course, is that the clots could break loose and travel to his lungs. There is too much risk in relying on medications alone to dissolve the clots. We will need to do another surgery for the placement of a Greenfield filter, which, in lay terms, is a cagelike device designed to stop clots from going to the lungs."

I swallowed hard. "He needs more surgery? Is he strong enough for that?"

"We hope so. At this point, there is very little choice. The clot could move into his heart at any time, causing a heart attack. However, he is refusing any further surgery. He is extremely agitated and emotional. We were hoping that if you talked to him, you might be able to calm him down and convince him to sign the consent form. If he will not sign, the fact that he is heavily sedated, and therefore not fully rational, makes it acceptable for either of you to sign the forms as his next of kin."

The doctor picked up his clipboard and stood. "He is, of course, still in ICU, so you'll have to go in only two at a time." He stopped in the doorway, turning back to us. "Remember to keep things calm and pleasant. Talk about things in the future he might look forward to. If you have any unresolved family issues, now is not the time to bring them up."

I wondered what I could possibly say. Daddy didn't think much about the future. He lived one day at a time, and told us he figured he'd die before he got old. Maybe refusing the surgery was his way of making that prediction come true.

Drew and I looked at each other as the doctor turned and left the room. Nate grabbed his crutches and stood up, starting toward the door.

Drew followed him. "I'll go in with him."

I watched the two of them disappear around the corner, knowing my turn was next.

CHAPTER 21

EUDORA

I lost my courage as soon as I started into that armory building. I took two steps in, then ducked into the shadows behind the door and waited a few minutes until I heard Jenilee's truck leave. Then I turned and slipped out of the armory. For a long time, I paced back and forth on the steps, tryin' to decide what to do.

"You're bein' foolish, Eudora," I muttered to myself. "Out here, pacin' around like some silly girl. Just go in and say it. Get it over with. Just go in there, stand by that old man's bed, and bury the past. Look him right in the eye and tell him you forgive him and you want him to forgive you, and you want to go on from here. It ain't a shameful thing to ask for forgiveness. How else you gonna get that man out of your head?"

The truth was, I wasn't sure that forgiving him would do the trick, but I was ready to try anything. That man had been haunting me, and I was tired of it.

Every time I lay down to go to sleep, somewhere in the dark of midnight he'd come, and I'd see him the way he used to be—with that mop of blond hair falling over his blue eyes, and that big smile, white against his sun-browned skin. In my dream, I'd feel the way I used to feel back then, with my heart flippin' over and my insides fluttering. He'd take my hand, and we'd go into the old Bijou Theater and watch Judy Garland sing "Somewhere over the Rainbow," and I'd lean my head on his shoulder and think it was the most beautiful song I'd ever heard. . . .

In the morning I'd wake with the words to that song on my lips. I'd touch the side of my face and almost feel him there. My mind would stay trapped in the past for a minute or two. Then one thing or other would bring reality back to me.

I would lay there feeling that old pain about everything that happened between him and me.

How could he have run off with my sister, Ivy? I'd wonder. *Did he ever feel anything for me back then? Why do I even care after all these years? Why do I care so much?*

The only thing I could think to do was bury the past, forgive and be forgiven, and hope that was what Ivy would of wanted.

I took a deep breath, straightened my arms, clutched my fists at my sides, and walked into the armory, ready to say it.

June, I think we need to bury the past once and for all. I don't want to sit around stewing and feeling bitter toward you anymore. I want you to know I forgive you, and I want you to forgive me. We'll go our separate ways, and that's that. . . .

But as soon as I went into the armory building again, my courage went out of me a second time. I walked right past June and went to work filling the gaps on the picture wall, like that was what I come there for.

"Morning, Eudora," he said. I could tell he was wishing I'd come over there and talk.

"Mornin', June." I tried not to look at him, but I noticed that he was sittin' up in bed with a TV tray in front of him, sortin' pictures, peeling the damp ones carefully apart, and laying them on the floor to dry.

"I got some more pictures sorted out for ya here. I figured, I was sittin' here, I might as well make some use of myself. I figure by the end of the day I can have all these bags sorted through."

June, I forgive you and I want you to forgive me. . . . "Well, that's all right, I reckon, but ain't you about ready to be heading home? You look like you're getting around better."

"Ain't much to look forward to at the old house." He sighed, a long, slow, sad sound that come from somewhere deep inside him. "Drew said the doors blew open in the storm, and the place is a mess. Guess I can't quite get my mind around the idea of going home and tearing into all that."

Me either. June, I want to bury the past. "Well, I hope Drew got your doors closed up good."

"Um-hmm. I reckon he did." He paused for a minute, and I heard him shifting on the bed. "Well, good mornin', Doc Albright. How are you this morning?"

"Doing well, June." I looked up to see Dr. Albright come in the door and stop by the medicine shelves, looking for something. "I just came in to pick up some things that I left in here. I'm on my way back to St. Louis this morning."

I stopped what I was doing. "You're not leaving this morning?" I wanted to talk to him about my worry that my mind might be slipping. Him being a doctor in a big-city hospital, he might know what to tell me.

Dr. Albright nodded, preoccupied and in a hurry. "Afraid I have to. The sheriff's deputy got my car out of the mud and brought it back here, so I finally have transportation. I'm needed at home." Something in the way he said it told me there was more to them last words.

*Ask him, Eudora. Ask him now, or you ain't gonna get
the chance. See what advice he's got about it, anyway.*
"Doc?" *You know if you don't ask him, you ain't ever
gonna get the courage to go to some other doctor and get
looked at.*

"Yes?"

"Do you have a minute?" *Now or never, Eudora.*
"Just a minute to talk, I mean?"

He pulled his golf hat off and scratched his head,
looking past me at the old letters on the wall. I'd seen
him stand there and read them two dozen times in the
past days.

"I suppose so. Sure. What was it you wanted to talk
about?"

I saw June and the two other old ladies who had spent
the night watching us. The last thing I wanted was for
everyone to hear me. "Why don't we take a stroll?
Maybe go down the hill and get a cup of coffee? Looks
like the men are making up one last breakfast before
they pack up the van. Ain't too many people left, but I
reckon the ones still here will be glad for the food."

Dr. Albright nodded. "I think they're trying to use up
the open containers of things before they pack up.
Come on, we'll see what they've got." He motioned toward the door, and I hurried to catch up with him.

I waited until we were on the front steps to say anything. Finally I took a deep breath and let it spill out of
me. "Doc, if I told you somethin', it would be just between you and me, right?"

He nodded, giving me a serious look.

"Well, I . . . talked to Jenilee Lane about the internship program," come out of my mouth. I don't know
why, because I thought I was all set to ask him about my
problem. "She's interested, all right. She said she'd have
to see what happened with her father these next few
days, but she could sure see where that program could
give her a chance in life."

The doctor smiled, seeming greatly pleased. "I would guess that you had a lot to do with her seeing the possibilities. I'll have my office get the admission forms together and send them to Jenilee, care of Dr. Howard. He'll be able to help her fill them out."

A smile sneaked onto my face. "Well, anyhow, she's pretty excited by the idea, but . . . well . . . I just want to make sure about somethin' before I go pushing this any farther. There's something I'm a little concerned about."

He frowned, looking at me from the corners of his eyes.

I pushed on before he could say anything. "Well, I'll just spit it out. I noticed, and not just once, that you give little Jenilee the strangest look. I can't quite put a finger on it, but it was just . . . well . . . I just wondered what it meant. I wanted to make certain you didn't have nothin' . . . well, nothin' . . . inappropriate in mind. She's just a little twenty-one-year-old girl from a small town, and you're a rich man twice her age, so you can see why I'd be concerned."

The doctor raised an eyebrow, looking offended. "Mrs. Gibson, for heaven's sake. I'm a married man."

"Well, that don't always make a difference."

"And a Christian."

"I've known a time or two when *that* didn't make a difference, either." I glanced heavenward, hoping lightning didn't strike. "Forgive me for sayin' it, but to some folks Christian is just a word. I guess I was wonderin' if you were one of them kind of folks, or if you're the kind who would help a young girl like Jenilee just because she's had some hard turns in life, and she deserves a chance. I ain't tryin' to offend you, but when I want to know something, I generally just come right out and ask."

The doc chuckled. "Well, I would hope I'm the latter kind of person."

His smile faded just as quickly, and he stopped walking. We stood there for a long minute, and I watched all the hard edges of him chip away like dried mud flaking off a calf's hide. Finally he let out a long breath and his arms fell limp at his sides.

"Lately sometimes I wonder which kind I am. I wonder how I came from being young and filled with a desire to help people to what I am today—just another middle-aged man wondering every day if I can drag myself through the same routine for one more time." He put the knuckles of his hand against his lips and closed his eyes for a minute, laughing under his breath. "It's pretty funny if you think about it. Here I am, driving hard to make chief of surgery before I'm forty-five, and all the while, I can hardly force myself to go to work." He pointed toward the motor home. "The only reason I came here was because my car got stuck in the mud. When I got here that night and started treating people, I thought—actually thought—'Boy, this will look good to the hospital board.' The sad truth is, that was why I sent the message for the church relief crew to come, because I wanted to make sure I had an audience for my heroics. I thought it would look good on my résumé— board member of a big church, successful doctor, country club member in good standing, family man, wife and three kids, adjunct professor of medicine, disaster relief worker. The whole package, you know? The perfect package?"

I shook my head. It didn't sound perfect to me. "A man in a perfect package wouldn't be out behind the building on his knees cryin' like a baby. That's what I think."

He nodded, his eyes a map of pain and confusion. He didn't seem to care that I seen him break down behind the armory. "You see, that's it. That's the problem. It's all an illusion. It's evaporating faster than I can make smoke, and pretty soon everyone's going to see that I'm losing my wife, I'm losing my kids. I've lost my faith. I'm not even sure how it happened—just a little bit at a time, I guess, one day after another while I was working to become the biggest and the best, and she was home getting the kids dressed, so she could take them to school without me, soccer without me, church without me. I come home, they're all in bed; I don't even stop to look in the girls' room anymore. Don't even go up to bed anymore. I just fall asleep in the chair for a few hours, then get up in the morning, and do it all again, and hate it all a little more."

"Well, that ain't much of a life," I said. "Why don't you think about doin' something different? What I mean is, if that don't make you happy, then why is it ever gonna matter if you get to be chief of surgeons? If it don't make you happy, and it don't make your family happy, what's it worth?"

He stared at me for a long moment, drawing in a slow, labored breath, then letting it out again, taking on a look of peace. "I think that's what I've finally figured out. I read those old letters, and I thought, 'There's nothing in my life that's strong. I've built a house of straw.' But I'm not sure I have what it takes to tear it down and start over."

I reached over and give his hand a squeeze, because I knew how he felt. "I'm not sure I do either, to tell you the truth, Doc. But I figure you start with the people you love. That's the foundation. That's the only thing that lasts. You always gotta keep tending them bottom blocks."

The doc nodded. "I think that's what I've figured out too, these last few days. It started the moment I walked in here and saw Jenilee. For just a minute she looked so much like my wife when I met her back in med school. It took me back in time. I remembered how I felt back then, how we all used to sit around and talk about saving the world. I see that fire in Jenilee, and when I look at her, I can feel that piece of myself coming back. It isn't just her I want to see have a chance. I want the chance to get that fire back myself. I want to put my life back together, and my marriage back together. I want to get to know my kids before they're gone. I've got three girls—eight, thirteen, and sixteen. When I come home, nobody even bothers to look up from the TV anymore."

"Then get rid of the TV," I said. "Them girls will thank you one day."

I reached out and stopped him just before we come within earshot of the breakfast line. "Doc, I got something else I want to ask you. Something I ain't talked about to anybody these past couple of years. It probably ain't your specialty, but I figure you come from a big hospital, so you ought to know some about it. Besides, if I don't ask you now, I ain't ever gonna get the courage."

A wrinkle of worry crossed his brow. "What is it?"

I looked at my feet, watching them old black grandma shoes scrub in the dirt. "Well, Doc, my mama got dementia when she was about my age, and I think now I got it, too. Sometimes I can't recall things that happened. I'm forgettin' people's names." I didn't look up. I just kept staring at them old black grandma shoes. "And the last few days I been . . . well, I been seein' an angel that looks like my dead sister. I wondered . . . well, I guess I wondered if there was any way to tell if I was getting old-timer's disease, or if I'm just an old lady with a bad memory and a good imagination?"

He was quiet for what seemed like the longest minute of my life. I stood there with my heart rapping so hard, I thought I might have a heart attack, and then it wouldn't matter whether I had dementia or not.

"It isn't at all my specialty," he said finally, "but I can tell you that there are a number of treatments for Alzheimer's, including drugs and nutritional supplements. You should be checked by a specialist in geriatric medicine, however, because memory loss can also be the result of a minor stroke, low hormone levels, or even electrolyte imbalance. If you have been noticing virtually the same level of symptoms for two years, the doctor will most certainly want to investigate possibilities other than Alzheimer's. Alzheimer's is typically a progressive disease."

"Oh," I muttered, not knowing what to think. "And what about the angel, Doc? Ain't that a little strange?"

He wrote a phone number on the back of a card. "Here is the name of a good geriatric specialist at the hospital where I work. Call his office and schedule an appointment." Our eyes met, and he smiled deep into my soul. "And as for the angel, who can say? We've seen our share of miracles, haven't we?"

I took the card. "Yes, Doc. We certainly have."

"There's nothing to be gained by sitting around fearing the worst. Call and make an appointment with the specialist as soon as possible."

"I'll do that, Doc. I'll do that right away." I reached out and grabbed him in a bear hug. "I'll do that, Doc. I surely will. Oh, thank you. I feel like the weight of the world's been lifted off my shoulders."

I turned loose of him, and he stumbled around. He turned red in the face, but smiled. "Glad I could help."

"Oh, you did help! You helped more than I can say!" I spun around and headed up the hill, feeling like I could of outrun a jackrabbit in the fifty-yard dash. "Thanks, Doc!" I called over my shoulder. "You send them forms for Jenilee. And take care on the way home. Turn off that TV and kiss them girls, you hear?"

"I'll do that, Mrs. Gibson!" he hollered, sounding like he had the wind in his sails, too.

By the time I got to the top of that hill, my heart was pumpin', and I was puffing like a steam engine. I burst in the door to find June standing by the picture wall, leaning on the back of a chair, looking at the old letters. Hunched over that chair, crooked, weepy-eyed, and unshaved, he looked old and tired.

"June Jaans," I said, and he jerked back like he thought I might slug him. "I got something to say to you, and I don't want you to say a word until I'm done."

"All . . . all right," he stuttered. "Should . . . should I sit down?"

"No," I said, catching a whiff of him now that he was out of that bed. "You come with me. You need a bath and a shave, and I'm gonna take you back to your house so you can have both. We'll talk on the way. I got some things to say."

June was speechless. He stood there flapping his gums, looking at me like my head had popped off my body and rolled across the floor.

"Come on, I'll help ya," I said, moving to get under his shoulder by his bad leg. "My mind may be going, but my legs are stout. Come on. One step at a time. That's it."

We made our way toward the door, one baby step at a time, June and I. Who would of ever thought it?

I could hear the garden club ladies whispering in the back of the room. When we got to the front door, there was Mazelle Sibley with one of her sandwich trays. She dropped her mouth open, lost her balance, and spilled the sandwiches all over the steps.

"Eudora!" She gasped. "Why . . . what in the world?"

"I'm helpin' June back to his house. He's healed up enough, and it's time someone helped him get home." I lifted my chin and looked her hard in the eye, because I wasn't about to deal with any of her snooty attitude. "Come on now, and help me get him down these steps."

She jerked back like a cat bein' fed castor oil. "Well, I *surely*—"

I didn't let her finish. I pointed a finger at her and kept going. "Mazelle Sibley, you've known this man all your life. You gonna just stand there and take a chance on him falling down?"

"Well . . . I . . . I guess . . . I suppose . . . I suppose not." She got under June's other arm, and together the two of us moved down them steps with June slung between us like a side of beef. He didn't dare say a word, I think, just hung there and groaned a little while we got him down and put him in the car.

I had to shoo Mazelle out of the way to shut the door. She was standing there, gap-mouthed, lookin' from me to June and back again.

"Thank you very much, Mazelle. You got a high sense of charity," I said, then stuck my chin up, walked around the car, and got in. "You might want to go pick up your sandwiches now," I called out the window just before backing the car out.

June looked at me wide-eyed as we started out of the parking lot.

"Don't say anything." I sounded meaner than I meant to, but I didn't want June to start talking and muddle my mind now that I knew what I needed to say. "I got something to say, but just give me a minute. I don't want to say it here."

June folded his hands in his lap and sat silent in his seat while I drove out of town. He watched me, his hands kneading the worn fabric on the knees of his old brown pants. I glanced at them pants and thought they needed washing and mending, and I could do that.

June sniffed when I pulled the car onto Good Hope Road. He looked around at the destruction brought by the tornado and shook his head, like he didn't want to believe it. He barely seemed to notice when I pulled off the road about a mile before his house and drove down the old gravel path to Good Hope Cemetery.

When we got to that place, tears come into his eyes, and he laid his head back against the seat, blinking at the sky out the window.

I stopped the car outside the fence, right by Ivy's grave. I looked at the headstone with that picture of a mother and baby carved in it. A lump welled up in my throat, and I didn't think I'd be able to talk at all.

"I been . . ." My voice was just a whisper. "I been keeping this hatred inside me all these years. I been most of my life with that small, dark thing inside me, and I want to let go of it. Here. Now. It's time, June. I want to let go of the past and move on from here. I been wrong to carry these mean feelings in me all this time. I want you to know I'm sorry. I'm sorry I stayed away from Ivy after the two of you run off. I'm sorry I wasn't with her when she was pregnant and afraid. I know she needed me then, and I turned my back on her because, the truth was, I was in love with you, and it hurt me awful bad that she was the one you really loved. It wasn't right of me to hang on to that all these years. I hope you'll forgive me."

Tears filled my eyes and I watched them drip onto the flowered fabric of my dress. I held my breath, wondering what he would say, here at the place where Ivy and their baby daughter were buried. "Sometimes I think if I would of been there for Ivy . . . well, maybe the baby would of . . ." I sobbed, not able to finish the sentence. *Maybe the baby would of survived. . . . Maybe Ivy would of survived.*

I felt his hand move slowly over mine, his fingers warm, damp with his own tears. "I ain't never held anger toward you, Eudora. Ivy didn't either. She loved you, and she never forgave herself for what her and I done, running off and getting married like that."

I shook my head, laying my face in my hand. "Oh, June, I should of understood. I should of seen that the two of you were in love, but the thing was, I just didn't, and then when it happened, when the two of you run off, I just couldn't get past it."

June reached out and took me in his arms, and I remembered the way he felt all those years ago when we were young.

"I never thought about how you felt after you lost them both." I sobbed. "I just thought about myself, and how hurt and angry I was. I never thought about how hard it was for you to put your wife and your only child in the ground and say good-bye."

"It was a hard time," he whispered against my hair. "I was glad to go off to the war and forget about Ivy and what happened here. I thought I would forget about you, too, but I never did. I never forgot you, and I never had the guts to tell you that Ivy's baby wasn't mine."

I pulled away from him, hearing those words in my mind, seeing them in his eyes. "But, June . . ." I whispered. "June . . . how? How could that be?"

He sighed, his hand trembling as he wiped his eyes and gazed out the window at Ivy's grave. He shook his head. "Even all these years later, I can't say, Eudora. I . . . I don't know. Ivy took that secret to her grave. There was a world of guilt and shame in her, and she didn't want to talk about it to anybody. Not even me. I wouldn't of known she was pregnant except I caught her out behind the USO dance that night, crying and talking to a lady about getting rid of the baby. I took her away from there, and we run off and got married." He touched the window, tracing the outline of her headstone. "Neither one of us thought about what would come of it."

I looked at Ivy's grave, shaking my head, feeling everything I had believed all these years tumbling down around me like Doc Albright's house of straw. "My God, June," I murmured. "My God. My God."

His face hardened, and he wiped his eyes. Rolling down his window, he took a breath of the air, which was just beginning to warm and smell of afternoon. "It's all in the past now, Eudora," he said, leaning back in the seat and looking at me. "It ain't like either of us have to regret our lives. We had good lives, both of us. Not the lives we might have had, but good lives."

I turned away from Ivy, away from the past, and thought about my life. I thought about Olney and his trains. I thought about the farm, and the children we made, and the grandchildren who ran to me with their arms open. I understood that if I had gone a different path, none of that would be. All of the things that mattered to me, all of the things that would last, would never have come into being. The other life, the one I could have lived with June, might of been good, but so was this one, and it wasn't over yet.

"Yes, we have," I whispered, slipping my hand into June's, feeling our fingers twined together like it was all those years ago. "We've had good lives. I don't suppose a person can ask God for much more than that."

"I don't suppose."

I sighed, feeling peace settle over me. It isn't every woman who gets to go back after all those years and hold hands with her first love. "You know that song you asked me about? The one that Dorothy sang?"

"Um-hmm," he murmured.

"I remembered the name." I looked at the old trees, thick with glossy green, and felt like one of them, just opening to a new summer. " 'Somewhere over the Rainbow.' That was it."

I felt his fingers squeeze mine, and I heard the words to the song. I wasn't sure if he was singing quietly, or if I was just remembering the way things used to be.

CHAPTER 22

JENILEE

It seemed that hours passed while Drew and Nate were in Daddy's ICU room. I sat there thinking about my father and me. I couldn't remember the two of us ever having a real conversation about anything. Daddy barked instructions, and I did what I was told. Daddy criticized, and I tried to do better. That was pretty much all there was between us. There was nothing to prepare us for talking about the future, or surgery, or Daddy's life.

What are the right words? I thought. *What words can I say that will change his mind? What can I say that will change him? Is it possible for things to be different now?*

That hope wound through me like the line from one of Nate's fishing poles—invisible, strong, twisted around every part of me.

He's reeling you in, Jenilee, a voice said inside me. *How many times are you going to let Daddy do this to you? You're asking for something he doesn't have to give. . . .*

But still there was that hope. That part of me that

wanted my father to change. If it could happen to Mrs. Gibson, couldn't it happen to him?

I stood up, pacing to the window to clear my head.

Darla glanced at me, twisting her hands in her lap. Finally she got out of her chair too. "I can't just sit here. Would you like a cup of coffee or anything?"

"No, thanks." Eating or drinking anything seemed impossible.

She paused in the doorway, turning back to me. "Jenilee, I want to thank you for what you said on the phone . . . for what you told me about Drew. It really made me think. It made me think that I've been looking at our relationship only from my own frame of reference. I thought that when Drew didn't want to talk about the past, when he didn't want to get married or have me meet his family, that meant he didn't love us. I never, ever considered that, in his mind, he was trying to protect us."

"Drew's a good person," I said. "It's just that you were trying to make him face things he's spent the last eight years running away from. It's hard to go back."

"I know." Darla sighed, folding a tissue in her hands. "I think I started to understand that after I came here the first time and sat with Nate. All he could think about was how mad your father was going to be when he woke up. You know, Drew never told me what his childhood was like. He just said he was estranged because he went into the army against his parents' wishes. I thought that was such a stupid reason to stay away from your family. I told Drew I wanted to get married, and I wanted him to invite his family to the wedding." She shook her head, meeting my eyes. "He refused, and that night I packed up all our stuff, and I left."

I sat down and pressed my hands into the warmth between my legs and the sofa, not sure how much more I should say. "He loves you and the kids, Darla. I know he does."

She nodded, looking down. "I know he does, too. Thanks, Jenilee." She walked out the door, leaving me alone. I sat in the silence, listening to the low hum of machines, wondering what was happening in Daddy's room.

Finally I heard Drew and Nate in the hall. I rushed to meet them at the doorway. Nate didn't stop, just limped across the room on his crutches and collapsed on the sofa, sobbing with his head in his hands.

"What happened?" I whispered to Drew.

His dark eyes glittered like chipped flint. "Daddy hasn't changed," he told me.

That explained everything.

I turned and left the room, walking to ICU with a sense of purpose, rehearsing in my mind.

I stood in the doorway of Daddy's room, wondering if he was still awake. His eyes were closed, his chest rising and falling slowly. The oxygen mask had been removed, and the only sounds in the room were the low hum of the machines and the rhythmic beating of the EKG.

The face in the bed looked eerily recognizable now.

"Daddy?" I whispered, moving forward. "Daddy?" I leaned close to the bed, my fingers resting against the hollow of my neck, feeling the dashing pulse there.

Daddy's eyelids opened suddenly, and I jumped back. I stood staring into his dark eyes, looking for a hint that anything was different from before.

He curled his fingers against the white sheet, motioning me closer. "N-Nate?" he whispered, his voice hoarse, barely there.

"Nate's in the waiting room," I answered, leaning closer.

"Don't . . ." He paused and swallowed hard, his eyes rolling back again. I felt his hand grab my arm, his grip stronger than I would have thought. "No . . . more surgery. I told . . . Nate."

I swallowed the hammering pulse in my throat, moving my hand down to clasp his. "You need surgery, Daddy. Just once more. Nate needs for you to get better. He blames himself for not going for help sooner. It's tearing him apart. He needs for you to get better."

"No . . . more surgery." His voice was louder, his grip tighter on my fingers.

Nausea knotted my stomach, and I looked away from him. "You have to have the surgery, Daddy. If you don't, you're going to have a heart attack. You need to sign the consent form."

His eyes closed, and his lips parted to form words, but no sound came out. Finally he whispered, ". . . not signing that paper. You're not signing either."

"Yes, Daddy," I said, staring at the pale, drawn figure in the bed and realizing he no longer had power over me. "I am. I'm signing the paper. It's the right thing to do. For once, I'm going to do what's right."

I didn't know if he heard me or not. His hand fell to the bed, and he lay silent, unmoving except for the rise and fall of his chest. I sat on the stool by his bedside and waited to see if he would wake again. When he didn't, I left the ICU and walked slowly back toward the waiting room.

Drew met me in the hallway. The question in his eyes passed between us without words.

I shook my head, saying, "No change. He won't sign the form."

Drew's head dropped forward, and he made a rueful sound. "I don't want Nate to know Daddy wouldn't sign the form. He blames himself too much already. If Daddy doesn't make it out of this surgery, he'll be sure that was his fault, too."

I nodded, getting Drew's point. We moved further away from the door to talk. "You're right. It will be better for Nate if he thinks Daddy committed to the surgery willingly."

A low sob disturbed the silence in the hall, and Drew glanced over his shoulder toward the waiting room door. "He's too emotional, Jenilee. Darla wants us to take him back to her house until the surgery is over. Her place is only a couple of miles away. We need to get Nate out of here. Have them get the form ready, and I'll sign it before we go."

"No. I'll sign it." I didn't know why I felt the need to be the one. Perhaps because I had promised Daddy I was going to do this one last thing for him. "You take Nate to Darla's. I agree he shouldn't be here. If Daddy doesn't make it out of this surgery, I don't want him to feel in any way responsible. I'll stay here and sign it, then be here in the waiting room until the surgery's over."

Drew cocked his head to the side, surprised. "Are you sure? Jenilee, I can stay."

"No. It's all right. You go to Darla's and be with Nate and your kids. I want to be the one to stay." I tried to put words to the feelings inside me. "I just feel like . . . this is something I need to do for Daddy. Tell Nate I'll see him when the surgery is over. I'm going to go down to the nurses' station and sign the forms there, so they won't bring them down here where Nate will see." I turned and walked away without giving him a chance to argue. I don't think he would have anyway. The look on his face said he understood.

Daddy's nurse met me inside the ICU door with a clipboard. I took the papers without saying anything, signed my name, and handed them back.

She looked at me sympathetically. "It'll be a little while before we take him to prep, so if you want to sit with him now, you can."

I nodded, then turned and walked to Daddy's room and sat silently on the stool by the bed as time passed. My mind clouded with a mix of bitter memories and hope for the future.

I touched Daddy's face, trying to see in him the man

Mama had fallen in love with. Mama always said he was different before the war. She talked about how he used to play guitar with a band and smile at all the girls, and how she knew the first moment she saw him that she was in love.

She always believed that lost part of him would come back home. I sat for a long time, wondering if there was a part of him we had never known, wondering if we would ever know it.

"Hello . . . miss?" A voice startled me from my thoughts, and I realized a nurse was in the room with me. "It's time to take your father into prep now."

"All right." I stood up stiffly and left the room, walked to the waiting room, curled up in one of the cold vinyl chairs, and closed my eyes.

My mind drifted away like one of the canvas-and-twig sailboats my grandfather used to make for me—not settling anywhere, just drifting, floating somewhere between the reality of the hospital waiting room and the farm pond behind our house.

I could see Drew and me as children playing in the water, Nate just a baby wading in the shallows, clinging to Mama's fingers. Mama's laugh filtered through the dappled sunlight like music. Her eyes met mine, and she smiled. There was no pain in her eyes, only love.

Behind her, an angel stood on the shore, a beautiful angel with soft gray eyes and dark hair that fell in curls to her waist. She raised her hands as if to embrace us, as if to say that everything would be all right now. . . .

The sound of rubber-soled shoes squeaking on the floor jolted me awake. I sat up, catching a startled breath as a candy striper stopped a few feet away. "They've taken your father into surgery. They're anticipating two hours, but we'll keep you informed as the surgery proceeds. Would you like a glass of water or anything?"

"No, thank you," I said. "I'm fine."

When she was gone, I called Drew.

He answered the phone in a whisper. "Everyone's resting," he explained. "Amber just came out here and fell asleep on the couch with me."

I pictured Drew smoothing his daughter's long, dark hair, thinking about all of the things that would be different for him and his children.

"Stay there," I whispered. "Let Nate sleep. I'll call you as soon as Daddy is out of surgery, as soon as I know something."

"All right. You're sure you're O.K.?"

"I'm fine. I really am. Good-bye, Drew." I hung up the phone and realized it was true.

I closed my eyes, and for the first time since I was a little girl, I prayed. I prayed for all of us—for Nate, and Drew, and me. For Mrs. Gibson and Mr. Jaans, for Doc Howard and Dr. Albright, for all the people whose pictures hung in the Poetry armory. For the two little girls who had been LifeFlighted from Poetry, for the Andersons now reunited with their tiny baby girl. I prayed for Daddy, who waited on the borderline between death and a life he didn't seem to want any longer.

I prayed that we, like the town, would emerge newer. Stronger.

I imagined what the future might be. Poetry, built again, block by block, rising slowly from the earth, a testament to the will of its people. Proof that the best things in our lives rise from the ashes of the worst.

I closed my eyes and drifted into sleep again, to the stream behind our farmhouse. The angel was gone, but all of us were there. Together . . .

The sound of a tray banging in the hall awakened me, and I bolted upright in my chair, realizing that my body was leaden, and over an hour had passed. Afternoon sunlight was coming in the window, and somewhere not far away, I could hear the staff picking up meal trays.

I stood up to go to the nurses' station and ask why no one had brought word of Daddy.

The doctor met me in the hall. "I was just coming to see you."

I looked into his eyes for a hint of what he was going to say. "I . . . I wondered what was happening."

"Let's go in the waiting room and sit down to talk." His voice was steady, giving no clues.

I sat on the corner of the sofa, watching him, unsure of what I wanted him to say.

He sat on the edge of the coffee table and set his clipboard aside. "Your father is in recovery. . . ."

The way he ended the sentence told me there was more. The words unsaid could change everything.

"He is very weak, and there was a great deal of blood loss and a possible slight stroke during the surgery. As he recovers, we will have to evaluate the damage caused by the stroke." He looked down at his hands, rubbing the palms together. "With time and therapy, he may return to an active life. A lot of what happens now will depend on his attitude and willingness to cooperate with therapy." He met my eyes, and I knew he understood more about Daddy than I thought. "The best thing would be to transfer him to the V.A. hospital for long-term recovery and therapy. He will still be close enough for family members to visit him, and the contact with other veterans may be good for his morale."

I looked away, consumed by guilt. It was like the doctor was offering me a way out and I was taking it.

He must have understood. "I think his chances of recovery will be slim to none at home. He needs further monitoring and physical therapy, as well as help recovering from long-term depression and alcohol addiction. Surely, you must be aware of that."

I nodded, feeling guilty, feeling that we should have done something to change things years ago.

"I'm sure that's the best thing to do," I said quietly. "I

think it's going to be hard for Nate to accept. He and Daddy are"—I wondered what word to use, and finally finished with—"close."

The doctor rubbed his forehead tiredly. "I realize this is a hard thing to accept. I probably won't be here when your brothers arrive, but Dr. Ineli is familiar with the case and can answer any questions you may have. I'll stop by my office and call your brothers before I leave, so that I can explain the outcome of the surgery and the prognosis to them. I'll tell them you're waiting here for them, if you'd like me to."

"Thank you, Doctor. That would be good." I tried to picture what they were doing right now, what they were thinking. When the doctor called, would they feel the way I did, caught between hope and fear, not knowing which to cling to?

The doctor patted my hand, then stood up.

Have faith, I heard, but I wasn't certain he had said it.

I sat for a long time, thinking, waiting for Nate and Drew to come. Finally I heard them in the hall, and I stood up. Nate came through the door first, his eyes red and swollen.

I helped him to one of the sofas, then sat beside him and put my arms around him. "It'll be all right, Nate," I whispered. "It will. We'll make it work."

Drew came into the room and sat down too, resting his hand on Nate's shoulder. "It's the right thing, Nate. Daddy's going to have therapy to help his recovery, the same way you're going to keep coming here for therapy on your leg, so you can play baseball next year. It's just like the doctors told you—the therapy sessions won't be easy, but without it, your leg isn't going to heal right. Therapy at the veterans' hospital is what Daddy needs to heal."

I met Drew's eyes and saw a mirror of my own hopes and fears. "We'll work it all out, somehow," was all I could think to say.

Drew nodded. "Darla and I did a lot of talking last night, Jenilee. I know you're looking into that medical internship program, and I think that's a great thing for you, but to do it, you're going to have to move away from Poetry. I think we should put the farm up for lease to make the payments until Daddy gets better. Darla and I talked to Nate about staying with us for a while." Drew's eyes told the rest of the story. He and Darla were getting back together, and they wanted Nate to come and live with them, and not just temporarily. "He'll be close to the hospital for his therapy."

Nate wiped his eyes with the heels of his hands. "The school here won state in baseball last year. Darla knows the coach because she does social work at the school. She said she'd call him for me, and . . ." He paused, then turned to me, afraid, insecure. "Do you think all this is O.K.?"

Something inside me tightened, like a fist squeezing the breath from my lungs. I rubbed a hand over my stomach, aching inside. My heart didn't want to let go. All our lives, Nate and I had been clinging to each other to stay afloat. Now that we had found the shore, it was hard to loosen my grip.

I bit my lip, nodding, then said, "I think it's fine, Nate. I think this will be the best thing. I'm going to miss you, that's all."

Nate smiled one-sidedly. "I'll only be a couple hours away." But I could tell his feelings mirrored mine.

"I know. It's just a change." *It's you and me going our separate ways. Things won't be the same after this.*

"We needed to change." He sounded older, more mature, not like the carefree kid he had always been. "You said so yourself."

"I know." I stood up, grabbed his face in my hands, and kissed him on the forehead. "I know." I stood up, afraid that if I stayed any longer, I would break down. I wiped my eyes and swallowed hard. "I . . . need to go home and take care of things. I'll ask around about someone to lease the farm."

Drew sighed, seeming relieved. "Why don't you take my truck? We've got Darla's car and my old Jeep. Nate and I can stay here and wait for Daddy to come out of recovery, then come on down to Poetry in a day or two to pick up things for Nate and Daddy, and help get the farm ready."

My resolve wavered. "Is that all right with you, Nate?" Part of me wanted him to say no, but I knew that was selfish. I looked at Nate, nearly as tall as Drew now. He wasn't a child anymore. The storm had changed him, just as it had changed me. He had grown up.

"That sounds all right." He raised his face, his blue eyes so like Mama's. "I'll see you in a day or two, Jen."

I left the room, knowing that everything would be different now.

As I drove home, even the tornado-scarred landscape, so quickly changed, was changing again. Along the roadsides, debris was being cleaned, homes torn down, buildings repaired, trees cut down, branches hauled away. In town after town, people were building anew. Towns just like our own—small, imperfect places beneath which hid the potential for something larger, something stronger, something we may never have seen, if not for the disaster.

Had I not suffered the loss of everything I thought would matter, I would have missed everything that truly mattered in my life. . . .

I thought of the words from the old letters as I drove through Poetry, passing the buildings on Main Street, where the debris was being cleared and new blocks laid, driving slowly to the armory, where the baseball field was once again just a field, and the place where the glittering motor home had been was now just a shady spot under two threadbare oak trees. I thought of our house, and the fact that it would be empty when I got there.

Loneliness needled inside me, and I pulled into the armory parking lot instead of going home. Parking the truck, I looked around the lot, amazed at the number of cars there. People were coming into the armory with boxes, walking out with sacks and various belongings in their hands.

I climbed from the truck, hurried up the steps, and stood in the doorway. A sense of wonder filled me as I watched people moving around the armory, some taking down pictures, some putting up pictures, some just looking at the pictures, some staring at the walls in amazement, some overcome with emotion. So many people, only a few of them familiar, most of them strangers.

The last of the cots was gone, and even Mr. Jaans was no longer there. I looked around for Mrs. Gibson, but she was gone, also.

Near the doorway, the letters still fluttered in the breeze. An elderly couple stood in front of them, their hands clasped as they read the words, the man leaning heavily on a carved wooden cane. He touched his wife's face, and she smiled, resting her head on his shoulder.

I moved closer. "Are the letters yours?" I asked.

They paused for a moment, seeming surprised by the question.

Finally the woman shook her head, her eyes glittering with emotion. "No. We read about them in the St. Louis newspaper. We just wanted to see them for ourselves, I guess."

"I don't suppose you ever found out who wrote them?" The old man looked at the letters, sighed, then turned back to me.

"No." I watched as a young couple read the letters, holding their baby between them. "Sometimes I wonder if we'll ever know."

The old woman smiled, her face soft, peaceful. "I don't think it matters who wrote the words," she said, then turned to her husband, her face filled with love and hope. "It only matters what the words say."

Slowly, hand in hand, they turned and walked out the door. He limped as he walked, leaning on his cane. She intertwined her arm with his and slowed her steps to match his as they made their way into the sunlight.

"Good morning, Jenilee." I recognized Doc Howard's voice, and I turned to find him coming across the room toward me.

"Oh, Doc!" I ran forward, hugging him so hard I nearly knocked him off his feet.

He laughed in his throat, hugging me back. "Well, my goodness, you'd better take it easier than that on a fella just out of the hospital," he said as we moved apart.

"I'm just glad to see you're back. I'm so glad you're all right."

"Well, I darned near had another heart attack when I heard you were talking about going away to medical school." He grinned, poking me playfully in the shoulder. "All these years I been trying to get you to go to vet school, and in three days some outsider steals you away. How is that fair?"

"Sorry." I chuckled. "Anyway, you never know. I may be back. This medical school thing may not work out."

Doc shook his head as if he knew otherwise. "You'll be fine. You just do your best, and you'll be fine." He pointed a finger at me. "But if you ever get lonely up there in that big city, you give a me call. I'll be here."

"You'd better be." I meant it. "You take care of yourself, all right? No more big adventures."

"Let's hope not." He glanced around the room as if he'd suddenly remembered something. "Well, I'd better get home for lunch before Mrs. Howard comes after me with a dog collar. I'll stop out at your place later on and check on you."

"You don't have to do that, Doc." The thought of people dropping by our house still seemed strange.

He patted me on the head the way he used to when I was a kid working for him. "I know I don't, but I will."

I followed him out the door and climbed into Drew's truck. A sense of peace and renewal filled me as I left the armory and drove toward home. For the first time in my life, I turned down Good Hope Road feeling as though I belonged there.

The gate was open as I passed Mr. Jaans's place. I pulled into the driveway and coasted up to the yard fence, where the Gibsons' car was parked. The door of the house opened, and Mrs. Gibson appeared with a broom, sweeping a cloud of dust out the door.

She saw me and set the broom aside, hurrying down the steps to open the gate.

"Oh, Jenilee!" she cried, reaching for me as I climbed out of the truck. "I've been wondering about you all day, and now here you are."

I stretched my arms out and slipped them around her ample body, smelling the scent of vanilla and freshly baked bread. For a moment I thought of my own grandmother.

We held each other for a long time. Finally she released me and stepped back, her face growing serious. "How's your father?"

I wondered how to answer the question. "He's out of surgery. I guess the rest is up to God."

Mrs. Gibson smiled. "It really all is, anyway."

"Eudora!" I heard Mr. Jaans's voice from inside. "Someone's got to help me out of this blamed bathtub. I'm stuck in here."

"Just a minute!" she hollered, then turned back to me and blushed. "Someone's got to look after the old fool." She chuckled sheepishly; then she called over her shoulder, "Just sit in there and soak awhile. It'll do ya some good."

I laughed under my breath, then remembered something. "I brought you something." I hurried to the truck and returned with the stack of notebooks.

Her eyes widened and brimmed with tears. "My note-books," she breathed, taking them from me.

"I found them in your cellar. I guess you forgot you took them down there."

"I guess so." She shrugged, as if it didn't matter any-more. "Next time my house is about to be blowed away by a tornado, I'll have to stop and make myself some notes about where I'm leavin' things."

We chuckled, and Mr. Jaans hollered again from in-side. "Good Lord, woman, I'm shrivelin' up like a prune in here!"

Mrs. Gibson blushed again. "That man." She rolled her eyes, looking exasperated. "I suppose I better go tend to him." She set the notebooks on the corner of the porch, then turned back to me. "Dr. Albright is sending them internship forms to Doc Howard's office for you. I want you to promise me you're going to fill them out."

"I am," I said, knowing she was asking about more than just the forms.

She touched the side of my face, her eyes filled with a love that warmed every part of me. "Then some good will come of all this."

I laid my hand over hers, thinking of everything that had changed the moment the wind blew us together. "A lot of good came of it."

"You go on home. I'm going to get this old man out of the bathtub," she said, lowering her hand. "I'll be down to your place in a little while with some supper. We can sit and talk."

"That sounds good. I have so much to tell you." I turned to leave, comfort settling over me like an old quilt. "I have your stained-glass window at home. Drew saved it for you."

"My dove?" she cried. "I thought it was ruined. I saw it in the dirt."

"Some of the glass needs to be replaced, but the dove is still there."

"Oh, Jenilee, what would I do without you?" She clapped her hands together, turned, and hobbled up the stairs. "My Lord, who knew everything would work out like this."

Who knew everything would work out like this? I thought as I climbed into the truck and drove away. *Who knew?*

A dust devil crossed the road in front of me as I drew close to home. I stopped to watch it pass as it lifted bits of paper from the grass in our pasture, swirling them high into the air, like butterflies in a spring dance, until finally they fell free and floated to earth again, landing on the lawn of my grandparents' old house.

I pulled the truck onto the side of the road and climbed out, squinting at the papers through the heat waves of the afternoon sun. Watching them flutter in the breeze, I slipped through the fence and moved closer, wondering if maybe . . .

My feet moved faster, until I was dashing through the grass, leaping over stands of milkweed and black-eyed Susans as I had as a child, rushing toward a place that was quiet and safe. As I came to the yard, I saw them all around me. Letters. Letters of every size and shape, on aging bits of paper of every color, spilling from what remained of the old white house, covering the grass, intertwining with the flowers.

I knew the handwriting without touching them. I stood, just looking, just listening to the low rustle of their voices. My grandparents' voices. A part of what I was. The best part. The part that hoped, and loved, and believed, and belonged to a family.

I moved to the decaying wooden swing, still hanging from the elm tree near the tumbledown porch. Sitting carefully on the edge, I untangled a piece of plain brown paper from the wooden slats. Brittle with age, it had once been torn from a sack of feed or flour. I turned it slowly in my hands, touching the neat rows of cursive writing that seemed too fine for the carelessly torn scrap.

> *Today, I harvested fruit from the vines we planted. I stand now in my kitchen, washing the fruit as I gaze out the window. In the field, I can see you with the horses among a sea of Queen Anne's lace, bathed in the summer sunshine, lifting our amber-haired daughter high on your shoulders. I want to tell you that there has never been a better moment in my life than this simple, quiet one, but you are too far away to hear me, so I will write this little note to you. Today as I harvested, I saw a moth in a cocoon among the vines. All day as I worked, it labored to break free. If not for something you told me once, I would have helped it to come more easily into this world. But because of you, I know. I know that even the struggle is a gift. It is God's way of giving a simple creature of the earth the strength to fly.*
>
> *I am in awe of God and His wonders.*
>
> *Your beloved,*
> *Augustine Hope*

Looking across the grass, I imagined a cloud of Queen Anne's lace, imagined my grandfather there among the horses. I imagined that he was smiling at me, as I sat there among those letters, so long trapped in that silent house, now set free by the wind.

Good Hope Road

❖

LISA WINGATE

This Conversation Guide is intended to enrich the
individual reading experience, as well as encourage us
to explore these topics together—because books,
and life, are meant for sharing.

CONVERSATION GUIDE
NAL
ACCENT
INCLUDED

A CONVERSATION WITH
LISA WINGATE

❖

Q. Good Hope Road deals with the effects of a disaster on a community. How much of the book was inspired by the events of September 11, 2001?

A. The answer is twofold. I began writing *Good Hope Road* long before September 11. The book was originally inspired by a devastating tornado that swept through Oklahoma City the day after I had been there speaking at a conference and visiting friends. When I saw coverage of the tornado on the news, I kept thinking, "Dear God, we were just there." My husband and I started trying to call friends and loved ones, but the phone lines were down. As we watched the TV coverage, trying to discern which areas had been hit, the stories about the community banding together gave us a sense of hope. There were so many powerful images, but one in particular stayed with me—that of a girl pulling photographs from the debris near a rural home and saying she didn't know who they belonged to, that they might have been carried from miles away. It was probably only a minute or two of news footage, but it haunted me. Inspired by that image, I began writing Jenilee's story.

By September 11, the manuscript was completed, and I was about to begin revisions. That September morning, the book took on a completely new meaning for me. In the wake of those horrible events, during those few days when we didn't know what might happen next, I needed to believe that the human spirit, that a community of people, could overcome even the worst tragedy. I wanted to create a book that would celebrate the best in human nature and the ability of good to triumph over destructive forces.

Q. *Why do you choose to write books in the first-person point of view?*

A. I like the closeness to the character that first-person point of view provides. I like the feeling that you're hearing a real person, not a third-person narrator, tell a story. I often get so wrapped up in the characters and their stories that I forget they aren't real people living out their lives somewhere. First-person point of view doesn't work for every story, but for many of my stories it helps create the impression of a personal narrative being told to the reader (and actually, to the writer) in a very intimate one-on-one fashion.

Q. *How much of the book is inspired by your own experience?*

A. Well, I grew up in Tornado Alley in northern Oklahoma, so from an early age, I knew about tornadoes and the need to run to the " 'fraidy hole" when funnel clouds were reported on the news. I've gotten close to a tornado or two, but I've never actually been in one, and I'd like to keep it that way.

The characters of Eudora Gibson and Jenilee Lane are composites of people I have known, and the town of Poetry could be any small town—its people old-fashioned, stuck in their ways, sometimes critical and stubborn, yet beneath their gruff exterior, filled with compassion and determination.

Like the people of Oklahoma City and New York City, the people of Poetry rise to the occasion when challenged. I hope that their triumph will leave readers feeling uplifted. It is always my intention, my desire to write stories in which characters grow to a fuller understanding of their world, themselves, and their spirituality. I like stories that end happily, and even though happy endings are sometimes criticized as being "pat" or unrealistic, that is where my heart goes as a writer, as a reader, and as a human being. I want to believe that all things are possible, in writing and in life.

Q. Good Hope Road deals with many important themes. Which ones do you hope will generate the most discussion?

A. The important issues in *Good Hope Road* are those that the characters struggle with during the days after the tornado—the need for the support of family and community, the need of every individual to be accepted and valued, the need to leave the past behind to move toward the future. The novel also explores the idea that God brings together people who can learn from one another, the difficulty of escaping marital and family abuse, the ability of faith to sustain people through difficult times, and how struggle can bring out both the best and the worst in individuals and in communities.

Q. When you speak to readers, via personal appearances and e-mail, what questions do they most commonly ask?

A. First, they want to know whether future stories will revisit the family in my first novel, *Tending Roses.* The answer is yes. The characters from *Tending Roses* make a brief appearance in *Good Hope Road* and are connected to Jenilee and her family through Jenilee's grandmother, Angeline, and her sister, Rose, the grandmother in *Tending Roses.* In the future I would like to investigate the past relationship between Rose and Angeline and explore what caused the family rift that has separated the descendants.

Readers also ask where I get my story ideas. I have to confess that ideas can come from almost anywhere. In *Good Hope Road,* the impetus was a flash of news footage. *Tending Roses* was inspired by my relationship with my grandmother and the life lessons she shared with me when I became a mother. I found the germ of an idea for *Texas Cooking,* which NAL published in the fall of 2003, in a conversation with my husband about the old-fashioned wit and wisdom found in the small-town cafés of central Texas. The novel I am now writing was first inspired by my family's move to an area that borders an intersection long called the Crossroads. On one corner is an abandoned store, known as the Crossroads Store, which has a fascinating and colorful history.

People also ask how long I've been writing. I always answer, "All of my life," but I know many writers who began writing very late in life, including a friend of mine who was first published at seventy-five years old. As for myself, I can't remember a time when I didn't write. My first grade teacher in Peaslee Elementary, Northboro, Massachusetts, first put into my head the dream of someday writing for a living when she wrote on my report card that she expected to see my name in a magazine one day. From then on, I hoped to write a book that would be published, and that people would read it and in response send a note, a prayer, or simply their good thoughts.

So, as I sit here on the porch writing these words on a quiet summer day in Texas, and as you sit reading them where you are, we are fulfilling a childhood dream, you and I.

QUESTIONS FOR
DISCUSSION

❖

1. *Good Hope Road* describes a community recovering from the destruction caused by a cataclysmic natural event. Have you experienced anything similar in your own life or do you know people who have? How might one's experience of destruction caused by an act of war, as on September 11, differ from one's experience of a natural disaster?

2. Although the townspeople have ignored Jenilee's plight throughout her life, she instinctively comes to the aid of her neighbor, Eudora Gibson, after the storm. On the other hand, at first, Jenilee doesn't think to bring emergency supplies from home to the center of town. Why does she behave inconsistently in this regard? Is one act instinctual and the other a learned response? Where does the instinct to help come from? Do other characters in the book have it? Do you and the people you know? How does one learn to become a caring member of a community?

3. The storm and the days afterward prove to be important turning points in the lives of Jenilee Lane, Eudora Gibson, and Dr. Albright. Why are these three characters so changed by their experiences? Can you compare their experiences to an important turning point in your own life?

4. Of all the items she finds in the debris, Jenilee is most fascinated by the photographs. Why? What do they symbolize for her? Compare what she does with the photographs to what people in real communities have done with photographs after great tragedies—for example, in Oklahoma City after the bombing of the Federal Building; in Littleton, Colorado, after the school shooting; in New York City after September 11. Why do you think that Jenilee feels, and the people of these real-life communities felt, such a strong need to publicly share those photographs? Discuss the impact of the photographs on the community.

5. At the beginning of *Good Hope Road*, Jenilee Lane is a young woman whose abusive family situation and limited circumstances have led her to expect very little from life. By the end of the book, she sees new possibilities for herself. Discuss the specific events in the novel that bring her to a place where she can see beyond the present to a brighter future. Why is her transformation so difficult? Do you know people like Jenilee? What efforts have been made to help them and what have the results been like? Why is it so difficult to change people's expectations of themselves, and where does our responsibility lie in helping them?

6. For much of the novel, Jenilee is angry at her brother Drew for having left her and their younger brother, Nate, alone to face their abusive father and ill mother. Was Drew wrong to leave the family? In what ways has he both succeeded and failed to overcome the limitations of his upbringing? In what ways are the responses of Jenilee, Drew, and Nate typical of children raised in abusive homes?

7. Don't read this question if you haven't already finished the novel. At the end of *Good Hope Road*, Jenilee's father is still

very ill, but if he recovers from surgery, the expectation is that he will be placed in a veterans' hospital for long-term care, thus freeing Jenilee and her brothers from his undermining influence. If a facility such as the veterans' hospital did not exist, what effect might that have on the futures of Jenilee, Drew, and Nate?

8. Many of Eudora Gibson's problems in life are the result of bitterly held resentments regarding past events. She concludes that God has been letting hardships come to her in order to prod her into "turn(ing) over the reins" of her life. Do you agree with her assessment? Why or why not?

9. Dr. Albright arrives on the scene with an unfriendly, all-business attitude, and shows little concern for his patients as people. How does he change in the course of the novel, and what specific events provoke that change? What changes do you think he intends to make when he returns home? Will he succeed?

10. The story of the moth struggling to escape its cocoon begins and ends the book. Why do you think the author chose to frame the book with this image? Is it effective?

The NAL Accent series by Lisa Wingate
that began with
Tending Roses
and continued with
Good Hope Road
concludes with

The Language of Sycamores

For an excerpt, read on . . .